THE BALLAD OF HOUSE DRACONIS

NOBILITAS OFFICIUM
FIDES AETERNA

THE BALLAD OF HOUSE DRACONIS

The Glory Road

Book One

Casey Cooper

Publishing Services provided by Paper Raven Books LLC
Printed in the United States of America

First Printing, 2025

ISBN (Paperback) 978-1-966512-00-4
ISBN (Hardback) 978-1-966512-01-1

N
VEDA LOWLANDS
CASTLE DRACONIS
THE BLACK MOUNTAINS
THE KING'S VALLEY
RAINBOW VALLEY
THE MYSTY MOUNTAINS
FAIRINHORST
FAIRINLAN
THE BARRIER PEAKS
THE GREAT SOUTHERN DESERT

Leaf and Stone

The earth moves... The oceans quake...
The planets changing tide... Then from the oceans...
Come the mountains... Where sweet waters hide...
There's water flowing down the rocks
Flooding Leaf and Stone...
Cascading from the hidden springs...
Among the mountain's bones.

The time will come... the time will go...
Leaf and stone remain...
Lightning strikes the path before...
And nothing stays the same...
Cycles changing... rearranging
Like the wind spun colored dawn.
The hand of Fate will write the tale
And time will carry on...

Mountain goat climbs up the mountain...
Thru clouds and fog alone.
Climbing high on misty mountains
Above the Leaf and Stone.
Eagle floating from the mountain...
No earth, just clouds below.
Alone with just a star to guide her...
High Above the Leaf and Stone.

THE BLOOD OF DRAGONS
(THE ANTHEM OF HOUSE DRACONIS)

From the Blood of Dragons the seeds of Kings are made
In the darkness 'fore the dawn the pawns become afraid
Afraid of all the things to come in History's fiery ride,
And as the towers tumble down proud men will lose their pride.

Then from the Blood of Dragons the seeds of Kings are made,
And with the spells of magic might men will be amazed.

From the Blood of Dragons the seeds of war are born,
Men will strive to overcome with armor, steel, and horn.
As so it is with Honor then even more with shame,
Black hearts will try to rule the day with treachery and pain.

Then from the Blood of Dragons the seeds of Kings are made,
And with the spells of magic might men will be amazed.

Then from the Blood of Dragons the seed of Kings are made,
From the darkness 'fore the dawn, a kingdom shall be saved.
History will proclaim the torch of honor burning bright,
And on the Road to Glory we march on to the light.

Then from the Blood of Dragons the seeds of Kings are made,
And with the spells of magic might men will be amazed,
Men will be amazed...

THE PROPHECY

King's Blood flows like Dragon's fire...

Yet from the Darkness... Light!!!

Young Falcons' flight begins in peril

As Black doth conquer White,

But Mystic Flames shall banish night

And wake Stone Giants at time's hour.

From Crystal Eyrie comes the Spell

To bring a new light unto flower.

Things to see with eyes of stone,

Blood and fire, earth and bone.

Everywhere to go, but home…

Wander lonely, all alone…

Learn to see through eyes of stone...

Eyes of fire, wood, and bone...

Cast your fate upon the foam

To sail through Time, to sail alone...

Dawn brings the day, new comes the light...

The Oracle ends now... with the night.

CONTENTS

Act One

Duka's Birthday

PROLOGUE

AARON

Twenty-one years before the present day
12/1/1950 ar
At the prenuptial celebration of Crown
Prince Aaron deDraconis,
The Great Horned Owl Tavern.
In the City of Phoenix, Veda Lowlands.
6:04 p.m.

Crown Prince Aaron deDraconis arrived at The Great Horned Owl tavern nearly a full hour before the prenuptial celebration was due to begin. His uncle, the Duke Baird deDraconis, told him and his brother Bretton to be at the tavern by seven o'clock sharp. Once they would have traveled to the tavern together, but now … Aaron shook his head sadly. Ever since Brett and Andune had their falling out, Brett just hadn't been the same. For over two years, his brother had been distant and cold. Sometimes downright hostile.

The Owl was within a stone's throw of Phoenix Castle and the unofficial watering hole for the off-duty castle staff and guards. There were a handful of people sitting at several tables within the common room, and none of them seemed surprised to see the prince enter. One of the guards waved and several more nodded, but traditionally, no one acknowledged his rank and just went about their business. The Owl was one of the very few places the princes could escape the formalities that went with their rank.

The bartender caught his eye and nodded his head towards the hall in the back. Aaron bobbed his head in acknowledgment, walked across the room and down the hall to the closed door at the end. He hesitated for a moment, then lifted the latch and pushed the door open to come face to face with a redheaded Fairborn warrior. It was Jaek, one of Andune's liegemen.

The warrior seemed to expect him, for he gave a bow and stepped to the side. Standing by the door on the far side of the room was his twin, Taur. The two were nearly identical in looks, garb, and demeanor. Their only difference in appearance was Taur's hair was blond instead of auburn.

The Fairborn sitting at the table in the room's center was not Andune, as Aaron had expected. There was a family resemblance, however, and Aaron guessed it must be his sibling. Sitting on the table was a polished wooden box, the top marked with runes Aaron didn't recognize. He walked into the room and nodded.

The Fairborn stood and bowed. "Prince Aaron, I am pleased to make your acquaintance. I am Tirinvo Naurfindl of Fairinlan. I know you to be a friend of my brother."

Aaron sighed. "I haven't seen Andune in over two years, not since he and my brother had their … their misunderstanding. I hope he is in good health?" He looked at the Fairborn warriors. "I thought Jaek and Taur were his bodyguards?"

"As far as I know, my brother is fine," Tirinvo responded. "But he and my father, King Farnir, have had a falling out and Andune has left Fairinlan. My father has since named me his heir and removed Andune from the royal succession. I haven't seen him for a few months myself. The twins are my liegemen now."

"That's terrible!" Aaron shook his head. "Whatever could have happened?"

"It was personal." Tirinvo motioned to the empty chair at the table and sat back down in his vacated seat. "I understand you are to be married soon?"

"In two weeks' time. On the Solstice, I will wed Lady Evelyn dePenrodyn," said Aaron as he sat across from the Fairborn prince.

"Congratulations. The Fairborn wish you well. I heard the news when I came to visit you at the palace. I had suspected as much since I had been sent to give you this." Tirinvo indicated the box with the runes. "I had an encounter with your brother in the entrance hall of the palace. He was not inclined to allow me access to you without inspecting your gift. As the contents of this are for your eyes only, I refused to acquiesce to his request and left. One of the palace guards overheard our conversation and directed me to await you here and assured me he would inform you of my desire to meet."

"I am sorry, Prince Tirinvo," Aaron sighed. "My brother and I are not as close as we once were, but he feels strongly about his duty to the family. Overly so, perhaps. I was given the message and came as soon as I was able. My Uncle Baird is feasting me here this eve for my bachelor's celebration."

"Think nothing of it, Prince Aaron. As is traditional, I have brought you the cryswords of Fairinhorst for your offspring." Tirinvo picked up the box and presented it to Aaron, who reached across the table and took it from his hands.

Aaron looked at the Fairborn prince with a quizzical smile. "This feels heavier than just two cryswords." The crown prince of House deDraconis unhooked the catch and opened the polished wooden box, and time slowed to a crawl. Instead of the expected two, or possibly three, dull grey short swords, there were four. Each with a faint tinge of color, a lighter gray, red, green and blue. "This … this is unexpected … this can't be right!"

Aaron looked up and met the sympathetic gaze of the Fairborn prince, who spoke gently, "Your uncle expects you will receive the green sword, Prince Aaron."

"No! Four sons? A blue sword? This can't be right." He looked imploringly at the Fairborn prince. "My uncle Cameron taught us that those chosen to bear the Star live long lives. And so he has. He is nearing his eightieth year. He told me I would likely receive a gift of white, red, and green cryswords, but a blue sword? The last deDraconis to bear the double dragon birthmark, to carry a blue sword, was false to the House. A coward. … Worse, a traitor..." He trailed off.

The Fairborn prince shook his head. "Is this what Archduke Cameron has taught you? It's not my place to correct your uncle, Prince Aaron, but let me say this; I have known several generations of your House, and there has never been a coward among them."

"But a blue sword means a wizard. There are no more human wizards."

"It seems there will be, Prince Aaron." Tirinvo looked into Aaron's eyes and smiled. "My cousin, Varyan, was gifted with a blue crysword. He is a noted bard and healer."

"We don't need a bard in our family." Aaron shook his head.

"I doubt fate has the path of a bard in mind for your son."

Tirinvo looked to the open door that led back into the inn's common room. "I must go. I hear your brother's voice. Prince Bretton has made it very clear that I am not a welcome sight to his eyes. I shall not give him cause to spoil your celebration."

The Fairborn prince reached over, closed, and latched the

sword box. "I wish you a blessed marriage, my friend. To you and yours be happiness and strength." The Fairborn prince turned and walked to the alley door. Looking back, he nodded farewell and he and his liegemen strode out into the dusk of evening, closing the inn's door behind them.

Aaron stared at the glossy wooden box. *I'm going to have four sons,* he thought, a numbness filling his entire being. *Four sons.*

"Here you are." Prince Bretton stalked into the room and looked around, his eyes falling on the polished wooden box. "I see you met with the elves."

Aaron raised his eyes to gaze at his brother. Brett wasn't as tall as Aaron, but was stockier and more muscular. He gazed down at his seated brother with a scornful look in his eyes.

"Brett, you know you only belittle yourself calling the Fairborn names. You make yourself look rustic and crude."

"I'm a warrior. I don't mince words and I don't care what anyone thinks of my attitude. The Fairborn are arrogant backstabbers who would sell us to the Beastmen if it suited their whims."

"That's not true. They are our allies, not our foes."

"Bah, think what you will, but someday you will see the truth. It's near time for your dinner to begin. Uncle Baird sent me to summon you. Come on." Brett turned and walked out of the room, leaving Aaron to collect his thoughts. He picked up the wooden box and followed his brother back to the common room.

CHAPTER ONE:

BIRTHDAY MORNING

1

NIGHTMARES

ARTOS

The present day
9/15/1971 ar
The Autumnal Equinox
5:37 a.m.

CROWN PRINCE ARTOS awoke with a start, his heart racing as though it wanted to burst. As his eyes darted around his room, his crysword appeared in his hand, summoned from where it hung in its scabbard on its peg on the bedpost. It was a pure white crystal blade that he had grown accustomed to wielding over the last four years. The room was empty except for himself.

Oh, just a dream, he thought, *a nightmare. A doozy of a nightmare.* He laid the short sword down beside him on the bed, glanced across the shadowed room, and located his timekeeper where it hung on the wall. A dull golden glow on the right side showed the sunrise was soon to greet the day, as the silver orb of the moon neared the left edge.

"Light," he called out, and the glow panels in his room's ceiling glowed with a soft warm radiance.

Swinging his legs out of bed, he sat up, stretched, and gave a prodigious yawn. Quickly grabbing the clothes he had laid out the night before, he drew on his trousers, then pulled a warm loose shirt over his head, belted on his crysword, and then sitting on the bed once more, he slipped his feet into his supple, calf-high, moccasins.

"That's right," he spoke to himself, memories of the nightmare fleeing his thoughts. "It's the Fall Equinox. Lil-Bro's fifteenth birthday. Might as well get going. Sunrise is only a few minutes away. At least it won't be another totally boring day." He shuddered, thinking of the upcoming coming of age banquet and the inevitable Grand Ball that would follow. He'd have to act all royal and pretend he liked the stuffed shirts that would be attending. His cousins once removed, twice removed, first cousins twice removed, or second cousins once removed. Sighing, he shook his head.

Some of the offspring of the other Great Houses thought being the crown prince and heir to the Dragon Throne was a glamorous life. Ha! If they only knew the truth of it. Just one tedious day after another; get up, go exercise, go to class, exercise again, day after day. At least the weekends were a little better, with no classes except horsemanship, which was fun. No, being the crown prince wasn't what they thought at all. Why would anyone want the job?

"Ah, well. Count Darrellyel should be there. I like him. He usually has interesting stories to tell. Let's go see if Bort is up." He knew his younger brother probably would be. Bortis was an early riser, unlike Carimus, the next youngest, who would sleep the day away if given the chance. And Duka? Hard to say. Lil-Bro was usually up and about when Artos went to gather his three brothers to start their morning routine. To his surprise, his youngest brother was standing in the hall outside the door as if he was waiting for Artos to emerge.

"Morning, Lil-Bro—" he broke off his greeting, seeing the expression on Duka's face. "What's wrong? Has Bort been picking on you again?"

"No, I had a nightmare. I couldn't get back to sleep, didn't want to. I just got up and waited for you."

"How long have you been waiting? You could have knocked and woke me up. I wouldn't have minded."

"It's only been a little while; a few minutes. I didn't want to disturb you. I'm not a crybaby."

"Of course, you're not. What was the dream about? I was having a nightmare just before I woke up, too. Was it the trophy again?"

"I don't remember. It was just something bad. People were screaming and shouting, terrible things were happening, but I don't remember what exactly. I just had to get up and come wait for you."

"Well, don't let it get to you. Everybody has bad dreams sometimes. They don't mean a thing. Let's go get Bort and Cari and get the day started." Duka sighed and nodded. Artos patted his brother on the shoulder as they walked down the hall to get their brothers. *Being a big brother is more satisfying than being heir to the throne,* he thought. *Why would anyone want the troubles Father puts up with?*

At the base of West Dragon Falls, a small, shadowy form slipped from the water of the loch and disappeared into the jumble of loose rocks and flotsam at the base of Castle Draconis.

2

THE EYRIE

DUKA

6:03 a.m.

SLAP, SLAP ... SLAP, SLAP. Duka's feet kept the beat as he jogged up the Winding Way. His brother Carimus, elder by a year, lagged somewhat behind him. The sound of his feet echoed those of his brother as they jogged upon the yielding stone floor. Their elder brothers had already passed out of hearing as they challenged each other to be first to the top. As usual. Twice a day, before breakfast and before dinner, the four brothers ran from their rooms on the Princes' Level up to the Eyrie and then back, a distance of almost a mile each way.

"Hey, Duke! Did you ever look at this?" called out Carimus.

Duka slowed his jog and looked back to see his brother kneeling on the floor, peering where the wall and floor met. He stopped jogging and walked back to stand beside his brother. "What? I don't see anything unusual ... just the floor and the wall."

"That's what I mean. The wall is solid, hard stone," Carimus slapped the wall to make his point. "And the floor is soft, sort of squishy, and yet it looks just like the stone of the wall, and there is no crack between them."

Duka bent over and examined where the floor and wall met. Carimus chose that moment to leap to his feet. Giving his younger brother a sudden shove, he sprinted away up the ramp.

With a surprised shout, Duka fell to his hands and knees. "You beast, Cari!" He laughed as he leaped to his feet and tore up the ramp after his sneaky brother. Duka was more than a match for Carimus in a long race, but his slender brother was very much his master in a sprint, and Duka was the last brother to reach the castle's top.

Bursting into the Eyrie through the tingly but invisible qulan seal that surrounded the castle's exterior, Duka gasped in the cool September air as he stopped and caught his breath.

Standing to the side of the entrance to the Winding Way was his oldest brother, Artos. Carimus peeked around him, a wide grin plastered across his face. Bortis, his remaining brother, was near the door to the western guard's quarters, engaged in a conversation with McArn, a sergeant of the guard, the Captain of the tower.

"Hey slowpoke, about time you got here," quipped Carimus.

"I would have been here sooner, but I speared a wild pig on the ramp, and I had to butcher the carcass, you know?" replied Duka. He eyed Carimus's location. "Is there some reason you're hiding?" Duka glanced around the empty Eyrie in mock fear. "Is there something dangerous loose up here? A rampaging pigeon, perhaps? Another wild pig?"

"Hiding? I'm not hiding," Carimus stepped up beside his eldest brother. "Why would I be hiding?"

Artos chuckled. "Let me guess, Lil-Bro. Cari told you there

was something wrong with the everlight stripe and when you stopped to look, he took off like a scared bunny and beat you to the top? Right?"

Carimus made indignant sounds as Duka grinned at Artos, "No. He had me bend down to look at where the floor and the wall meet and then gave me a push. He knocked me to my hands and knees, then he bolted ahead. The only way he could beat me was to cheat."

"I didn't cheat! No rule says I couldn't ..." He trailed off as Artos laughed and then, with a sheepish smile, he concluded, "Well, there isn't."

Artos shook his head, "Bort used the everlight. Bit of advice. Don't mention this to Uncle Brett. I speak from experience. Uncle Brett was up here talking to Sergeant McArn that day. When I scolded Bort for cheating, he overheard me. Did Bort run an extra lap for his behavior? No. On the other hand, I had been caught with my guard down. So, I ran two extra laps. For my own good, you understand. To imprint the lesson."

Duka shook his head. "I hadn't planned on saying a word. It's embarrassing to be tricked by a weasel."

"Hey!" said Carimus, stiffening with indignation. "Weasel? No one made you stop and look, fool."

"You won't get me that way again," Duka slapped Carimus on the arm. "Let's go out and see if we can spot any of the other families on the way here for tonight."

"Tonight?" asked Artos with a voice tinged with innocence. "Is there something special going on?"

Laughing at his eldest brother, Duka walked to the southern door and out onto the battlements.

As he looked out across the King's Valley, he pictured in his mind his home, as it would appear to those approaching the castle.

Castle Draconis looked more like the rocky peak they had carved it from than the fortress it was. There were battlements, the airship docks, and here at the top, the Eyrie. A keen eye would discern several score arrow slits and even a few stained-glass windows, but the home of the Family deDraconis looked more like a crag than a castle. The quantimasters of millennia past had done their work exceedingly well. The gatehouse across the causeway looked more like a castle than the Great House behind it.

Coming up beside Duka, Artos scanned the King's Valley, along with his youngest brother. Carimus had stopped and was standing a few yards behind them, his eyes closed as if in concentration.

"It's way too early, Lil-Bro. Nobody will show up for your birthday feast for hours and hours yet." Artos laid his hand on his little brother's shoulder.

"Nobody's going to show up at all." Cut in a fresh voice, "Sorry Spare, the weather-sensor told McArn an hour ago. There's another autumn storm blowing this way and it will be here a wee bit after sundown. If we were back in the lowlands, they might try if the airship pilot thought he could get over it, but up here? No way." Bortis strode up and joined his brothers at the parapet. "Father will probably have your coming-of-age ceremony at the Solstice, back in Phoenix." Bortis shrugged. He was a few inches shorter than Artos, but with slightly broader shoulders, a wiry wrestler's build.

Duka looked doubtfully out at the cloudless sky and then back at Carimus. "Cari?" he asked uncertainly.

"He's right, Duke," Carimus opened his eyes and shook his head. "There's angry weather off ... off somewhere ... To the east, I think." Carimus gazed toward the Black Mountains and shrugged.

"Like you could tell, Cari," said Bortis. "I suppose you're a weather-sensor now?"

Artos placed his hand on the hilt of his crysword and closed his eyes in concentration for a few moments. "Yes, I think so … it feels like … like … rubbing your hand on fur and feeling the static charge. I could probably farsee it on the screens. Well … maybe not yet. It can't be too close. Across the mountains, probably." He pointed to the east, then nodded at Carimus. "Has Uncle Cameron been working with you on weather-sensing now, too, Cari?"

Carimus nodded, looking proud. "I've been practicing. He says I'm very strong with all the nature quans. It comes easier to me than to him even, but don't tell him I told you so."

Bortis snorted. "We need to get going. Back down the Way, let's go!"

"You're wrong, Bort!" said Duka, pointing to the south. "Look!"

The brothers looked. Three riders were approaching, tiny figures in the distance.

"Oh wow. That'll be a grand party alright. Come on. We'll be late for breakfast." Bortis made his way back toward the Eyrie doorway, with Artos and Carimus close behind. Duka watched the riders a moment longer and a feeling of uneasiness swept over him. Was there something bad coming with those riders? Bad news perhaps? No, the feeling he had was closer to home. Something felt wrong, but he wasn't sure what. Could it be connected to the nightmare that had woken him up? It was a beautiful morning, cool and crisp. There wasn't anything he could place a finger on. Maybe he was sensing the storm Cari said he felt approaching. He shrugged, turned, and followed his brothers back inside and began jogging down the Winding Way.

3

BREAKFAST

ARTOS

6:46 a.m.

ARTOS WAS THE FIRST of the brothers to reach the dining hall after showering and changing from his exercise. His father, King Aaron, was alone at the table when he entered the room.

"Good morning, son," the king gave him a somewhat distracted smile. "Did you have a good run?"

"Yes. I beat Bort to the Eyrie, but he beat me back down."

His father nodded. "I'm glad we have a minute alone. We don't have much chance of that, it seems. You are nearly twenty. It will soon be time for you to marry and set up a household of your own. We will have even less time then. You will be concerned with your wife and starting a family of your own."

Artos stopped in the middle of sitting down and looked at his father, then finished settling into his chair. "I haven't given much thought to marriage, Father. I'm in no rush."

Aaron gave a small sigh. "It is time you consider your duty, Art. You are not just anyone. You are the Crown Prince of Veda.

There is a destiny you are born to; a leader of men along the road to glory. You bear the dragon and crown birthmark; you carry a white crysword. You do not just belong to yourself. I watch you when you attend the council meetings. There are times when you look as though you wish you were a thousand miles away. Do not think the other heads of the Great Houses do not scrutinize your every move, every gesture. You have a destiny to rule when I am gone. A duty to our line. You are not a child. Do not act like one."

At that moment, Carimus and Duka came hurrying in, pulled out their chairs, and sat down.

"Good morning, boys. Happy birthday, Duka," said the king, turning his attention away from his firstborn. "I'm afraid I have some bad news. We won't be having the large celebration tonight we had planned. The weather sensors have detected an early autumn storm coming this evening. We have been in contact with the other Houses. Only your grandfather and the deEagledons are close enough to risk the trip. There will be your birthday dinner and you'll receive your birthday gifts, of course. But the guests will have to leave early to beat the foul weather so there won't be a Grand Ball."

Duka nodded from where he and Carimus sat across the table from Artos. "I'm not really a dancer, father."

"A man is judged by many things, Duka. Grace is far from the least important. But no matter, we will make it up at the Winter Solstice. You shall have your official ceremony then."

At that moment, Bortis rushed into the room and hurriedly sat next to Artos, just as the chime that signaled the seventh hour rang forth.

Aaron glanced at his second son and shook his head. "I'm glad you could join us, Bort." Bortis nodded back to his father as the servitors appeared from the kitchen, bearing trays of eggs, fried potatoes, and crispy bacon. Others began filling the glasses with milk and the cups with steaming, hot coffee. Conversation stilled as everyone's attention turned to their breakfast.

Chapter Two:

The Bonding

4

BRETT AND BORT

BORTIS

7:50 a.m.

AFTER WOLFING DOWN his usual breakfast and being excused from the table, Prince Bortis hurried back toward his room with the goal of spending a few minutes practicing summoning his sword. It came so easily for Art and Cari. Why was it such a struggle for him?

Turning off the royal stairway and into the hall that housed the princes' bedrooms, he came face to face with his uncle, the Duke Bretton, Grand Marshal of Armies of Veda.

In a swift motion, his uncle summoned his crysword to his hand, its crimson blade glinting as it sliced through the air towards his abdomen.

With a surprised shout, Bortis jumped back a step, his hands raised to block the blow. The red sword stopped inches from his outstretched fingers.

"That's a good way to lose your hands," his uncle remarked coldly and slid his crysword back into the sheath on his belt.

Bretton stood an inch under six feet and was solidly built. His hair was steel gray, as were his mustache and well-trimmed short beard, which ran from ear to ear. His eyes were gray as well and never at rest. Anyone could tell just by looking that he was always at the ready. A small scar lay upon his left cheek and brow, having narrowly missed his eye.

"Why didn't you summon your sword to block?"

"You … you surprised me," stammered Bortis, as he held out his hand to summon his sword.

"A warrior needs to always be alert. Do you think a bandit is going to politely wait for you to draw your sword and fight a formal duel? Take an extra lap before practice this afternoon."

A drop of sweat beaded on Bortis's forehead as his red-bladed crysword appeared in his hand. The look of disgust on his uncle's face made his chest tighten with emotion. He nodded, "Yes sir, I understand."

"You're still having problems summoning your sword?"

"I summon it … well … I call it to my hand like you taught me. It doesn't want to come. It fights me!"

"A crysword is not alive, Bort." The look in his uncle's eyes was almost one of pity. Somehow, pity was worse than disgust. He looked down and shoved the sword back into its sheath.

"A crysword is a tool. It is the most important tool you will ever use. That you will ever own. How will you be able to defend yourself or anyone else if you cannot wield it properly? At sword practice today, I will have Artos oversee the others, and you will work on summoning your blade."

Bortis nodded dumbly, unable to speak. How humiliating that would be. He could already picture the smug look on Cari's face when their uncle made this announcement.

"You were born with the sword and dragon. That birthmark

means that one day you will be protector of the realm. It is the duty you were born to. You must overcome this problem."

Bort nodded again. "I know, and I will. I know I must. I won't let you down."

Bretton sighed. "It is not me you would be letting down. Your brother will depend on you. No matter what happens, you must be the rock his rule will stand on. Now, be on your way. Get ready for class. Go. I will see you at swordsmanship practice." His uncle brushed by him and walked down the stairs.

5

CLASS

DUKA

8:30 a.m.

THE ARCHDUKE BISHOP SUPREME Cameron deDraconis was a thin, fussy man. A part-time teacher to the brothers, he instructed them in politics and the protocols of their station. Also, the basics of quanti-magic, the day-to-day uses, such as turning on the lights in their rooms or adjusting the temperature of their showers. Although he was their great-uncle, he did not seem elderly, but someone who still had much vigor and energy. His hair was gray, streaked with white, as was his thin mustache and goatee. He frequently paced back and forth in front of his students as he lectured and used his hands with sweeping flourishes to add emphasis to his words. Duka often thought his great-uncle reminded him of a stork with his long, thin legs and his way of peering at his pupils, as if they were tasty fish and he was choosing his dinner.

He was pacing when the brothers entered his classroom. "Ah, you have arrived. Happy Birthday, Prince Duka! A special day. Today you have come of age. You'll begin the bonding of your crysword. An auspicious day."

Duka thought his uncle looked more nervous than happy. The room smelled like the air before a thunderstorm and the hair on his forearms stiffened. He smiled and gave a respectful bow. "I thank you, Archduke Cameron. It is indeed my fifteenth birthday." He straightened and with a more somber look said, "I'm afraid you are mistaken about my bonding with my crysword now, sir. Father informed me at breakfast that because of tonight's storm, he won't be having my coming-of-age ceremony until we are back in Phoenix. At the solstice," Duka shrugged.

"Nonsense! I know your father postponed the official ceremony. Of course, he has. We can't have you missing all the pomp and all the young girls now, can we?" Cameron laughed, and Duka again was reminded of a bird. A loon, perhaps? "No, no. That has nothing to do with you bonding with your sword. You will begin bonding with your crysword today, this very hour, in fact." Cameron gestured at a polished wooden box sitting on his desk. "I have it awaiting you now, but first, yes, first, we will review a few things. These things must be done properly, you know. Prince Duka, we shall begin. What is a crysword?" He noticed the brothers were all still standing just inside the room. "Well, what are you waiting for? Sit down, sit down." He paced around behind his desk and stood before the screen of light blue crystal that took up a good deal of the wall.

Artos, Bortis, and Carimus all sat down. Duka stopped alongside his desk to recite. Carimus gave his younger brother an encouraging smile and then paid attention eagerly, while Bortis just looked bored.

"A crysword is a short sword made of colored crystal," began

Duka. "It is as strong as the best steel of the Forge-folk. It serves the person to whom it is bonded in different ways, depending upon that person's ties to the quanti. Just about anyone can use theirs to start a fire, or know the direction. With some people, it can be a fearsome weapon, while to others, a handy tool." He sat down.

"Harrumph." Cameron cleared his throat. "Are you sure of everything you just said?" He peered at Duka, again reminding him of a hunting stork. Duka remained silent but nodded to his great-uncle. "Actually, everything you just said is correct, to a point. But also, much of what you said is wrong. Do any of you know what Prince Duka said that was incorrect?" He peered eagerly at the other three. "Prince Artos, do you? Prince Bortis? Now, having had a moment to reflect?" He continued without waiting for a reply, "No! A crysword is not as strong as steel. It is stronger. Harder too. Not all cryswords are short swords. I know of at least one that is a rapier, another a quarter staff, and there are tales of others as well. There are stories that some quantimasters of old could even change the size and shape of the blades they wielded, but that's probably just that ... stories. The Queen of the Fairborn court wields a crysbow and a few of the other nobles of her court as well. Then there is the crysaxe of the Thain of the Forge-folk. So, no Prince Duka, a crysword is not always a short sword, or even a sword.

"Ah-ha, next. The uses of a crysword ... Now it's true they can be used as fire starters, yes. But that's really a pretty minor use of the quanti and as a compass ... well, yes, but any scout could figure the directions from the placement of the sun or by the stars. Duke Bretton, your uncle," he paused and peered at the brothers as if they might need time to remember who their uncle was, "he can use his crysword to truesee and, as a terrible swift-sword of vengeance, it is true. My brother, Duke Baird, taught him well. He always said young prince Bretton would be a masterful warrior with his sword. It is almost a shame there is little use for his mastery anymore. But with the Beastmen problems largely in the past, it is mostly bandits your uncle need deal with and he would hardly need to call upon the power of the quanti to deal with the likes of that.

"Now I know Prince Duka is untrained in crysword lore, but which of you three can tell me the most important feature of a crysword?" He paused again and looked at Artos, Bortis, and Carimus. "Well ...?"

"Oh!" Carimus suddenly sat up straighter. "I know. Once a person has bonded with their sword, they can always call it to them. Even from another room."

"Excellent. Very good, Disciple Carimus. Yes, once bonded to your crysword, it is yours forever after and no one can keep it from your hand should you call it to you. Even if mountains should stand between you. A crysword bonds for life and when the owner passes away, his crysword crumbles to dust." The Archduke was always careful to call each of the brothers by their title, prince, except for Carimus who, to Cameron, was always either Disciple Carimus outside of services to the church, or Acolyte deDraconis during services. Prince Carimus had been born with a birthmark of the four-pointed star above the head of a dragon upon his right upper arm where it joined his shoulder, showing his destiny was to be the eventual head of the church. One day, Carimus would graduate to Brother deDraconis and be ordained as a deacon and then a priest as he continued his training to take his great-uncle's role as both secular and spiritual head of the Church of the Four, the High Church of the land of Veda.

"Prince Bortis, would you care to give us a demonstration?" Cameron stood beside his desk and held out his hand.

"Huh?" said Bortis with a start. "Me? You always have Art do that."

"Shall I ask Prince Artos to give the demonstration, then? Are you unable to show Prince Duka how you are bonded with your crysword?" Cameron folded his arms and tilted his head to the left and stared at Bortis, once again reminding Duka of a stork.

"No. I can do it. You know I can." Bortis stood from his desk, glaring at Duka as if being singled out was somehow his fault.

"Your crysword, sir," said Cameron, again holding out his hand. Bortis unbuckled his sword belt and handed it to his great-uncle.

"Very good! Did you see, Prince Duka? He didn't unsheathe his blade but handed me the crysword still within its sheath. This is the safe way to give your blade into the care of another. Never hand a person a naked crysword." He turned and walked behind his desk, pulled a drawer open, and placed the sword belt with the sheathed sword within. He shut the drawer and walked around to the front of the desk, and nodded at Bortis. "You may proceed."

There was a thin sheen of sweat on his elder brother's forehead. Bortis nodded to their great-uncle and held out his left hand, his fist nearly clenched as if the hilt of his sword were clutched there. He let out his breath, then slowly drew another in, concentration written upon his face. With a *pop*, a short sword with a blade that looked as if it were forged from ruby was in Bortis's hand. He waved it in triumph, a look of relief on his face.

"Good, prince Bortis. Now, Prince Artos, please demonstrate

a quick draw for your brother."

Without moving from his seat, Artos held out his right hand as Bortis had done with his left. There was another *pop* as Artos's diamond white crysword appeared in his hand, and another *pop* from the direction of Carimus, who could not refrain from copying his elder brothers, his crysword looking as if it had been carved from the heart of an emerald.

"Disciple Carimus," said Cameron, "I do not recall asking for your assistance." His slight smile dispelled any thoughts that he might really be displeased. It was no secret that Carimus was his favorite prince. He walked back behind his desk and retrieved Bortis's sword belt and handed it to him. Duka's eyes turned to the polished wooden sword box on his great-uncle's desk.

"You may sheath your blades, gentlemen," rang a new voice. Everyone turned to the door where their Uncle Bretton now stood. He nodded to Cameron, "Pray forgive me, Uncle, for interrupting your class. I won't be a moment. I must address the young gentlemen."

Cameron nodded graciously. "Of course, Nephew." He twirled his hand at the four brothers. "They are all yours."

Bretton deDraconis gazed at his nephews in his usual soldier's stance.

"I know it will disappoint you all terribly, but I'm canceling your afternoon classes with me. No sword practice today." He looked back at Cameron. "If you please, Uncle, could you arrange your schedule to give your afternoon instruction to Cari and Duka directly after lunch and then meet with Aaron and I in the Hall of Mirrors at three o'clock?"

"The Hall of Mirrors? Is it a Council meeting then? Oh, of course, I shall attend."

"Yes." Bretton nodded. "Aaron received a request for a concourse from the Darrel this morn. One of your druids brought it just a few minutes ago. A big man who looks as though he would have made a fine Sky-knight if he hadn't turned to hugging trees."

Duka's uncle favored the sect of the Sky over the sect of the Earth, but still, he thought his uncle's contemptuous tone was stronger than he had noticed before. Duka had met a pair of druids when he had visited the Lord of House deDarrellyel. They had seemed like fine men, healers, and scholars of nature.

"He brought other news as well. It seems we will receive a few elves for dinner tonight. They are coming for his banquet, not knowing it's been canceled," Bretton gestured at Duka.

"Fairborn are coming tonight?" interrupted Duka, forgetting his manners.

Bretton gave Duka a stern look. "I just said that, didn't I, Prince Duka?"

Duka glanced down and nodded. "I'm sorry, sir. I didn't mean to be rude."

His uncle acknowledged his apology with a brief nod and continued speaking to Cameron. "The concourse is at four. We shall have a few guests attending with us, and Aaron wants us to have a short meeting before then. Artos, Bortis, you two plan on attending me directly after you have lunch."

"Who are the guests?"

"Count Eagledon, Count Penrodyn, and the Canon. The Canon is a cousin of Count Stephan, and he has been at their castle awaiting the airship trip back next week."

"Ahh, yes, Pietro told me he was finishing his rounds of the diocese here in the King's Valley, that he would journey back to Phoenix after the equinox. How fortunate he chose to end his pilgrimage here this year."

"Yes, Count Stephen, his family, and a few retainers will be here for Duka's banquet tonight. Count Estel sent word he would be in attendance as well." Bretton glanced at Duka. "Some people have all the luck, eh, nephew? Not only do you get a birthday party today, but another party to share with your brother Artos on his birthday." He looked at Artos, "Lady Elaine will accompany her family. Your father is of a mind that she will be a good match for you. Think upon it." With a brief nod to the brothers and a slightly deeper bow to Cameron, Bretton turned and strode from the room.

For a long moment, the silence was palpable, each lost in their own thoughts.

"Close your mouth, Art," said Bortis. "Or are you hoping to snack on a tasty bug or two?"

"I do not believe Duke Bretton should be speaking of this," Cameron said with a disapproving frown. "Marriage is a serious matter and between people of high rank, especially so. Oh no, no, no."

"So it's not true then, is it? Father wouldn't just arrange such a thing without telling me, would he?" Artos looked at his greatuncle, his face pale.

"Oh, I expect it's true. But Duke Bretton was totally out of place to mention it. Now, where were we? Oh yes! Prince Duka, step forward, please."

Duka slid from his seat and glanced at his eldest brother as he walked up to his great-uncle's desk. Artos' face was pale with surprise. He tried to remember Count Eagledon's eldest daughter. *Oh yes! The twins, Ellis, and Elaine deEagledon, that's right. She's not hideous. I wonder what's up with Art?* Duka stepped up on the raised part of the floor and stood waiting, his heart racing in anticipation. His own crysword. What would it be like? Would it be red like Bort's or green like Cari's? Maybe his would be golden? Or maybe … maybe it would be colorless… He hoped desperately it wouldn't be. His great-uncle seemed to take forever to open the box. He carefully unhooked a latch and stood there with his hand on the lid, as if he didn't want to open it. *That's it! It must be colorless, and Uncle Cameron knows, and he doesn't want to open the box and reveal my disgrace.* Cameron swallowed hard as he opened the hinged lid. Duka looked inside.

The box had been designed to hold four swords. Three empty places showed where his brothers' swords had once lain, and the fourth spot held a sword. Duka's heart fell. The sword awaiting him looked nothing like the cryswords of his brothers, no gemlike radiance, just a dull bluish gray sword.

"Take up your crysword, Prince Duka," said Cameron. Was that a slight quaver in his voice? "Take it and hold it before you with the blade pointing to the sky. Empty your mind of all distractions. Feel the quanti in your soul and align them in your mind with the quanti in your heart and the quanti in your sword."

Duka looked from the dull gray sword to his great-uncle. Cameron was now holding his own crysword, its emerald beauty almost too much to bear. Duka clenched his teeth and quickly reached out to grab hold of the grip. Since there was no hilt wrap as was typical in all the swords Duka had ever been trained with, the grip felt hard, rough, and a little gritty. But as he held his blade before him, the hard, gritty feeling was replaced with a soft, smooth, comfortable grip made for his hand. The quanti of the crysword merged somehow with the quanti deep within his being, deep within his soul.

"It usually takes a while for the—eh?" Cameron gasped.

"Duke. It's beautiful," cried the voice of his brother Carimus at the same moment.

"Very nice, Lil-Bro," said Artos. "You should take a look at it."

Duka realized his eyes were clenched tightly shut. He slowly opened them. The bright blue hued short sword in his right hand was the most beautiful thing he had ever seen. If Artos's crysword was diamond, Bortis's ruby, and Carimus's emerald, then his was sapphire. "I'm bonded," he said with wonder in his voice, and he was.

6

THE AFTERMATH

ARTOS

9:05 a.m.

Artos felt numb as his great-uncle fussed with some things in a desk drawer. Marriage. His father had said he should think about it. Well, he was thinking. He wasn't ready to marry. It seemed his father had already picked his bride. That wasn't right! He took a deep breath. Had the room gotten warmer? The ozone smell was even stronger than it was before. Is this what it means to be crown prince? Not being allowed input on the most important details of your life? Would being king be any better? Artos had attended some council meetings with his father. He had seen the Council try to force their will on King Aaron. His father had the last word unless the entire council overruled him, but the arguments, the infighting, the shouting, and blustering. Was being king even worth the trouble? Would he be up to it? Did he even want to try?

Duka stood motionless, looking dazed, his eyes still transfixed upon his newly bonded sword. He remembered how shaken he had felt after his own bonding, and his accident immediately after. Artos got up from his desk and walked up to stand beside him. Duka shook his head and reached his left hand up toward the sword.

"Lil-Bro, DON'T! Don't touch the blade."

Duka stopped and turned his head toward Artos, a puzzled look on his face. "Ah … okay, why?"

Artos held up his left hand with the palm facing his little brother, revealing the large white scar that ran across his four fingers. "You don't want to make the same mistake I did, Lil-Bro. You have to train yourself to always keep your sword exactly as sharp as it needs to be. Or rather, how dull, most of the time. Uncle Brett will show you." Artos carefully drew his sword from its sheath and held the edge pointing upwards so Duka could examine it.

"Prince Artos, I must step away for a short time. You are in charge of class until I return. No shenanigans. Train your brother about basic crysword safety. I won't be gone overly long, but I must speak with King Aaron." The Archbishop hurried from the room.

"Whoa. What got Camy all riled up?" asked Bortis, looking at Artos.

"Yeah," chimed in Carimus. "He looked upset."

"No," said Artos, shaking his head and sheathing his blade. "He looked scared. I mean, worried, scared. Not terrified, just distressed." He thought for a moment. "Cari, how long did it take you to bond with your sword?"

"Ahh ... oh ... About an hour or two? Maybe ninety minutes? I'm not sure. You know what it's like. Oh," Carimus stared at his younger brother.

"Yeah." Artos nodded. "It was something like that for me,

too." He shook his head and looked at Duka. Puzzled, he gazed back and forth between Artos and Carimus.

"Hey, Bort, how long did it take—" Carimus began to ask.

"Never you mind, how long it took me!" barked Bortis. "I bonded, didn't I?"

"Hey. Calm down, Bort," said Artos, looking at Carimus. "It takes some people longer than others, Cari. It means nothing." He looked back at Duka. "And some people can bond pretty quick, I guess. Really quick." He shook his head again, his mind filled with questions. He remembered his great-uncle telling him he had bonded exceedingly quickly at just over an hour. It had taken Bort several days.

"Okay Lil-Bro, first we need to get you a sheath for your sword." Artos looked around the room, trying to think of the nearest place to find one.

"Hey, Spare." Bortis rummaged about in the clutter inside his desk drawer and pulled out a well-used leather scabbard. "Here, you can have this one. I outgrew the belt, but it should fit you just fine." He stood up and handed it to Artos, a look of gratitude on his face, and gave a slight nod. He then sat down again, leaned back, and closed his eyes.

"Thanks, Bort," said Artos.

"Thank you, Bortis," repeated Duka a moment later.

Artos turned to Duka. "Okay Lil-Bro, as I said, Uncle Brett will train you to use it. He will train you and train you and drill you. Then he will train you and drill you some more. Oh, and also, he will train you and drill you and train you and drill you. And did I mention he will train you?"

Duka smiled a little. "Why do I feel you are trying to tell me something, Art? Come on, just tell me."

Artos smiled back. "I know you know all about sword safety,

but that's for a regular sword, not a crysword. Your sword now knows it is your sword, and it won't like anyone else touching it. It's more for show than anything else. I mean, you can use it to help you focus when you use the quanti, but you have to be careful and keep thoughts disciplined. That's a big part of what Uncle Brett will teach you, how not to hurt yourself by accident."

"Cryswords aren't alive, Art," said Bortis. "They're just tools. Fancy tools."

"Yes, I know, but it helps if you think they are, at least for me," retorted Artos.

Bortis just snorted.

"Now think about the wooden practice swords we beat each other with every day. See it now? A nice, rounded edge and point, dull, and boringly safe. Picture it and think about your sword." He looked from Duka's face to his new sword. Then, just for a moment, the sapphire appearance of the crysword flashed to the brown of seasoned oak, exactly the look of the swords the brothers used daily to practice with at the pells. Then it was gemlike again.

Artos stood dumbstruck. Not believing his eyes.

"What did you do, Duke?" Carimus's voice cracked.

Duka looked at his sword. "I made the edges rounded, Cari. I did it!" Pride showed in his face, mirrored in his voice.

"Hooray," interjected Bortis, still sitting with his head back and his eyes closed, "let's have a parade."

"Shut up, Bort," snapped Artos, still gazing at the blue sword in Duka's hand. "Duke, did you … were you looking at your sword? I mean, did you see that?"

"I saw it, Artie!" Carimus's voice was shrill with excitement. "It changed to wood and then back."

"Huh?" said Duka, looking at Carimus. "What? That's crazy." He glanced between his two brothers. "Wood? Really, Cari, wood?" he examined his sword closely.

"Lil-Bro, he's not pulling your leg. Weren't you looking at it when you were thinking about the edge?" Artos handed Duka the sword belt Bortis had given him. Duka slipped the blade inside, fastened the belt around his waist, and tied the leather strap around his right thigh.

"No. My eyes were closed. I can't picture things in my mind with my eyes open, at least not while concentrating on them. Wood? Really? You're telling me I turned my sword to wood and then it just turned back? 'Cause I wasn't trying to. I wouldn't! Why would I?"

"PRINCE DUKA DID WHAT?" Their great-uncle was back. Bortis sat up with a start, and the four brothers all turned to look at the doorway. Cameron stood there aghast, a scabbard in his hand. And he wasn't alone. To his left stood their Uncle Bretton, his face impassive. To his right, their father, the king, looking at the brothers with concern.

"Prince Duka did what to his sword?" Cameron repeated more calmly. "Where is it?" His eyes darted around the room.

"Duka, you are not trained yet," their Uncle Bretton rudely cut in, interrupting his uncle. "You are forbidden to attempt any magic with that sword. Do you understand?" He crossed his arms and stood waiting, staring at Duka.

"Yes, sir, I understand. But I wasn't trying to do any—" Duka stared at the ground.

"No magic! Until I have you trained." Bretton turned and strode out.

Artos turned to his father, "Sir, he was only following my instructions so he could put his sword safely away and—"

"I specifically told you no shenanigans, Prince Artos," Cameron interrupted. "I wasn't out of the room fifteen minutes and—"

"It's alright Uncle Cameron," said Aaron, as he studied Duka. "Are you all right, son? Is your sword damaged? What happened?" No one spoke. "Anyone?" His sons looked back at him, mute. "Artos?"

"I was telling Lil-Bro ... er, Duka, the safety basics, that's all," Artos began. "It happened so fast, I thought I might have just imagined it, but Cari saw it too."

"That's right, Father," said Carimus anxiously. "Oh, and the room smelled like a thunderstorm."

"I can smell the ozone, Cari. The classrooms always smell that way, but it is stronger than normal. Thank you." Aaron turned to look at Bortis. "What did you see, Bort?"

"Nothing. I wasn't looking at Spare when it happened. I just smelled the rain, err, ozone, I mean, and heard Cari scream." Bortis snickered a little.

"I didn't scream," started Carimus, ready to argue with his elder brother.

"Enough!" said Aaron, "Duka?"

Duka gazed into his father's eyes. "It was like Art said. I mean, I ... I didn't see anything. I had my eyes closed and was concentrating on how the blades of our practice swords are round with dull points. Then Cari screamed."

"I didn't scream ..." Carimus began, but stopped as his father looked at him, then muttered softly, under his breath, "I didn't."

"Well, I think we should just put that sword back in the box and think upon this," said Cameron.

Artos saw the stricken expression on Duka's face and was about to protest.

"No, Uncle," said Aaron. "It's too late for that." He looked back at Duka. "You understood what your Uncle Bretton said?" Duka nodded. "I want you to promise me that until you are trained to use that sword properly, you won't try to use any magic with it. Your word, sir."

"No Father, I mean, yes Father, no magic. I promise, you have my word, sir." Duka nodded and Artos patted his little brother on his arm reassuringly.

Aaron glanced over his shoulder at the timekeeper on the wall above the door of the room and then at his uncle.

"I see you don't agree with me, Uncle Cameron, but like it or not, Duka is bonded to that sword. He has promised, and I trust my son's word. He is a deDraconis. What I would not like to find is how he might react in a dream-state, feeling separated from his bonded sword. Can you be sure he might not try to call it to him, or worse, try to use it in a nightmare? No," he shook his head. "I do not believe we should try to separate them now. Do you?"

Cameron deDraconis sighed and bowed his head, his lips moving in a few words of silent prayer. "No, I was wrong. You are correct, King Aaron. I hadn't thought it through. I had not thought it would be so swift and it scrambled my wits. I still have some time to … to … I hadn't planned a lesson for this morning. I had thought we would spend it with Prince Duka, trying to bond. But I'll think of something. You will see me at the Hall of Mirrors. I shan't be eating lunch today. I have much to think about." He stared at Duka. "Lessons to plan."

King Aaron looked back at Duka. "May I see your sword, son?"

Duka mutely nodded and drew his crysword from the sheath and made as if to hand the hilt to his father.

"No, Son. I just want to look. You hold it." Aaron gazed a moment at the shining sapphire blade. "It's beautiful, Son. Thank you."

Duka sheathed the blade. Relief showing on his face.

Aaron nodded, "Until three then, Uncle." He turned and walked from the classroom.

Flustered, Cameron walked back behind his desk. "Well, what are you three doing standing about? Sit down, sit down. We shall proceed. Yes, yes." He paced back and forth behind his desk. "Duka! What did you do wrong when the king asked to see your sword?"

The three brothers all returned to their desks and sat down. Duka's right hand kept reaching out and touching the pommel of his new sword as if to reassure himself his sword was still there. Artos looked down at his right hand and smiled as he realized he was doing exactly the same thing.

The dark form slowly moved from one shadow to another, one crevice to another. Slowly climbing the rough, rocky exterior of Castle Draconis, never moving with anything but slow deliberation. Never emerging from the shadows ...

7

CARI AND CAMERON

CARIMUS

11:30 a.m.

AFTER HIS BROTHERS all fled the classroom, Carimus approached the desk where his great-uncle was sitting and stood patiently, waiting to be noticed. After a few moments, Cameron looked up and saw him standing there.

"Yes, Disciple Carimus, is there something you need?"

"No, Uncle. I just wondered if there was anything you wanted me to do?" Carimus saw the deep worry on his uncle's face and felt uneasy. The archbishop seldom looked so distressed.

"Thank you for asking, but no. I don't have any chores this morning. I have some reports to look over. It seems there has been an increase in the amount of children born this year with the taint. A child with horns or a tail is just not fitting. Not to mention the harm a child with horns or fangs could do to another innocent child. It is so distressing to have to remove infants and young children from their parents, but the greater good sometimes requires harsh measures." He shook his head. "If we were less vigilant, there is no telling what havoc would ensue."

"We can't let Beastmen run loose," agreed Carimus. "They will be happier with their own kind, in Renn." He repeated the words he had heard so often from the elders in the Sky sect.

His great-uncle smiled at his words, giving him a feeling of pride. "You are a wise lad. I wish more of the people would understand. It would be unforgivable for us to allow these things to go unchecked. Unforgivable. And of course, there is always the chance of something even worse."

"An Abomination," agreed Carimus. "Has there been a report of one being born?"

"Oh, no! There hasn't been an Abomination born in many years. Many, many years," he repeated with a slight shudder. "I have never had to deal with such a thing, and I hope I never do, nor you either. I believe we have been spared from that horrible occurrence. Hopefully forever more. If any of those creatures still live, they know better than to approach the lands of men. The fate of Tomung has deterred them from venturing forth from whatever holes they cower in, hidden in the eastern wastes."

"And good riddance," announced Carimus, taking a step closer to the desk and examining the lid of the polished wooden box sitting there. The box which had held the crysword of his brother. "What do those runes mean, uncle?"

"Eh? What runes?" Cameron saw where he was gazing. "Oh, those. Those are the runes of the witch of the Fairborn who holds the secret of creating the cryswords. They are just decorative. Pay them no mind."

"They are like the runes on my bracelet. The one the

Fairborn gave me years ago."

"Oh yes, I remember that. They hold no meaning that I'm aware of."

"Doesn't anyone else know how to craft cryswords?"

Cameron appeared to think a moment before answering. "I do not believe so. It is something they keep for themselves. I believe both the Fairborn and the Forgefolk have craftsmen who can work with the crystal for some objects. But the secret of creating the cryswords is known only to the artisans of the witch. I believe some of our people have petitioned for the secret in the past, but she is greedy and keeps it for herself. Beware such evil, Disciple Carimus. The hoarding of such knowledge is certainly a sin."

Carimus nodded knowingly.

"Go get ready for your midday meal." The archbishop rose from his chair. "Your uncle said there was a druid here. I should go and find him. He mentioned it was a large man. I wonder … could it be …?"

"What's that, sir?"

"Oh, nothing, nothing. Off with you now. I shall see you and Prince Duka in class, after lunch. Be off." Cameron made shooing motions with his hands, and Carimus turned and left the classroom.

8

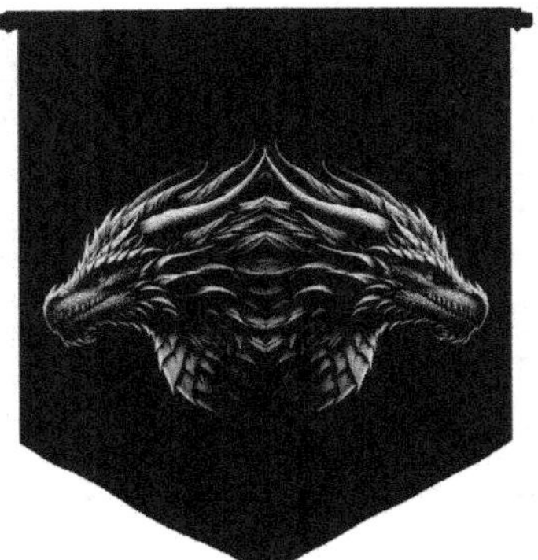

THE TROPHY

DUKA

11:43 a.m.

WHEN ARTOS AND BORTIS turned off the Winding Way on the level which held their quarters, Duka continued down until he arrived at the landing that led to the entrance of the Great Hall where his birthday banquet would be celebrated that evening.

The double doors were open wide, and a gentle breeze wafted into the spacious room. Although no servants were present, Duka could see their handiwork in the clean tablecloths neatly draped on the wooden tables lining the walls, ready for the delicious food and beverages slated to appear for the banquet in another six hours.

He walked the length of the room and climbed the few steps to the raised portion of the room where the dragon throne and three large tables were situated. The royal family and the noble guests from the other Great Houses would be seated there for the festivities. He reminded himself that the hall would have few guests tonight due to the storms that were due in the early evening. This didn't trouble him, for unlike Carimus, he was a bit of an introvert and never comfortable in large crowds.

Stopping next to the throne, where his father presided over the gatherings that occurred a few times a year during the royal family's stay at their summer home, he turned his eyes up to examine the grotesque mounted head of the Abomination Tomung, its lifeless eyes staring back at him. The silver collar which held the trophy glinting in the glow of the everlight globes mounted around the room. To his horror, the eyes slowly blinked, then fixed their gaze upon him.

"So, they are throwing you a bone and having a party for your birthday," came a dry, rasping voice from the mouth of the creature. "How special." Its lips barely twitching as the words came forth.

"What are you?" cried Duka, taking a step back. "How can you speak? You're dead."

"Am I? Speaking, I mean. Of course, I'm dead. I've been a prize hanging on a wall for centuries. Are you imagining things? After all, you don't have any function in your family. Perhaps you have gone mad. You aren't needed for any important position like your brothers. You are useless. A spare in case something happens to one of your important brothers."

"I am not useless!" Anger pushing his fear aside. "I am not!"

The trophy chuckled, a hoarse, raspy laugh, then its eyes glazed over and became lifeless once more.

Duka stared up at dead eyes and the face mocked him as it had ever since he first saw it years ago.

"Duke? What are you doing?" It was Carimus from the doorway. "I thought I heard someone shout. Was that you?"

"I ... I was just trying to see if there was an echo," said Duka, looking around shamefaced. "It doesn't. I mean, there isn't …" he trailed off.

"Of course not," said his brother as he walked across the room. "It would mess up the orchestra if they were playing for a ball. Uncle Cameron told me the builders designed it to have no echo. You knew that."

"I was just testing …"

"Well, stop fooling around. We need to go upstairs for lunch. Come on." Carimus walked toward the side passage, which led to the stairs that went up to the royal quarters, waving his arm imperiously. "We don't want to be late."

Why did I lie? Cari knows I hate that thing. He followed his brother, taking a quick look over his shoulder at the mounted head as he left the hall. He thought he saw it give him a quick wink in response.

It won't be long now, thought the trophy. Three hundred years of suffering will soon be over. I can read the signs in the mind of that fool Duke Bretton. I will have my revenge. The wedge I have kept between the king and his brother, the grief from the suicide of the king's wife, those are nothing compared to what is coming.

Soon … soon … soon …

Chapter Three:

Meetings and Arrivals

9

LUNCH

ARTOS

11:52 a.m.

WHEN ARTOS LEFT HIS ROOM to attend the midday meal, he was determined to have a discussion with his father concerning the idea of marriage to Elaine deEagledon. *It will be the best time*, he thought to himself. Uncle Cameron said he would be absent, and with only himself and his brothers present, he felt certain he could explain that he just wasn't ready for marriage.

His plans were dashed when he entered the royal dining room, for his father was not alone. A guest sat across from Carimus and Duka, a large, dusky skinned man in the green robe and gold sash of a druid, his robe shabby and travel-stained. They were having an animated conversation, and his two younger brothers were listening attentively.

"No, Cantor Aubrie, I do not believe we are heading for another large confrontation with Beastmen," King Aaron made a sweeping motion with his hands. "There may be a few isolated pockets of the creatures in the Mountains of Myst, but not enough to be more than a nuisance. I'm assured so by my brother. Twice, this last summer he went forth on expeditions in answer to reports of pillaging Beastmen and both times it was only bandits. Undoubtedly, they inhabit the Black Mountains in swarms, but ever since my great-grandfather, King Alexavier cut the head off the Abomination Tomung and threw his body into the Dragon Sea to feed the fishes there, it took the heart and soul from the Beastmen. Ever since, they have cowered in the eastern wastes and have feared to show themselves in civilized lands. My ancestors slaughtered thousands of the creatures. The mounted head of that traitor still graces the Great Hall to this day. It is my family's greatest trophy and a clear warning to any who would seek to disturb the peace of our land."

Artos noticed Duka's slight shudder at the mention of the mounted trophy, and he tapped his brother on the shoulder as he sat in the vacant chair beside him. He whispered to him, "Was that what your dream was about, Lil-Bro?"

"It wasn't a dream. I was as wide awake as I am now when it laughed at me. Hanging there on the wall." Duka looked defiant. "I know no one believes me. But it's true. That head is still alive. I don't know how it could be, but it is. I hate that trophy. When you're king, please destroy the horrid thing."

Cantor Aubrie shook his head, "Wishing away a problem will not solve it, King Aaron. Count Darrellyel will discuss this at today's concourse. I beg you, do not lightly dismiss the Darrell's words."

"Stanley! It is you." Cameron deDraconis bustled into the room and nodded at the head of the Earth Mother's sect. "My, oh my. I could hardly believe it when a servant asked me what the kitchen should prepare for the Archdruid's meal, as if he didn't eat like any other man. I have been looking for you. What brings you out of the forests and here to our home?" He sat down at King Aaron's right-hand side, leaving one empty seat between him and Artos.

Two empty chairs sat at the head of the left-hand side of the table. The first chair to the King's immediate left had been vacant for fifteen years since the death of his wife, Queen Evelyn Draconis ne`dePenrodyn. The next chair was reserved for Duke Bretton, but he seldom took lunch with his brother, or any other meal for that matter. Artos and Bortis constantly argued about the Queen's chair. Artos believed it was because of sentiment. His father missed his wife and wished her chair to be left empty in tribute to her. Bortis insisted the chair was kept there, so King Aaron and his brother didn't have to sit next to each other. Artos knew there was formality and coldness between his father and his uncle, but was sure his reasoning was correct.

At that moment, Bortis hurriedly entered the room and sat just as the great chime that signaled noon rang out through the castle. King Aaron lifted a brow at his second son, but said nothing as servants began bringing lunch into the dining room.

"Glad you could join us, Bort," said Artos, grinning at his brother. He wondered how his father and uncle could feel coolly toward each other. Bort was a pain in the neck at times, but he was his brother, after all.

"Got to keep up my strength," replied Bortis, slipping into the vacant chair between Artos and his great-uncle.

"Would you do us the honor of blessing the meal, Cantor?" asked Cameron to the Archdruid.

"I would be most happy to, my Lord Cameron," said the druid. He pushed back his chair and stood up. He waited until everyone rose to their feet, then the Cantor made the diamond

Sign of the Four as he spoke the Blessing;

"By Leaf and Stone, we ask Earth Mother Veda to smile upon her children."

"By Leaf and Stone," repeated everyone.

"By Sun and Moon, we ask Sky Father Quai to grant us his favor and watch over the lands."

"By Sun and Moon, by Leaf and Stone," repeated the assembly.

Everyone sat as the servants served the soup and salad.

The Cantor looked across the table at Artos, "It's been well over a dozen years since I was last here at Castle Draconis, and since I last laid eyes on you, young sir. You're looking well." His gaze took in the other three brothers. "All of you." He turned to King Aaron. "You have raised them right, Aaron. A fine-looking group of young gentlemen, not like those wastrels of House deAnson or House deHerndar." He shook his head, a look of mild distaste upon his weather-beaten face, "It's good to know some Houses still follow the old ways."

"Youth is a time for training and discipline," interjected Cameron. "They will have time to enjoy their positions after they have learned their responsibilities and earned their places."

"My sons are not over-worked Ser Cantor," Aaron smiled, lifted a spoonful of soup to his lips, and everyone began their noontime meal.

"My father and my uncles," he nodded in Cameron's direction, "taught Bretton and I that the way of a leader is to lead by example, not to shout platitudes and demand that those he leads do as he says, and not as he does."

"Your father, Attios, was a good man, Aaron. It was sad that he and your Uncle Baird met such untimely deaths. I still have to wonder how a vine-crawler of such size was even in Oakwood, and no one was aware it was present until after the accident." The Archdruid shook his head, sorrow plainly evident upon his face.

Aaron nodded. "Yes, it is fortunate that Uncle Cameron is not a hunter. Brett and I should have been there that day as well, but we had been forbidden to join at the last minute. We had gotten into an argument which almost resulted in us coming to blows. Uncle Baird sent us to do some tasks for Uncle Cameron instead. We were with him when the news reached us." The king shook his head sadly. "Without his guidance, we would have had a much harder time adapting to our new stations."

"A terrible day, just horrible!" agreed Cameron, looking down at his soup. "But what could we all do except to carry on?"

"The beast must have wandered down from the mountains. It couldn't have been there long, or some of Count Reginald's foresters would have reported it. Count Reginald, Stephan's father, was also lost that day, as you surely recall?"

"Indeed, I do. In fact, all the hunting party was killed that day except Count Boris Anson, weren't they?" asked the Cantor.

"Yes, well, he and two of his retainers escaped to bring us the news, although he wasn't the Lord of House deAnson then. He wasn't even the heir at that time. His elder brother, Lord Winston, wasn't as lucky and died with the rest of the hunting party. His father, Count Willyam, passed away a few weeks after Lord Winston was killed. The shock of losing his heir was too much for the old man." Aaron shook his head. "We organized a great hunt, then. We found the disgusting creature and destroyed it. Count Penrodyn led the hunt, and all the families joined in ... well. All except House deSpryngdal, of course. Countess Maria sent her regrets for our father's passing, but stated it was her opinion that the vine-crawler was just doing what vine-crawlers do and if they hadn't disturbed it, nothing bad would have come to pass."

Artos was shocked. He knew the story of his grandfather's passing, although he was only a few years old when the event took place, but he had never heard this about House deSpryngdal before. "Why didn't you order her to help, Father? That is unforgivable. That she would refuse to help is … is monstrous."

"She wouldn't have helped, young Artos," the Archdruid answered. "My Aunt, well, she's really a cousin, but anyway, she has very strong feelings on such matters. Do you know that most of her line will not even eat meat?"

"What?" asked Bortis. "Not eat meat? What's wrong with them?"

The Archdruid smiled at the outburst. "Ah, young Bortis, you must learn, my son, to allow others to have their otherness. Some feel that the taking of life is not justified to merely fill your stomach. You and I may agree that a cow or a chicken is serving its intended purpose to be our soup." He lifted his spoon and then took a sip. "Delicious soup, Aaron. I am grateful to the chickens who gave their lives for such wonderful broth." He looked back at Bortis. "But not everyone feels the same. Do not be overly hasty to judge someone just because their tastes and ideals are not exactly the same as yours. The world would be so very dull if we were all exactly the same."

"I suppose," muttered Bortis, but Artos could see he didn't agree.

"Eat," said Aaron. "Let us find another subject to discuss while we sup. Something less gruesome, perhaps."

Artos could see his father was not inclined to discuss that matter of House deSpryngdal's eccentricities. What use was it to be king if you could not enforce justice?

10

DUTIES

ARTOS

12:57 p.m.

FOLLOWING THE END OF LUNCH and the servants clearing the dishes, Cameron stood and motioned for Carimus and Duka to join him. "Stanley, as it is Thirday, it is my day to instruct the young gentlemen. Yes, yes, the rest of the week they belong to their tutor, Master Elaer, when they are not practicing their warcraft with their uncle, Duke Bretton. Normally he would have them sweating today from noon until three, but today is an unusual day, most unusual. Would you care to join us in the classroom? Or perhaps you would prefer a nap in a guest room?"

"Actually, I would ask that you and the Cantor attend me," said Aaron. "I have things I would discuss with the both of you." He looked at his eldest. "Artos, I want you to take Cari and Duka with you on whatever duties your uncle has assigned to you this afternoon."

"Yes, sir," Artos answered and looked at the two youngest. "Come on, you two." He exchanged a knowing glance with

Bortis. Both thought their uncle would not be happy to have his orders changed, but Aaron was king, so whatever task Duke Bretton had for the two eldest brothers, it was now to be shared among all four.

As the four brothers walked out of the royal dining hall into the hall that led to the Winding Way, Artos realized that there was no need to search for their Uncle Brett. He was waiting for them where the hall opened to the great ramp that wound up from the base of the castle to its peak like a giant's corkscrew. Artos hurried to him.

"Here we are, Uncle Brett. Father has asked me to watch over Cari and Lil-Bro ... err Duka, as he wants to discuss matters with the Cantor and Uncle Cameron." He eyed his uncle warily, expecting him to be angry.

"What? Oh, no matter. They may as well be learning this along with you two. Come along." He turned and started up the Winding Way at a quick jog. As usual. The four brothers fell in behind him, all knowing better than to ask their gruff uncle "unnecessary" questions.

They soon reached the landing that led to the airship docks. Stepping through the invisible, but noticeably tingly qulan seal, they emerged on the enormous landing dock. The *Dragon Queen* was being loaded this week for the upcoming trip back to Phoenix. Artos felt the familiar twinge of regret he felt every fall. They would soon leave their summer home for the royal palace in Phoenix, and he really preferred their summer home to the official residence of the House of deDraconis. Phoenix palace was close to the sprawling horse farms of the lowlands, but he always hated to leave this residence. He sighed.

The balloon that kept the ship aloft was being stowed away. The house retainers in their black-and-gold uniforms reminded him of hornets as they swarmed over the airship. Extra mooring lines secured the royal airship firmly to the docking posts. "They must expect tonight's storm to be pretty bad," he observed to Duka. "They've only loaded about half of what's being taken back down to Phoenix, but they can't continue until they re-inflate the balloon."

"Bortis, you and Cari wait here," Bretton pointed to a spot near the door. "When Count Penrodyn's ship arrives, you are to greet him as representatives of the House and invite him into the Castle. Remember your manners, be respectful to your grandfather, and usher him and his entourage through the qulan." Bretton looked at Carimus, "No fooling around. Understand?"

"Yes, sir," the two answered in unison.

"Good. Bort, you are in charge. Take Count Estel to his family's rooms. That's on the floor above your quarters, as you recall. They won't be staying as we planned earlier, but they still need a place to refresh and prepare for tonight's feast. Tell Count Penrodyn that a servant will be sent to escort him to the four o'clock concourse, and that the birthday feast will take place as soon as the concourse is finished. Questions?" Unlike his uncle, Bretton waited to see if there were any questions.

"We're to welcome Count Penrodyn and his group to our home and invite them through the qulan. Then we are to escort them to their family's quarters and inform the Count that a servant will fetch him for the concourse and that the Spare's birthday feast will begin right afterward," Bortis rushed through, reciting his instructions back to his uncle. Then stood waiting to see his uncle's reaction.

Bretton looked at Bortis and gave a small smile. "Close enough." Bort was Bretton's protégé. He could be harder on him than his brothers one moment, then nicer to him than anyone else the next. Apparently, this was a 'nice' moment.

"You two come with me." He looked at Artos and Duka, turned, walked back inside, and began jogging up the Winding Way.

"Are we going to the Eyrie again?" Duka softly asked.

Artos started jogging after his uncle. "It looks like it. Come on." The two brothers followed their uncle to the top of the castle, through the qulan into the Eyrie. Their uncle was waiting for them at the ramp's end. As soon as they stepped through the seal, he motioned them to wait where they were, strode over to the doors to the guardroom, and stepped inside.

Twelve round wooden beams, well over a foot in diameter, ran like spokes in a titan's wagon wheel eight feet above the floor of the circular tower that was the Eyrie. Each beam was fifty feet long, from the wall to the twenty-foot diameter pillar in which they were embedded in the center of the room. A ladder carved into the stone pillar rose to the watch post above the pigeon cote at the tower's tip, sixty feet above the Eyrie floor. Ten feet above the floor in each of the four cardinal directions was a window fifty feet tall and equally wide, open to the outside air. To the east and west were stout wooden doors that led to the quarters of the tower guard. To the north and the south were the doors that led out onto the upper battlements. "I wonder what Uncle Brett has in mind for us, Lil-Bro?" Artos chuckled and added, "I think I'll have to join Cari and start calling you Duke. You're not so little anymore. You are almost as tall as Bort and Cari, although Bort's shoulders are wider and Cari's a lot skinnier."

Duka grinned, "Hey, I don't care what you call me." His face sobered a little. "Except ... well, I don't really like 'the Spare.'" He shrugged.

"Ah, you know Bort. He doesn't mean anything by it. Heck, when he was six or seven, he used to call Cari 'Crier.' You remember that?"

Duka shook his head, "No, but it sounds like Bort. You know what Cari and I used to call Bort behind his back?" Art shook his head. "Bullybort."

"Ha-ha. That fits. He was a bit bossy to you guys before father caught him once and told him he'd have Uncle Brett handle it if it ever happened again. I think he was more afraid of Uncle Brett thinking badly of him than of any other punishment."

"A bit bossy? That's like saying water is a bit damp," Duka chuckled.

"I know Bort can be harsh, but he's not really mean. He just has a very strong sense of duty and when he thinks others are not living up to what he thinks they should, he gets impatient." Duka nodded, then pointed.

Artos turned and saw his uncle emerge from the guardroom, with Sergeant McArn following closely behind. As he was Captain of the Eyrie guard, the Sergeant wore a gold vest with his black and gold house uniform along with a red and gold sash. The two young men both unconsciously stood a little straighter as their uncle approached.

"Artos, you two wait here with Sergeant of the Guard McArn. We don't know how many of the elves will be coming. If there are more than a half dozen, don't invite them in and send Duka to find me. At once. I shall probably be in the courtyard awaiting the deEagledons' arrival. Do you understand?" His uncle looked angrier than usual at the thought of the Fairborn. He knew his uncle didn't like them, though he didn't know why. They hardly ever visited. Artos couldn't remember them coming here or the Palace in Phoenix more than a few times during his lifetime.

"Yes, sir," Artos stated and was echoed by his little brother.

"The Fairborn are flying here?" asked Duka, the wonder obvious in his voice. "Not to the airship dock?" Artos would have nudged his brother in warning, but he was a bit too far away.

Bretton had been turning away, but at Duka's question, he turned back. "Yes, they will come … here. That's why I am stationing you … here, Prince Duka. Does that make sense to you?" He glared at Duka, who immediately flushed but had the sense to nod quickly and say, "Yes, sir." He remained staring at the ground.

"Good." Bretton started to turn away again.

Artos swallowed. "Uncle?" His uncle stiffened, stopped, and looked back at Artos.

"Yes?" Bretton's voice was very soft. "Do you have a question, Prince Artos?"

"Yes, sir." Artos nodded. "You gave Bort very specific instructions about what to tell Lord Penrodyn and where to take him, and I just wondered if you had any messages you wished me to deliver, sir?"

"Sergeant McArn will give you instructions concerning where to lodge the elves. As to any message I would give them, you can tell them to take a swim in the Dragon Falls for all I care." He turned and stormed off down the Winding Way.

"Oh, laddie, ye should be knowing better than to talk to the Duke about the Fairborn," said Sergeant McArn as soon as their uncle was gone from hearing. "Ye know how he feels about them."

"No, McArn, we don't!" Artos spread his hands wide in

frustration as Duka shook his head to show that he, too, did not know. "I mean, we know he dislikes the Fairborn, but why? No one ever talks about it."

The grizzled guardsman sighed and signaled the brothers to follow him, and he walked back to the guardroom.

"It was almost two dozen years ago and a sad thing it was, too. Sit down, young Lords. Make yourselves comfortable. We likely have an hour or two before the Fairborn arrive."

The two princes looked around with interest. It had been a few years since Artos was last in the guardroom off the Eyrie, and Duka had never been there before. On the north wall were four large screens made of the same light blue crystal they had in their classroom, but unlike the class screen, their eerie glow showed they were active, although the screens appeared empty. Seated on a chair before the screens was a young man in the black chain mail of the house guard with a red-and-gold sash over his right shoulder, showing he was trained in the use of quanti by the Sky Church. His attention focused on the empty screens.

"I take it everything is still clear out there, Corporal?" asked McArn, walking over to stand next to the seated guardsman.

The young man shook himself and then grinned at McArn. "The air is clear as only air can be, Sergeant." Then, noticing the two brothers, he jumped up and bowed. "Excuse me, my Lords. I didn't expect another visit from royalty so soon on the heels of the Duke."

Artos waved off the apology. "It's quite all right. Don't let us interrupt your duties." Artos scratched his chin. This young guardsman looked familiar somehow. There were only a score over a hundred guardsmen at the castle and probably sixty more at the gatehouse. He had undoubtedly seen him before over the course of the summer. He couldn't put his finger on it, though.

"I'll be relieving ye for a bit, corporal. Go take a break, have a snack. Leave me a wee bit o'privacy with the young Lords. We have a few duties to discuss."

"Sure." The young man grinned. "I know when I'm not wanted, Sergeant. I'll survive … somehow." He feigned a distressed look, his hand laid flat over his heart. He grinned again and walked toward the barracks door on the other side of the room.

"Aren't we related?" Duka's words startled Artos and, from the look on their faces, both Sergeant McArn and the young corporal as well.

"I wouldn't have been so bold as to mention it, Lord, but yes, we are cousins, but I'm just a guardsman in the service of House deDraconis, and proud to serve. I was tested as a youngling, of course, as all children are, and I was found to have a small measure of quanti control. I had thought perhaps to be an airship pilot, but my control is too erratic, but I can farsee with the screens as well as any. So here I am." He bowed once again, then turned to walk away.

"How are we related?" blurted Duka. Art could hear McArn fussing, but Duka chose to ignore it.

The young corporal stopped, looked back at the brothers, then smiled faintly. "My father was the third son of the fourth son of your Great-Uncle, Duke Baird. Only a first son and perhaps his first son, if merited, may become a Barron and an officer in the Guard. Any other children are out of title. It makes sense, my Lord. If it were otherwise, after a few hundred years there wouldn't be anyone in the world who wasn't a Lord." He smiled a bit sadly. "When I was a child, I wished my father had

had the good sense to be born a first son." He shrugged. "As I grew older, I came to realize that wishes wouldn't change the course Fate sets before you and all you can do is be the best you that you can be." He nodded to the brothers and Sergeant McArn and left the guardroom.

Artos looked at the Sergeant who merely shrugged. Duka nodded, then stepped closer to the screens and looked at them intently. "I had no idea," said Artos, "Uncle Brett doesn't have any children. He never married, so the thought never occurred to me." He looked at McArn. "I know we have a lot of cousins among the other Houses. I guess I never really thought how many of the guard would be."

"Aye, laddie. Probably every officer and most of your guardsmen are related to you in some fashion. Lad. Ye are probably related to half the guardsmen in every Great House. There are only seven Great Houses and mostly, the children of the heads of the Great Houses only marry children of the other Great Houses. Lad, there's only so many bodies to go around. Only seven Great Bloodlines anymore since House deYung turned rogue. There is blood of that House mixed in with all the rest, though you'll not find many who'll be willing to admit it."

"Let me tune in and check the screens, lad, and then …"

As McArn turned back to the screens, Duka looked away from them and said, "The screens are still clear. I just checked."

McArn tilted his head a bit to the side, "Did ye now lad? Well, I have me duty and it means I still have to check."

"I understand," said Duka, and he walked back to his brother's side. Then, in a soft voice, he said to Artos, "But they are clear. To the north, you can look right across the Loch O' Wrens to Starstone Tower, right through the fog. You can scan to the mountains of Myst in the West from House deEagledon to House deAnson. The South screen scans from House deHerndar to House deDarrellyel in the Black Mountains, and the West screen scans from House dePenrodyn all the way to the ruins of Blachaas and the skies are clear."

Artos stared at his little brother. "You saw all that, that quickly and easily? I thought it took weeks of training to farsee with the screens. You're telling the truth, aren't you?"

Duka nodded. "I wouldn't lie to you. You're the only brother I have who always treated me fairly. You always have. You think I don't know that?" Duka smiled a bit sadly.

Before Artos could think of an answer, McArn stood up from the chair and walked over to the brothers. "The screens are indeed clear, Master Duka. We have time for a wee bit of history." The grizzled veteran shook his head. "It be not my place to be a-telling you this, but ye have a right to know your own history and King Aaron, bless his soul, he should be the one, but in truth, I'm not sure he ever learned the whole story. The real story. He wasn't there, ye see? But I was. I was one of Prince Bretton's guard back then."

He looked at the brothers with a troubled face. They both nodded, pretending they understood, and he continued, "As I were a-saying, it was about two dozen years ago and King Aaron ... well, he was Crown Prince Aaron then and he and his brother, your uncle Duke Bretton, he was Prince Bretton then o'course, they were fast friends then, just as close as two brothers could be." The senior guardsman held up his hand with the first two fingers tight together. "Then one day their good friend, Stephan deEagledon, brought his twin sister Stephanie to reacquaint her with Aaron whom she hadn't seen in over ten years. She had been fostered with ... um. I forget with who, but it doesn't matter. She hadn't been around since she was a little girl, and Aaron and Bretton were little boys. King Attios' marriage hadn't been a happy one, and he foolishly vowed that he would let Aaron pick his own bride. How quickly that proved a mistake."

Artos stirred uneasily, and Duka met his gaze and raised his brows.

"I'm pretty sure the deEageldon's plan was for Aaron and Lady Stephanie to fall in love and get married. Well ... Aaron fell for her alright, but so did Bretton. Lady Stephanie liked them both, but I don't think she ever loved either of them. Aaron and Bretton both attempted to win her heart. If one gave her a gift, the other had to top it. If Brett took her riding, then Aaron had to take her dancing. I think she enjoyed the attention, at first, but then she realized what it was doing to the two brothers, and she broke it off with both of them and disappeared from their circle for a while. Then one day, she went to a dance in Phoenix at the deDraconis Palace. It was a Summer Solstice ball and I think she believed that Aaron and Bretton would be here, in the Kings Valley for the summer, and Aaron was. Bretton, however, had gone to Phoenix on some business. He saw Stephanie at the dance. She was dancing with the Fairborn Crown Prince Andune. He was someone Bretton didn't care for much, I guess. He didn't hate the Fairborn before then ye see Lad? Well, he caused a scene. He attacked the prince. He drew his crysword and struck afore anyone could react. Prince Andune pulled his blade and struck him back. Then we pulled Prince Bretton back and the Fairborn guards were in between them and it were over. Prince Bretton was a master swordsman, still is o'course. He had never been marked by an opponent afore that day. He was humiliated, and had that scar upon his cheek to remind him that some others were blade masters, too. I was never sure after which burned him more. That Lady Stephanie rejected him or that Prince Andune marked his cheek."

Artos blinked in surprise. He had been told his uncle's facial scar was from a hunting accident.

"He blamed Aaron for introducing Lady Stephanie to the Fairborn Prince," continued McArn. "I dinna know how fair that be, but he blamed him anyway. When Prince Bretton returned to the Valley, he went straight to Viscount Stephan and told him that his sister was disgracing her family. Stephan got his father to demand she return home at once. She, however, was a strong-minded lass, and she ran away with the Fairborn and was never seen again after, although there were rumors for years. I think the Duke still blames his brother to this very day. And he hates the Fairborn for stealing his love."

Artos nodded, his expression troubled. "I guess that explains why Uncle Brett always calls them elves. You don't think that Prince Andune is coming tonight, do you? That would explain why he is so touchy today."

Sergeant McArn shook his head. "No lad, I believe they both died years ago. But you never hear much news about the fair folk. They tend to look down on us and a lot of people resent 'em for it. They are a bit standoffish. Snobs, a few of them are, but they're all kinds." He shrugged. "Just like us. Truth be known, I have a few relatives I don't be caring for much either."

"Who wants a hot cinnamon bun?" asked a cheerful voice. The young corporal had opened the door from the barracks and stuck his head into the guards-room, the smell of fresh rolls quickly filling the room. "Agnes just brought a fresh baked batch up from the kitchens and I thought maybe you young lords might care for a wee snack?" his eyes twinkled. "If not, I can probably force myself to finish the lot of 'em."

"Bring 'em on lad," said McArn. "If I'm not mistaken, the two young lords look like they could manage a bite or so." He chuckled. "Or maybe young lads don't like cinnamon buns these days?"

Artos's mouth was already watering in anticipation. The buns smelled heavenly. "I think we could force ourselves. Yes, thank you. They smell wonderful."

The young guardsman carried in a tray upon which was a steaming jug that added the scent of fresh coffee to the already fragrant air.

"Agnes is the best pastry chef in the castle," said the corporal as he set the tray down on the table beside the brothers. "Enjoy." He strode back to the barracks, shutting the door behind him.

Artos gazed upon three coffee mugs and a large plate, upon which were six golden brown buns crossed with large stripes of white frosting.

Artos greedily took one of the golden buns and took a large bite of rich cinnamony goodness. "Mmm! These are delicious! As good as we get at our Sunday breakfast!"

Duka nodded, a crumb of frosting falling from the corner of his mouth as he chewed enthusiastically.

Sargent McArn nodded and took a sip of the steaming coffee. "Aye, they should. Agnes is the one who bakes em fer ye. We do get a few treats now an' then. Agnes does tend to spoil Shawn, and the rest of us get to share his booty."

Artos swallowed. "Should she do that? We won't say anything, of course. But mightn't she get in trouble bringing treats to a corporal of the guard?"

The grizzled veteran smiled, "Oh lad, I don't think anyone would say anything. Agnes is Shawn's mother, you see? As long as she works her magic in the bakery, who would be so small to deny a widow giving her only son a treat?"

"She does magic?" Artos looked confused, and he looked at the hot buns as if they might run off the plate and hide.

"There be all kinds of magic lad, an' what Agnes does with the dough is truly taste bud magic." The Sergeant picked up a bun and looked at it. "Dinna ye think so?" He took a large bite.

Artos nodded in agreement, finished his roll, and grabbed a second. "What do you think Duke?" He noticed his brother was sitting with his eyes closed. "Duke?"

"The Fairborn are coming from Darylhaas, aren't they, Sergeant McArn?" asked Duka, opening his eyes and turning to the Sergeant.

"What? Aye, lad. They would be coming up from that direction. Do ye think I should be a looking for them now?" He smiled indulgently at Duka.

"There are four of them ..." Wonder filled his voice, "and they are flying here on eagles!"

11

THE FAIRBORN ARRIVE

ARTOS

2:42 p.m.

Sargent McArn hurriedly dropped the remains of the bun he was eating and strode over to the screens. He stared intently at one of them for a long moment.

"Ye be right lad …" he whispered, "They'll be here in less than an hour." He turned and looked back at Duka. "Yer uncle has been teaching ye farseeing lad." He shook his head. "I thought ye were funning with me. Ye do know how to read the screens."

Duka shook his head. "Uncle Cameron has been saying he was going to begin my extra instruction, like he does Sevenday afternoons with Cari. But we haven't started yet. He was waiting for me to bond with my crysword." He put his hand on the hilt of his new sword. "I think I'm ready."

McArn looked at Artos as if for confirmation. Artos was just staring mutely at his youngest brother. He turned and met McArn's eyes, shook his head and shrugged, just as puzzled as the guardsman.

"Is something wrong?" Duka looked back and forth between the two of them.

"Nothing's wrong Lil-Bro, I mean, Duke. It's just that it usually takes Uncle Cameron a little while to teach farseeing. You seem like you were born to it. I remember he worked with me at least a week or so before I could lock into them. I think it was the same with Cari. It took Bort a good month and a lot of extra hours with Uncle Cameron, but he finally managed. Don't tell him I told you that. He's sort of sensitive about taking longer than Cari or me to pick up that kind of stuff ..." he trailed off, lost in his thoughts.

"I don't know, it's just ... just there. I never had it happen with the screen in class. It must be something to do with how quickly I bonded to my sword. You think?" he looked at his older brother anxiously. "I'm not trying to do magic. Really. It's just happening without me doing anything. Do you think there's something wrong with me?" a touch of panic crept into his voice. "I promised Father I wouldn't try any magic. I didn't use my sword. I didn't even think about it!"

"Relax ... I'm sure it's fine. We'll tell Uncle Cameron, he's the family Loremaster. He'll know what's going on." Artos did his best to speak calmly, though his thoughts were all jumbled between thoughts of his father and his uncle and how fast Duka was adjusting to the ways of the quanti. In the back of his mind, there was a little voice that kept repeating over and over, marriage ... marriage ... marriage ...

"Be sure to be doing that. I think your brother's right lad, but be a-talking to yer uncle about it. Soon, today I mean, after ye two have finished yer duties and invited in the Fairborn and shown them to their quarters. Ye know where the Fairborn have their guest rooms, don't ye? Down on the twelfth level?"

Artos nodded. "There are a dozen suites there. No one ever uses that floor at all. It's been years since anyone stayed in those rooms. There's lots of empty rooms on every floor, but the Fairborn floor has been totally deserted as long as I can remember."

McArn nodded. "It's been over twenty years since that little trouble I told ye about. The Fairborn were never here a great deal even before that, but since Duke Bretton had his kerfuffle with Prince Andune, the fair folk have been rarer than a hen's tooth. A few messengers have dropped off missives fer the King from their king at Fairinlan, but I dinna think that any have stayed here more than one or two times. An' none fer a good many years now." He turned to Duka.

"Would ye be doing me a small favor, Lord Duka? Could ye be a-taking the plate and the tray back to Shawn in the barracks fer me, lad?"

"Sure," Duka replied, and hopped to his feet. He picked up the tray and walked out of the guardroom and into the barracks. As soon as he was gone, McArn looked to Artos.

"Lad, be sure that ye go to yer uncle and tell him about this. Shawn, he be good with the screens and I'm even better, more practice, ye know? But neither of us could have walked away from the screens, sat over here and eaten half a cinnamon bun, and suddenly be reconnected enough to know that the Fairborn were a-coming. I have to be within a half dozen feet or so an' gazing into 'em. He was twice that far away and … and ... well, it be worrisome, that's all." He broke off as the barracks door reopened and Duka walked back over and sat down.

"I was wondering Sergeant McArn," said Duka, "why don't we have any eagles to ride?" he looked at Artos. "Is something wrong?"

Art shook his head.

"Ah laddie," answered the Sergeant, "we think alike, you and me. I asked that very same question my first day o'duty here up top, ages ago." He ran his hand over his short-cropped gray hair. "I can only tell ye what my sergeant told me that day. He said, 'Them eagles don't like people, they only like elves.' Oh, he shouldn't have been rude about it, I know. But he dinna mean nothing, he was just a soldier." The guardsman shrugged. "I dinna think he was right myself. Over the years, I have seen them bring a message or two. I think they're like war-horses, they have a master who they love and trust and nobody else best be a-bothering 'em. Remember that, lads! Don't get too close to them. They could take yer head off as easy as you, or I ate them cinnamon buns. Snap! And yer body would be a walkin' around wondering where yer head went. That reminds me. I best be telling the watch the Fairborn are soon to be here. I'll be right back."

Artos looked at his brother as the guardsman walked out into the Eyrie. "I guess I should have warned you, but I wanted it to be a surprise. I didn't know you'd be able to see them coming like that. Five or six years ago, I saw one. Yes, it was six years. It was Cari's tenth birthday, so you would have been going on nine. I came up here with Father and went out on the battlements with him and we watched the Eagle fly up. There was just one." He shook his head. "I don't remember much more about it. Father didn't let me get anywhere near the bird. The Fairborn didn't stay. He and father talked, and he gave father something for Cari ..." Artos thought a few moments. "That silver bracelet with the runes on it that Cari wears once in a while. I think that was the gift. I'd have to ask him to be sure."

Duka nodded. "Maybe I could watch the screens." He pulled back the sleeve on his right arm and looked at the birthmark there. The double-headed dragon was the same as it always had been. "The dragon has two heads. Good for keeping watch." He looked at Artos with sudden, heart-wrenching sadness. "All of you have royal birthmarks that mean something. Your crown, Bort's sword, Cari has the star. You're going to be king, and that's good. You'll be a just king, wise and fair. Bort will take Uncle Brett's place someday as war leader, and Cari will take Great-Uncle Cameron's position as head of the church. But where is my place? There's no job for me. I'm useless. Maybe I am just … just …" He trailed off, gazing down and exhaled deeply.

"Duke …" Art looked at his brother, "you are not useless. You're not just a spare! We will figure it out. Father Quai and Mother Veda didn't put you here without a reason. We just don't know what it is yet, that's all. We're brothers. That's enough for now. We have time." He patted his brother awkwardly on the shoulder, and they sat together in silence.

After a short time, the door to the Eyrie opened and Sergeant McArn walked back in and walked over to the barracks door. "Come on out, ye lazy good fer nothing, Shawn. These screens won't watch themselves!" He grinned at the brothers. "We'll be a-waiting on the battlements now, lads. The Fairborn are just in sight now. It won't be long."

The brothers jumped to their feet and headed for the door. Artos was glad to see the sadness replaced with excitement on Duka's face. His thoughts remained troubled, however. He remembered hearing stories about how a great-great-great-uncle of his had once been born with the double dragon birthmark and bonded to a blue sword. He didn't remember the details, but it stained the family's honor. Or the uncle's honor, or something. Bort would know. History and fighting were about the only two things Bort did care about. Well, one thing he was sure of, Duka wouldn't ever do anything to harm the Family.

As the brothers and the guardsman stepped out on the battlements, a warm September breeze bore the faint scent of freshly fallen leaves. Autumn was in the air. Far off to the southwest, the trees of the Oakwood showed their changing hues. "Isn't it funny? We can see the Oakwood from here, plain as anything, but riding out across the causeway all you can see are the tops of the thousand-year-old trees and you have to ride a mile or so out of Brierly toward House deEagledon before you can see the rest of the forest."

Duka nodded, but he wasn't paying attention. His eyes were glued to the southeast, in the direction of House deDarrellyel. His little brother stiffened, and he pointed.

"There they are! Do you see them?" Duka's voice was charged with excitement.

Four specks against the backdrop of the distant mountains close to forty miles away to the south. As he watched, they grew in size. "I see them."

Soon, the four giant golden eagles glided in graceful circles above the top spire of the castle. Then one broke off and swooped down and around towards the opposite side of the Eyrie from where the three stood watching.

Sergeant McArn beckoned for the brothers to follow him as he hurried back inside. They arrived to a mighty flapping of wings as the Eagle slowed and landed on one of the oaken perches and folded its wings.

Artos expected some saddle like that of his war-horse, but instead, the majestic bird wore a vest of netting from which its wings protruded. Upon his back, with his legs entwined in the net, sat the Fairborn rider. He wore leather armor with a green cloak, pulled tight to keep it from flapping in the breeze. A short bow was strapped across his back, and a short sword was on his belt. His auburn hair was bound in a long ponytail, his features unnaturally smooth and even, almost pretty, Artos thought. His ears bore the pointed tips that earned his people the name "elf" among the rustic and rude.

"I hight Jaek Ka'Naurf," called out the Fairborn in a clear tenor, almost singsong voice. "I seek a safe landing for my Lord Tirinvo Naurfindl and his cousin, the Bard Varyan Beiniot. Also, my brethren, Taur."

"I be Jake McArn, Captain of the Eyrie Guard of Castle Draconis. I bid ye be welcome and enter!" called back the Sergeant.

The Fairborn held up his right hand with his fingers in a fist and nodded to the guardsman. He spoke to his steed, and the giant eagle hopped into the air as it unfurled its mighty wings. The Eagle and rider burst back out of the window and climbed up to join the others flying high above the Eyrie. Artos and Duka followed out the door and watched in awe as the four golden eagles broke formation. One after another, they flew back towards the windows that opened to the perches. The brothers hurried back inside and stopped by the entrance to the Winding Way. This time the eagles did not land on a perch, but angled between them and settled upon the floor of the Eyrie itself. Each rider slipped their legs from the netting. When their mounts crouched down, they slid off beside the wings. Once free of their riders, the four magnificent birds each made an effortless hop to land on the perch eight feet above the floor. One of the Fairborn called out to the birds in Espro. Artos wasn't fluent by any means, but he thought the Fairborn was telling the steeds to wait, rest, and sleep. What happened next amazed

Artos. The eagle the speaker had been riding cocked his head and made several screeching chirps as if arguing with the rider. And the rider answered back something about a storm and morning. Artos now wished he had made more effort to learn the Fairborn tongue. The Eagle chirped again as if mollified, closed its large golden eyes, and tucked its head down.

Duka's elbow poked hard into Artos's side. "Did you see that, Arty? The eagle talked back to him. They were talking," he whispered loudly, obviously excited.

"Straighten up. They're coming." Artos whispered back and stood tall and stepped forward to greet their guests. Duka stepped up and stood beside him.

"Well met!" Artos brought his fist to his heart and bowed his head to the leader of the four Fairborn. "I am Crown Prince Artos deDraconis and this is my brother, Prince Duka, and we welcome you to Castle Draconis."

Duka mirrored his brother's bow and added, "Welcome!"

The Fairborn crossed his arms and brought both his hands to his chest as he bowed in return. "Greetings. I am Crown Prince Tirinvo Naurfindl from the Fairinlan." He turned slightly to his right and nodded at the Fairborn standing there. "This is my cousin, Veryan Beiniot. Veryan is a noted bard amongst our people."

Surprisingly, Varyan had hair that was the purest white and wrinkles at the corners of his eyes. The kind of wrinkles his Uncle Cameron had. *This must be a Fairborn elder*, he thought, *though he doesn't look old.*

"These others are my liegemen, the twins, Taur, and Jaek Ka'Naurf. Who are also cousins. They have been my bodyguards ever since I became Crown Prince," Tirinvo said with a somewhat rueful smile.

"You weren't born Crown—oof!" Duka started to ask before Artos's elbow poked him in the side.

The Fairborn Prince didn't look offended by the personal question. Rather, he gave a small chuckle. Artos noticed he didn't answer, however, but changed the subject. "So, it is your birthday we are here to celebrate, Prince Duka? Congratulations upon your ascension." He glanced at the hilt of the sword at Duka's side and then, Artos noticed, at Artos' sword hilt as well. He then looked at the Winding Way and back to Artos expectantly.

Oh yes! Artos remembered his duty. "If you come in peace, please enter our home. "

The Fairborn Prince bowed again and turned and stepped through the qulan field into the Winding Way.

Duka repeated the formula to the bard, and Varyan followed his cousin. Then the brothers each repeated the formula to allow entrance to the two bodyguards of the Fairborn Prince. Nodding farewell to McArn, the two brothers stepped through the qulan together and led their Fairborn guests down the Winding Way to the twelfth level of the castle. Stopping at the doorway to the first suite on the north side of the hallway, Prince Tirinvo turned expectantly to Artos.

"You seem to know your way, Prince Tirinvo," Artos stated. "I shall inform my father that you have arrived." He gestured at the door to the suite. "Please refresh yourselves. The rooms have been made ready for your arrival."

"'Tis been a good many years since I last stayed here. It was shortly after your brother, Prince Bortis, was born, but I haven't forgotten the way. Give your father my deepest regards and tell him I wait to greet him with anticipation." The Fairborn Prince nodded to Artos and Duka and then nodded to his liegemen.

The auburn-haired twin opened the door to the suite and proceeded inside while the other three lingered.

As Artos and Duka walked back to the Winding Way, Duka looked up at his eldest brother and asked, "Will you have to do that too?"

"What's that? Do what?"

"Wait outside while your men check your room?" Duka looked back down the hall as they turned and proceeded down the Way. Then said with a troubled voice, "He can't think that we would set a trap or an ambush for him? Can he? No one else can pass through the qulan unless we invite them, so if there was something bad in the suite, we would have put it there."

"I don't know, Duke. I guess it's his men's duty, that's all. I suppose if I was visiting his king in Fairinlan, I would be expected to do the same. Uncle Cam has lectured us a lot about protocols, but I don't remember anything about that. Do you?"

Duka shook his head and the two brothers proceeded down to the Royal level in silence, each lost in his own thoughts.

Chapter Four:

The Birthday Celebration

12

THE BIRTHDAY DINNER

ARTOS

5:28 p.m.

ARTOS WALKED DOWN the King's Stairs toward the Great Hall, brushing a few stray hairs off the neat, sharply creased lapel of his black dress uniform. As he neared the bottom, faint strains of music wafted up the stairs. *Did Father summon an orchestra for Duke's dinner? He must have. I hear strings and horns.* He turned left at the bottom of the stairs and approached the hall from the south, the royal's entrance. The music was louder as he stepped up to the doorway and looked into the Great Hall. He first looked up at the orchestra gallery, but found it empty. Somewhat mystified, he looked around. The Fairborn bard sat on the speaker's dais at the west end of the Hall, next to the Dragon Throne. He held a small harp in his hands, a harp made of sapphire-blue crystal, a crysharp! At that moment, the bard sang, and his voice melded with the music with far greater volume than should have been possible, even for a trained bard. All the sounds of a full orchestra, all generated from the small instrument. Artos stood in awe and watched in wonder. The song he knew well, a hymn to Mother Veda.

The bard sang in a clear tenor:

"The earth moves... The oceans quake...
The planets changing tide... Then from the oceans...
Come the mountains... Where sweet waters hide..."

"Are you just going to lurk there in the doorway, Art?" Bortis appeared beside him dressed in his black dress uniform with its gold epaulets, braid, and trim, identical to Artos's sans the gold lanyards and starburst of the crown prince. "I don't think the deEagledons have come down from their rooms yet. You won't be able to hide from Elaine all night, you know. I don't see what you are so afraid of. You've known the twins since we were all children. If anything, she should be the scared one," he teased. "I remember you once put a frog down the back of her frock."

"Oh, no brother," Artos protested, "you were the frogger. I just kept her attention, so she wouldn't notice you held a frog until it was too late."

Bortis laughed. "Well, maybe I was. Shall we present ourselves to father?"

"We might as well." Artos bowed deeply with mock formality. "After you."

"As it should be," said Bortis, returning the mock-formal bow. He proceeded Artos into the Great Hall.

Artos looked around the hall. His father, great-uncle, the Cantor, and the Fairborn Prince were all standing near the head table, deeply involved in a conversation. His father seemed every inch the High King in his black dress suit with gold epaulets, braid, and trim, a golden sash with the House crest and the Dragon Crown upon his head. The Fairborn Crown Prince was clad in a tunic of bright, emerald-green silk, his guards standing unobtrusively behind him. The Cantor had changed out of his shabby robe and wore a dark forest green robe with a golden sash. Gaudiest of all was Uncle Cameron in his ceremonial garb, a robe made of alternating panels of crimson and forest green with a sash of black and gold, his golden bishop's mitre upon his head. *Darn it,* he thought, *I still haven't talked to Uncle Cameron about Duke and the screens.*

The lower end of the hall, to the east, had a surprising amount of people sitting or standing around, quaffing mugs of ale or sipping from glasses of wine. Artos realized his father had given leave to all the off-duty guards and castle staff to attend. This way, there were more than just a dozen guests rattling around in the large hall. He approved. *Father is clever. No wonder the guards and staff all love him. They get a feast, and Duke has more of an actual party.* He and Bortis took a few steps in their father's direction and when they caught his eye, they nodded. Their father returned their nods. Their filial duty fulfilled, they turned their attention to the gala. Artos paused near the dais while the bard played the music of an entire orchestra with the small crysharp.

On the western wall of the Great Hall, above and behind the bard, hung the Trophies; nine in all. They gazed balefully down at the people in the Hall. The four to his left were the least imposing, though in truth, they were rather frightful in their own right, the giant heads of a bighorn sheep, an elk, a ghost-walker ram, and a moose. On the right was a snarling peccary with tusks that exceeded five feet, a golden grizzly bear, a black ferret, and a fearsome-looking wolverine. In the middle, looking incongruously out of place among the giant heads, was an angry-looking man with curly black hair, the mounted head of the abomination Tomung. Remembering Duka's words, he examined the head of Tomung. It looked just the same as it always had. There was no sign of anything out of place as far as he could discern. *Duka's right*, he thought. *What kind of trophy is the head of a defeated enemy?*

Bortis came up and handed his brother a mug. Artos took it and gave a careful sniff before taking a drink. It was cider.

"What's the matter," teased Bortis, "did you want something stronger?"

"You know father doesn't approve of you children drinking ale. I expect that after my birthday in Rastous, I'll drink ale with Father and Uncle Brett while you, Cari, and Duke are still drinking cider." He smiled indulgently. Bortis snorted.

Suddenly, there was a loud fanfare, and both brothers turned in surprise. The Bard was now playing the opening bars of 'Hail Penrodyn', the anthem of that House. The elderly, but still spry, Count Estel strode into the Great Hall through the northern doorway leading to the stairways, which led up to the two floors set aside for the other Great Houses. His entourage accompanied him: his two sons, one daughter-in-law, and a dozen house retainers. All the men were clad in somber black with white vests, the lady, and her maid in white gowns with black lace, their House colors. The Count glanced around and then strode to stand next to the Cantor in order to join the conversation with those standing near the main table. *Grandfather looks troubled*, Artos thought. *I wonder if there's more trouble with Beastmen in his demesne. Starkeep is on the edge of the Black Mountains, after all.* His sons, Walter, and Johan, along with Walter's wife, Ruth, made their way over to the buffet and secured drinks. On their way, they nodded politely to the brothers, who both responded in kind,

"They didn't bring the kids along tonight," mused Bortis. The four dePenrodyn children—three girls, and a son—were about the same age as the deDraconis sons. "I wonder why?"

"I guess they're worried about the storm," Artos replied. "It's a thirty-minute flight back to Starkeep, and then they have to secure their ship. Oh, I almost forgot. They moor their ship right inside the keep, don't they?" Bortis nodded and sipped his cider. "Nevertheless, they still will have to fly back home, and the wind will be against them."

Carimus and Duka had both entered the hall. Like Artos and Bortis, Duka was dressed in his dress uniform of black with gold trim. Carimus was wearing his crimson robes with his black and gold deDraconis sash, as befit his role as an Acolyte of the Sky Church. They stood with their brothers.

"Say, Cari, isn't that the bracelet the Fairborn sent you for your birthday?" Artos asked.

Carimus glanced down at his left wrist, as if in surprise. "Yeah. That's where it came from. It just felt right to wear it tonight." He shrugged. "Why?"

Artos nodded. "I was telling Duke about the first time I saw a Fairborn riding one of their eagles and I remembered that was why they came that day. To deliver your birthday gift."

Artos glanced around the Great Hall once again. This time he found his father gazing at him, with a look as if to say, *Why aren't you acting more like my heir?* With a nod of his head at the dePenrodyns at the buffet, he turned back to his conversation.

"I guess we better go talk with our aunt and uncles. Father just gave me 'the look.'" He started in their direction, Bortis falling in beside him, with their younger brothers trailing behind. The Great Houses customarily addressed any member of an older generation as "Aunt" or "Uncle," but in this case, it was literal as their late mother Evelyn was sister to Walter and Johan. The four had not taken more than a few steps when Veryan gave another flourish on his magical instrument. The trumpet fanfare of "Fly Eagles, Fly Free" rang out, announcing Count Eagledon, his family, and retainers. Count Stephan, with his wife, Countess Renee Eagledon ne'deHerndar, entered the Great Hall accompanied by his brother, Baron Jon, and the Canon of the Sky Church, the Grande Bishop, Ser Piedro Neubre and his aide. Their eldest children, Viscount Ellis, and his twin sister, Viscountess Elaine, followed them. The deEagledon men were wearing dress uniform suits with blue-trimmed silver jackets over red shirts and trousers. The Countess and her daughter wore silver gowns with red vests and sapphire buttons. The Canon and his aide wore the crimson robes and golden sashes of the Sky Church. Several retainers in the silver and red House deEagledon uniforms completed the grand entrance.

"You lucky dog," muttered Bortis, stopping so suddenly that Carimus bumped into him from behind.

Turning to look at his brother, Artos noticed Bortis was staring at Elaine deEagledon as if he had never noticed her before. He had to agree Elaine looked very nice, quite lovely, in fact. But still …

"No! I do NOT agree with you, Count Penrodyn," exclaimed the angry voice of Uncle Bretton.

Startled, Artos turned back to see his uncle walking away from the discussion his father and the rest were having. *When did he come in? What is he so angry about now? Is he going to ruin Duka's birthday dinner?* Artos twitched uneasily, his thoughts jumbling together in his mind. Bretton stalked over to the buffet table and poured himself a goblet of the golden fire brandy, which he gulped down and then refilled. He nudged Bortis. "What do you think has Uncle Brett so worked up?"

"Huh?" Bortis looked at Artos. "What are you babbling about?"

Artos nodded his head at their uncle, who was now standing alone, glaring at the Fairborn bard. He had finished the House deEagledon anthem and was now playing an airy, lively tune. A few of the couples on the main floor moved to the dancing area. Most of the others in the Great Hall were tapping their feet in time with the beat.

"You know Uncle Brett, he doesn't like elves. So what? You watch, he'll find some reason to leave early. If it wasn't Spare's birthday, I bet he wouldn't even have come tonight." Bortis tugged at his arm. "Come on. Let's go talk to Ela … err … Ellis."

Resigning himself, Artos took a deep breath and followed his brother toward the deEagledons. Carimus and Duka followed along behind, snickering.

"Well met, Count Stephan, Lady Renee," said Artos, bowing to the couple. His brothers all followed suit. "Ser Neubre, you grace our House," he said, bowing to the Canon.

"So good to see you again, Grande Bishop Neubre," added Carimus as the brothers all mimicked Artos's lead.

"Hello, Baron deEagledon, Viscount Ellis, Viscountess Elaine," continued Artos.

"Prince Artos! Good to see you again," boomed Stephan Eagledon, turning, grasping his hand, and giving it a hearty shake. "I expect it won't be long before you join us at the bastion of power, wot? Leading the nation is an awesome responsibility, but fear not. You will always have my advice when you need it, my boy. Never fear! Lovely get together, wot?" He nodded to the other brothers. Then, looking at Bortis, he boomed, "Happy Birthday, Happy Birthday!" He looked back at Artos. Before Artos could explain that it was Duka's birthday, not Bort's, he found the Count's arm around his shoulder, and he was forcibly turned to face the twins. "You remember my son, Ellis, wot? And who could forget my lovely daughter, Elaine? You young folk go mingle … eh? Go dance to this lovely music. We old folks will leave you alone now, wot!" He released Artos, leaving him face to face with Elaine while he smiled at his wife. Taking her hand, the Count followed his brother and the Canon to join King Aaron and the others by the main table.

"Subtle, isn't he?" said Ellis deEagledon and burst out laughing. "Oh Art, the look on your face, priceless."

Elaine deEagledon's face was bright pink. "We all know Father has the tact of a giant moose. Just shut it." Her face grew even more red, and she stared at the floor. Her dark blond hair falling forward around her face.

"It's all right, Elaine," Artos pretended to throw a punch at her twin, who stepped back, still chuckling.

"Come on Bort," said Ellis. He looked at Carimus and Duka. "Sammy and Junebug told me to say hi to you two and wish Duka happy birthday. Father didn't want to bring more than one carriage with the storm blowing in tonight and so they had to stay home. It was crowded enough with the six of us … Wot!" he mimicked his father and grinned. "Come on. Let's leave the two lovebirds alone … Ooof!" he gasped as his sister elbowed him hard in the side. If anything, her face was even redder than before.

"Ellis! You beast. Shut up!" she exclaimed, looking as though she was about to burst into tears of embarrassment.

Ellis pulled at Bortis. Carimus and Duka followed along,

heading towards the buffet table and the dePenrodyns there.

"I'm sorry, Prince Artos, my brother isn't any more tactful than Father," Elaine gazed up at him shyly.

"It's nothing, Elaine, and hey, it's still Art. We've known each other since we were little kids, no reason to get all formal."

She smiled hesitantly and nodded. "When did your father tell you? About us, I mean? Father has barely talked about anything else since midsummer. At least to me. Mother too." She shook her head. "I have to say I was relieved when they told me it was to be you. I was so afraid I was going to be sold off to that fat Floyd deAnson. He gives me the creeps." She looked at Artos expectantly. *Since midsummer?* he thought.

"Um ... Well, actually, Father hasn't told me much of anything." Horror flashed in her eyes. "Father first brought up marriage this morning."

Elaine looked relieved. "Oh, thank the Sky! I thought you didn't know about their matchmaking, and then what would you be thinking about me?"

"I have to say, Elaine, I'm still trying to get my mind wrapped around the whole idea of marriage. Really, I had thought very little about it. I mean ... don't you want the freedom to decide for yourself? Not that I don't like you!" He hastened to add. "It's just so sudden, for me, I mean."

Elaine looked him in the eyes. "Mother has been telling me for years that she and Father would pick my husband," she looked at the floor. "You can always refuse, you know. Men always have more say in these things. It's the way of the world." She sighed.

"What do you mean? You could refuse too. You are not a slave."

Elaine shook her head. "I keep forgetting. You grew up in

a household with no women around. It is not the same for us as it is for you. Women are expected to do what their parents decide for them. The only alternative I would have to marriage as my father directs is to run away. Like my aunt did before I was born. I couldn't do that. I enjoy having nice things and a comfortable home. Ellis may be offered some choice in who he marries. I will not."

Artos did not know how to reply and stood silently for a moment. "Can I get you a glass of cider?" he said, desperate to change the subject.

Elaine looked up and nodded. "Yes, please, that would be nice."

As they walked toward the buffet tables, Artos noticed Bortis standing and speaking with Ellis, who was talking to him about something at length. Bortis nodded, mumbling at the pauses, but Artos could see that his brother's attention was not on Ellis. Bort's eyes were focused upon Elaine as he watched them approach the table laden with beverages.

13

SOME FRESH AIR

ARTOS

6:co p.m.

The full silver moon was rising over the Black Mountains in the east as the red September sun sank slowly between the peaks of the Mountains of Myst in the west. A faint rumble of thunder sounded in the distance as, in the shadows above the lonely western watch post, something stirred.

IN THE GREAT HALL, a chime rang out six times, signaling that it was time for Duka's birthday dinner to begin. On the speaker's dais, the Fairborn Bard Veryan finished a song with the last notes of a trilling arpeggio. As the guests walked to their tables for dinner, the Bard began the familiar resounding notes of "Blood of Dragons," the deDraconis House anthem. A cheer went up from the guardsmen and staff, and when the bard began the chorus, almost everyone in the entire hall sang the refrain:

"And from the blood of dragons, the seeds of kings are made …
And with the spells of magic might, men will be amazed …
Men will be amazed."

Artos saw his uncle scowl and step over to speak to the
king. Whatever his father said failed to mollify the angry duke.
"It's disrespectful, I tell you. Bah! I need some fresh air." Bretton
turned and stormed out of the Great Hall. Artos shook his head.
Bort was right; there he goes.

Artos's father composed his features and strode to his
chair at the head of the main table. He stood behind his chair
and waited as the guests searched for their assigned places
with a placard holding their names. After a few moments, the
guests all stood at their places. Artos stood across from Elaine
deEagledon. *What a surprise*, he thought to himself as he nodded
and smiled at her politely. Duka, he noted, was to be seated
at his father's right hand, the seat of honor, between him and
Uncle Cameron. The deEagledons, the dePenrodyns, the Canon,
the Cantor, the Fairborn Prince, and his Bard, who had left the
speaker's dais, completed the company at the main table with
the six members of House deDraconis. Six instead of the seven
there should be, since Duke Bretton failed to return. Leaving
two empty chairs on the king's left, at the head of the table. The
always vacant queen's chair and that of the recalcitrant duke.

When everyone was looking his way, the king began to
speak. "Welcome, my friends, to House deDraconis and the
birthday dinner of my youngest son, Prince Duka." His father
waited for the polite clapping to subside, then continued. "My
son is fifteen years this day, and if you will, please join me now
in a toast celebrating his Ascension."

The serving staff passed out glasses of the bubbly beverage,

Vhert, a gingery flavored drink, with a mildly euphoric effect. When everyone in the hall was served, the King raised his glass, and everyone followed his example. "To Prince Duka deDraconis!" he exclaimed and drained his glass.

"TO PRINCE DUKA," shouted everyone. They all downed their drinks, set down their glasses, clapped, and cheered. Artos clapped as hard as anyone, happy for his little brother.

14

THE WESTERN WATCHPOST

BRETTON

6:13 p.m.

The western watchpost was a lonely station. A small guard room within with a short crenelated battlement outside, carved from the crag itself. The western falls made it a noisy and damp post, and many of the guardsmen regarded a post there as punishment duty. The sound of the water as it rushed past on its journey from Loch O Wrens to Dragon Loch far below was relentless. Mist was ever-present, as was the smell of water. Sometimes, when the sun was setting, a lovely double rainbow would grace the scene. It was said that rainbow watching caused Queen Evelyn's fatal accident fifteen years before. There were scandalous whispers of a double suicide, but no one knew the details as both the Queen and the guard on duty had apparently fallen to their deaths in the loch three hundred feet below. Some insisted the post was haunted, that there was an eerie sense of being watched and even that strange feeling that some described as "someone treading upon your grave."

<><><>

"Take a break, guardsman. I want some air, and I want it alone," Bretton strode out of the guardroom onto the battlement, startling the on-duty guard, who quickly spun around. Upon seeing the Duke, he came to attention and bowed.

"Good evening, Lord Bretton. I didn't expect to see you this evening, what with your nephew's dinner an' all."

"Are you deaf?" snarled Bretton as he strode out onto the small watch post. "Go away. Don't come back for at least thirty minutes. Do you understand?" He glared at the guardsman, who managed a quick nod that rapidly turned into an awkward bow. The guardsman then scurried back into the inner guard room. He paused there and looked back. The Duke was still glaring at him. He raised his hand, pointing to the doorway that led up to the guard's barracks three hundred feet above the watch post. "Go!" The guardsman did not even try to answer. He just ran to the open door and started up the stairs.

Bretton stalked over and slammed shut the door that led up to the barracks, then opened the nearby door leading to the long passageway running all the way to the Airship docks on the eastern side. No one was in sight. Good. Everyone was either on duty or at the stupid dinner, fawning over the damned elves. He slammed the door much harder than necessary, walked back out onto the battlements, and stood leaning on the wall, looking down at the turbulent waters far below.

"Have you reached a decision yet, Duke Bretton?" hissed a voice from somewhere off to his left. He scanned the bleak, empty rocky wall. "I am afraid you really need to decide soon." Now the voice was to the right side, but that way looked just as deserted as the left. Far off thunder rumbled, warning of the upcoming storm.

He rotated around, held out his hand, his crysword

appearing in his grasp. The red blade glinted in the last rays as the sun slid out of sight behind the Mountains of Myst. He scanned the rocky walls of the castle, but the shadows that filled every nook and cranny grew darker as the light fled.

"Where are you?" Bretton demanded. "Who are you? What do you really want? Damn you!" He backed until he stood within the qulan's tingly field in the doorway.

"We go over this every time, Lord Bretton." This time, the voice seemed directly over his head.

"I want straight answers!" roared the Duke. "Where is Stephanie?" His voice broke, and he lapsed into silence.

"I'm afraid she is not doing well, Duke Bretton. Not well at all. As I told you last night, she is cold and all alone. But I guess that isn't enough to allow you to give me that one small thing I need. I may as well go … Farewell." The voice receded, growing fainter as if the speaker were moving away into the dusk.

"Wait," whispered Bretton, his voice harsh.

"Yes?" the voice answered. "Are you reconsidering? Having a change of heart? You will grant me my little favor?"

"Why do you want the trophy? Give me a good reason and I'll get it for you myself. Tell me where Stephanie is, damn you!" he rasped.

"I keep hearing that Tomas's head is hanging in your Great Hall, flaunted, and mocked. I merely want to give him a decent burial. A man's head is hardly a fitting prize for your great Family to display. It's barbaric." The voice took a wheedling tone. "Is that such a hard thing to understand? What if it was one of your relatives? How would you feel, knowing it was being used in such a horrific manner? Would you not want to give it a proper ceremony and burial? Wouldn't you? I won't tell you anything unless you give me his head … or invite me in to fetch it myself. It would be foolish of me to give up my only bargaining chip. You have everything in your favor. I have only the location of a poor, lost woman. Surely you see my point?" The voice paused and waited.

"The mounting is twenty feet off the floor. I would have to get a ladder and, and … No! This is madness. Someone would see me carrying a ladder through the castle or notice me removing it. Even in the dead of night, a guardsman or a passing servant would see me. Impossible."

"This is why I offer to get it myself, Duke Bretton. As you see, I can make myself very unnoticeable. I have some skill at climbing sheer walls. It must be the better option? And if I am seen and caught? What do you care? I promise I would never betray the fact that you invited me into the castle. Who would believe me? No one would suspect Duke Bretton was involved. How could they?" wheedled the voice. "Just invite me into the castle and tell me the shortest route to your Great Hall. I will tell you Stephanie's whereabouts and you can quickly join her. I promise."

Bretton's head was churning. The thought of rescuing his Stephanie. The chance to be a hero in her eyes once more. To erase that humiliating memory of that doubly damned elf prince. The goblets of fire brandy burned in his belly as strongly as the desire to be a hero in his beloved's eyes burned in his heart. He didn't know why Stephanie's memory had come to haunt him so much in the last few weeks, but the thought of her, cold and alone, drove him to despair. The chance to be her champion once again. He could. He would! He must … He must.

Bretton bowed his head, sighed, and in a soft voice whispered, "Forgive me, I … I must." He raised his head and recoiled in surprise. Standing just a foot away from him was a small, spindly figure, barely four feet in height, wrapped in a gray, hooded cloak, head bowed down, features hidden in the shadows of the garment. Raising his crysword, Bretton almost stumbled while stepping back from the doorway into the guardroom. Gripping his sword, he concentrated on trueseeing. Nothing changed, no illusions. This was the speaker's real form. *Hardly a threat*, he thought, but he still held his sword at the ready.

"I invite you into my home," he spoke, barely above a whisper. The cloaked figure glided forward through the qulan field, into Castle Draconis. In the distance, thunder rumbled once more.

15

DINNER

AARON

6:04 p.m.

King Aaron Draconis surveyed the Great Hall. The tables in the lower reaches of the hall were mostly empty, even with the off-duty guards and staff with their families. Still, it was much better than it would have been if he hadn't invited them all. Drat the damn storm anyway. Duka was a good son and deserved better than an empty hall for his ascension birthday dinner.

Cameron worried far too much. So what if Duka bore the double-dragon birthmark? The fact that he bonded so quickly to his blue sword could be to their advantage. Cameron was head of the Church and the schools that oversaw the teaching of the quanti-craft. He needed to stop leaning so heavily on Ser Pietro and the Sky sect and direct the forming of a new school for quanti usage. One not so heavily controlled by the Church. Aaron could foresee Duka being just the person to head such a school. Eventually. Assuming he could find a teacher to give him the knowledge to do so. Crown Prince Tirinvo had already told him his bard had some suggestions along those lines. He glanced fondly at Duka sitting next to him.

"You set a fine table, Aaron, wot?" said Count Stephan, interrupting his thought. "We will have to put our heads together when we get back to Phoenix and begin planning for the Solstice celebration." He nodded in a self-satisfied way and gave the king a knowing wink.

"Aye Stephan, we shall. I'm sure we both have some ideas to make it a momentous affair."

Aaron turned his attention to his slab of medium-rare roast beef, carved off a bite, and delivered it to his mouth. Delicious.

Brett would have called it a mouth-watering piece of cow, back in the day, back when they were still best friends. So long ago now.

Aaron swallowed and sighed sadly to himself, glancing at the empty chair his brother should have been filling. Damn the man, this was Duka's birthday. Couldn't he just get over this? It had been over twenty years and Brett showed no signs of forgetting his imagined snit with his brother and with the entire Fairborn race.

He glanced at his first-born, saying something to Stephan's daughter Elaine, who was seated across the table from him. Good, they were getting along nicely. The deEagledon girl was well trained by her mother. *The Sky knows it can't be from Stephan*, he thought. *He thinks I don't see how he believes having his daughter married into my family will add to his power. Once she is a Draconis, she will be mine, not his. He will learn, but by then it will be too late.* He continued eating his dinner.

A few minutes later, he felt a brief stabbing pain in his chest, and he sat up with a start.

"Is something wrong, father?" asked Duka, stopping in

mid-motion delivering a fork of beef to his mouth. "You look pale."

Aaron looked at his son and shook his head. "It's nothing. I just swallowed too big a mouthful. Remember that, and always chew your food well," he admonished.

"I will, father," said Duka and returned his attention to his dinner.

Aaron glanced at Brett's empty chair and frowned. *Damn that man. It's not your nephew's fault. Where is he?*

16

TO JOIN STEPHANIE

BRETTON

6:20 p.m.

Bretton kept his sword at the ready. The creature before him appeared frail and helpless, but it had somehow climbed a sheer rock wall of over three hundred feet. *This creature is far from helpless*, he thought.

"What manner of creature are you? Show yourself," Bretton moved back another step and moved his crysword back and forth defensively.

A thin, pale, grayish hand emerged from the creature's robe and slowly drew back its hood. It was female, though she resembled no woman Bretton had ever seen before. Her bald head was egg-shaped with gray skin and white arched eyebrows. A light blue tattoo adorned both of her cheeks, and her lips were full and red. Two golden posts garnished her earlobes. But her eyes, her eyes, drew his attention. They were large and white as if she were sightless, but she gazed up into his eyes, studying him as carefully as he was watching her.

They stared at each other for a long moment.

"Where is my Stephanie?" he whispered, as if talking loudly was impossible. "You promised."

The creature placed the fingertips of her two hands together and bowed her head slightly, as if in prayer. Then she raised her head to stare into his eyes. Once his gaze locked with hers, a long black needle extended quickly from her fingers and pierced him through the chest. He was frozen in place. The sharp, lancing pain intensified as the life drained from his body.

"I promised you would join her," she whispered. "As you now will, in death." Bretton's final look of horror faded as he crumpled to the floor. His crysword dissolved into reddish-gray dust.

The creature shivered, trembled, and began to change and grow. In moments, the form of Bretton deDraconis stood over the body of what was once Duke Bretton. Raucous laughter rang out from the guard post.

17

AFTER DINNER

ARTOS

7:28 p.m.

Fidgeting, Artos finished his dessert. His dress suit was always uncomfortable when he had to wear it for a long period. At least Bortis was keeping Elaine engaged in talk. Though he was only listening with half an ear, they seemed concerned with very inconsequential matters. He looked around the hall. Everyone was enjoying themselves now that his uncle had left the room, although he couldn't help but notice that his grandfather Estel kept complaining. Apparently, the villages in his demesnes were too underpopulated to farm enough crops, and the situation was only getting worse.

"What do you think, Art? Should we do that when we get back to Phoenix?" asked Bortis.

"Hmm? What did you say, Bort? Sorry, I was daydreaming, I guess." He realized his brother, Ellis, and Elaine were all looking at him expectantly.

"I said when we get back to Phoenix, we should all go riding together. You know, horses, saddles, that kind of thing? Like we do every Sixthday, only without someone telling us where to go, what to do, and when to do it," Bortis replied.

"Oh, yeah, that would be fun. We could—" His father vigorously tapped a silver mug with his spoon, interrupting his thought.

"May I have your attention? Attention please!" called out King Aaron and the murmur of voices faded away throughout the Great Hall. "As is customary on such occasions, we shall now make a final toast to my son. Usually, we would begin a Grand Ball after such a fine birthday feast, but due to the rising, inclement conditions, we shall forgo that this evening so that Count Stephan and Count Estel can depart and reach their homes before the storm arrives. The esteemed Bard, Veryan, has graciously offered to entertain any of you who wish to remain."

The gathered guards and staff cheered, knowing they could finish any food and drink that remained while they listened to the Fairborn bard. "Speech! Speech!" they cried out to Duka, who was standing beside his father.

Aaron nodded to his youngest, and Duka nervously cleared his throat. "I ... I thank you all for coming." He glanced toward the table near the dais where many wrapped packages lay, waiting to be opened. "And I would like to thank you for all the birthday gifts." He looked at his father, who smiled and then raised his glass.

"To Prince Duka deDraconis!" he stated loudly.

"Prince Duka!" roared the crowd, downing their drinks.

Artos moved to hug his little brother, but had to make way for the Greatdruid, who reached his little brother before he did.

"Prince Duka," said the Cantor. "I almost forgot. Because of the storm, the Darrell could not be here this evening, but he asked me to deliver a gift to you and to tell you he would be present in Phoenix at Prince Artos's birthday on the Solstice to celebrate your official Ascension." He reached into a pocket in his robe and pulled out a small, polished wooden box, which he offered the prince.

Duka took the box and opened it. Artos peered over his shoulder. It contained a shiny copperish amulet shaped like the head of a great horned owl. It hung upon a fine silver chain.

"Thank you, sir," said Duka. "It's very nice. I like owls."

"You needn't thank me, Prince Duka. I was merely the messenger for Count Glendon. The Darrell would have liked to have given it to you himself, but it wasn't to be, due to the oncoming foul weather." The Cantor clapped him upon his shoulder. "Fare ye well, lad. May Mother Veda watch over you and keep you safe. I must go. Count Estel has asked me to travel with him to Starkeep to discuss matters of import. Be safe, and you too, Prince Artos." The large druid hurried off after the dePenrodyn family.

"Did you see, Art?" said Duka, as Artos stepped up. He held up the open box. "It's an owl." Duka smiled, obviously pleased.

"Yes, here. Let me help you with it." Artos reached into the box and, pulling out the amulet, clasped it around his little brother's neck. "Very nice! Happy Birthday, Duke." He hugged his little brother.

"Artos, may I have a word with you?" Artos's father beckoned him from where he stood with the Fairborn prince. He nodded and walked a few steps to stand before Aaron, Duka trailing along with him.

"Son, I am happy to see you and Elaine getting along. I have asked Prince Tirinvo to attend your birthday celebration at the solstice, and he has agreed to come and ask his cousin to perform more of his wonderful music." Aaron looked at his son expectantly.

"That would be nice. Thank you, Father, thank you, Prince Tirinvo." Artos nodded to each.

"That will be great," enthused Duka. "Bard Varyan is very good. I wish I could play my guitar the way he plays his crysharp."

"Me too," Artos agreed. "I wish I had a crysharp." He smiled wistfully.

"Hmnn, I hardly think you would have the time to devote to such an instrument, even if you had one." Aaron shook his head. "Count Stephan and I agreed we will have a three-fold celebration at the solstice. We shall have Duka's formal ascension." He reached out and tousled Duka's hair. "Your birthday, of course, Artos, and we shall use the occasion to announce your betrothal to Viscountess Elaine." He nodded dismissively to his sons and turned to continue his conversation with the Fairborn prince.

"Congratulations, Prince Artos," said Tirinvo. "I wish you a blessed marriage, my young friend. To you and yours be happiness and strength."

"But Father!" Artos stiffened. "I wanted to talk with you about this."

"There is nothing to discuss. Stephan and I have agreed. This is for the best, son, not only for you, but for Veda as well. Believe me, you will come to thank me for this. Now take your brother and go enjoy the music." Aaron waved his hand in the bard's direction and turned away again.

"But, but ..." Artos began, and then stopped as his father turned and gave him a piercing glare.

"Come on, Art." Duka pulled on his arm, and he allowed

himself to be drawn away. The castle seemed to spin around him, and the air got very thin. "Look, Cari is watching the bard." Artos followed numbly.

"Isn't he something, Cari?" asked Duka, as they stopped to stand beside him. "I wish I could make music like that," he added wistfully.

Carimus nodded absently as he watched the skilled Bard. "Yes, he's superb. I wonder how long it took him to master it?"

Varyan finished the song he was playing, and the brothers clapped with enthusiasm. The bard stood up and bowed to the brothers. "Prince Carimus, I see you have on your rune bracelet. Does it bring you comfort?"

Carimus looked down at his left wrist and shrugged. "I'm not sure why I even put it on tonight. It was lying on my dresser, and I noticed it. It just felt right. I don't hardly ever wear it, really."

The bard pursed his lip and gave a slight shrug. "Among the Fairborn, to be given such a gift is considered a great honor. I should have stayed and given it to you myself, but I was under orders not to stay here that day, some six years ago. I am sorry." He glanced over at King Aaron. "The Runes have several uses. They have ties with quanti-magic and can be used to foresee the future if one has the proper gifts in the quan."

"It was you. I was there when you gave it to my father," said Artos. "I didn't remember the rider until just now. I was paying more attention to the eagle."

"You were what, thirteen then, I believe, Prince Artos?" he said, smiling. "It's not surprising that my steed was more interesting to you than me. There are those who would still say Cloudbreaker is far more exciting than a mere Bard." He looked to the hall and announced, "I will be taking a quick break, but

I will play more songs after I have a drink." Many in the hall clapped and not a few cheered, raised their cups, and whistled as they continue to eat, drink, and be merry. He smiled at the royal siblings, then carefully put his sapphire crysharp into his belt pouch.

Carimus watched with amazement. "How did you do that? Your crysharp is much bigger than that pouch. But you just put it right inside. It's magic, isn't it?"

Varyan nodded. "The holding pouch was a gift from my teacher many years ago." Smiling, he untied the leather strip that held the velvet bag to his belt. "This is not a gift, Prince Carimus. Excuse me for saying so, but I must. Take the pouch and examine it." He held it out to Carimus, who gingerly took it as if it might be dangerous.

"It feels empty," he exclaimed. "What happened to your crysharp?"

"Open the bag and look within," said the bard.

Carimus peered inside. "I don't see anything."

"Go ahead, reach inside. It's not dangerous."

"It's empty. And barely big enough for my hand," Carimus exclaimed as he withdrew his hand and looked to the bard in wonder.

"You may examine it, Prince Artos," said Varyan.

Carimus handed the pouch to his brother, who felt the bag from the outside, nodded, then put his hand inside and withdrew it.

"It's empty alright, but we saw you put your crysharp inside. Where is it now?" asked Artos.

"Somewhere between worlds, I would guess," replied the bard. "Give the pouch to Prince Duka now and let him look."

Artos handed the small velvet bag to Duka, who took it and

said, "It's not empty. I feel something inside."

The bard smiled, "Well, Prince Duka, it is your birthday, after all. Inside is my present to you. Take it out."

Duka hesitantly pulled out a small black velvet pouch with silken drawstrings. "A pouch, and it's not empty either."

"Is it another magic bag?" asked Carimus excitedly. "What's in it?"

"No," replied Varyan. "Putting a magic bag inside another magic bag would be a recipe for disaster. But the contents have some minor magic of their own."

Duka opened the drawstring, reached inside, and pulled out a small tile of wood, which he examined. "There's a Rune on it."

"Yes, Duka. There are twenty-five rune-stones within. One is blank and the others each has a Rune inscribed upon one side. May I see what you have drawn?"

Upon seeing the Rune, the bard frowned. "Well, it takes some time for the Runes to become attuned with their owner."

Carimus, who had craned around the bard to look at the tile, exclaimed, "It's the same as one of the Runes on my bracelet."

Varyan nodded, still looking grave. "Indeed it is. The Rune is Hagalaz. The Rune of disruption. I need to excuse myself, young lords. I must have a word with Prince Tirinvo. Is there anything I can play for you tonight, Prince Duka? It is your party and so if you have anything in particular you would like, please ask and I shall endeavor to do it justice for you."

Duka returned the smile and replied, "Whatever you please is fine with me. It is all magnificent."

"Will you leave your crysharp to your son to follow in your footsteps?" asked Carimus.

"Alas, my son does not seek to be a bard, Prince Carimus.

His talents lie elsewhere. Besides, when I pass from this world, my harp will turn to dust, just as your crysword shall follow you back to the earth from which we all come." He shrugged. "I need to wet my throat. Singing is dry work. I shall return shortly, my young lords." And he strode off to the buffet tables in search of a beverage.

Carimus frowned and turned to his brothers. "That's not true. I wonder why he said that?"

"I would think he would know Cari. Besides, why would a crysharp be different from one of our cryswords?" Duka asked.

"I do know. And I can prove it. Come on, I'll show you." Beckoning his brothers to follow, Carimus headed towards the Royal entrance to the hall.

Duka tugged at Artos, who allowed himself to be pulled along, still somewhat in a daze, between thoughts of magical bags and the suddenness of his upcoming betrothal.

18

THE HALL
OF MIRRORS

ARTOS

7:47 p.m.

CARIMUS, PUFFED WITH IMPORTANCE, led the way, with Duka still pulling on Artos' sleeve until Artos finally tugged his arm free. Duka looked at his eldest brother with concern as they walked past the stairway leading up to the royal quarters.

"Are you okay, Art? You look funny," Duka said.

"I'm fine, Duke, just fine …" he trailed off as he realized where Carimus was leading them. "The Hall of Mirrors, Cari? I don't think we are supposed to go in there without Father or Uncle Cam. I don't think we even can. That's a warded door, isn't it?"

"I can open it, Art," said Carimus with confidence. "Uncle Cameron keyed the plate to my hand this summer when he was giving me lessons in using the House Screens." Noticeable pride filled Carimus's voice. "I think he planned to have me key the three of you once I officially become Disciple or something."

They neared the end of the hallway and stopped before the

sturdy stone door that led into the Hall of Mirrors. A small, light blue crystal square sat where a knob would be on an ordinary door.

"Why are we going in there, anyway?" Artos asked, "What's so important?"

"You'll see, just wait. I'll prove to you the bard was wrong." Carimus placed the palm of his hand on the crystal square and concentrated for a moment.

Noiselessly, the door swung inward, revealing the council chamber of Castle Draconis, the Hall of Mirrors. Carimus gave a sigh of relief, leading Artos to believe he hadn't been as confident as he portrayed. The brothers stood in the doorway, peering around nervously, half expecting their great-uncle to appear and scold them for sneaking in somewhere they weren't supposed to.

The hall was well lit, with four everlight globes hanging from the ceiling. Although it was not huge, the octagonal-shaped room's seven mirrored walls made it seem almost infinite. Even the inside of the entrance door was a mirror. Only the westernmost wall straight across the room from them was without a mirror. Instead, it was the dark gray stone of the castle and home to eleven large crystal screens. One large screen at the top, above two rows of smaller ones. A row of four screens above another row of six.

All the screens were the familiar light blue color, save for two rectangles of black which had been painted over.

Above each of the smaller screens was the sigil of the Great House to which it aligned. The rising eagle for House deEagledon, the obscure intertwined circles which were the archaic sigil of House dePenrodyn and the rest. These sigils were etched into the wall and easy to read, even from across the room.

Those screens which had been painted over also had their etchings obscured with black paint. Art remembered his father telling him one of the blacked-out screens had been aligned with the now-defunct, traitorous House deYung. Artos wasn't sure what the other screen was aligned to, but he thought perhaps it had something to do with the black mark on the family honor, bound up with the last deDraconis to be marked with the double dragons and to wield a blue crysword. He glanced at Duka, wondering how much of this he knew.

His brother peered around the room curiously. Artos realized this was the first time Duke had ever seen the inside, as neither their father nor their great-uncle would have introduced him to the workings of the chamber yet.

"Why are some of the screens blacked over?" asked Duka, as if reading his mind.

"One of them is the screen that communicated to House deYung," Art answered. "They painted it over after the rebellion. I'm not really sure about the other. Did Uncle Cameron tell you, Cari?"

"I asked him," said Cari. "But he only said it was something he would talk to me about later. I could tell he didn't want to talk about them."

"What did you want to show us, Cari?" Duka asked.

Carimus looked around guiltily, then beckoned his brothers to follow him. He walked around the room, to his right, following the wall, avoiding the rows of benches and the oaken table with the control panel their great-uncle would normally sit, next to the king in the center. Stopping beneath the rightmost screen by a plain wooden stand upon which stood something covered with a black silken cloth. He whisked off the covering and pointed to the transparent block sitting upon it. "There!

See, I told you. The crysharp isn't like our swords." Within the cube was a sapphire-blue crysharp, twin to the harp played by the Fairborn bard.

"I didn't know that was there." Artos stepped closer and inspected the case. It appeared to be made of some transparent material. Glass perhaps? He rapped on the side. From the solid thunk, he decided it wasn't hollow, but a block of some clear, dense material with the crysharp embedded within.

"Maybe it was destroyed, Cari," he ventured. "Maybe the stuff it's encased in just keeps its form as it was?" He tried to lift the block and found it was far too heavy to pick up comfortably.

"Let's ask the bard," said Duka excitedly. "I'll bet he might even know whose harp it was."

"We can't do that," said Carimus quickly. "We're not supposed to be in here, remember? Varyan would be sure to ask father about it if he doesn't know whose it was and maybe even if he does. It must be precious."

"He's right," Artos agreed. "In fact, we really should go back to the Great Hall before someone comes searching for us. You want Uncle Cam to find us in here? Or worse, Uncle Brett? Besides, you should be opening your birthday gifts by now. Father will wonder where we are. Come on."

"He's wondering that now," said a fresh voice. The three brothers all jumped and turned to see who had caught them. "How the heck did you get in here anyhow?" Bortis stood in the doorway with his arms crossed, trying to look stern.

"Bort!" cried Duka. "Come and look at this, quick. Then we'll go. You know a lot of the family history. Who did this belong to?"

Bortis sauntered across the room, peered at the crystal block, then shook his head. "I dunno? It looks like the harp the bard's got, doesn't it? Wonder why it's stuck in here? I guess it's broken or something. Come on, Father sent me to look for you guys. I was about to go upstairs, but I heard voices down here instead. Come on." He turned and hurried back towards the door with his brothers close behind.

"I still think we should ask the bard," said Duka, as Carimus pulled the door shut and applied his hand to the blue square.

Carimus just shook his head and hurried after his older brothers, Duka following along.

Artos stopped at the doorway into the Great Hall. The bard had returned to his stool and was playing again. His father stood near the main entrance to the hall, the Fairborn prince beside him, still deep in their discussion. Bortis hurried ahead, back to the buffet table. Artos shook his head in wonder. His brother was a bottomless pit when it came to food. *I couldn't eat another bite*, he thought ruefully.

Carimus and Duka caught up with him at the doorway. Carimus pushed past and made his way back to stand near the bard to watch him play. Duka lingered next to him in the doorway. His attention was not on the bard, but on the trophies hanging above and behind him.

"He was watching me, Art; I could feel his eyes on the back of my head throughout dinner. Promise me you'll destroy that thing. Please."

Artos nodded. "I promise. When I am king, I will have that traitor's head removed and buried."

"No! Not buried, destroyed. It should be burned, and the ashes scattered far and wide. I just know it must be completely and utterly destroyed."

Duka was almost in tears now, and Artos quickly patted him on the shoulder. "Alright, that's what I'll have done. We'll soak it in oil, and I'll let you start the fire."

"I don't want to even be that close to it. Or you to be, either. But we must watch to be sure it is gone. I'll never feel comfortable until I see it destroyed."

"Artos!" Father had seen his sons standing in the door and was calling him to his side, anger evident on his face. "Come on. It's time to escort the Count and his family to the Gates."

Artos gave Duka one more reassuring pat on his shoulder and hurried to where his father beckoned.

Just as he reached his father's side, the Fairborn bard gave another of his flourishes and began playing the deEagledon anthem once again. At the same time, the Count and his entourage, along with Canon Neubre and his two retainers, entered from the north side of the room and began making their way towards the Great Hall entrance and the Winding Way.

"Where have you been hiding? Count Penrodyn has already left. Never mind. Just straighten up," snapped the King. "Hurry up. Go join them and escort them to their carriage. Show them out the main gates. Remember, you are acting for me and the Family, do not shame us."

Artos wondered what had his father so worked up? *We weren't gone that long.* He composed his features and even managed a smile and a nod to Elaine as he joined the family group. He fell in beside Ellis and Elaine. His father walked up beside the Count, Countess, and the Canon, the Count's brother and the Canon's men falling in at the rear.

"Well, Art," said Ellis, "we'll be seeing you back in the lowlands. Elaine and I will let you know when we are free to join you for an afternoon of horseback riding." They walked out of the Great Hall and began the trek down the Winding Way to the main courtyard, one floor below. "It will probably be in a couple weeks, before the weather turns too foul for such things."

"What's that? Oh, yes, riding, of course." Artos felt at a loss for words as his thoughts caught back up with how his father had taken control of this part of his life. "Eh … umm. Bort's birthday is coming up in a few weeks. Maybe we could go then?"

"What about my birthday?" asked Bortis, who had come up from behind to join them.

"We were trying to decide when to go riding together," said Ellis.

Bortis nodded. "Does that sound good to you, Elaine?" Art noticed Bortis's eyes were drawn to Ellis's twin more than anything else.

"That would be fine with me," she answered.

"Good! It's settled then. Art and I will make the arrangements with the horse-master at Armida, our ranch outside Phoenix," said Bortis, with more enthusiasm than Artos felt. But he nodded and smiled as if he thought it was a grand idea.

After making two revolutions down the Winding Way, the party exited to the inner courtyard and walked to the large iron-bound oaken door that led to the outer courtyard where the deEagledon carriage and outriders were waiting. A corporal of the guard stood at attention. At a nod from King Aaron, the guard thrust his right hand into the light blue crystal box mounted on the wall. With a slight grating sound, the three oaken beams securing the door slid into their sockets in the stone wall and the large door swung open. Waiting on the other side was the carriage, and the six mounted deEagledon guards. Two more saddled horses awaited the Canon's entourage. The driver sat at his post while the three footmen waited beside the door, ready to assist the nobles to their places within.

"Grand party, Aaron! Wot?" said Count Stephen. "Too bad the beastly weather that is coming made it such a small gathering, eh? We'll do it up proper at the Solstice and celebrate the betrothal with a grand time, wot? With a proper orchestra and a royal ball." He reached out and clapped Artos on the shoulder with a knowing smile, then followed his family inside. The Canon followed behind after a few polite farewells to the King and the Princes. The footmen closed the door and assumed their places upon the carriage as the Canon's guard mounted their steeds.

Thunder rumbled in the distance as King Aaron turned to his eldest. "Escort your future in-laws to the outer gate. Attend your duty. You have been lacking in grace tonight and don't think I haven't noticed. We shall have a talk about this on the morrow. You were born to be king after I am gone, Prince Artos. It's time you began acting that way." Aaron walked back through the door into the castle proper, leaving Bortis standing beside Artos. The two brothers exchanged glances, and Bort shrugged. Artos signaled to the driver of the carriage to begin toward the gate.

Another corporal of the guard stood waiting at the main gate leading from the castle to the causeway, which lay across Dragon Loch.

Artos walked up to the guard and nodded to him. "Open the main gate, Corporal." With a nod, the trusted guard thrust his right hand into the light blue crystal box mounted on the wall. The dragon tattoo on the back of his hand glowed slightly with the energy of the quanti. Only a guard proven loyal at the mid-summer testing bore the dragon tattoo on his hand that allowed the gates to be opened.

With a rumbling sound, the steel beams reinforcing the iron-bound oaken doors slid out of sight into the stone wall, the massive gates swung outward and the steel portcullis beyond slowly rose into its nesting place in the dark stone above. The brothers' skin prickled as the qulan separated around the opening.

The guard remained with his hand within the crystal box until the carriage and the mounted riders had left the castle onto the long causeway that led to the far gatehouse and the town of Brierly beyond. Then he withdrew his hand from the box. The portcullis slowly lowered as the enormous doors silently swung closed, the steel beams sliding back into place. The prickly feeling on their skin disappeared.

The two brothers turned and walked back to the inner gate. Closed now, as both gates could not be open simultaneously. The magic of the quanti that controlled them would not allow it.

"Ever wonder what would happen if you or I tried to open the gate?" asked Artos. "We don't have the mark that the trusted guards do."

"We don't need 'em. Uncle Brett told me any of us could open them if we stuck our hand in the lockbox. The quanti respond to our blood. I asked him about that last summer."

"I know. I just wondered if you did."

"I also asked him why we needed all the bars and beams and gates since it's just the qulan on all the upper doors, like the airship docks or the Eyrie." Bortis gave his brother a challenging look. "You'll never guess what he said."

"I was just wondering that myself, well not about the other ways in, but why we need all the extra stuff on the front and the river gates when the qulan would keep anyone out who wasn't invited in." Artos raised a brow. "What did Uncle Brett say?"

"He said it was because they were 'suspicious fools.' His exact words," Bortis said, shaking his head. "Come on, I want to see the look on Spare's face when he opens my gift."

"Why? What did you give him? And you really need to stop calling him the spare. He really hates it. He does."

"Oh, back off," snapped Bortis. "You know, I don't mean anything by it. You know it."

Artos took a step backwards, surprised by the anger in his brother's voice.

Bortis shook his head as if clearing his thoughts and softened his voice. "Heck, he's a decent kid. I just like teasing him sometimes, that's all. Anyway, I wrapped up a big old rock, and put it in a box and wrapped up that box and put it in another box and wrapped that one up—"

"I get it. But that's not funny, it's mean!"

"No, it's not mean, it's funny. I got him a real gift. There's a nice sword belt and sheath for his new sword wrapped around the rock. I just want to watch him to open all those boxes before he gets to it. That's all. Come on."

Sighing and shaking his head, Artos followed his brother as the inner gates swung open for them, attended to by the trusted guardsman.

19

WHAT'S WRONG WITH ME?

BORTIS

8:50 p.m.

As Bortis led the way back to the Great Hall, his mind was jumbled with emotion. *What's wrong with me? I almost hit Art.*

It was crazy. It seemed like whenever Art and Elaine spoke to each other, he wanted to punch his brother in the face. To push him away from her. He'd never felt that way before, even when Art beat him at some contest or another. He had always taken it in stride. After all, he won a fair share of them himself. He was a better shot than Art with a bow, could beat him three times out of five in a contest with swords, and won almost half of their twice daily foot races. *Where is this anger coming from?* He knew he could be hot-headed. His uncle had often counseled him to control his emotions. "A warrior who loses his temper usually loses the battle shortly after." He prided himself on his control, or he had, until today. *I will control myself.*

Why did seeing Art and Elaine talking to each other set his teeth on edge? Elaine was to be Art's wife. That was a good thing, wasn't it? Wasn't it?

When Art had stood with his back to Bort, directing the guardsman to open the gates, a thought had crept into his mind. He could reach out and give Art a push as the carriage began moving forward, and his brother would fall and be crushed, or even killed by the large iron-rimmed wheels of the deEagledon carriage. That such a thought could even enter his mind unnerved him. He loved his brothers. It was his duty was to protect them. He walked back to the Great Hall, wrapped in silent thought.

20

THE PARTY'S OVER

AARON

9/16/1971 ar

12:44 a.m.

"THAT WAS MY FINAL SONG," announced Varyan. There was some scattered applause from the remaining members of the castle staff still in the Great Hall. With the announcement, they began to disperse, leaving the last few serving maids to begin the cleanup.

Aaron marveled that the Fairborn bard had managed to play so long and so well. He had regaled the hall with ballads, lively airs, and rousing chanties for hours.

Carimus and Duka were seated in nearby chairs. Carimus was nodding off and Duka was wide awake, still watching the Fairborn bard with rapt attention. Bortis was garnering snippets to munch on as the maids were clearing the buffet tables of the last remnants of the feast. Artos was seated next to his younger brothers, a stony expression on his face, still looking as though he wanted to argue about his upcoming betrothal. Aaron sighed and shook his head.

His Uncle Cameron was also looking as though he was ready to fall asleep in the chair where he sat next to Aaron. He reached over and tapped him gently on the shoulder.

"I'm awake! Not asleep," said the archbishop, sitting up a little straighter.

"Yes, uncle, I know. I just wanted to point out that Prince Tirinvo wished to have a conversation with us tonight, and I believe he is ready for that now."

"Well, it's about time, although I can't imagine what he feels we need to discuss that couldn't wait until tomorrow."

Crown Prince Tirinvo had been down on the main floor with his two liegemen speaking with the guards and even dancing with a few of the unattached serving maids. With the bard's announcement, he was coming back towards the raised end of the room with his two ever-present bodyguards close on his heels.

Aaron stood and stretched, then turned to the bard who had wiped off his crysharp and returned it to his magic belt pouch. "That was a magnificent performance, Ser Varyan. We owe you our undying thanks for such wonderful entertainment."

"It was my pleasure, King Aaron," said the bard with a bow. "An entertainer lives to entertain. It is I who should be thanking you for the opportunity."

"Bortis," called the king, "escort Carimus and Duka to their rooms. It's well past all of your bedtimes. Don't think you can sleep in all morning tomorrow just because we were lax with you tonight. You know your uncle will expect you to run your morning laps before breakfast, same as usual."

Upon seeing the dismay on their faces, he chuckled. "Breakfast will be served an hour later than usual, however. Off to bed with you. Go." Turning to Artos, who was starting to follow his brothers, he held out a hand to stop him. "Artos, I know this betrothal came as a shock for you. Trust me, son. Someday you will understand. This is for the best. Elaine is a lovely girl and you and she will find happiness. I am sure." He placed his hand on Artos's shoulder and gave a gentle squeeze. "Go to bed son, we will talk more tomorrow after breakfast." He watched fondly as his four sons walked to the royal entrance and were gone.

He called for wine and the servitors brought the last few bottles from the buffet and several glasses, pulled the corks and left them on the side tables. Then made their exits. He dismissed the last of the guards, leaving the Great Hall empty except for Cameron and the four Fairborn.

"You have fine sons, Lord Aaron," said Tirinvo as he joined the king and the archbishop. He and Varyan drew up chairs to sit across from them, his retainers standing a few feet behind him. "Where is Duke Bretton? I never saw him return to the hall this evening."

"My brother has solitary habits," said Aaron as he sat back down. "I imagine he is prowling the battlements somewhere. I hoped he would return, for Duka's sake, but am not surprised he didn't. He still holds your brother at fault for some imagined slight from long ago."

Aaron saw Tirinvo's liegemen glance at each other when he spoke, then stoically stare off into space. *They know something,* he thought, *but of course, they were there that night with Andune. I wonder if I might catch one of them alone and ask him what really happened?*

"No matter," said the Fairborn prince. "This only concerns him marginally. You said you were concerned with finding a proper teacher for young lord Duka,"

"What!" said the archbishop and sat up sharply. He turned to Aaron. "You never said anything to me about asking the … the Fairborn for advice on this. What is the matter with the Sky Church quanti school? It was good enough for you and your brother, was it not? It is a fine school, a fine school that will teach them everything they need concerning the use of the quanti."

"Uncle, neither Brett nor I bonded with a blue sword. A wizard's sword. Duka will need someone who knows the ways of wizardry. Something we have lost in our part of the world."

"But … but wizards aren't to be trusted, Aaron, you know that. You know what happened … before. Besides, there are no more wielders of blue."

"Excuse me, Lord Cameron," said the bard. "You have watched me perform all evening with my crysharp. My blue crysharp."

"And you wish to train him? No! Duka is not going to be a bard," said Cameron sharply. "The church will train him."

"Uncle," said Aaron. "Let us hear what my friends have to say. There is no harm in listening."

"I was not suggesting that I be a teacher to the young man," said Varyan. "You misunderstand me. There are still people who wield the blue. I am not alone."

"You can't be suggesting we send Duka to Her? To learn with the Fairborn?" Cameron was shaking his head vigorously. "It's out of the question. Absurd!"

"As a matter of fact, I was not suggesting you send Duka to Fairinhorst," said Tirinvo. "I was thinking of somewhere much closer."

"No," said Cameron. "You can't mean that. That avenue is long gone, dead and buried."

"I respectfully suggest it is not gone," said Tirinvo. "I also think it would be of great benefit for all your sons, Aaron, to have this opportunity. Not just young Lord Duka."

High above in the orchestra gallery, a dark figure watched from the shadows and listened to the conversation below. When it became apparent the argument would not conclude quickly, the figure retreated from the gallery. There was work to be done on the lower level. Much lovely work. She would return in a little while to have a meeting of her own with the king and his uncle. Thunder boomed in the distance. The storm had arrived.

21

MAYBE YOU COULD GUARD ART

DUKA

12:50 a.m.

THOUGHTS OF SLEEP were far from Duka's mind as he marched up the royal stairway. It had been a terribly exciting day. Bonding with his sword, meeting the Fairborn, and listening to the bard. And of course, his birthday dinner and his gifts. He glanced down at his new sword belt and sheath. It was beautiful leatherwork, almost worth going through layer after layer in the package to reach it. It was wonderful to have his own crysword now. He wasn't the odd one out anymore.

"Say Duke," said Carimus from where he trudged alongside him. "I was talking to Taur, you know, one of Prince Tirinvo's guards."

"Yes?"

"They are his cousins. Did you know that?"

"Yes, Prince Tirinvo introduced them to us when they arrived."

"Oh ... Well, did you ever think that maybe that could be the job you could do? You could be Art's most trusted bodyguard when he is king!"

"And what am I? Chopped liver?" said Bortis from behind them.

Carimus flinched from the caustic tone of Bortis's voice. "No, I didn't mean Duke would replace you. But you will have many other duties besides guarding Art."

Bortis just snorted as he followed them up the stairs.

"You would have to get Uncle Brett to give you more training, of course," Carimus continued enthusiastically. "But he is going to start with your crysword training soon. Maybe he already has it in mind!"

"I don't know, Cari," answered Duka slowly. "I'll always have Art's back, of course, but I think there is something more for me to do. In fact, I know there is, there must be. I just don't know what it could be yet."

For a moment, a vision of him fighting a terrifying figure flashed through his mind and he heard the roar of many voices chanting his name. He stumbled on the step and almost fell, then felt the firm grip of Bortis, steadying him from behind.

"Hey, careful Spare, you don't want to make a trip to the infirmary this late at night."

Duka steadied himself and nodded. "You right, I don't. Thanks, Bort."

Thunder rumbled as the brothers reached the top of the stairs and made their way to their rooms, ready to retire for the night.

CHAPTER FIVE:

THE ESCAPE

22

WHAT'S HAPPENING?

ARTOS

9/16/1971 ar

2:20 a.m.

ARTOS AWOKE FROM ANOTHER NIGHTMARE. Or was it the same one? Fuzzy from his slumber, he thought the pounding noise was thunder. The storm had come rolling in just before the brothers had retired for the night and the rolling booms of thunder had ushered him to sleep.

Not thunder. Someone was banging on his door. His first thought was Duka had experienced another nightmare and had come to wake him as he had told him to. He disentangled himself from his blankets and, with his mind still befuddled from sleep, walked to the door and opened it.

A sudden wave of sound washed over him, confusing him even more. Crashing sounds and the baying of beasts intermingled with the cries of men and the ring of steel against steel.

Tirinvo stood outside his door. His hand still raised.

"Artos, dress yourself. No time to explain. You are in grave danger. Beastmen have breached the castle. I promised to get you to safety." He pushed into Artos' room and pointed to the trousers Artos had laid out on the chair near his bed, ready for the morning's run.

"What? Beastmen in the castle? How?" Artos mumbled as the Fairborn Prince pushed him toward his pants. The tumult coming from the hallway befuddled his sleep clouded mind. This could not be real. Was he still dreaming?

As Artos pulled on his pants, Tirinvo looked into his wardrobe, grabbed an old hunting jacket, which he tossed to land on the bed beside him. Then he grabbed Artos's sword belt off its peg on his bedpost and laid it next to the jacket. "Quickly. Your boots. Put on your boots." Not knowing what else to do, Artos complied, pulling on his moccasins as Tirinvo hurried back to the open door to look out into the hallway.

Just as the Fairborn reached the door, a monstrous figure loomed into view, blocking the doorway.

Artos had heard tales of Beastmen all his life but had never actually seen one in the flesh … until now. Wearing only a ragged pair of tattered gray trousers, and covered with coarse black fur, the creature had the head of a snarling boar, complete with four-inch tusks jutting from its foaming jaw. A rancid stench filled Artos's nostrils, combining the worst elements of sweat, wet fur, and blood. In its hand was a short sword, its blade dripping crimson drops on the hall floor.

As quick as thought, a slim rapier with a blade of pure white crystal appeared in Tirinvo's right hand and smoothly slid into the chest of the boarheaded Beastman, which groaned and fell onto the floor in Artos's room with a thud. The Fairborn prince stepped over the still twitching body and looked into the hall.

"Come on, Artos. That one was alone, but more are sure

to follow. There isn't much time. They are overwhelming your guards in the lower levels. Come on. By the Mother, hurry!"

Artos stood, buckled his sword belt around his waist, and rushed to the door, stepping over the fallen creature, his heart pounding rapidly. Then stepped out into the hallway to see his Carimus and Duka emerge from their rooms in the care of Tirinvo's twin liegemen.

A moment later, Bortis and the bard darted from Bortis's room. Bortis had dressed himself in his leather hunting armor and jacket. Art and Tirinvo fell in behind them, and they all hurried toward the hall's end at the Winding Way.

Carimus, being pushed along by Taur, was still in his pajamas, his jacket flapping open, and his moccasins unlaced. He looked dazed, unable to grasp what was happening. Duka was in better shape. He appeared scared, but determined.

When they reached the Winding Way, the noise was worse. The castle reverberated with loud peals of thunder from the storm, the clash of steel against steel, and the howls of ravening Beastmen. Veryan looked at Tirinvo and shouted something in Espero that Artos didn't recognize, but the Prince nodded, and he and the blond-haired bodyguard pushed the four brothers before them up the Winding Way toward the eyrie.

"Run! For your lives. Run!" the Fairborn Prince kept repeating. Carimus abruptly shrieked and began sprinting up the way. The other brothers followed.

Suddenly, from behind came an extraordinary noise. A thundering CRACK as if a bolt of lightning had struck within the passage behind them.

"What was that?" screamed Carimus, slowing down, only to be pushed into sprinting again by Tirinvo's liegemen.

"Veryan is making them wary of the Winding Way. Hurry. He and Jaek can't hold them back forever," Tirinvo shouted out as he and Artos brought up the rear of the fleeing group.

With Carimus leading the way, he, Duka, and Bortis all burst through the qulan seal into the rain-swept Eyrie at the castle's top. The Fairborn bodyguard came to a sudden stop just before the hidden barrier and looked at what awaited on the other side.

The grim faces of a few tower guards stared at him through the barrier as he slowed to a stop. Most held their swords ready and looked at the Fairborn with fear and suspicion. Bortis was yelling for McArn incoherently. Duka had his arm around Carimus, who was white with shock.

Artos waved his arms and he and the two Fairborn passed through the invisible seal into the chill of wind and rain that swept in through the Eyrie's enormous windows. The guards were clamoring for information. McArn pushed through the guards. "WHAT'S GOING ON?" he demanded.

Artos opened his mouth to answer and then realized he didn't know how to answer the captain of the tower. Fortunately, Tirinvo answered in his stead.

"The castle's breached. We don't know how, but there is a hoard of Beastmen following us. My cousins are holding them back, but they can't for long. The king ordered me to get his sons to safety. Guard the entrance, but please, let my men through when they get here."

McArn assessed the situation and began barking orders. "Johnny. Kurt. Williams. Watch the Way. The rest of you, go grab your bows. Wake the rest of the guard. Hurry! Kincaid. You and Dony barricade the stairs down in the east guard room. Thomas, you and Sonny do the west. Leave someone to watch each of the stairs, then grab your bows and join us back here. GO! RUN!" The well-trained guards sprang to do his bidding. McArn turned back to Tirinvo. "You'll be taking the Lads then?

On your Eagles?"

Tirinvo called out to the giant eagles, and they all hopped down from their perches where they had sheltered as far from the wind and rain as they could manage. He looked back at the Sergeant and shook his head. "No. They can't handle double loads in weather like this. The Eagles shall take the princes, and my men and I will stay here with you." With a grim expression, McArn nodded and strode over to the men he had stationed at the mouth of the Winding Way, drawing his sword as he went.

Tirinvo turned back to his steed and spoke to it in Espro. Then, after the Eagle seemed to object highly, he spoke louder, and the bird bowed his head and nodded. All the birds then kneeled to allow themselves to be mounted. As soon as they did, Taur picked up Carimus and placed him upon one of the Eagles' back. Taking his arms and legs, he wove them into the netting that was the bird's saddle. All the while talking in Espro to the steed. Tirinvo helped Duka aboard another of the Eagles, then turned to Artos as Taur then helped Bortis mount.

"Your father is gone, Artos. His last words to me were to get you to safety. You must stay safe to become king. I am sorry, but you must go now!"

Artos froze with shock at Tirinvo's words, then numbly allowed himself to be mounted upon the giant bird. "Windrider will take you to safety, Artos."

Tirinvo redrew his rapier and turned away, shouting something in Espro.

Windrider gave a harsh cry that the other eagles echoed, and one by one, they leaped up, unfurling their wings. They shot into the air and out the eyrie's windows right into the teeth of the driving wind and rain. Then it was all Artos could do to hang on to the net harness, buffeted by the wind as they flew up into the dark sky, the icy rain soaking him to the skin.

23

FLIGHT

ARTOS

2:40 a.m.

LIGHTNING ARCED ACROSS THE SKY as the four golden eagles, whipped by the gusting wind, struggled to gain altitude through the driving rain. Artos held on tightly to the entwining netting, his saddle, and whispered a heartfelt prayer to the Sky Father that his little brothers could hold on and ride this out. Dazed and confused, his mind churning, he tried to digest the events of his last moments at the castle. How could there be enemies in their home? How had Beastmen gotten past the qulan? It was impossible! It went against everything he knew, everything he had ever learned.

He tried to look around, but the night and windblown rain made vision almost impossible. Only when the lightning arced through the clouds, could he see. There, a little way ahead, were the forms of two other birds, and to his right, he could just make out Bortis, soaked and bedraggled, gazing back in his direction, across the empty air.

CRACK!—BOOOOOOM!

Artos held on for dear life as Windrider pulled back, swerved wildly, and then spun around through the air. Purple afterimages blinded him, and his ears rang from the sound. That lightning had been in the direction he had just seen his two little brothers! The smell of ozone was overwhelming. He buried his face against the feathered back of the giant bird and clung to the netting, gasping for breath. In a moment, the eagle pulled out of spiral and began climbing again. He looked around, but found he could not see anything. The wings of the mighty eagle struggled as they angled upwards. If his legs weren't wrapped in the netting, he might have slid back and fallen into the darkness below. A sharp pain pierced his ears as they popped with the pressure change. He clung to the strands of the net grimly, his hands burning, the netting cutting into his legs as his weight pulled him backward.

Soon things became level again, and the pummeling rain diminished. Artos was now engulfed in a black fog. Of course. Windrider was now up into the clouds, wings still flapping mightily. Where were the rest? The eagle angled upwards again, though not as sharply as before. They burst up out of the clouds, revealing stars and moon above him. A blast of air spun the giant eagle around like a wind-blown leaf and he saw another of the eagles whisk past on a powerful gust, as out of control as he felt. Then his steed spiraled down into the fog of the cloud once more.

Artos cursed. Which brother had he just seen? There had been no one else. Were his other brothers even still alive? Had the lightning spared him and Bort flying behind the others? Had it struck Cari or Duka? Or both? Despair filled his heart. Would this nightmare never end? It seemed as if he had been clinging to the back of Windrider for hours now, though he knew it couldn't have been that long.

Tirinvo had said he was sending him to safety, but where? Artos knew he was somewhere above the mountains, but that was not reassuring. Would the eagles take them all the way to the Lowlands? The Mountains of Myst held many dangers. Besides bandits and Beastmen, most of the creatures there were extremely dangerous, vine creepers like that which killed his grandfather, giant wolves, weasels, bears, and many more. The land itself was treacherous, with many narrow, steep trails and deep ravines. The perpetual fog which cloaked the mountains and gave them their name made travel dubious at best.

Artos shivered with more than just the cold. He clung to the netting with aching hands, his legs growing numb. The smell of wet feathers filled his nostrils, the sound of Windrider's wings contesting with the wind. At least the rain had stopped. There was a damp, dark mist surrounding him. The thunder and lightning were now only memory, thanks be to Sky Father Quai. Was the fog around him growing lighter?

Without warning, Windrider flew out of the cloud. The moon was ahead, and the stars shining down, but fainter than before. Dawn must be approaching.

Artos searched the sky for some sign of his brothers. There! Ahead of him was another of the golden eagles, with the still form of Carimus, looking like a wet rag strapped to the giant bird.

"Art!" cried a faint voice from above and behind him. He twisted around, looking for the source. There, the face of Bortis peered at him over the wings of his mount some ways to his rear. Two brothers.

Where was Duke? Artos looked all around, and his heart

sank. There was no sign of Duka.

Windrider screeched loudly, causing Artos to grip the netting even tighter. The cry was repeated from ahead and behind, but only by two eagles. The bird shrieked again, but only the wind responded.

Carimus's steed made a great circle and fell in beside Windrider to Artos's right as Bortis's mount drew closer on his left. Windrider screeched again, then angled down into the mist below, and the other two birds echoed his call and followed closely behind.

Oh no. Have the eagles finally reached the end of their strength? Are we crashing here in the mountains? His breath caught in his throat, and his heart beat so quickly he thought it would burst.

The top of a vast tree rushed by to his left, just beyond Bortis. The eagle cried again, and Artos heard a faint echo. Was it another bird, or was a cliff rushing up to brutally end their flight? The fog grew lighter as dawn approached, and another immense tree whizzed past.

The eagle tilted to his right and circled even faster, plummeting downwards in a rapid spiral. Then it landed on the ground with a bone-rattling jolt. The fog and the dim light made it hard to see, but it appeared they were in a clearing, a grassy field of some sort. With a whooshing sound, the other two eagles landed nearby. Artos untangled his legs from the netting and said a silent prayer, thanking Mother Veca for being back upon her solid ground once again. The night's events flooded his mind and despair washed over him. *Where is Duka?*

ACT TWO

THE MAGIC MAN

Chapter Six:

Donel

24

THE MAGIC MAN

DONEL

9/15/1971 ar
The Crystal Tower
The Autumnal Equinox
5:37 a.m.

DONEL, THE MAGIC MAN, woke with a start, his heart racing. *That was a nasty dream,* he thought. It had been a doozy of a nightmare, too much blood, ravening Beastmen, total chaos. He rubbed a hand over his well-trimmed goatee and looked across the room. A pair of amber eyes gazed back at him solemnly. *Good morning, Liv. When did you come in?*

Donel received the picture of a haunch of rabbit. *Brought you breakfast*. He sent a thought of gratitude.

Tossing off his blanket, he swung his legs out of bed and sat up, stifling a yawn and stretching. When he looked again, he was alone in the room. He shrugged, pushing his silvery hair out of his face, and tucked it behind his ears. Liv wasn't much for conversation. Too bad, he thought. A bit of company after a nightmare like that would be welcome. Oh well.

I hope that was a glimpse of something from the future or the distant past, but I don't think so. I think the time foretold by the

Prophecy is upon us. He sighed to himself.

He had dreamed better dreams recently. After all these years of being the sole resident of the crystal tower, guardian of Hellesgate, he had dreamed of students coming to learn from him. Liv was good company, but it was not her destiny to take his place as Warden, as the Keymaster. As always, he had eyes watching and waiting for the one who was.

Teaching the girls had been fine practice, but they had other issues to deal with, and he had known from the start they wouldn't remain his pupils for long.

Those poor fools up in the valley. Their forefathers had sealed their offspring's doom many years ago. There was nothing he could do. The King's Valley was far beyond his reach. All he could do now was wait.

"Time to cook some breakfast, I guess." He spoke to himself sometimes, a habit some would think hinted of madness. He stood up, pulled on his robes, and walked from his bedroom to his kitchen where some fresh rabbit lay waiting to be fried. Glancing down at his shabby black robes, he shook his head. *Time to request a new robe. I should have done it a few months ago.* He chuckled. *I wouldn't be making any points from my appearance, I bet. I'll send a request to Maria, but by the time she has a new set of robes finished and sent back to me, it will be midwinter, at least. Oh well. It's not like I have to impress anyone, or anyone to impress. Liv doesn't care.*

Reaching the kitchen, he found a large hunk of bloody meat, easily enough for a dozen meals. "I should have known it was a giant rabbit. Well, I won't freeze the extra. I may make some rabbit stew with the extra," he muttered to himself. He skinned the haunch and hacked off enough for his breakfast. Gingerly trying to spare his robes from messy bloodstains, he picked up the rest and carried it to the chill cabinet, where he placed it on the bottom shelf. "I wish I had a few chickens. A couple of fried eggs would taste good this morning," he said with a sigh, trying to remember the last time he had eaten fried eggs.

Donel took the rabbit steak and sprinkled on some salt and a few herbs and then, with only a thought, adjusted the griddle top of his stove to searing heat. After a moment, he tossed the steak on. The smell of the frying rabbit made his mouth water. "What else do I have that would go well with fried rabbit?" he asked the air. He walked to his larder and poked around for a few moments before picking out a handful of watercress and a few mushrooms. He sliced the mushrooms, tossed them next to the frying rabbit, and flipped the cut over to sear the other side. Going back to the larder, he selected a few green onions, a carrot, and a green pepper and set them down next to the watercress beside his sink. As he made his watercress salad, he had a feeling it was going to be another long day. Well, his gardens needed some attention.

After a productive morning in the gardens below the crystal tower, Donel finished his lunch and pondered the afternoon. I wonder who called for the council meeting? Either the Darrel or the deHerndars, I bet. If it was the deHerndars, it would be more of their bellyaching about "bandits," trying to get Bretton to do their dirty work again. Trouble is, he's so obsessed with finding the West Wind he'll probably believe them. Again. And if it's the Darrell, the council will just ignore his problems with Beastmen and say it's just bandits. He sighed. "I suppose I need to eavesdrop either way. No helping it."

He washed his plate, dried his hands, walked back through the large common room, and climbed the spiral stairs to the upper floor. Arriving in his library, he stopped at an empty nook and placed his hand upon one of the bumps on the crystalline wall. A wall section slid aside, revealing another stairway leading higher into the tower's upper reaches.

Upon reaching the top floor of the tower, he impulsively turned down the passage to his left and walked to the apparent dead-end. Again, Donel placed his hand upon a protrusion on the side of the wall. A section of the blue crystalline wall quietly slid open. He walked out into the cooler air of the Roost.

Stepping softly so as not to wake Oswald if he was asleep, he turned right and entered a dim alcove. Oswald's preferred perch. Sure enough, there was Oswald, his eyes tightly clenched against any light that filtered in from the sunlit afternoon sky beyond the Roost. He silently retreated into the tower hallway, placed his hand on the proper spot, and closed the door. "I'll stop by this evening and bring Oswald a bit of rabbit," he said to himself as he walked back down the passage.

When he reached the junction, he turned left, walked a few yards, and again opened a sliding door. He walked into a small room with three of the walls covered with crystal screens. A room he sometimes referred to as his "eavesdropping post." He settled into the comfortable chair on the slightly raised circular platform in the center of the room. As always, his attention went first to the large screen on the center wall, the screen which displayed the bright red flames that danced forever before the door to the Hellesgate. The prison of which he was the perpetual warden, his duty, and his curse. As usual, there was no change there. Hopefully, there never would be. Glancing down beside his seat at the black onyx pad with numerous bright buttons of crystal that controlled the screen's access, he thought a moment, then placed a finger on one of the buttons and held it a few moments. Almost immediately, the screen below the rose-crossed lily flashed, and then the face of Countess Maria Spryngdal appeared before him.

"Hello Donel, I was expecting your call. As soon as the chime for a council rang this morning, I told myself, you would look in. And here you are." The elderly face smiled at him knowingly. "It's no use asking you what's going on. You're even less in touch with the Houses than I am. I suppose you want to record through my screen again?"

Donel bowed his head to the Countess of House deSpryngdal. "Well met, Maria. Yes, I was hoping you wouldn't mind. I can listen in without your help, but to record it all, well …"

"It's no problem, my dear. Of course, I will have my screen blank, and my recording light will be lit, so they never know if I'm actually watching or recording to watch later. Yes, I know it really bothers the deAnson in particular. Sometimes I'll cough just to see him jump," she chuckled wickedly.

"Thank you, Maria. I like to have these things on record. Sometimes someone will say more than they mean, and it's good to have their words recorded, so you have it when they deny it later. Not that I ever have needed to, but I like to be prepared."

"I know, Donel." A look of sadness appeared in her eyes. "Have you thought of speaking with young Aaron? He isn't the fool his great grandfather was. It's past time for reconciliation, long past."

"I'm afraid it's too late for that. Bad things are coming. Soon I'm afraid. I wanted to warn you. Keep your people close over the next few days. I had an awful dream this morning, all blood and beasts." He shook his head. "I had hoped it would still be years away and that I would have a student trained before anything would come to a head, but I fear it's not to be."

"Don't worry about my House, Donel. My warders are ever vigilant. Beastmen fear my demesne, as well they should. They know that if they cross my borders, they won't leave." There was an angry glint in her eye now, and her lips were a thin line as she thought about his words. "That reminds me. I know you might need a few things from me. I sent you some new clothes and a few other things a tenday or so ago. The Darrell should have passed them on to Andune by now. I expect you'll get them shortly if you haven't already?" The elderly lady arched a brow in question.

"I don't think I have, but then I didn't look to see if Oswald had any packages in the Roost. I'll look this evening. Thank you, my dear. You are too kind."

"Oh, tish. We here in the Valley owe you far more than you ever ask in payment. A few clothes and a few ropes are nothing to me. Don't be silly!" She glanced away from the screen. "It's about two hours until the council. I'll leave you connected so they won't notice later. Take care." Her screen went inert before he could answer.

"Well, nothing to do but wait, I suppose. I'll go see if Oswald has any packages waiting for me in the roost."

Chapter Seven:

Daughter of the Wind

25

WHAT DO WE DO NOW?

9/16/1971 ar

5:54 a.m.

Artos slid from the back of the giant eagle, grateful the flight was over. He rubbed his aching legs and looked around the fog-shrouded clearing. "Where we are? Where's Duke?"

Both his brothers followed his example and dismounted. Carimus promptly fell to the ground. "Oh," he moaned. "My legs are asleep." Both brothers turned to help their little brother back to his feet.

Windrider spread his wings with a harsh cry and gave a mighty leap into the air. The other eagles echoed his cry and followed his example. The three giant eagles circled once above the brother's heads then disappeared, climbing into the mists.

Artos stared in dismay at where the eagles had been standing. He should have done something, but what? No matter, it was far too late now. The eagles were gone. They were abandoned here in this fog-shrouded valley, somewhere. Lost and alone.

Artos and Bortis looked at each other helplessly. The eagles had set them down in a clearing of wet, knee-high grass. Art had seen thousand-year trees nearby as they circled to land, but none were visible now, though the fog seemed to be lessening with the approaching dawn.

As yet, the gray light of morning revealed little of their surroundings, but the fresh scent of rain-soaked leaves and evergreens filled the air. There was also the distinct smell of a large body of water. Close to where they stood, Artos could see some fallen logs making a triangle on the ground, surrounding a cleared circle of small smoke-blackened stones. The peaceful setting was totally at odds with Artos' turbulent emotions. He tried to collect his thoughts. He was the elder. It was his responsibility to figure out what they needed to do. Where to find food and shelter.

"Someone has had a fire here," said Bortis, as he walked through the calf-high, rain-soaked grasses and examined the ring of stones. "Hasn't been used for a while, though. I think. Hard to tell after all this rain."

Artos could tell Bortis was trying to appear cool and collected, though the slight waver in his voice proved his younger brother was just as unsettled as he was. He walked over and sat down on one log and stared at the ground in despair. His thoughts churning. "The fog should burn off as the sun rises," he trailed off, shivering. "We need to dry off. Our clothes are soaked and it's freezing."

What was he doing? He couldn't just sit here. He jumped up. "Bort, Cari, find some wood. We need to get a fire started so we can dry off before Cari gets pneumonia." He looked around, but there was no obvious firewood in the wet grass. "Cari, you stick close to Bort and look over that way." He pointed to where some trees were peeking through the fog. "I'll look over here. Don't go too far. We don't want to lose each other." His heart wrenched. *Where is Duka? Is he even still alive?* His memories of the wild flight they had just endured were fresh in his mind, thunder and lightning all around them. *Was that Duka's eagle I saw spinning away out of control in the wind? Had he been struck by lightning?* Whispering a prayer to Mother Veda, he walked through the wet grass, his pant legs soaking, and scanned the earth for dead wood. A whoop from Bortis drew his thoughts back to his surroundings, and he turned and ran back the way he had come.

"Hey, Art! I found some wood. Over here!" Bortis broke off as Artos came running out of the fog. A small, neatly stacked pile of deadwood was standing between a pair of birch trees with brightly colored trunks and foliage. A piece of oilskin lay on the ground beside it.

"Who found it?" came the indignant voice of Carimus beside Bortis.

"Yeah squirt, you found it, relax." Bortis gathered up some of the smaller branches to take back to the circle of stones. "They're even dry. They were under that oilskin," he said as he pointed to the discarded covering. "Someone had a camp here once. Lucky for us."

"Yeah, lucky," said Artos. "I wonder who it was? Oh well, let's get a fire going and some dry clothes." He drew his crysword and cut the cloth into three pieces and carried them back with him to where the fire circle awaited. Bortis was already stacking the dry wood in the stone circle. As soon as he was finished, he drew his crysword, stuck the blade between two smaller branches, and screwed up his face in concentration.

After about thirty seconds, Carimus made as if to speak, but

Artos quickly shushed him with a shake of his head and a look of warning.

A few moments later, a trickle of smoke rose from the wood where the sword lay. Bortis leaned in and gently blew, rewarded with a small tongue of flame as the dry wood caught and started burning.

"Okay, off with those soaked clothes. Spread them out to dry. Keep a watch and don't let them burn." Artos led by example, pulling off his drenched jacket, his pajama top, and finally his trousers. He laid them out on the log near the fire and wrapped himself in a piece of oilskin. His brothers followed suit, and soon all of their wet clothes were steaming in the cool morning air.

The brothers sat together on the logs, still numb with the events of the night. As their clothes dried, the fog slowly vanished, revealing the surrounding landscape. They were in a large clearing on the east side of a large lake, surrounded by a forest of evergreens, mountain oak, and colorful rainbow birch. A scattering of the enormous thousand-year trees intermixed with the rest. The shadowy forms of mountains lay to the east, with the sun peeking between two tall peaks. To the west loomed more mountains, with the lake running between them as far as they could see. The morning bird song with the gentle rustling of the fall foliage made for a pleasant atmosphere instead of the earlier, tomblike quiet of the fog-shrouded predawn. *What do I do now?* Art thought, his mind dark with despair.

"What are we going to do, Art?" Carimus suddenly jumped up and looked around wildly. "We're lost. I have no clothes, only my pajamas. We have no food, and we don't even know what happened at home or where we are. And … and Duke! He just disappeared!"

"We're in the Rainbow Valley," said Bortis, and pointed at the multi-colored trees that surrounded the open meadow. "Uncle Brett told me there aren't this many rainbow birch in one place anywhere else." He pointed in the lake's direction. "So that's Lake of the Setting Sun. I'm pretty sure, anyway. Uncle Brett brought me here with him on a patrol last summer." He furrowed his brow, worried. "I think this is bandit country now. I asked him this spring if we would come by here on the summer patrol. He said no. Not enough farmers in these parts anymore. This valley has gone wild." He looked as though he were going to say more, but looked at Carimus, shook his head, and became quiet.

Artos looked up, glanced at the lake, and nodded. He locked gazes with Carimus, took a deep breath, and spoke as calmly as he could. "We are going to do our duty, Cari. We have been in training all our lives, and now we'll put that training to use." He cleared his throat. "The last thing Tirinvo told me before he sent the eagles on their way." He looked down and wiped his forehead. "Before he sent us away, he told me, father is gone. I have to become the king now." Artos' voice broke, "We owe Father ..." his voice trailed off.

"You think? ... You mean ..." Carimus looked dazed. "No ... it can't be," he choked.

Bortis cleared his throat. "You heard the cries. They were celebrating. They were in a frenzy. I ... I hope the Elf was wrong. Uncle Brett wouldn't die easily."

"Neither would Father, nor the Fairborn," said Artos. "Did you see Prince Tirinvo's sword?" He looked at Bortis, but Carimus answered.

"I saw his sword. A white crysword." He looked at his eldest brother. "It was a rapier. And pure white, like yours."

Artos stood up, thinking of the maps he had looked at in class. "We're probably sixty miles from home, as the crow flies." He felt his shirt. "Clothes are dry enough. Get dressed." He pulled on his outfit, as did his brothers. "Put the fire out, Bort, would you?"

"It's more like eighty, I think." Bortis scattered the remains of the fire in the circle and then tossed loose dirt over everything. "And double or more by road. Probably way more. We didn't come straight here last summer, but it was a three-week trip. And we were riding," he trailed off. An owl hooted not far off.

"We have no food," Carimus gestured with both hands. "Nothing to hunt with. You say there are no farmers around here. How will we stay alive? And we've lost Duke," his voice becoming shrill. "He must be out there somewhere alone. His eagle will have ditched him, too. We have to find him!" He looked around wildly, as if expecting his little brother to appear from between the trees.

"We'll find him, Cari. And we'll get home somehow." Artos looked over Carimus's shoulder at Bortis, who looked back with a slight shake of his head. "Don't worry, Bort can make a bow and arrows, and I know you were taught the most lessons of the land, what's safe to eat and what's poison. We won't starve." He looked around the clearing. The sun was shining, birds singing, and yet something made him feel uneasy. More than just being lost and far from home. Was something watching them? Hunting them? "Let's go closer to the lake. I could use a drink, and we need to find some saplings for a bow." He started walking towards the lake shore, angling towards the forest with its yews, fir, and cedar trees.

Carimus sniffed, then nodded and turned to walk towards

the lake. Bortis leaned toward Artos and whispered, "And just what am I going to use for a bowstring, Artie?"

"The first thing we'll need to do," said Artos, ignoring Bortis, "is find some yew staves, make some spears, and use a couple of the more suitable branches for bows. Then we'll need some gut to make bowstrings."

Bortis gave his brother a sardonic glance and looked around uneasily.

Artos looked at his brother. "Why would Tirinvo send us here? Is he expecting to follow us somehow?"

Bortis scowled. "Did he? Or did the eagles just fly until the storm let up, and they found a clearing where they could dump us?"

"No, I heard him tell Windrider two things. He said, 'The Setting Sun.'" He looked to see if Carimus was listening and lowered his voice. "And he said 'west' and 'wind'."

Bortis furrowed his brow and scowled. "You mean like the bandit chief? That West Wind?"

"I don't know. Maybe. Maybe he was telling Windrider to watch out for him, or maybe just telling him not to fight the storm and go where the wind took him. Since the storm came from the east, that would be to the west. I don't speak Espero very well," Artos shook his head. "Nothing makes sense. What happened? How did those beasts get into our castle? Surely the qulan can't have failed." He looked to his brother like he expected Bort to explain the inexplicable.

Bortis glanced around uneasily, as if he expected an attack to suddenly spring from the trees. "Beats me, Artie. It must make sense somehow ... it happened. You heard the foul things. They were in the castle ... somehow." He beat his clenched fist into his other hand. "We have to get home. We ... we ..." He trailed off, the frustration showing on his face. "We have to do something! I just don't know what. I wish Uncle Brett were here. He'd guide us."

Artos just shook his head and hurried after Carimus, who was now almost to the thicker evergreen trees by the lake shore.

26

SAFE AT LAST

CARIMUS

8:20 a.m.

As Carimus neared the lake shore, the rainbow birch gave way to a thick cluster of evergreens, towering cedar, colossal fir, mighty pines, and thick groves of juniper. He pushed between some bushes and scanned the trees and there! The red berries that mark yew trees, the bowyer's favorite. A pair of thousand-year pines stood tall beside them. Those yew trees were what Art wanted him to find. There was rustling in the branches as he approached. He looked up into huge yellow eyes that stared back at him unblinkingly. He screamed in terror.

He heard his brothers' feet swishing through the grass as they ran up behind him.

"What is it, Cari?" asked Artos.

"What's wrong, Squirt?" asked Bortis simultaneously.

"A Demon!" he screamed, pointing up into the thick overhang of branches above him. "A Demon!"

"Tchokk! Tchokk, tu-whooo!" A loud call came from the

branches above him as Artos and Bortis ran up beside him, their cryswords in hand. Huge golden eyes peered down at the brothers through the branches. The eyes were separated by white markings like back-to-back Cs in a circle of gray.

"Tchokk. Tchokk. Tchokk. Tu-whooo," it hooted again.

Bortis burst out laughing. "It's only an owl, Squirt. A big owl," he added, looking up through the branches.

"It's laughing at me!" exclaimed Carimus, staring up at the enormous bird. The giant owl peered back, taking in the brothers with eyes reflecting more intelligence than a normal bird. Then with a final "Tu-whooo-wooo-wooo" it leaped to a higher branch and then another. In a flurry of wings, it launched itself into flight.

"Just be glad it wasn't hungry, Squirt!" quipped Bortis. "You'd probably be a fair meal for a bird that big."

Artos tried to watch which direction the bird flew off in, but the thick foliage of the evergreens blocked his view.

"Here are a couple of yew trees, Art," said Carimus proudly, forgetting his fear. "I found them."

"So you did. Good job, Cari," said Artos. "We can cut some shafts for spears and bows, but first, what's safe for us to eat? It's too late in the year for blueberries and I know we can't eat the yew berries. Have you seen any fruit trees here?"

Carimus's brow wrinkled. Then he walked over to stand by the base of one of the thousand-year pines. On the ground were a few scattered pinecones, each nearly four feet in diameter. "I wonder?" He muttered to himself. Then, to his brothers' amusement, he began to tug and yank at the woody cone. "Yes! Yes, it is, it must be," he cried out, pulling at the huge pinecone. The pleasant smell of pitch became much more apparent as the giant cone fell apart, releasing large white seeds.

"Pine nuts! We can eat these. We're saved now, Artie," he cried, picking up one of the grapefruit-sized seeds.

At that moment, an arrow with dark brown fletching thunked into the tree beside Artos' ear. "Keep your hands in plain sight!" called a melodious voice from the thick brush in front of Artos. "Leave your little swords right where they are."

27

BANDITS!

ARTOS

8:20 a.m.

Bᴏʀᴛɪs's ʟᴇꜰᴛ ʜᴀɴᴅ reached slowly toward his sheathed crysword. THUNK. An arrow with bright green feathers came from another direction and plunked into the tree beside him.

"That means you too, moron!" came a second voice.

Artos froze. Both voices were higher pitched than a grown man's. *Are some boys targeting us?* Artos wondered. A third arrow embedded itself in the tree above the head of Carimus, standing frozen with fear on his face. A red-feathered arrow from a third direction.

"Steady, Bort, Cari," said Artos, "We're surrounded. Just hold." His gut clenched, the sickly bitter taste of fear in his mouth. He scanned the surrounding brush, looking for a glimpse of the people with the drop on them. The thick evergreens were obscuring his view, the smell of the pines suddenly becoming much less attractive.

"Well, well, well … what have we here? Out on a picnic,

boys?" A cloaked figure with a hood pulled close around their face stepped from the brush, bow in hand, with an arrow notched and aimed directly at Artos.

Artos took the measure of the situation and held up his empty hands. "We aren't here to hurt anyone. Just relax. We're travelers, passing through and looking for a bite to eat before moving on. No need to aim that arrow at me. We're not bothering anyone."

The Archer shrugged the hood back from her face and smirked. "I'll decide when to stop aiming my bow. Thank you. I am relaxed, never fear. We don't care too much for outlaws here in the valley."

Artos froze in surprise. The girl facing him had long red hair, bright green eyes, and was breathtakingly beautiful. Her bow never wavered. The arrow held taut on the string.

"Outlaws! We're not outlaws. You're the outlaws," said Bortis, anger evident in his voice.

The girl chuckled. "Which house do you ... 'travelers' come from? Anson or Herndar?" She glanced at Carimus and did a quick double-take. "Travelers wander around in pajamas now? Who are you, and why are you here?" She inspected Artos. "Looks like you're wearing your jammy tops, too. What's the story? The truth, please, my father takes a dim view of liars, and so far, I have little to tell him that rings of truth." She waited, her bow now pointed toward the ground, but the arrow was still notched on the taut string.

"Who's your father?" countered Artos, "We heard this valley was unoccupied now. The rightful holders have been driven away by bandits. Bandits like you, maybe?"

"Bandits?" said a new voice in angry tones as another girl stepped into view, her bow aimed at Bortis. "Raiders in the pay of House Herndar, you mean? When my parent's farm was razed, we followed the vermin back through the mountains. A few miles up the pass, away from here, the leaders changed back into their House colors. Blue and yellow, they were. I'll never forget those colors, never forgive them either." Her gray eyes blazing with rage, she shook a black braid away from her eyes. "Just give me a reason to shoot, pretty boy. Go ahead."

"Easy, Cat. These boys don't look like raiders. Too soft," said the first girl. "We'll let father sort them out." She glared at Artos again. "Your name, please? Or shall I tell my father you are a bunch of lazy boys who got themselves lost in their pajamas?"

Artos stood still, surprised. When the girl turned her head, he glimpsed a dainty, slightly pointed ear. "You're a Fairborn!" he exclaimed.

"No, she's not. Worst luck. Only half." A third girl stepped into sight. "But I am. Want to make something of it?" The third girl was also dark-haired, but unlike the other girls, her ears were decidedly large and pointed.

"My father is Fairborn," said the first girl. "But my mother wasn't. She escaped from one of your 'Great Houses' and found her freedom and her husband, my father. You may have heard of him. He's known as The West Wind."

Bortis gasped, "Bandits! I knew it."

"Shut up, Bort." Artos turned back to the first speaker. "We have no money, nothing of value to give you. Just let us go on our way and leave us alone. We mean nothing to you."

"Well, that's no lie, anyway. You mean nothing to me. But my father will be the one to decide your fate. This valley is under his protection now. If he had been around when those raiders burned Cat's parent's farm, fewer of them would have returned to their House, if any. One last time, your name. I already know theirs. Bort and Cari. So, who are you?"

Artos made a quick decision. "I'm Art. Now, common courtesy would demand you give me yours."

The leader arched a brow, faintly amused, but seemed to decide. "I'm Angel. My Fairborn friend is Joy, and that's Cat." She pointed at the angry girl, who still held an arrow aimed at Bortis. "I don't think she likes you, Bort. I'd move really slow and careful like. She can shoot almost as good as me. Now Cari, I want you to fetch two pine nuts for each of your friends and then two for yourself. Each of you hold one nut in each hand. Do it!"

Carimus twitched, but then looked to Artos for direction. Artos nodded. "Go ahead, Cari." Carimus nodded back with a doubtful expression, but finished pulling the giant cone apart, revealing more of the pale nuts. He handed the first two to Bortis, who looked angrier by the minute.

"Don't try anything, pretty boy," said Cat. "I could put an arrow in your heart before you could throw one of those. Just try me."

"Relax, Bort," said Artos. "This is all just a misunderstanding. We'll be okay." He hoped it was true, but he had to keep Bortis from doing anything rash. He didn't doubt for an instant that Cat could fire her arrow before Bortis could even begin to do anything. From the scowl on Bortis's face, he knew it too, and it was making him even angrier.

When all three of the brothers were holding a pine nut in each hand, Angel said something in fluent Espro, and her companions both nodded. Joy responded in a questioning tone. Artos listened carefully, but couldn't make out the meaning. When Angel answered, he caught two words: 'no' and 'four', but he had no idea of the context.

Angel replaced her arrow in its quiver and slipped her bow on her back. She then pulled a small knife and some twine from a belt pouch. "Okay, we're going to make sure no one gets frisky with their little swords. I'm going to put a loop around each of your wrists and tie them together. Not tightly, but enough so you can't get your swords out quickly and maybe get hurt. Or I can take your sword belts?" She arched a brow as she looked at Artos.

"Bort, relax," said Artos quickly, before his hot-tempered brother could reply. "Go ahead." He nodded to Angel.

"But, Artie," Carimus stopped when Artos looked at him and shook his head. "Oh, alright." He held his hands out as he held his two pine nuts, a look of comprehension on his features.

Angel quickly and efficiently wrapped a loop of twine around both of his wrists, so he was forced to hold the pine nuts about eight inches apart or closer. She was true to her word, and the twine was not uncomfortably tight. She repeated the process on Carimus and finally on Bortis.

"Okay, we have about seven miles to go. The four of us will watch you closely, so let's keep this nice and easy, shall we?" Angel pulled her bow off her back, re-notching an arrow.

"Four?" said Artos, looking around at the three girls.

"I think she means me." A fourth girl stepped into view. "I'm Vix." She smiled. She, too, had red hair with an arrow notched and ready. "I would have tried to only wound you, Bort, but accidents happen." She shrugged.

Angel took charge then. "Cat, you lead the way back to Swan's nest. Joy, Vix rear guard. Let's go. I'm going to walk a few steps behind you, Art. Just follow Cat. Cari, you follow us, but don't get too close, about four or five paces behind me. Bort, you follow Cari. Everyone understand?" She paused a few seconds, looking at each of the three brothers. Waiting for them to nod. "Good, let's go."

Cat gave Bortis a sour look, then walked back in the direction the brothers had come from. When she reached the edge of the forested area, she paused and scanned carefully in all directions, including the sky. *I wonder what dangers there are flying around? I don't think giant owls attack people, do they? Bort probably knows. He was here before, with Uncle Bret last summer. I'll have to ask him when I get a chance.*

Artos walked behind Cat, noting she was careful to watch where she placed her feet. She avoided the low-hanging tree branches he had only pushed aside. He tried to mimic her path as closely as possible. These girls seemed to be very adept in their manner, moving noiselessly through the thick underbrush. They were obviously at home in the trees. They walked out of the wooded underbrush near where they had dried their clothes that morning, and he heard Angel say something in Espro, and one of the girls behind him answered.

"Well, at least you didn't leave a fire smoldering. But I will have to replace our sheet to keep the wood dry. Do you just slice up things for fun, Lazy-boy Art?" said Angel from behind him. Disapproval dripped from her words.

"I'm sorry for cutting up your oilskin," Artos replied. "We were soaked through and had to dry our clothes. I didn't feel like sitting around naked while they dried. I was worried Cari might catch pneumonia or something."

"Just like a bunch of lazy boys, you left the rest of the firewood out to get rained on. Vix will tidy up after you. I expect you're used to having people clean up your messes," Angel sounded disgusted. "You made it very easy for us to find you. Good thing no one is hunting you."

Artos opened his mouth to reply and then had a sudden disturbing thought. "Err, yeah. Good thing." Tirinvo had sent them here for a reason, and he had said west wind. Did he intend for them to be captured by bandits? *Just what is going on?* He continued to mull it over as they walked along.

They had walked about a mile and a half when suddenly, from behind, Joy cried out softly, "Rashwe!"

Angel answered, "Mana nostale?"

Joy replied. "Essie, i wilya yenya us!"

"Everyone down. Now! Into the grass. Move!" The urgency in Angel's voice convinced Artos, and he dropped his pine nuts and ducked into the waist-high prairie grass. Carimus dropped behind him. Then an angry "Hey! … Ooof!" as Bortis followed suit, apparently helped by one of the girls behind him.

"Bort. Cari. Be still," Artos said softly. "Wait."

He heard the rustle of the dry stalks as the girls also hid in the tall grasses. He rolled onto his side and tried to look up at the sky, but the sun, at its afternoon height, hindered his gaze. After what seemed like an hour, one of the girls said, "Clear." With the rustle of the grasses, Angel appeared, standing over him. She extended her hand and helped him to his feet. She then turned and helped Carimus to stand. Bortis struggled to his knees and then to his feet, unaided. He glared at Vix, standing nearby, trimming her nails with a sharp-looking dagger.

"Any problems?" asked Angel.

"Nope. Bort was a real good boy as soon as I showed him my knife," said Vix innocently. Bortis continued to glare, but didn't say a word.

"We best get under cover, Angie," said Cat. "I don't see how that harpy could have missed us. Raptors can count the freckles on a field mouse's nose. We're too exposed out here."

"Yeah," agreed Angel. "We've only got about a half-mile till the trail to the nest. You boys can leave the pine nuts. We're going to run for a bit. Be good boys, 'cause we'll be behind you, and we can shoot as we run, never doubt it. Follow Cat. Let's move!"

Cat immediately loped off through the thick grass. Artos looked at Carimus. "Come on Cari. You can do it!" Only after his little brother started running did Artos follow. Bortis quickly pulled up beside him. They could hear the rustling of the prairie grass behind them as the three girls followed. Cat was a good twenty yards ahead of Carimus, who was a few yards ahead of Artos and Bortis. The remaining girls were a few yards to the rear. Cat suddenly broke to her right and dashed in between a pair of large rainbow birch. Carimus followed, and Artos slowed to let Bortis go first through the gap in the trees.

As Artos reached the opening, he stopped and turned. The three girls ran spread out in a row behind them, Vixen to his left, Joy on the right, and Angel in the middle. Right behind Angel, swooping in with talons like huge meat hooks, was the raptor! Artos didn't have time to think. With a cry that might have been defiance or maybe simply fear, he threw himself at the bandit girl. He crashed into her, knocking her down, and fell beside her. The bird's claws slashed through his jacket sleeve and he felt a searing pain. Two bow strings sang, and the giant bird shrieked with pain and crashed into the rainbow birch near Bortis and Carimus.

Vixen was at Angel's side in an instant, pulling at her arm. "I'm sorry, Angela! I never checked behind us. It's my fault! I was watching ahead. Did it get you? Are you okay?" The bandit girl was almost in tears.

Joy was kneeling beside Artos, looking with dismay as

blood gushed from the rents in his jacket. She pulled a wad of cloth from somewhere and expertly pressed it tightly against the wound while muttering in Espro. Then, remembering, she switched back to the common tongue. "It's not spurting. It's a nasty gash, but you'll be okay. Can you sit up? We can't stay here. We've got to get under the trees." Bortis was suddenly beside her on Artos's other side, helping him up, his hands free from each other. The broken ends of the twine showed he had snapped the binding like string.

"Are you okay, Art? Are you okay?" he asked repeatedly.

Joy held the wad of cloth to Artos's arm, and Bortis half-pulled, half-carried his brother as Vixen helped Angel up. They all hurried beneath the cover of the trees where Cat and Carimus stood. Cat was scanning the sky, but Carimus only had eyes for his brother and the blood that drenched his jacket.

"Art! Art!" he cried. "Don't die. We already lost Duke. We can't lose you too." Tears ran down his face as the events of the past day all descended upon him at once. He shook with sobs, his face white with shock.

"I'm not going to die, Cari. It's just a cut. I'm alright. Bort. Help him!" Artos cried out.

"I've got him." Angel wrapped her arms around Carimus and held him as he sobbed. "Joy is a healer, Cari. Art's going to be just fine. Really. He's in good hands."

Artos wasn't so sure. His legs suddenly started wobbling. If it weren't for Bortis holding him up, he would have sunk to the ground.

Joy seemed to know what he was feeling, though, and she pulled them a few more feet under the sheltering trees, indicating for Bortis to let him sit down on the ground. She pulled off her pack and rummaged through its contents. "I need some water. Vix, Cat, your canteens, please." She continued to hold the bloody rag over the slash, looking at Angel. "You okay?" she asked with concern clearly evident on her face.

"I'm fine. Thanks to Art." Angel held the still shaking Carimus. "He's going to be okay, Cari. Is he your brother? Don't worry. Joy is the best."

Carimus nodded, his face still buried against the bandit girl. His sobs turned to inarticulate moans, then died away. He sniffed and rubbed his eyes, his hands still bound. Quietly, Angel reached out and untied his wrists.

Joy spoke to Bortis. "I need you to hold this pad in place while I cut his jacket and shirt away from the wound. That's it, firmly. Cat, I need some yarrow. Gather me a few handfuls. Vix, better keep watch in case there's another harpy out there."

"Already on it." Vix gazed back out into the open meadow behind them.

The Fairborn healer cut away the sleeve of Artos's shirt and jacket and then gasped. She spoke a few words in Espro that caught Angel's attention. Angel caught her breath, staring at his arm—something Artos was trying very hard not to do. Then he realized what she must be seeing. There, on his upper arm, right over the bloody bandage Bortis was holding, was his birthmark, the crown above the head of a dragon.

Angel looked from the birthmark to his eyes, but the question she asked wasn't the one Artos expected. "Who's Duke? I thought Cari was talking about his dog. There were four of you, weren't there? The Magic Man said to watch for four."

"Magic Man?" asked Bortis. "Who the heck ...?"

"Angel!" Cat crouched near the body of the fallen raptor. "You'd better look at this."

Angel disengaged from Carimus, who had stopped sobbing, but was gasping for breath. She gently pushed him to a sitting position on a nearby fallen tree trunk, speaking to him in a calm, reassuring voice. "Just rest here, Cari. Art is going to be fine. Joy has everything under control." When he nodded, she hurried over to Cat, a few yards from the still twitching giant bird. "What is it?" she asked.

"Watch it. It's still alive, though not for long, I'd say. Look at its left leg. Right above the talons." Cat pointed. Around the bird's leg was a shiny ring of some black substance. At that moment, the bird gave a convulsive shudder and stopped twitching, dead at last.

Angel stepped closer, pulled out her dagger and looked at the band on the bird's leg. As she reached out to probe it, the ring dissolved into black dust and drifted to the forest floor.

"What the?" exclaimed Cat, watching intently. "What just happened?"

"It died," said Angel.

"No. I know it died, but I meant—" said Cat.

"I know what you meant," cut in Angel. "Get some of that yarrow for Joy." She pointed at the herb growing near the carcass. "Oh, and good shot." She pulled a green fletched arrow free from the breast of the bird and handed it to Cat.

"Not as good as Joy's," Cat replied, pointing at the red-feathered arrow which had pierced the bird's left eye.

"Yeah," Angel nodded. "Another bullseye to Joy, so to speak. Take her the herbs and bring back one of her vials. An empty one. Dry if possible. I want to collect that dust. Father will want a look at it."

"What is it? Do you know?" asked Cat. Angel just shook her head and reached to pluck the red-feathered arrow from where it had lodged.

"What is that thing? It's horrible." Carimus gazed at the dead bird.

"It's a harpy eagle, a giant one. And it's out of place. They usually live in the Black Mountains, not in the Mountains of Myst. They hunt by sight, and the fog here keeps them away. It's been sighted a couple times over the last few weeks, though." She shook her head. "Something's going on, something bad. I have a feeling ..." She looked at Carimus. "You feeling better?"

"Yes. Thank you. I guess I acted pretty badly. I'm sorry I broke down." He held up his wrists.

"I think we're past the prisoners part, Cari. I'm not going to bind you again. We're going to my camp. We'll eat some dinner and try to sort this out. That okay with you?"

Carimus sighed with relief. "Yes, I'm starving. I need some new pants too. I ripped up the legs on these pretty badly."

"Susi's about your size. We'll find something for you to wear. Provided you promise to tell me what the three of you are doing here and why you are wearing your pajamas?"

"That's for Art to decide, I think, but I'm sure he will." Carimus nodded confidently.

"Sixteen stitches, so far," said Cat as she handed Angel a small glass bottle. "Art's asking for you, Cari, and Bort's ready to explode because you ran off. Better go back over there." She pointed to where Joy was still working on Art's arm. Sure enough, Bortis was glaring in his direction with a scowl on his face.

"Oh, Bort always looks like that. Well, not always. He was all googly-eyed at Elaine deEagledon last night, but he is bossy. I think he's jealous that she and Art are going to be betrothed." He turned and walked over and sat down on the log again, closer to his brothers.

Angel and Cat looked at each other with surprise. "Elaine Eagleton? Isn't that …?"

"Yeah, she is." Using her dagger, Angel began scraping up what she could of the black dust and transferring it to the glass vial, careful not to touch it with her bare hands.

28

THE SWAN'S NEST

CARIMUS

4:45 p.m.

THE SHADOWS WERE GROWING LONG when the three brothers and the four girls reached the camp. Artos was wearing his right arm in a sling Joy had made for him. Carimus could see the trip was not an easy one for his brother. Every stumble or slight misstep caused him to shudder. But Bortis walked at his side or directly behind him as the narrow trail they followed through the birch wood dictated, and helped whenever he could. Carimus knew Bort worried more about Art than he did for his other two brothers, but he understood. Art was to be the king, after all.

Joy followed behind them. Whenever Artos staggered or swayed, she let out a low whistle, and Cat, still leading the group, would stop, letting him have a few brief moments of rest.

Carimus walked near Angel, asking her numerous questions about the various trees and shrubs they passed and the few small animals he sighted. Carimus could tell it surprised her when he often added bits of knowledge concerning many of the plants after she had named them. It was clear he knew a great deal about many things without ever having seen them himself.

"Are you going to be a teacher, Carimus? You seem to know a great deal about these plants and things."

"No," he answered in a self-important voice. "I'm in training to be a priest. I am an acolyte of the Sky Father. And next summer, I am to be receiving training from the Cantor of the Earth Mother as well."

"Both sects?" Angel arched a brow. "Isn't that unusual?"

Artos cut in. "Cari, stop pestering Angel. She probably needs to be watching for another raptor or something."

"Oh, it's alright, Cari," answered Angel before he could protest. "You can ask me whatever you want. My girls will let me know if there's anything I need to know about. How are you doing, Art? It's not much further, and there's nothing too dangerous around Swan's Nest. Oswald keeps an eye out for us. There were a half a dozen farmsteads in this part of the valley until the raiders burnt them out last year." Bitterness filled her voice. "The Herndars think the people of the valley are going to default on their taxes, but they're wrong! They paid 'em last midsummer with good silver. It surprised the Herndar tax collector down in Koelbey when they answered the roll and paid right on time. They'll do it next summer too. The Herndars aren't going to cut down the forest here like they have done in the lowlands."

"I'm doing okay," Artos answered. "I'm just a little dizzy, and my arm hurts like the blazes, but I've had worse. I broke my wrist last summer when my horse spooked and threw me. It hurt worse until we got it set, and Unc ... ah, the Priest cast a restore and set things right."

"Good thing you had the silver to pay him," Angel replied.

"I hear the Sky Priests don't give their spells away to just anyone. Or did you find a druid? Druids will usually barter a spell for a meal or just give it away for free if the need is great."

At that moment, Cat came hurrying back down the path and called softly, "Angel, come quick. Oswald's been hurt. He's at the nest. Ava just told me."

"Oh, no." Angel hurried ahead with Cat, leaving the three brothers to continue on with Joy and Vix.

"We're only about another mile to the nest, Art," said the Fairborn healer. "Think you can handle that with no more stops? They might need me to help with Oswald."

"I can make it," answered Artos. "You can go on if you want. Vix can guide us there if you need to go ahead."

"No, Kae is there. She's my sister. She's the healer who taught me. If I were needed, Cat would have said. Angel wouldn't be pleased if I left Vix alone with the three of you. Not that Vix can't handle herself, but it's the company's rules."

"The company?" asked Bortis.

"We're the Daughters of the Wind," replied Joy. "And Angel is our leader, although my sister is older. We hunt bandit raiders and Beastmen now, mostly. Before the raiders and the Beastmen showed up, we formed our band to help protect the farms against the occasional nasty creature coming into the valley from the mountains. It let the men keep up with their crops. Now and then, a giant boar or weasel would wander in. Still do, in fact, but they're not as important now as they were when there were farmsteads here."

"So, you hunt and kill dangerous animals?" asked Carimus.

"Kill? No, not if we can help it. We try to herd them back where they belong, away from people. Killing is always a last resort. It is one thing to kill in defense, or because you need food to live. But it is another thing to kill just because you are afraid. I think it's shameful, as do the rest of the Daughters. With the Beastmen, something has gotten them riled up. They used to stay in the Black Mountains, away from the demesnes. A few tribes lived here in the Mountains of Myst, but they stayed away from people as much as they could, until this last year. Now they are running wild. Something's changed, and not for the better."

"What could cause that?" asked Carimus. The Fairborn girl merely shook her head and shrugged. Bortis glared back at Carimus, scowling and shaking his head, but when he shrugged, his brother just looked away. *Bort's mad again. What did I say?* Carimus shook his head and sighed.

Soon, the trail led them to a grove of oak trees surrounding a small clearing. Two other paths led away in different directions. In the middle was a small fire pit with a triangle of fallen logs around it. A fire was burning beneath a pot from which a meaty smell was emanating. When he caught the delicious odor, his mouth started watering instantly. Carimus looked around for the camp, but except for the fire, he saw no sign.

Vix was watching him, and she chuckled. "You are looking in the wrong direction. Look up."

At that moment Joy gave a sort of hooting call and a ladder made of some light-weight white cord dropped from above. She quickly scrambled up as the brothers scanned the trees. Carimus saw there were several platforms in the trees with walkways connecting them. "Tree houses!" he exclaimed.

"Angel says to send the boys up and put them in the dining hall for the time being," said an unfamiliar voice. A girl with long blond tresses was looking down from where she had dropped the ladder. "Susi has some stew cooking and there is fresh-this-morning flat bread."

A chord with a small hook on the end dropped from another spot. "Hey Vix! Hook the stew pot for me, would you?" came yet another voice from a different spot, and Carimus spied another blond head and mischievous eyes peering at him through a square hole in one of the larger platforms.

Vix slipped her ever-present bow upon her back, picked up a potholder that was lying on one of the logs, and with a small grunt took a hold of the simmering pot's handle, lifted it off the fire, and carried it over next to the cord. Setting it down, she deftly hooked the handle, looked up, and said, "All yours, Susi." A winching sound followed, and the pot slowly rose into the trees.

"Up the ladder, boys," said Vix. "Oh … Art, your arm. Can you climb with only one? We can pull you up … maybe?"

Artos carefully removed his arm from the sling and flexed it experimentally, wincing a bit as he did. "I think I can climb a short way if I use my left arm to do most of the work. My legs are fine, tired, but fine. Cari, Bort, if you guys hold the ladder steady from down here, it would help a lot. Okay?"

"Sure, Artie," said Carimus, as Bortis just walked over and grabbed the rope ladder with each hand and stood waiting. Carimus quickly joined him and Artos slowly and carefully climbed the ladder up into the trees, one rung at a time, his left arm doing all the work. Just using his right to hold the rungs.

When he reached the top of the ladder, the tall blond girl helped him to the wooden walkway. Carimus followed his brother up into the trees.

29

REVELATIONS

BORTIS

4:55 p.m.

Bortis watched as the tall blond girl helped Artos leave the ladder and nodded to Carimus to go next. He could faintly hear her words to him from where he stood as Carimus followed Artos.

"Hello, I'm Rachel. Follow me and we'll get you fed. Cat told me you probably saved Angel's life from that Harpy. Thank you."

When Carimus was about halfway up, he followed at the urging of the one called Vix. *What does she think I'm going to do? Run away and leave my brothers in the hands of bandits?* Art was still in shock from his wounds, and Cari could not stop showing off for the bandit girl leader. As usual. He paused, reaching the walkway, panting a little from the exertion after the long climb.

Artos was following the tall blond girl, Rachel, into a hut built around the bole of the largest oak tree in the grove, and Carimus was about halfway between them. He looked down and saw that Vix was almost up the rope ladder and nearing the walkway. She grinned at him in that infuriating manner, her normal expression. He scowled back, then turned and followed Cari to the hut.

When he entered, he was surprised to see finely crafted furniture. There were two large tables, each with places for eight people. Two couches, and several comfortable chairs, were scattered around the large room. There were plates and bowls set for seven people. A slender girl was ladling stew into the bowls as he entered. He recognized her as the face calling for Vix to send up the stew.

"Have a seat. I hope you like rabbit stew?" she asked. "We have some flat-bread and apples as well," she continued without waiting for an answer. "If you don't like stew, you're out of luck, but who doesn't like stew? It has a few carrots an' taters in it as well, but it's mostly rabbit, 'cause we don't get too many vegetables an' what we get go right in the stew pot. So there you go. Sit down, sit down. Just pick a spot an' sit. First come, first served."

Artos had chosen the nearest chair to the door and sat there breathing heavily. The day's events had taken their toll on his brother. Bortis walked over and sat beside him. "How you doing?"

Artos nodded and gave him a little smile. "I'm okay. Just need a meal and some rest."

Bortis looked around the room. The girl Rachel stood by the door as if she was on guard. The bowls, plates, and even the cups were all made from wood, as were the spoons beside each plate. Each was covered with scrolled carving and was quite beautiful to look at. The furniture was decorative as well as sturdy. *These girls did not make all this stuff themselves. I wonder where the rest of the bandits are hiding?*

Vix came in and sat across from him, still smiling with her infuriating expression. "This will taste better than the field grass, Bort. I promise!" He glowered at her, and she just smiled even more.

Susi went to each place and poured water into the cups before taking a place for herself. "I'm Susi, Cat's little sister. That's Rachel, by the door. Ava and Sherri are out on patrol and won't be back till later. Eat, eat, no need to wait." Her face became more serious. "Angel, Joy, and Kae are up with Oswald. I hope he's not hurt too bad. He barely struggled in here, a nasty cut across his back. No telling when they'll eat." She looked at Carimus. "What's your name? I'm fourteen an' the youngest of the Daughters," she grimaced. "That's why I usually get stuck with the cooking. But I'm good at it. Don't you think?"

"I'm Cari," he answered when she paused for a breath. "That's Bort, and he's Art. And it smells delicious." He then started spooning the stew into his mouth. Bort was already eating.

Artos was struggling to eat left-handed and was finding it awkward, but manageable. "It smells very good, Susi. Thank you. We hadn't eaten since yesterday, so a hot meal is most welcome." He managed a few bites and then asked, "Who's Oswald? Is he someone's brother?" Bortis listened carefully, pretending to be uninterested.

"Oswald's our scout." Angel came in the door. "He lost a bit of blood, and he won't be flying for a few days, but he's going to be fine, just a nasty scratch, a lot like yours, Art. Not too surprising. It was the same harpy that got you."

"Oswald can fly?" asked Carimus, his eyes wide.

Angel smiled. "Yes, and he's not even a demon, either."

Carimus looked horrified. "An abomination then?"

The Daughters all looked at each other and laughed.

"That's not funny!" Carimus cried.

"We'll take you up to see him after dinner, Cari. You can judge for yourself," said Angel.

"Oswald the abomination!" giggled Susi. "Oh, I don't think he will enjoy being called that, Cari. It's not nice!"

Bortis and Artos exchanged puzzled glances, as lost as their little brother at the girl's humor. Bortis guessed Oswald was some kind of bird, a falcon perhaps.

Two Fairborn soon followed Angel into the hut. Joy and another with dark brown hair, who Bortis guessed was her sister, Kae. She was carrying a jar, which she opened as she walked up to stand behind Art. The air suddenly smelled of roses, or maybe lilac. Bortis couldn't decide.

"If I may look at your shoulder for a moment, Art?" she asked. "I have some balm that will help it heal. And it will soothe the pain, too."

His brother nodded and pushed back his chair from the table as Bortis watched suspiciously.

"No need to get up," she said. "Just let me smear a little of this on the bandage for now. I'll take a look at it later, after you have finished eating. This will soak right through, and you should feel its effects almost at once."

She dipped a finger in the jar and wiped a small amount on the bloody wrap. It must have helped, because Bort saw his brother relax as soon as she smeared the glop on his wound.

"Yes, that feels good. Thank you."

"You can be angry with me, Art," said Joy. "I usually have some almas in my pack, but my jar was dry. I forgot to refill it the last time I used it."

Artos shook his head. "You stopped the bleeding, and that

was the important thing."

"I was careless, and am angry with myself, even if you are not," she replied. "The yarrow stopped the bleeding, but the almas would have made your journey here far easier on us all. I won't forget again."

"Yes, sister, I'm sure you will remember now. It is an ill feeling to reach for a healing measure and realize you do not have it when needed," Kae said.

The group finished their meal in relative silence. Cat talked quietly with Susi about chores, while Angel, Joy, and Kae shared a few words in Espro, which irritated Bortis to no end. *What are they planning?* He glanced at Artos. Bortis could tell he was trying to follow their conversation. Vix and Rach remained quiet.

"Are you ready to meet Oswald, Cari?" asked Joy.

"I guess. Are you coming Art?"

"I don't think Art would like to make the climb up to the roost this evening, Cari," said Kae. "Besides, I need to finish treating his wound. He can make the climb tomorrow if his arm allows."

Bortis spoke up for the first time since entering the camp. "You can wait until morning too, Cari. We stay together." He glanced around, expecting someone to challenge him.

"As you like. I'll go check on him then," said Joy, and she left the table.

Susi gathered up the dishes and tableware. "Remember Vix, you're on kitchen duty tomorrow."

"Sorry Susi," said Angel. "Vix, Rach, and Joy will head out with me early tomorrow, taking our guests to Blue Spires, to the Magic Man. I'll make it up to you later. You and Kae will hold down the Nest. Ava and Sherri will stay on patrol, and I have a special errand for Cat."

"Oookay," said Susi, sadness in her voice.

"No," said Bortis. "We have to go home."

"Bort," said Artos, "are we just going to walk there? Tirinvo sent us here for a reason. He must have."

Bortis pushed back his chair and jumped to his feet. "I don't care what that elf did. We need to go home!"

"Elf?" Ice coated Angel's voice. "I see."

"Bort," groaned Artos, "shut up. Just shut up for once."

"Why? You think these bandits are going to help us? We can't take a walk off to go visit some 'magic man.' What are you thinking?"

"I'm thinking we need help. We can't just walk back to the castle and chase away the Beastmen!" shouted Artos, standing up and facing his brother.

"No, we go to Eagle Roost and get Count Stephan to help us. You know he will. He has to! It's his duty."

"Eagle Roost! They won't even be there in a few days. They were leaving for the lowlands in another day or two. And how do we know they weren't attacked too? They don't have a qulan. We have to find out what's going on."

Bortis realized what they were saying and looked around. Eyes like saucers, Susie stared at the arguing pair from where she had stopped clearing the table. Carimus gaped, gazing back and forth between his arguing brothers. The rest of the girls were sitting stony-eyed except for Kae, who tried to keep a smile off her face.

She stood up and picked up her jar of almas from the table and unscrewed the top. "May I look at your shoulder now, Prince Artos?" she asked. Susi gasped.

Artos sat back down and nodded. The Fairborn healer had him lean forward and removed his torn jacket. "Susi, if you can patch this tonight, I'll do the cooking tomorrow and the washing up as well," she said, laying his jacket on the table.

"Deal!" Susi finished stacking the used plates and bowls on a small table next to the tree trunk in the room's center. She then gathered the jacket and held it up, shaking her head. "I'll need to wash out the blood stains first. Sis, will you go down to the spring with me so I can get started?"

Cat looked at Angel, who nodded and said, "Thank you, Susi. I wouldn't ask you to do it tonight, but we will be leaving at first light." She looked at the brothers one by one. "I won't force you to go, but the Magic Man thought you might be coming here. He sent word with Oswald yesterday that you might show up soon and that's why we were out looking for you. Except, he said, there would be four of you. That's why we thought you were raiders or lost from Anson or Herndar or something. It was stupid of me not to realize we were looking for you, even if you were one short. What happened to the other? Cari called him Duke."

"We don't know," said Carimus. "We were flying together, the lightning crashed, and Duke was gone. Just gone." Tears glittered in his eyes. "He's lost and all alone." Bortis laid his hand on Carimus's shoulder and just shook his head.

"Cari," Artos said, "we will find him. His eagle may just have been blown in a different direction. Arrggh!" he gasped as Kae pulled the bloody bandage free from his wound. Surprisingly, it didn't hurt nearly as much as he expected. The almas she had applied to the bandage had soaked through and the caked blood wasn't stuck to the wound.

"Sorry, Artos," said the Fairborn healer. "I wanted to get that off while you were distracted." She stroked a clean rag smeared with the healing balm over the wound, cleaning away the rest of the dried blood. She then used a wet cloth to finish cleaning the area. "Good, neat stitches. The yarrow stopped the bleeding pretty quickly. My little sister does good work."

"I had an excellent teacher," said Joy as she entered the room. "Oswald is asleep. He won't be flying for a few days, but I think he'll be good as new before we know it." The two Fairborn sisters exchanged a brief smile.

Angel sighed, "I'm glad he's going to be okay, but I wish we could use his wings. If Duke is wandering around the Valley somewhere, we need to find him. Soon."

Kae spoke a few words in Espro, which left Angel shaking her head. "It's too dangerous, Kae. What if there's another harpy?"

"We only spotted that one. If there were more, we'd have seen them … probably."

"Probably," repeated Angel. "But we don't know for sure. I don't think you should."

"Angel, even if there is another harpy, I will be safe if I leave now. They don't fly by night. There might be someone out there lost and alone, maybe injured. I am going."

Bortis watched and listened with interest. Was there going to be a disagreement between the bandits? Could he use it to his advantage somehow?

"I'll join you, sister," added Joy.

"No. Angel needs you to travel with her in the morning. You were out all day today, while I sat here at the Nest with Susi. You need to rest for the journey to the Spires. It's over fifteen miles and a lot of it is uphill. I'm fresh." She deftly bandaged Artos's arm back up. "You will be sore for another day or so, Prince Artos, but you were lucky it didn't damage the muscle or sever a large blood vessel. Joy will keep an eye on you, but you'll be fine. I'm sure."

Artos nodded. "How did you know …?"

"That you are a Prince? Let's just say an 'elf' told me about you and your family a while back," she smiled. "It took me a little while, but I remembered the names. Artos, Bortis, Carimus, and Duka, I believe?"

Art nodded.

"Now, I should go and look for Duka. If he is nearby, I may have a chance, not a good chance mind you, but a chance to find him."

Bortis cut in, "It's night. How could you possibly find him in the dark? He isn't stupid. He's not going to be wandering around calling for help."

Kae looked serious. "I don't think I will find him. But the moon is rising and just past full. I'm going to go look, anyway."

Troubled, Angel signaled with a toss of her head that she and Kae should go outside. As she left, she looked at Artos. "I'd like a few words with you when I finish with Kae. Then we will give you a room to sleep, and you can decide what you are going to do. Come with me in the morning to see the one person who may be able to help you. Or rush off like fools." She looked hard at Bortis, who stared back at her defiantly. Then she, Kae, and Joy walked out of the room onto the walkway. Their muffled voices could be heard speaking in Espro for a few long moments, and then Angel walked back in.

"Cat, Susi, the moon's rising. You can slip down to the spring and wash that jacket. Whatever they decide, Prince Artos will need it in the morning, so please sew it together as best you can. Thanks."

The two sisters nodded to their leader, and taking the jacket, they left the room.

"Okay, Vix, Rach, would you two please ready the guest room for our three guests?"

"But, Angel, I can do that myself, or Rach can. I mean ..." Vix started, then looked pointedly at Bort.

"I wish to speak to them alone, Vix. It will be alright." She turned and looked at the brothers. "You aren't planning on attacking me, are you, Prince Artos? Prince Carimus? Prince Bortis?"

Artos shook his head and Carimus said, "Of course not." Bortis glowered, but remained silent.

"You see, Vix. Go ready the room, please."

Rach and Vix exchanged a glance, nodded, and left the room.

Angel walked back over to the chair she had sat in for dinner, pulled it away from the table, and sat down. She looked at Bortis, who then also sat back down.

"Kae is the eldest here, by a good many years. I really can't tell her what to do like the rest of the Daughters. She was a friend of my mother, just as her little sister, Joy, is to me. I don't like anyone going off by themselves right now, but she is right. If your brother is somewhere in the valley, if anyone can find him tonight, it's Kae."

Bortis made a dismissive snort.

"Believe me, Bort, I will be just as glad to see you gone as you will be to go. I am risking my father's anger to send you to the Magic Man. My father's orders are for all strangers to be sent to his camp at Alfhiem." She looked at Bortis. "Elfhome. He calls it that on purpose. I asked him once why he gave it such a spiteful name. He said it was a remembrance. But he would never say what it was remembering."

She looked back at Artos. "My mother always told me to

listen to the Magic Man, that he wouldn't steer me wrong. And he never has. He was my teacher for a time. He's always been a friend, so I am willing to risk my father's anger. He asked me to bring you to him. If you decide to go your own way … Well, I probably owe you my life, Artos. That harpy would have pierced me through, maybe broken my back with his attack. So I owe you, and I pay my debts. Now, I am asking you to please explain how you came to be here. You have mentioned flying on eagles and Prince Tirinvo. This troubles me. Why isn't he with you?"

"He said the eagles couldn't carry double loads in the storm. They had trouble in the wind and rain, just carrying us. I am sure he was correct. Windrider went back, I think. They flew off in that direction. I don't know."

Artos then proceeded to tell Angel the tale. Carimus and Bortis sat silently and let him talk.

After Artos finished, she shook her head. "Once more, I will say I think you need to tell this story to the Magic Man. Prince Tirinvo is his friend. Perhaps he will be waiting for us there. And maybe Duka as well, although I do not wish to give you false hope, Cari. Tirinvo and the other Fairborn may have escaped your Eyrie and found the missing Eagle, and all of them may be at the Crystal Tower. The Magic Man's home. I do not know. Come, we all need to rest."

She stood and led them out onto the walkway and to another of the platforms with a smaller hut upon it. Vix and Rach were sitting on a bench outside the door. Upon seeing Angel, they waved, then stood and walked away on another walkway towards a hut at a different tree.

"Sherri and Ava are walking the perimeter. If there is any danger, or if Kae returns with news, we will wake you. You are my guests here tonight. Sleep well. We will wake you at first light to hear your decision." Angel let them enter the hut, closed the door, and walked away.

30

DECISIONS

ARTOS

8:oo p.m.

INSIDE THE SMALL HUT were three pallets with a blanket laid out on each. Otherwise, the room was empty, save for the slight scent of cedar. The only light was the moonlight shining in through a small window. Carimus sat down on the nearest pallet with a sigh and began removing his boots. Bortis, however, turned to Artos, "Are you out of your mind?" he hissed with an acidic glare. "You think these bandits are harmless just because they're pretty girls? Wake up. We don't know if half the things they are telling us are true. Raiders from House deHerndar burning farmsteads? Come on, Art."

Artos ran his left hand through his hair. "Bort, father has had me sit in Phoenix's mid-winter council meetings the last few years. Two years ago, House deHerndar asked father to allow them to raise taxes in their demesne. House deAnson was the only House that backed them after father refused, and they called for a vote. Count Charlton was angry. I remember he puffed up and said father didn't understand finance. Father said he wouldn't allow small farmsteads to be taxed off their lands."

"So what? How does that prove anything?"

"Isn't this valley within the deHerndar demesne?"

"So what? You don't know this was where they wanted to increase taxes two years ago, and we know that there have been bandits in these mountains for years. Uncle Brett hunted them."

"I don't think these girls are the bandits Uncle Brett was hunting."

"She admitted her father was the West Wind, the worst bandit in the whole Mountains of Myst! They call themselves the Daughters of the Wind. What more do you need?" Bortis began pacing back and forth in the small space like a caged beast.

"So, what do you want to do? Capture them? Kill them? Let's hear your plan. You heard Angel. We are free to leave in the morning if we want. Is that what you want?" Artos realized he was talking louder and lowered his voice. "Or are you just mad because some girls captured you? I bet if you ask nicely, they would even give you a spare bowstring, maybe even a spare bow, and you could start walking home. You might get there before your birthday, maybe. Just what do you want?"

Artos sat down on one of the empty pallets and tried to unlace his moccasins with his good hand. Their little brother had lain down and was watching Bortis pace, his eyes struggling to stay open.

"Cari, what do you want to do?"

"Me? I don't know, Artie ... I think we should go with her." He looked imploringly at Bortis. "You heard her, Bort. Duke might be there. I don't know."

"I was behind you when that lightning struck. You two were ahead of us. Then that bolt crashed, and when I could see again … there … there was just you and Art. I'm sorry, Cari, but you need to accept he is probably gone." Bortis's voice was tight.

"No! He's not. I would know. I can still feel him, Art. He's out there somewhere. Lost and alone." Tears glittered in his eyes, and he sat upright.

"Cari. Calm down. I hope you're right. We just don't know." Artos tried to stand up, but with only one arm, he was unbalanced and fell to his side. Fortunately, his uninjured side, but it still knocked the wind out of him.

He felt strong hands grip him as Bortis helped him roll over onto his back. "Stay down, Art. Rest. You too, Cari."

Bortis shook his head, sighed, then pulled the blanket to cover Artos. "After we go see this magic man, then what? I think we are being taken for fools. But I can't see any better options. We should have never let that elf rush us out of the Castle. For all we know, Uncle Brett rallied the guard and killed off the beasts. We don't even know if there were any Beastmen. I didn't see any. It could all be some plot to kidnap us. Did you ever think of that? She said this magic man knows Tirinvo and told them the day before yesterday that we would come. How could he know unless it was planned?"

"I sure heard the Beastmen," said Carimus. "Something was howling. You heard them too, Bort!"

"I heard something. How do we know it wasn't the bard and his crysharp? Who knows what black magic he could have done? Brett and father could be looking for us now. They could be worried sick. Or worse …" He trailed off, then whispered, "The elves might have murdered them."

"I don't believe that!" Artos struggled to his good elbow.

"You may not have seen any Beastmen, but I did. One of them burst into my room after Tirinvo came in and woke me up. I was dressing when it charged in. Tirinvo killed it. He was father's friend. They knew each other before we were born. It doesn't make sense, Bort. Tirinvo was outside the qulan when he sent us off on the eagles. He couldn't even get back inside. Think!" He lay back down. "I think we need to go see the magic man. So does Cari. Are you going to come with us, Bort? Or go off on your own?"

"You know I can't do that, Art. It's my duty to protect you two, even if I think you are being fools." He sat down, unlaced his moccasins, then laid down and pulled the blankets over him.

Art put his head down and adjusted his blanket. As exhaustion overtook him, he heard a honking sound outside, as if a goose or swan were nearby. *Do geese fly around at night?* he wondered. It was his last thought until a soft knocking woke him many hours later.

Chapter Eight:

To the Blue Spires

31

THE JOURNEY TO
THE BLUE SPIRES

ARTOS

9/17/1971 ar

7:54 a.m.

A soft knocking penetrated Artos' deep and dreamless slumber. As he awoke with a start, his first thought was that he was awakening from a terrible nightmare. Looking around the small barren room the reality dawned. Sighing, he laid his head back down and tried to lose himself in sleep once more, but the knocking repeated.

He sat up and realized that although his arm was still stiff and sore; it felt nothing like it had the night before.

"Who's there?" he asked, just as Bortis sat up with a gasp.

"It's me. Susi. Angel asked me to tell you it's time to prepare for the journey to the Magic Man. If that's where you're going. Anyway, it's time to have breakfast. I'm leaving you some things. I mended your jacket, and I have some of my old clothes for Carimus to try on. And Rach sent one of her old flannel shirts for you. Angel said you needed a shirt, and Rach is the tallest Daughter. It might fit. It was baggy on her, she said.

Anyway, they are outside the door. I have to scoot. Hurry up. The porridge will get cold." Artos heard the soft sound of her feet as she padded away.

The air was chilly outside the blanket, and when he opened the door to the hut, there was a pile of neatly folded clothing stacked before the door. To his surprise, sitting beside the neatly piled clothing was a silvery-colored basin with a few clean rags lying on the bottom, with a large jug standing beside it. Upon picking up the jug, the sloshing told him it was filled with water to allow them to wash up before they dressed.

Using his left arm, he carried the jug inside. "Hey Bort, get the rest of the stuff, will you? I'm still sore, but it feels much better than yesterday."

Bortis threw off his blanket and gathered the items from outside the door, grumbling softly to himself. He set the basin down in the center of the room and tossed the rest of the items on top of the still snoring form of Carimus. "Wake up, Squirt."

The form buried beneath the blankets rolled over and continued snoring. Bortis then grabbed the blanket and yanked it from his brother, finally awakening him. Carimus sat up and rubbed his eyes. He realized where he was, and a look of sadness pushed the sleep from his features.

"It wasn't a dream, was it? We're still here, and Duke's still lost."

"Maybe we'll find him today, Cari," said Artos. "Maybe he will be waiting for us at the Magic Man's tower."

Artos tried to pour some water from the jug into the basin, wincing from the soreness in his arm. But when Bortis attempted to take the jug, he turned away. "No, I can do it, Bort. I need to work out the stiffness." He managed to fill the basin half full and set the jug down. Picking up the clean rags, he handed one to Bortis, still fully dressed in his leathers. He tossed another to Carimus and removed the remains of his torn pajama top.

"Wash up, Cari. Susi left us some clothes to try on after you clean up." He looked at the stubborn glare from Bortis and shook his head slightly. "At least wash your face, Bort."

Bortis hesitated, then removed his leather top and the undershirt beneath and washed off the dried sweat. Artos smiled to himself and silently joined him. Carimus waited till his brothers were done and then looked at the dirty water with a grimace.

"Oh, for ..." Bortis walked to the door, opened it, then took the basin outside and poured it over the edge of the walk. He set the basin down and slopped the rest of the water from the jug into it. "There you go, princess. All fresh and clean."

Artos was trying on the gray flannel shirt. It was a little tight across the shoulders, but otherwise was a pretty good fit. He reminded himself to thank Rachel for the gift.

Carimus looked at the rough cloth pants and the flannel shirt left for him, shrugged, and put them on, drawing a laugh from Bortis. "It's a good thing you were wearing your moccasins, Cari. Those pants don't go but halfway down your calves."

"Yeah, but I am. It's better than wearing torn pajamas, anyway," answered Carimus, as he finished his lacing.

Artos had a start on his younger brother, but was still the last, by far, to finish dressing. He was just tying his boot strings when Angel appeared in the doorway. "All dressed?" she asked, though it was apparent they were.

"Yes, thank you, Angel," said Carimus. Artos nodded with a smile. Bortis just glowered and remained silent.

"Glad they fit. Have you reached a decision yet?" she asked, looking at the brothers one by one. "We need to get started soon if you are coming with me to the spires. You'll have time to gulp down some porridge, Cari, but I'm afraid we need to skip taking you up to see Oswald. He's still sleeping and probably won't wake up for hours yet. He'll be flying to the Magic Man's tower in a day or two, though. You can meet him then. Shall we go to the common hall?" she asked as she turned, without waiting for a reply.

"You seem to assume we are coming with you," growled Bortis.

"I don't think you are fools, that's all," she replied over her shoulder. "Am I wrong?" She continued walking towards the large common room hut.

Artos cut in before Bortis could answer. "We decided we'll go. It seems our best choice at the moment."

Three steaming bowls of porridge waited in the empty common room. Artos looked at Angel, but she anticipated his question. "We've all eaten already. Ava and Sherri got back from patrol about an hour ago. They're sleeping now. Susi knows the schedule and had a warm meal prepared." A troubled expression crossed Angel's face. "Kae's not back yet. If she has any news for me after we leave, she knows how to get it to me. Never fear, Cari. If we find Duka, you will know as soon as possible. Now eat. We need to hit the trail." She looked out one of the two windows, staring at the red fall foliage of the oak trees surrounding them.

The three brothers had almost finished their porridge when the door opened, and a form hidden behind an armload of backpacks walked into the room. "I have your pack, Angel," came Susi's cheerful voice. "And I packed some flatbread and jerky. We talked, and Cat, Sherri, and I all decided we could loan our travel packs to the boys, so they have something to carry their food. Cat said they have to give them back when they're finished, though, and they can't have them if they aren't going with you, Angel. But I told her they were. Where else would they go? I hope you don't mind?" She peeked out and gave a timid smile to Angel.

Angel looked at the youngest member of her band and smiled at the sight. "We're only going fifteen miles or so, Susi. But thank you." She looked at the brothers.

"You are too kind, Susi," Artos quickly replied. "We thank you for your thoughtfulness." He stood up and reached for a backpack to help her unload. "Cari, why don't you stack up those bowls for Susi, save her a little work?"

Carimus stood up, placed his bowl into Artos' empty one, and reached for Bortis's bowl, only to have his hand slapped away.

"Not done yet, Squirt. Wait a minute, sheesh." Bortis spooned the last of his porridge into his mouth and then placed his bowl onto the stack. "Okay, done." He stood up and eyed the backpacks Susi was setting on the other table.

"Thank you, Cari, but Kae's doing my chores today since I did the sewing last night." She handed one pack to Carimus. "This one's mine. Try to be careful with it. I still haven't used it for anything yet. But it's got a coil of spider rope and my canteen. You'll have to fill the canteens. I didn't have time. There's some flat-bread and dried jerky. It's rabbit too, just like the stew last night. It's good for munching on a hike." She paused for a breath.

"Thank you, Susi. Please get Vix and Rach for me? Ask them to wait at the ladder's foot. I'm guessing you already gave them their supplies?" said Angel.

"Sure, I'll tell 'em. And of course, they have some bread and rabbit jerky too," she answered as she headed back out the door.

Angel looked at Artos and Bortis. "You have any problems with being lent a backpack? Either of you?" She spoke to them both, but her eyes were on Bortis.

"No," Artos answered for both of them, taking one and holding it out to his brother. Bortis slowly reached out and took it, handling it as if it were a serpent ready to bite his hand. "We thank you again," said Artos. "I hope we can make good the promise to return them without any problems."

"We can carry them back from the spires. That's not a problem if you don't bring them back yourselves. I'd get the canteens out now before you put them on," she eyed Carimus, who had already fit the straps over his shoulders. He looked shamefaced, swung the pack around, untied the leather closure tie, and looked through the contents. He found the leather water bottle, pulled it out, and closed the pack.

"I wonder why they call it spider rope?" he asked.

"Because it's woven from spider-silk," answered Angel.

Bortis gave a derisive snort. "You can believe that if you want, but Uncle Brett told me it's just a silken rope, that's all, Cari."

Angel looked as though she was about to make a retort, but seemed to change her mind.

"Everyone have their canteens?" she asked instead. Although both Carimus and Artos had found theirs, Bortis simply stood waiting. She looked amused and slipped her arms through the straps. "Let's go then. The spring is on the way. We'll pause there and fill them." And suiting action to words, she walked out ahead of the three brothers.

"Bortis, stop acting childish. Get the canteen and let's go," Artos matched his brother's glare. Bortis muttered beneath his breath, then rummaged through the pack, produced the canteen, clipped it to his belt, and shrugged his arms into the straps.

"We don't need packs and canteens to walk fifteen miles. We can do that in a few hours."

"Fifteen miles into the mountains, Bort."

"Whatever you say … whatever you say," Bortis said, shaking his head.

Art led the way, with Bortis following Carimus out onto the walkway, where the gray light of dawn continued to lighten the morning. The crisp scent of autumn leaves filled the air as thunder rumbled in the distance, but the ground below was shrouded in fog again.

Angel, Susi, and Joy waited at the top of the white cord ladder leading to the ground. Artos could just make out the forms of two others waiting in the fog below. Like Angel, Joy had a pack on her back, and on seeing Bortis and Artos approach, she began climbing down. Angel motioned to Carimus, and he followed the Fairborn girl down the ladder.

"How does your shoulder feel, Art?" asked Angel. "The climb down won't give you any trouble?"

"It's still a little sore and a bit stiff, but nothing like yesterday. Kae's balm works wonders!"

Angel nodded and waved Bortis to follow Carimus. After he reached the ground, she motioned Artos to follow. As he climbed down, he overheard her say to Susi, "Wake up, Ava and Sherri a few hours before noon. Keep an ear out for Kae. Keep the ladder pulled up, and when they go back out on patrol, you're in charge. Kae will need some sleep after her all-night sojourn." Susi replied, but Artos' attention was on the climb down. It was less than twenty yards or so, but with his stiff and sore arm, it felt double that distance, and he was happy when his feet were once more on solid ground. The ladder was being held steady by the tall blond girl Rachel. "I guess I owe you thanks for the shirt," he said. She nodded, but her attention was on holding the ladder steady as Angel followed him to the ground. When her leader was safely on the ground, she gave a soft hoot, and the ladder disappeared back into the air.

After filling their canteens at the spring just to the west of the oak grove, the group set off on the trail, back the way they had come from the day before.

After two miles, the trail split into two branches, and without hesitation, Angel followed the trail to the southwest. Artos realized he had never even noticed the split the day before. His attention then had been just on keeping his feet and walking. After another mile, the ground rose, and as the fog cleared, the oaks and rainbow birch gave way to larch and mountain pine. They were mostly normal-sized trees, but with an occasional thousand-year giant here and there.

"Glad the fog's clearing, but it feels like rain," Artos remarked.

Angel, leading the group, looked back over her shoulder. "We'll be climbing right back into it soon enough. These are the Mountains of Myst, after all. It feels like we are going to get another storm today, though. That will slow us down. There are no caves on the way, and only a fool stands under a tree in a thunderstorm. We may not have a choice, though. The trail is mostly through woods all the way to the spires." The girl's voice sounded troubled. "I may have misrepresented the distance, too. It's about fifteen miles as the crow flies, but the trail is longer because it goes up and down and winds a bit. Maybe another five miles or a bit more. Still, it's not more than a good day's walk. Sorry, I wasn't thinking."

"Are there clearings?" asked Artos.

"A few small ones. We have to hope the rain blows over." As if to spite her, the thunder rumbled again, but no rain fell. "We may get lucky, or we may get wet."

As it turned out, they got both. A brief shower blew through about the time they reached the end of their trek through the valley proper and were about to begin the climb up the rocky trail into the mountains. They waited nervously under the dubious shelter of the mountain pine, but no lightning disturbed their wait. After about twenty minutes, the shower turned to a drizzle and then a fine mist. Artos envied the four girls their hooded cloaks. The boys' jackets kept their clothes fairly dry, but the same could not be said for their heads, and Artos' hair was plastered to his scalp. Drops of water kept seeping down his neck, not enough to soak his new flannel shirt, but more than enough to make it damp. The pine was a poor excuse for a roof, and it seemed no matter where beneath the boughs he stood, the rain still trickled down upon him.

"We should head out," said Angel at last. "I think the worst is past. Are you boys ready? The trail gets pretty steep in another mile or so. I'm glad you have sensible boots. Hard leather soles would make this a slippery climb, but your moccasins should make it easier."

Artos noticed that all four girls were wearing ankle high moccasins of soft leather. "We do … we did a lot of running every day. Uncle Brett made sure we had proper footwear. The Winding Way would have been difficult to run up and down in hard boots. I'm glad we all put on our moccasins instead of the shoes we were all wearing at Duke's birthday dinner. They wouldn't have held up well out here in the valley."

Angel nodded and led the way, Joy behind her. Vix and Rachel stayed at the rear. Artos walked behind Joy with Carimus between him and Bortis.

"How's your shoulder feeling, Art?" asked the Fairborn healer over her shoulder. "Let me know if it bothers you."

"It's a little sore, but it's so much better than yesterday. It's healing very well. Thank you."

"I'll take out the stitches later then, if they look ready. I'm thinking they will. Almas is a very good healing salve."

"Indeed it is," he agreed, and trudged on.

The trail zigzagged upward into the mist-shrouded Mountains of Myst. Their party was soon higher than the tops of the regular trees, though not those of the thousand-year trees, some of which were nearly one thousand feet in height. Then Vix urgently called out.

"Angel! Look back across the valley. By the Mother!"

The entire party turned and looked back towards the east. Swooping down from the fog shrouded mountains across the valley from where they were climbing was a gigantic crow. Suddenly, the scale of the sight became apparent, and Artos realized the size of the bird. The giant golden eagle he had ridden would seem like a sparrow beside an eagle in comparison.

"Sky Father preserve us. How far away is that ... that thing?" he asked.

"Stand still, everyone," said Angel. "No motion. It must be fifteen miles away, at least, Art. Crows have good eyes, but they're not like an eagle's. It won't notice us if we don't give it some motion or anything shiny to notice. I hope ..." she trailed off, transfixed by the sight.

When the bird turned away from them, she said, "Vix, keep watching. When it turns back, whistle. Everyone, follow me. We want to get over the ridge as quickly as we can but be careful. Watch your step. We don't want any broken legs." She turned back to the trail, climbing again at a quicker pace.

Artos pushed Carimus in front of him and followed closely behind. He mentally thanked his Uncle Brett for insisting on the twice-a-day trek up and down the Winding Way.

Twice, before they reached the top of the ridge, a quick whistle from Vix stopped them. They all froze in place until the monstrous bird circled away.

When they crossed the top of the ridge, Angel signaled a stop out of sight of the crow and moved to the back of the group. Falling to her hands and knees, she crawled to where she could keep watch and waved at the two rear guards. She only had to whistle once as Vix and Rachel climbed to join them. Soon after, she had waved them to proceed, she stood up and said, "It's gone. It flew up back towards the east."

She kept watch in case it reemerged from the fog enshrouded peaks, but there were no more sightings by the time Vix and Rachel rejoined the group.

"Glad you kept a close rear watch, Vix. Keep it up. Okay everybody, we'll be climbing into the mists soon, but that doesn't mean we can let down our guard. No unnecessary talking. Sounds do strange things here in the mountains. Especially when we get to the Blue Spires."

"What are the Blue Spires?" asked Carimus.

Angel grinned. "You'll know 'em when you see them, Cari. Trust me. Okay, I'll lead, with Joy second, Cari, you next, then Art or Bort. Rach, you and Vix as before. Can you boys all whistle?"

Artos nodded. Bortis looked disgusted and muttered, "Of

course." Carimus chose to demonstrate and whistled three notes to prove his ability.

Angel whistled two brief notes, one low and one higher. "I'll whistle that if I see or hear anything. It means freeze and look sharp. If you notice something I don't, you whistle. Let's go."

Angel set off down the short slope, then began climbing a steep switchback up the side of the mountain before them to the west. She set a steady but somewhat quicker pace than when they had first set out into the mountains. Soon they were climbing into the mists from which the mountains were named. Artos lost sight of Angel and could barely make out Joy in front of Carimus. Glancing behind him, he could just make out Rachel behind Bortis. *At least no birds can see us now.*

Soon after, the mountain pine appeared through the fog as they followed the trail into the mountains. Occasionally, the mists would part, revealing they were following a mountain valley that wound higher into the peaks.

After a few hours Angel reappeared before him, standing beneath the trunk of a towering thousand-year pine. When everyone was together, she motioned for all to follow her and led the way to a hollow formed by a pair of huge roots that made a ringed area about ten yards wide.

"Rest break," she announced. "We'll be seeing the spires in another half mile or so, Cari. Sit down and rest for a bit. Nibble a little jerky and then we'll push on."

She pulled off her pack, rummaged around inside, and produced a waxen paper with a few sticks of Susi's rabbit jerky. Pulling out a stick, she carefully re-wrapped the rest and replaced it in her pack. She placed the pack on the ground beside her as she sat on the pine needle covered ground and leaned against the root.

Vix was carrying her bow with an arrow loosely notched when she entered the root circle. Bortis remarked, "Watching for raiders?"

Vix smiled back sweetly. "You never know." Putting the arrow back in her quiver, she set her short bow down as she pulled off her pack. She pulled out some jerky, sat down and leaned against the root.

Carimus was already munching on a stick when Artos found his supply and removed it from his pack. Joy joined him.

"How's the arm?" she asked.

Artos realized that he hadn't noticed any stiffness in a while, and he rotated it slowly.

"It's not hurting anymore. The stiffness is gone, too."

"Good. Take off your jacket and shirt and let me look at those stitches, then."

Artos complied, and she scanned at his arm and nodded. "Looking good. You heal well." She opened a small vial, and the rose/lilac scent of almas filled the area. She smeared a tiny amount over the stitches, pulled a small knife from her pouch, carefully cut each stitch, and deftly yanked each one out.

When she was done, she nodded to herself once more. "Not even a scar to show for your misadventure, Art. Probably no one will ever believe you when you tell them the tale of being wounded by a harpy."

"Of course, they'll believe him," said Bortis with a scowl. "He's of House deDraconis. We don't lie."

Joy looked startled by the outburst. "Excuse me, Prince Bortis. I was not casting aspersions upon Prince Artos' honor."

"Relax, Bort. She didn't mean anything like that at all," said Artos, frowning at his brother. He turned back to look at the Fairborn. "I wish to thank you, Joy, for your immediate first aid and prompt care. You saved me from much worse blood loss with your quick actions."

"My sister Kae was an excellent teacher, Art. She is very skilled and has tended many wounds in her life. She has done her best to see that I have learned as much as I could."

"Best eat your jerky, Art. I see Bort isn't hungry. His jerky is still in his pack," said Angel. "We still have a good five or six miles to go and it's pretty much all uphill. No more steep climbs, though. The worst was back there when we left the valley. The mountain vales we'll be following wind upward among the spires and lead to the Crystal Cave, the entrance to the Magic Man's tower. Stay together. It becomes a maze when we enter the Blue Spires, and it would be all too easy to get lost in the mist and the spires."

Artos began to eat his jerky. Bortis quickly hunted through his pack for his snack as well. Though amused, he wisely decided not to call attention to that fact.

Carimus had finished his stick, and after a sip from his leather canteen, started asking questions. "I thought these were the Mountains of Myst? Why do you call this area the Blue Spires? All the rock I have seen is gray."

Angel smiled. "You'll see pretty soon, Cari. Trust me, you will know."

Vix added, "I'm looking forward to seeing them too, Cari. Neither Rach nor I ever came this way before. I don't think any of the Daughters have, except Joy and Kae."

Carimus looked surprised at this revelation. "Really? Joy said you herded beasts back into the Mountains."

"We used to, Cari, but that was always to the north, south, or east. The mountains are much steeper this way and I don't think any bears or boars ever wandered into the valley from this direction."

"Most predators shun these vales," added Angel. "The ones that live here don't stray into the valley. They live on the bighorns, the mountain rabbits, and the elk. Come on, finish up. We need to get moving again before another rainstorm blows in. Let's go." She jumped up, pulled on her pack, and waited impatiently as the brothers finished their snacks. As soon as they were ready, she started off.

"Same order, same rules. Keep it quiet. Keep your eyes and ears open."

Artos leaned in close to Bortis. "You have to admit, she knows how to lead, Bort." His brother answered with a scowl, a snort, and a push to get his brother moving as he shook his head in disgust. "She's a bandit, brother. Remember that," he whispered.

"With good ears," whispered Joy back over her shoulder.

After about fifteen minutes of hiking, the group rounded a turn in the trail just as a small gust of wind twirled away the mists around them and revealed the first of the Blue Spires standing before them, a group of three blue crystal obelisks. Behind them were dozens more. The spires stood well over a hundred feet tall, and the brothers all stopped and gazed at them in wonder. The individual spires each seemed to be a single huge crystal, although the bases seemed to be multitudes of smaller crystals, all fused together.

"Takes your breath away, doesn't it?" said Angel with a grin. "I know it did me, my first sight of them. And these are smallish. In the heart of the Spires, some are nearly a mile in height," she shook her head, "I still find them amazing, and I've seen them many times."

Artos and Bortis both were speechless.

Carimus looked at Angel. "Is this where cryswords come from? Are they forged somehow from these crystals?"

Angel looked amused. "No, I asked the Magic Man that same question some years back. He told me that there's some connection. Just as a nugget of gold or silver is similar to a steel sword forged from iron. He said that long ago, the quantimasters forged things from this crystal. He didn't say what. It's a lost art. Let's move on. We have less than five miles to go now. Stick close, the fog will get thick again. There are still dangers here in the spires. Some you will hear as they approach, but some are as quiet as the night breeze." Even as she spoke, the mists closed in about them and they could no longer see further than a few yards around them. The blue crystal spires fading away into the mist.

32

THE MAGIC MAN

BORTIS

4:44 p.m.

The mist cat perched a dozen feet above the ground on the gnarled root of a thousand-year mountain pine. Its gray fur was a swirl of muted tones, allowing it to blend perfectly into the mist. It sat all but invisible and watched the path that wound between the spires. Nine hundred pounds and four feet tall at the shoulder, the enormous cat was a fearsome predator, easily capable of bringing down a ten-foot-tall, two-ton giant bighorn sheep with a pounce and a quick strike to the neck. It was in hunting mode now and, except for an occasional twitch of a fluffy tail, remained motionless, ears cocked forward, eyes wide and alert. It had been listening to the approach of many pairs of feet for some time now.

THE TRAIL HAD WIDENED, and Angel and Joy walked side-by-side, with Carimus close behind them. Artos and Bortis came next, with Vix and Rachel still in the rear. Vix watched what was behind the group as much as she did the path ahead.

Suddenly, out of the fog, appeared a huge cat. Landing six feet before Angel, it stared at the group with enormous amber eyes. Drops of dew sparkled on the big cat's gray whorled coat, and its fluffy tail swished like a banner above its hindquarters.

"Look out!" yelled Bortis, his ruby crysword gleaming in his right hand. He grabbed Carimus by his jacket collar, pulling his younger brother behind him.

The mist cat crouched and growled a deep, threatening rumble, its tail switching back and forth.

Artos stepped up beside him, his white blade in hand.

Angel looked back at the brothers. Her face seemed to shift between anger and amusement. "Put those swords away. I mean it. You're not in danger." She turned back to face the snarling face of the mist cat. "Hello, Liv. Good to see you again. I'm bringing these boys to see the Magic Man." She walked a few steps forward, reached out, and rubbed behind the right ear of the huge cat.

The cat relaxed slightly, but kept her eyes glued to the cryswords in the brothers' hands.

Angel looked at them again. "Please, put your swords away. Liv is a friend. She's the Magic Man's companion. Trust me."

Artos and Bortis exchanged looks. Before Bortis could say anything, Artos nodded to him and sheathed his weapon. "Put it away, Bort. I believe her. Put your sword away." Bortis hesitated, then giving Artos an "on your head then" look, slipped his sword back into its sheath.

The mist cat relaxed and sat back on her haunches, her head

even with Angel's, and allowed Angel to continue scratching behind her ear.

"Do you want to let him know we're here, Liv?" Angel asked. The cat gazed into her eyes for a moment, then turned and disappeared into the mist.

"She's very protective. She will tell him we're almost there. Let's proceed."

"Right, she'll just walk up and announce us, I suppose?" sneered Bortis.

"Something like that," said Angel. "Shall we go, or do you want to stay here and argue?"

"Was that a mist cat?" asked Carimus, excitement in his voice. "She is beautiful, but scary. I didn't know they were so big."

"Yep, that's Liv. She's alpha mist cat around this part of the Spires. If she accepts you, you'll be accepted by all her family. There are four or five more spread out around this part of the mountains. The Magic Man knows. Let's go, shall we?" She turned and started walking after the mist cat.

As they followed her, Artos glanced at Bortis and said softly, "Nice quick draw there, Bort. I think that's the fastest I've ever seen you have your blade in hand."

"Yeah, well, there wasn't time to do anything except react. I thought we were meat," Bort thought for a moment. "You're right, though. It just jumped into my hand. I've never summoned it that easily before. First good thing to happen since … since … since Duka's party, I guess."

The thousand-year pine which the cat had leaped from marked the end of the thickly wooded part of the vale. More of the blue crystal spires jutted from the ground, and the trail wound between them. An occasional tree struggled to grow here and there, but they became fewer and fewer as they traveled through the crystal maze of obelisks.

Suddenly, a red spire appeared among the blue spires of the maze.

"We're almost there," Angel announced. "I asked the Magic Man why some spires were red, but he said he didn't know. Some just are. But another five minutes, and we'll be at the Crystal Cave."

"I thought you said he lived in a tower," said Bortis.

"He does. It's one of the spires, actually, but the entrance is a cave. You'll see," replied Angel.

Angel led the way into a clearing of the spires. The habitual mist was very light now, and Bortis could see some patchy blue sky. He placed his hand on the hilt of his crysword and used his direction sense to determine they were walking north. The circular area was about twenty yards across, and two more trails led out. One went to the north and one to the west.

On the east side of the clearing was a huge mound of blue crystal, with a dark opening at the base. The cave entrance was ten feet wide and a dozen feet high. The spire rising above it was not large compared to some others surrounding the area, and Bortis felt some relief. He had expected the tower of a wizard to be mysterious and grand. This was just another spire among hundreds. As he gazed at the entrance, he felt some unease. The opening was black and forbidding. He could easily imagine this was home to something dark and evil. Was something watching him? The prickly feeling reminded him of stepping through a qulan field, but his body wasn't affected. It was his mind, his soul. He remembered hearing someone say once that something felt like someone was walking on the site of their grave. He now knew what that person meant.

"This is it, huh?" he said. "Looks like a hole in the ground to me. Not some sorcerer's abode. Well, do we go in or what?" He strode toward the opening.

"I'd be careful—" said Angel, but it was too late.

There was a loud snap, and a blue spark struck Bortis square in the chest. He stepped backward, fell, and landed sitting on the ground.

"He has to invite us in," finished Angel.

"What was that? Are you alright, Bort?" cried Carimus as he sat on the ground, stunned.

"Are you okay, Bort?" asked Artos. He stepped forward to help Bortis to his feet. "Is it a qulan?" Artos looked at Angel. "I didn't know there were any others besides the one at Castle Draconis. How do we get in?"

"Yes," answered a voice from the darkness, "it is a qulan field. Castle Draconis isn't unique. There is a qulan at Starstone Tower as well, though it is a different type. There are several in the Fairborn demesnes as well. I am Donel, and only those I choose may enter the Crystal Cave."

A man with silvery-gray hair, a neatly trimmed mustache, and a goatee stepped into view. He wore a robe of black silken material and had piercing blue eyes. "Why are there only three of you? Prince Duka?" He looked at the group, a frown on his face.

"He's not here?" asked Carimus. "We were hoping he was."

"How could he be here? Didn't he flee the castle with you?"

"How do you know about us?" asked Bortis. "You seem to know a lot about it. A lot more than you should. Angel said you told her we were coming. How did you know? Tell us!" He placed his hand on the hilt of his sword.

"You must be Prince Bortis," he examined the group. "And

you, Prince Artos, and Prince Carimus. Angela and Joycel, I know well, of course. Who are your friends, Angela?"

"Answer me!" Bortis shouted and started forward. Artos caught his arm and held him from walking back into the qulan again.

"Bort. Calm down," said Artos, as Bortis glared, first at him and then Donel.

"Maybe he enjoys shocks and getting knocked down, Art," said Angel. She nodded respectfully to the Magic Man.

"Greetings, teacher. It is good to see you again. This is Sarah, who we call Vix, and Rachel. Before the trouble, they were living on neighboring farmsteads. They are my companions and members of my scouts."

"They are welcome." He looked at the brothers and said, "As are you, Prince Artos, Prince Bortis, and Prince Carimus." He nodded at each in turn. "I'm glad to put faces to your names. You must tell me where Duka is. But we need not stand here talking before my front door. I invite you all to my tower, to my home." Bort felt the static in his mind again. "Don't worry, Prince Bortis. It won't bite you again. Please follow me." He turned and strode back into the darkness.

CHAPTER NINE:

THE CRYSTAL TOWER

33

WITHIN
THE TOWER

ARTOS

5:00 p.m.

ARTOS LOOKED QUESTIONINGLY AT ANGEL. She nodded and gestured that he should proceed into the darkness after the Magic Man. There seemed to be nothing to do but to go in. Taking a deep breath and squaring his shoulders, he activated his direction sense and followed Donel.

Once inside, he realized it wasn't as dark as it seemed. A blueish twilight filled the tunnel. After a short corridor and a pair of modest stairways, the rough crystal passage had transformed into a square tunnel, ten feet tall and wide, which led to an archway with a massive oaken door. The door stood open, and the group walked inside. The room beyond was large and better-lit. Seven golden-colored wall sconces each held a pair of bright everlights, which reflected countless twinkling stars from the polished light-blue crystal walls and ceiling. A purplish rug, ten feet wide and twenty-five feet long, as if it were a giant welcome mat, ran across the center of the room to a long table against the far wall. Donel was standing a few feet inside, facing them.

"This is the cloakroom." He pointed to the wall to the west, lined with hooks. "You may hang your cloaks and jackets here." He pointed to a narrow table to the side. "You can place your packs there." He waited while they all complied. Bortis delayed until everyone else had hung up their outerwear, then hung his jacket next to Artos's.

Angel and the other girls also laid down their packs and bows.

"This is the first floor of the Crystal Tower. We are a dozen feet below the ground level here. There are cellars beneath, where I have my gardens. The common room, kitchen, freeze room, larder, and storage areas are on this floor, as is my bedroom. You are free to roam on this floor except for my room and the far storeroom. That room belongs to Liv when she chooses to sleep here. Come, I will give you the grand tour. Angel and Joy already know where everything is, of course."

After pointing out the other rooms, they ended in the commons. It was a large, carpeted room with a big wooden table set in the middle. There were nine chairs arranged around the table's perimeter, one at the head, two at the foot, and three along each side. Fireplaces in the north and west walls burned merrily, with well-stuffed chairs nearby and an oversized couch in front of the western one. Artos looked closer at one of the fireplaces, surprised as no wood was present to be consumed. The flames danced merrily above several crystal tubes that ran across the fireplace.

Donel noticed Artos examining them. "Flammable gas," he explained. "Piped in from somewhere underground. Gathering wood for the many hearths in the tower would be exhausting and time-consuming. There is no quanti-controlled central heating and cooling like at Castle Draconis. No need for it. The tower is large but nowhere near as big. There is a natural spring somewhere below as well. Water in the baths is quanti-controlled like you are used to. Vix, Rachel, Angel will show you how to adjust the temperature to your comfort. It may take a few lessons if you are not proficient in using quanti." He looked at the two girls and arched a brow. They both appeared uncomfortable, but nodded.

"Angel told us about it this morning before we left the nest," answered Vix. "Neither Rach nor I have been tested, so we will have to find out."

"Not tested?" asked Carimus. "Why not?"

"It's not uncommon for those living in the mountains away from the Valley, Cari," answered Artos. "Father talked about having the Church do more quanti-testing in the outlying areas, but Uncle Cameron said if the farmers aspired to be tested, they could come up into the Valley or go to a town in the lowlands. You know they prefer the Earth sect in the mountains, and druids don't do quanti-testing like the sky priests do. The druids test for abominations and look for the beast-born, but not for high quanti levels."

"Well, I think that's wrong, Art. I will change that," said Carimus, filled with self-importance, causing Artos to smile indulgently at his little brother.

"If you will follow me, we can go up to the upper level now," said Donel and walked over to where a pair of alcoves awaited in the northern wall. Each held a small stairway. The one on the left spiraled down, and the one on the right went up. He started up the stairs to the upper level, and the rest followed behind.

After a brisk climb, the stairs ended at a short hallway

that led south into a vast room, which caused Art to marvel at the sheer size. Bigger than the commons below, it was at least eighty feet long and wide. The ceiling was over a dozen feet above a gray floor, patterned with narrow black lines forming squares within squares. Towering bookcases running from floor to ceiling lined the walls. A multitude of everlights hung from the ceiling, giving the room a bright, cheerful glow, aided by an enormous fireplace in the southern wall. A square carpet occupied an area not far from the fire, with a large purple couch and seven armchairs grouped around a low wooden table with a polished light-blue surface. Scattered around the room were more than a dozen other armchairs, with another free-standing bookcase on the east side of the room.

"This is the library," said Donel.

"By the Sky!" exclaimed Carimus. "How many books do you have? This makes the library at the castle look tiny." Awe and wonder filled his voice.

"I never counted, Carimus. More than even I have read, and I have read many. There are books on music, language, history, and philosophy. Books naming the stars in the sky, the plants, and animals on the plains, and in the forests. Books detailing the birds of the air and fish in the waters. There is a catalog on those separate shelves listing books by subject and upon which shelf to find them. Without the catalog, it would be a task indeed to find anything. I will show it to you another time, and you may explore them to your heart's content."

"Thank you, sir. That's wonderful." Carimus gushed. Bortis made a derisive snort, although he looked interested at the mention of history.

"Please, everyone, find a seat and make yourselves comfortable," Donel said. "Before we dine, I wish to hear your tale of the last few days, Artos."

From the ring of armchairs positioned on the rug, Donel picked one before the fireplace, sat down, and gestured for them to pick a spot.

Carimus walked up to the low table and bent down to examine the surface.

"Yes, Carimus," said Donel, "the surface is a screen. It is keyed to me, however, and no one else can use it unless I choose to adjust it to them. Please sit down. We can discuss such things later."

"I hardly know where to start," said Artos as he sat across the circle from Donel.

Everyone except Bortis chose a spot and settled in. Bortis stood behind Artos' chair and remained standing with a scowl on his face. Artos looked back at his brother. "Don't hover there, Bort. It makes me nervous. You're acting like Uncle Cam when he was giving us a test, and he wanted to ensure we weren't peeking at each other's work. Sit down."

Bortis muttered a few words under his breath, sat down cross-legged on the floor next to Artos' chair, crossed his arms, a scowl furrowing his brow. "Better?" he growled.

Artos sighed. "Not really, but never mind. Be uncomfortable if you want. It's your choice."

"Begin at the start of your last day at the castle, Artos, and tell me everything you remember. Bortis, Carimus, if you have something to add that pertains to Artos's story, you may interject it, but I ask that you only add if you saw or felt something different. Please begin."

Artos took a deep breath and let it out slowly. "It was a hectic day. So much happened."

34

REVELATIONS

BORTIS

7:10 p.m.

"THEN WE BUILT A FIRE WITH THE WOOD, dried our clothes and—"

"I think you can stop there, Artos," said Donel. "You have an excellent memory. Do either of you have anything to add?" He glanced at Bortis and Carimus. The latter shook his head.

"I was riding a little way above and behind the rest," said Bortis. "When the lightning flashed, I didn't see it hit him, but it was closer to Duka than the rest of us. I think it got him. Cari says he can still feel him, but ..." he trailed off.

"But you didn't see them struck? They were just gone from your sight?"

There was an urgency in Donel's voice. *Why is he so concerned about Duka?* wondered Bortis. "That's what I said, wasn't it?" he said as he stood up, hostility back in his voice. "I say what I mean. What is it to you, anyway? Who are you? What are you up to? I want some answers." He glared at Donel.

Donel appraised Bortis for a moment, then turned his

attention to Angel. "I know you are no longer my student, Angela, and I cannot expect you to—"

"Teacher. When I left here two summers ago, I told you I had nothing more I needed to learn from you. I regret those hasty words. Oh, I know we did not part in anger, yet I feel I owe you an apology," Angel spoke from Donel's left.

"No, you owe me nothing of the sort. You needed to feel the wind and rain. To learn more about yourself. Everyone needs to do those things. If you are ready to learn more from me, you shall always have a place here, but you have a duty to your father that you must not neglect. You are his eyes and ears in Rainbow Valley. I do not think that now would be the time for you to return here as a student, but that time will come. Next spring, when the families return to the Valley, perhaps. We shall see." He smiled at her. "But now, I would ask a boon. There is some rabbit in the chill cabinet and vegetables as well. Do you think I could persuade the four of you to make a dinner for us this eve?"

"It was my turn for kitchen duty at the Nest," chimed in Vix. "So I can certainly help." Rachel nodded in agreement.

Angel jumped to her feet. "You have never cooked in a place such as this, Vix. You will be quite jealous when we finish, and you see how easy cooking can be."

The four girls headed to the stairs back down to the tower's first level, Angel still talking of the amazement Vix and Rachel were to feel once they learned the ease of quanti-cooking. They left Donel and the three brothers alone. Donel turned his attention back to Bortis.

"Let us get some things settled right now. You are a guest in my home, Bortis. I know you have been under a great deal of stress the last few days, but I will not tolerate any more rudeness. You may have been a pampered prince all your life, but now there are things that need to be done. I can and will help you and your brothers fix them. But I expect you to remember your manners and act in a fashion befitting a guest."

Bortis could feel the heat flush his face. "That's right! I am a prince, and Art is king. It is your duty to help us! Not to tell us what to do. We need supplies, and we need to make our way back home." He held out his left hand and strained for a moment. His crysword appeared in his clenched fist with a small pop.

Donel tilted his head and gazed at the angry prince. "Why are you so afraid of your sword, Bortis?" he asked gently.

"Afraid? I'm not afraid! How dare you speak to me that way!" shouted Bortis.

"Put. Your. Sword. Away," commanded Donel.

To Bortis's consternation, he found himself unable to resist Donel's words, and he thrust his crysword back into its sheath on his belt.

"Sorcery!" yelled Carimus, jumping to his feet, his emerald blade appearing in his hand.

Bortis felt Artos rise to his feet to stand beside him as well.

Donel looked at each of the three in turn. "There is no need for swords here. Put your sword away, Carimus."

Carimus looked wildly at Artos, unsure what to do, as Bortis tried futilely to draw his sword again.

"Put it away, Cari," said Artos, his eyes not leaving the face of Donel. "Who are you? What are you? What is going on?"

"As I told you," said Donel softly, "my name is Donel. I am the Earl High-Wizard of Veda, Donel deDraconis. At this moment, I am the highest-ranked lord in the Kingdom. We need to take steps to fix this situation. Now."

"LIAR!" shouted Bortis wildly, struggling to redraw his sword. "There is no High Wizard anymore. There hasn't been for three hundred years."

Donel fixed Bortis with a look that was almost pitying. Standing, he pulled back the sleeve of his black robe, revealing his upper right arm where a double-headed dragon's birthmark was plain to see. He held out his hand, and a sapphire crysword appeared in his grasp with a soft pop.

"Duke's birthmark," whispered Carimus, almost too softly to be heard, "and a blue-sword."

"Art, he's the traitor," said Bortis. "The one they disowned for refusing to help Alexavier against Tomung's rebellion in the Great War. You ... You should be dead, long ago."

Donel closed his eyes and shook his head. Without a sound, the sword in his hand disappeared. Carimus gasped. Donel turned to Artos. "I see this is going to be a long night." He looked back at Bortis. "If I release your compulsion, will you refrain from threatening me and learn some history before you act so rashly again?"

Bortis felt Artos's eye turn to him. "Bort, I think if he was going to hurt us, we would be powerless to stop him. Let's listen to what he has to say. Cari, put your sword away." He looked back at Donel. "Tirinvo told me father was dead, and I was to be king."

Slowly, Carimus slid his sword back into its sheath.

Donel sighed. "As of this morning, in all likelihood, except for Prince Duka, every living royal of House deDracconis is present in this room."

"You can't know that!" shouted Bortis. "Why would you say that?"

Donel sat back down with another sigh. "I have good reason

to believe so, Bortis. In a little while, I will show you. But first, it is time for you three to learn some history. There was a reason I could not go to aid Alexavier. That fool set in motion the acts that led to you being here now. Artos, until you are crowned and seated upon the dragon throne, you are not the king. You are the pretender to the throne, it's true. You were born with the crown birthmark. Is that not correct?"

Bortis stood numb as Artos nodded and then unbuttoned the flannel shirt he was wearing, exposed his right shoulder, and twisted it to better show the birthmark.

Donel nodded gravely. "I did not doubt you were who you claimed to be, Artos. Any of you. To me, your aura is more than enough. The moment you three passed through the qulan field, it was very apparent to me. You three were born to your destiny, and I was trained to sense such things. Long ago."

He shook his head. "I am afraid there are those who would be happy to see our House become extinct, Artos. Not from any personal hatred of you, but because they wish the power for themselves. What is worse, I believe there are other beings using those people. Others who do hate you, and all the Great Houses, as well. They would use your deaths to start an end to the Houses and to loose upon the world a terror that has not been seen for almost two thousand years."

"And just what would that be?" asked Bortis, disbelief dripping from his voice.

35

MORE IS REVEALED

ARTOS

7:30 p.m.

"Dinner!" called Vix as she walked into the library. "Your kitchen is a wonder, Magic Man! I wouldn't have believed what I saw if someone had told me about it." She looked at the group. "What's wrong? Isn't anyone hungry?"

"My history lesson can wait until after we have supped. You have traveled many miles today and are sure to be hungry," said Donel.

As if in answer, Bortis' stomach made a rumbling noise. Artos felt his own grumble in response. "Rabbit sounds good," he replied, and turned to follow Vix to the common room below. "Come on, Bort. Let's go eat."

Bortis looked as though he wanted to stay and argue, but his hunger won the battle of wills, and he turned and followed Vix to the stairs.

"Aren't you hungry, Cari?" asked Artos, when Carimus didn't move to follow his brothers. Looking back, Artos could see fear apparent in his eyes.

"What's wrong, Carimus?" said Donel. "I'm not a demon set to destroy you. I am who I say I am, your great-great-great-granduncle."

"How can this be? You look so young, and the Great War was long ago?"

"It is the magic of this tower, Carimus. Time passes, but does not affect those within its walls at nearly the same rate as those without. There are reasons for this, which I will explain later. But let us eat dinner. Come." Donel stood and Artos led Carimus to the stairs down to the common room below, where dinner awaited them.

At first, the dinner passed with little conversation except for requests for the salt to be passed or whether anyone wished for more gravy. Angel was the first to break the silence.

"Oh, I almost forgot, Teacher. I have something in my pack that I must show you. Remember, I told you of the harpy eagle which attacked Oswald?"

Donel nodded gravely, and she continued. "Later, we were ambushed by the same bird. It swooped in to attack me, but Artos knocked me aside and took a nasty gash from its talons. Cat and Joy killed the foul thing with their archery. It crashed to the ground and lay there, dying. Cat called me over to show me. It wore a band. There was a shiny black band around its ankle just above the claws."

"Did you retrieve it?" asked Donel, consternation in his voice. "You brought it here?"

"No, well … sort of. When the creature died, the band dissolved into dust. I gathered it up and put it in a vial. That's what I mean to show you. The dust, the remains of the band."

"It turned to dust? Like a crysword when the owner dies?"

asked Carimus.

"I gathered up the dust with the blade of my dagger and put it in an empty vial. As soon as we got here, I was going to show you. I am sorry."

"I will want to see it, of course. But, if it dissolved, I fear there will not be much I can learn from it. But the knowledge that it existed is disturbing news. It confirms my gravest fears. There are fell and mighty foes behind these acts." He fell silent for a moment, then continued. "I had thought perhaps the harpy might have been in the service of House deAnson. They have some strength in the nature quans. So do House deDarrellyel and House deSpryngdal, but they would not use birds to spy and attack. No Great House has the knowledge to craft black crystal and use it to bind creatures to its will. Those who have such knowledge are terrible in power and should be feared. They are the ones behind the attack upon Castle Draconis and the murder of your family, Artos. I am sure of that now. I had dared to hope that the attacks were from a different source. Such wills and egos which crave power never want to share it and do not work well together. We must act as though the worst has befallen us and strive to squelch their plans and quickly place Artos back in his rightful place."

"Haven't I said so?" asked Bortis. "We must return there at once!"

"And then what, Prince Bortis?" said Donel. "Will you just order them to leave? To run away from your terrible might? Will they cower before you and beg you to spare their miserable lives?"

"We will gather the other Great Houses behind us, of course. We will march to the front gates, open them, and the three of us will invite the guards from the other Houses in, and we shall slay the foul beasts. I don't know how they ever got inside, but they caught our guards by surprise in the dead of night after most had been celebrating the Spare's birthday and … and… what else can we do?"

"Prince Bortis. How many of the Great Houses do you think would trust you to lead their men into battle? How often have you led troops in combat? Just how many troops do you think there are in the King's Valley at this time, anyway? How many House guards must remain at their own castles' defenses, and how many could be spared to help you?" Donel gazed at Bortis with a slight, sad smile on his lips as he awaited an answer.

"It's their duty!" said Bortis with heat in his voice. "Art is High King. They have no choice."

"Would they follow you and him? Or would they say, 'Count Eagleton has more experience in these matters. He should lead the troops. Or Count Penrodyn, though he is getting on in years, should be in command.' Or would they say, 'We must convene a council of the Great Houses and vote for a war leader?' And having done this, they would say, 'Artos is too young to be king as yet. Oh, we shall make him the figurehead and have a council to rule the land until he is older.' Would they not? Once you let that dog run loose, you will have a very hard time putting him back in the kennel. An unfortunate accident to Artos and the council would control Veda ever after. Or so they would think." Donel pushed his plate away and looked hard at Bortis. "Artos cannot appear weak and beg for help from the Houses. Don't you see Bortis? That path leads to disaster. He must first recover his place, and only then can he call upon the rest of the Houses to finish whatever is starting now."

"But how?" asked Artos. "There are only three of us now that Duke is missing, and even if he wasn't, what could the four of us do against a horde of Beastmen?"

"Artos, you have me. I am the Earl High Wizard of Veda."

"You?" sneered Bortis. "The coward who refused to aid his king in the Great War of Rebellion? Why would you help now? Except to make Art your puppet." Bortis pushed back from the table, stood up, and glared at Donel.

Artos could see the pain on Donel's face as his brother spoke, and he felt he should intervene. But what if Bort spoke the truth?

"Why should we trust you?" Bortis continued. "Count Eagledon is to be Art's father-in-law. Count Penrodyn is our grandfather. I know they would help. It's their duty!"

A new voice cut in. "Count Stephan wants power, Bort. He wants Art as his son-in-law and to be a shadow power behind the throne. You can't trust him." It was Angel, and she looked angry.

All three bothers stared at her. Bortis was the first to recover. "Ha! How would you know what Count Stephan wants?"

"He's my uncle," she declared. "My mother was his twin and told me so. He and my grandfather, Reginald, planned for her to marry Aaron, but your uncle Bretton got involved, and things became a mess. My mother was the firstborn twin, and they reasoned the only way to keep her from becoming the head of the House was to marry her to Crown Prince Aaron."

"Was his twin?" said Carimus.

"She died. Two winters ago."

"I'm sorry. Our mother's dead too," he said sadly.

"Then you are the rightful head of House deEagledon," exclaimed Artos. "You could be the Countess."

"Why would I want to be? Except for House deSpryngdal, women don't head the Houses. It's been three generations since any other House has had a woman lead."

"It wouldn't matter," protested Artos.

"House Anson was the last and the Counts all feared her. Years before that, House deDarrellyel had a countess, but males dominate the firstborn in that line. House Herndar hasn't had a female head in over a hundred years. My mother told me she thought they found a way to control the sex of their children and shared it with Anson. My mother was first born, but my grandfather favored his son and wanted Stephan to follow him as Count."

Artos sat stunned. He'd never thought of such a thing. The idea was abhorrent.

"But my mother learned their plans. She saw what was happening between Aaron and Bretton. She overheard Reginald and my uncle bemoaning the fact that Bretton had interfered with their plans. So, she escaped and ran away. She met my father, and they fell in love."

Angel's voice turned bitter. "He took her to his people, and they rejected her. My Fairborn grandfather told his son he would disinherit him if he married my mother against his wishes. But he did anyway. So, King Farnir disowned him and named his younger brother the crown prince. Tirinvo never turned on his brother, though. They are still close. Why do you think your uncle declared my father an outlaw when all he ever did was defend the people of the mountains against the real outlaws and the Beastmen?!"

Bortis stared at her, speechless.

"That's why he didn't answer Duke," gasped Artos in surprise.

"What? Why wouldn't who answer Duke? What are you talking about, Art?" said Bortis, looking bewildered as he gazed back and forth between Artos and Angel.

"Prince Tirinvo," explained Artos. "He said Taur and Jaek had been his bodyguards since he became crown prince. Then Duke asked him if he wasn't always crown prince, and he changed the subject."

"The twins were my father's bodyguards first," said Angel. "They're my second cousins."

"Do you see why Artos cannot entrust his throne and crown to the Great Houses, Bortis?" asked Donel. "The Darrell would support his claim, I'm sure. House deSpryngdal as well and House dePenrodyn most likely. But Count Estel is a conservative old man and would feel Artos would need strong supervision until he has proven himself. House deHerndar and House deAnson have wanted more voice in how things are done for a long time. Angela has told you of the desires of House deEagledon. I do not doubt Count Stephan would back your claim as long as he is to be your father-in-law. I also do not doubt he would say you will need a firm hand to guide you. With his being that hand."

Artos stood up. "So, it's hopeless? Well, maybe that's good. I am not sure I even wish to be king. To have a marriage forced upon me with someone not of my choosing. I have sat with father at Council meetings. I can't control people like that. Count Boris Anson always talks to me as if I were a child, and Count Estel does pretty much the same. Count Charlton Herndar just ignores me. And now Count Stephan acts like I'm already married to Elaine, and I have never even met anyone from House deSpryngdal. The only one I like is the Darrell, Count Glendon." He slowly sat back down and stared at his empty plate.

Bortis pushed back from the table and jumped to his feet.

"Art, it is your duty! You bear the mark of the crown. You can't run from that."

Artos just shook his head silently as Carimus sat with his mouth wide open in shock.

"Artos, it is far from hopeless." Donel gazed at Artos with sympathy. "Yes, things are not looking good right now. But for you to give up would be far worse for Veda. A council running the land would be a disaster. Things that needed to be done would not get done. Things that should never happen would certainly happen. I know all too well hard choices are difficult, but running away is not an answer you can afford. Not if you care about Veda. The Glory Road is a hard road to walk, but sometimes hard choices are all we have. You are Artos Draconis. You are destined to be king. I believe this with all my heart and soul. You must believe in yourself. You have your brothers. Would you let them down?"

Artos sat motionless in the uncomfortable stillness that followed, staring at his empty plate.

Carimus broke the silence. "I believe in you, Artie! Duke does too, wherever he is. I will do whatever I can to help!"

"You know I have your back, brother," added Bortis softly for once.

"But what can I do?" Artos asked quietly. "The whole thing is such a mess." He raised his head and looked at his brothers and then at Donel.

"The first thing we do," said Donel, "is to go back to the library, and I will explain to you just how I can help. Then we shall plan our first step. All journeys begin with a single step."

"Rach and I will clean up down here," said Vix, and she stood up and started to gather the dirty dishes.

Donel shook his head. "No. I want you to come too. The

Daughters have a part to play in this as well. Just what? I am not sure, but I feel it is so. Leave the dishes for now. All of you go up to the library. I will join you shortly. Go."

Joy, Vix, and Rachel looked at Angel as Artos and his brothers stood up. She shrugged and then nodded that they should proceed. Joy led the way, with Bortis and Carimus following the three girls up the stairs. Donel took the other set of stairs, the ones leading down to his cellars.

Angel stopped Artos before he could follow. "Art, why did you knock me out of the way of the harpy?"

He looked at her with a question in his eyes. "Why? Because you didn't see it, and it would have injured you. Killed you even. What else could I do?"

She smiled a strange half-smile. "And that's why you should be the king. Carimus would have yelled at me to move," she chuckled. "Bort might have let it strike me and tried to escape in the aftermath. But you? You did what you believed was the right thing to do. Not thinking, just acting, to do what needed to be done. Your heart knows what you need to do. Don't let your head try to talk you out of it." She turned and walked up the stairs to the library, leaving him standing there thinking about her words and those earnest green eyes and how lovely they were.

36

DUKA

ARTOS

8:15 p.m.

A few moments after Artos settled into one of the comfortable chairs in the library, Donel followed him into the room, carrying a tray with a large jug and eight glasses. He set his burden down on one of the low tables and pulled the cork from the jug. He poured some of the beverage into each of the glasses and motioned for everyone to take a glass.

"Cider," he announced. "It should still be good. I cast a preservation spell." He sniffed the aroma from the glass he held and nodded as if satisfied.

"Help yourself," said Donel. "There's plenty for all, so don't be shy." He settled back into his chair.

"Bort, you asked me earlier why I thought there were no more members of House deDraconis within the castle. Now I will show you.

"The qulan field that surrounds the castle prevents scrying. Except for the Hall of Mirrors, which is open to the screens in the relays, Castle Draconis is virtually spy proof. With one exception. Cryswords. Not just any cryswords, but those swords belonging to members of a family can be detected by others of the same family. Those are connected by blood. Those of the same color sword, that is, those with similar regalos, can hone in very closely. Provided you can scry. I have that ability."

"So, we just take your word?" said Bortis. "You scried and there is no one there." He snorted in disbelief.

"Bort, back off," said Artos. "I want to hear what he has to say." Bortis just shook his head in disgust.

"Normally I would expect you to take my word, Prince Bortis. But I understand you do not know me and have no reason to trust what I say. So I will give you a demonstration."

Donel held his right hand before him and made a slight gesture towards the table in the middle of the circle of chairs, and the light-blue surface glowed.

"I knew it was a screen," said Carimus. "I never saw one used as a table before."

"Cari, hush," said Artos. Carimus gave his brother a hurt look.

Donel gestured and from the screen an obelisk of blue crystal sprang up, rising four feet above the surface of the table. "My crystal tower has a similar qulan field, but as we are inside, it wouldn't block me, but this is just a demonstration. If I was outside and I wanted to know if a relative of mine was inside with a red crysword, it would look like this." Donel pointed and a bright red spot appeared, looking as though it was within the crystal structure. "Or a green sword." Donel motioned again and a green spot appeared beside the red one. "Or white." A white spot appeared next to the others. "And of course blue." A blue spot appeared lower down, away from the others. "My sword is in my room on the lower level," Donel explained.

Donel waved his hand, and the vision disappeared.

"Now at Castle Draconis." He made a gesture with both hands and a miniature version of their home grew out of the screen, rising six feet into the air.

"I shall now scry for any red swords in the Castle." Donel moved his hand and concentrated for a moment. Nothing happened. "Green." Again, nothing. "And white." Artos held his breath, but nothing appeared. "There are no cryswords of my blood in the castle," said Donel sadly.

"Try blue," cried Carimus. "There is a crysharp in the Hall of Mirrors, a blue one!"

"That was mine, Prince Carimus. King Alexavier thought he could keep my crysword away from me by placing it in a block of leaded glass. He simply showed his own ignorance, as I could remove it or replace it at will. He painted over the screen, which was connected to this tower, which only blinded him, not me. I let him think he had some advantage. He was a fool."

"You can change the shape of your sword?" asked Artos. "Uncle Cam said that was just legend."

"I'm afraid your great-uncle was not as well versed in the use of quanti as he thought he was."

Carimus opened his mouth to protest as Donel waved his hand, and Castle Draconis disappeared.

"Duka!" shouted Carimus. "You're related to Duka! Can you find him?"

Donel looked surprised. "Carimus, of course! I cannot look for Duka, but I may be able to locate his crysword. I should have thought of that from the start. Sometimes I get too distracted to think of all things."

Donel stood beside the screen, staring down at it, and

concentrated. Everyone crowed around the table.

The great screen glowed with the soft blue light. Donel closed his eyes with a look of concentration on his face. Everyone watched the great screen with hope. A bright blue spot of light suddenly flashed into existence on the screen! A picture formed, and a room came into view. A bed with tall wooden posts stood in the center of the view. Hanging from a peg on the post was a sword in a sheath.

"That's Duke's room at home," cried Carimus.

"That's the new sheath I gave him for his birthday," muttered Bortis at the same moment.

A sick feeling filled Artos' heart. He looked at Donel. "He didn't take his sword." The look on Donel's face was one Artos would never forget. "He had just bonded that day. He wasn't in the habit yet of strapping it on every morning. I should have checked. I should have made sure he was wearing it. Cari, Donel, this is my fault!"

Angel laid her hand on his shoulder. "You were all rushing to escape, Artos. You said. Tirinvo was hurrying you all to the eagles. Don't blame yourself. Surely, he will summon it."

"He hadn't learned how to summon it yet," said Artos in a flat, dull voice. "And he promised father. He promised he wouldn't attempt to use any magic with his sword until he was trained. Not only is he lost, but he is lost without his sword. Oh, Duke."

There was a long silence as everyone tried to digest this latest development.

37

HISTORY

ARTOS

8:45 p.m.

"Okay, we didn't find where Duka is, but we still need a plan," said Bortis. He looked at Donel. "You said you could help us. How?"

Artos looked at Bortis in disbelief. "Bort ..." For some reason, Bort looked happier than he had in days.

"Look Art, he had his sword less than a day. He didn't know how to use it. This isn't as bad as you are making it."

"How can you say that?" yelled Carimus. "What's wrong with you?"

"Cari, think. What does seeing that sword tell you?"

"It tells me that Duke is lost, and alone, and he hasn't even got his sword!"

Artos suddenly realized what his brother meant. "Cari, he's alive! His sword is in his room. It didn't turn to dust."

"Oh ..." Carimus fell speechless, but had a new look of hope.

Donel directed everyone to sit back down.

"First you need to understand what you are facing," said Donel. "For that, you need some history. What do you know of Demigoran?"

"I thought you said history," said Bortis. "Demigoran is a myth. Something for when everyone is sitting around the campfire telling scary stories. A tale to tell children when they misbehave. You can't be serious."

"I was afraid that would be your reaction, Bortis." Donel glanced at Carimus, who was looking uncomfortable. "Carimus?"

"Well ... Uncle Cameron told me that there probably was something behind the myth, some horrible war leader who committed atrocities, so the legends transformed him into a demon. But since it was back at the dawn of history, we would never know the truth behind the myth. Like The Reckoning."

"Uncle Brett told me it was most likely pure nonsense," said Bortis. "And The Reckoning was some powerful quantimasters who almost destroyed everything. The church said it was the Sky Father and Earth Mother to keep the people in their place."

Carimus looked horrified. "Bort! You attend church every week. How can you say that?"

"This isn't about the Church," Donel cut in to halt the argument between the two brothers. "Please be quiet and let me show you what I know. I do not know everything about the time before The Reckoning or what exactly The Reckoning was, but I know some things and will tell you now. Please attend, and if you have questions, I will try to answer them."

"We live in the second age of Man," began Donel.

"More myths," muttered Bortis.

"Bort, shut up," said Carimus. Everyone in the room looked at the younger brother in surprise. Artos was secretly pleased at the shocked expression on Bort's face from the unexpected force in Cari's words.

"I want to hear this." The look on Carimus' face was a mixture of surprise and fear, as if he didn't believe he had just told Bort to be quiet.

"Thank you, Carimus," said Donel. "As I was saying. We live in the second age of Man. All that is generally known of the first age is indeed myth and legend," he nodded to Bortis and continued. "I had been taught a few things, but the assassination of my mentor, Denaryl deDraconis, interrupted my education. I had to leave off my studies and return here immediately and step into Denar's role. Fortunately, the assassin did not breach the qulan here. Not from a lack of trying, I assure you. Over a score of dead Beastmen lay strewn before the entrance, and someone was still trying to breach the door when I approached.

"But I stray from my tale. As I was saying, what we know of the first age is that it ended with savage wars. The Quanti wars. Arising from the ruins of those wars were fearsome beings. Wielders of quanti in ways that are unknown today. Dark and loathsome ways.

"The mightiest of these beings was Demigoran, and he claimed the world was his to do with as he liked. Indeed, if not for the two other fell beings who opposed him, he might easily have enslaved all our ancestors. Those two also thought they were more fit to rule the world, so they contested one another as to who would be master.

"Mighty Tiameng sought to claim the world, remove men, and replace them with those she held dear; the dragons and dragon-kin."

"Dragon-kin?" asked Carimus. "I thought those were fairy tales."

"They existed, Carimus, though never in any great number. None were known to have survived the Reckoning."

"Yeenaghou sought to use men and beast alike as his soldiers. He was the weakest of the three, but his legacy, the Beastmen, still plague the world to this day."

"The Three battled and lay waste to much of the world. Were they indeed demons? I cannot say, but I was taught that they were far more powerful than any man or woman before or after, and they were not alone."

Bortis snorted in disbelief. Donel chose to ignore him.

"No one knows the original purpose of this tower or even when it was constructed. It became a very special library, among other things. It is connected to the relay screens which serve the Council. Perhaps it's even the base for the relays, I do not know. It has a special connection with Starstone Tower. Many years after Starstone became the Wizard's school, instructors recorded lessons which could be replayed on the screens there. But those lessons are stored here. The head of the school often was forced to remain separate from the school itself and stay here with other duties, but he was always in close communication with the school. Before the school was shut down." Donel sighed.

"After Alexavier and his son closed Starstone and regulated the teaching of quanti-magic to the Sky Sect, I found myself with a great deal of free time on my hands. I decided to organize the lessons, catalog them for the day the school would reopen. For I was sure it would. It was then I made some interesting discoveries."

Artos felt an urge to comfort Donel. He still felt the sting of being cut off from his family. Artos could see the pain on his face. Hear it in his voice.

"I found records which predate the school. I have no idea

who recorded them or when, but it is a certainty they come from a time before the Reckoning."

Bortis crossed his arms and sat back in his chair, his skepticism evident.

Donel glanced at Bort, then made another gesture and an image rose from the screen. Faint and blurry, as if seen from a distance, the figure before them was not human. Two heads sat upon muscular shoulders and there was a pair of horns sprouting one to each side. The monster wielded a massive double-bladed ebony axe and was engaged in destroying something with it. Artos realized the creature was destroying a castle. The creature was a giant!

"Demigoran." Donel's voice was barely more than a whisper, but it rang in Artos's mind as if he had shouted it. Carimus gasped.

As Artos watched, the drama portrayed above the screen, the gate to the castle opened and men poured forth to battle the monster, looking like squirrels attempting to confront a bear. The monster's heads tilted back as if in laughter, then it shrank until it was merely double the size of those who swarmed around it. The creature then mowed down wave after wave of the hapless men, his axe cleaving them effortlessly.

Donel waved his hand, and the scene changed. A muscular, gray-skinned creature with two heads loomed over five figures clad in gray hooded cloaks, bowing down before it as if in worship. The monstrous figure held an ebony axe in one hand and a ball of glowing energy in the other. Where the creature's eyes should have lain were folds of wrinkled skin, but it was not blind, for in the middle of each of the monstrous foreheads was a single eye, one blue, the other brown.

"There were five who followed Demigoran. The Abominations,

terrible beings who served as his minions. Powerful, cunning, cruel, and delighting in death and destruction. They were named Mohattri, Babich, Kargyn, Anndr, and Tomung. Yes, that Tomung, whose head your great-great-grandfather so foolishly hung on his wall as a trophy and started the chain of events that led to your being here today."

Donel made a dismissive gesture, and the scene faded.

"Men were no more than sport to Demigoran. His true foe was Tiameng. Their battles lay much of the land to waste while Yeenaghou sulked in the shadows and sniped at them both. There are a few other records like this, but I will forgo showing them to you. It would serve little purpose save to leave you ripe for nightmares.

"There are also bits and pieces of recorded words of those survivors of this terrible age. From them, I have learned as much as may be known of the beginnings of our age."

Donel took a long drink of cider, then looked around. Carimus looked pale. Bortis still had a skeptical scowl. The Daughters glanced at each other, then turned back to Donel.

Artos met his gaze. "What happened to them? How did we escape destruction at their hands?"

"It was the Reckoning! Wasn't it?" asked Carimus. "The Sky Father intervened to save us."

"No Carimus, the Reckoning came later. The Gods waited to see how men would deal with Demigoran. And deal with him they did." Donel leaned back, paused a moment to collect his thoughts, then began.

"In the shadows, some men, powerful in the ways of the quanti, refused to serve as pawns in these terrible battles. They joined together and built an armory. Starstone Tower, hidden in the Mountains of Myst. They worked there to build weapons to use against the power-crazed Demigoran and Tiameng. They built strongholds using the quanti, then would attack one of the demons with the new weapon. Time after time, a new weapon would be designed, built, and installed at a new stronghold. Then they would attack. Time after time, the new strongholds fell."

"Castle deDraconis withstood the attack?" asked Bortis.

"Castle deDraconis never had one of the new weapons installed. After many failures, the quantimasters decided to change tactics. Instead of a weapon, they designed a trap, a trap of quanti-crystal, a trap which would be a prison. Choosing a time when Demigoran and Tiameng were weakened from battling each other, they lured Demigoran into the Mountains of Myst, sprang their trap and imprisoned him in a crystal prison, the Hellesgate. Then they turned their newest weapons against the weakened Tiameng, hoping to destroy her. But she was not destroyed. Instead, she fled off across the sea to the far north. As for Yeenaghou, they believe he was attempting to assassinate the weakened Tiameng and was destroyed in the fire meant for her. They believed the fear of being trapped like her foe kept Tiameng away for a time, and now she is sleeping In a prison formed as a part of The Reckoning somewhere in the north of Renn.

"Then, the people who had trapped Demigoran and caused Tiameng to flee found themselves the masters of Veda. They divided the lands into their own separate kingdoms. Shortly thereafter, they were battling among themselves, each group striving to master the rest. Soon they became no better than those they had deposed. The lands were again being despoiled, the strong were preying on the weak. Some men took weapons forged to be used against Tiameng and turned them on other men. The high Valley became the Kingdom of the family Darrellyel. They captured the Armory of Starstone and closed the highlands to all but their clan and stayed out of the wars in the lowlands. The Fairborn, believing humankind insane, withdrew to the lands of the southeast, thinking men would destroy themselves. The Forge folk soon followed suit and burrowed under the Sierra Mountains to the southwest to build the Kingdom of Deepearth. In the lowlands, men battled on, each group vowing to be supreme. Quantimasters caused floods and fires, avalanches, and lightning strikes. Then, one day, it was as if the earth and sky said, 'Enough!' and the result was The Reckoning. Rocks fell out of the sky, and the earth swallowed cities, but it was only the kingdoms of men that were targeted. The Fairborn and the Forge folk witnessed the destruction from their strongholds and were untouched by the devastation. They thought it was undoubtedly the end of men.

"It was then, when all seemed lost, that the forefather of our House, Austin Draconis, arose from the rubble. With his three brothers, he brought forth a message from the Four."

Donel moved his hands again and the images of four men arose above the screen, each with a birthmark of House deDraconis on their forearm. "They each bore a mark upon their arm. Birthmarks to show their destiny. The crown, sword, star, and double-dragon. They had the first cryswords and though there were those who doubted their message, none could deny the destruction that had ravaged the Lowlands."

"Where did they get their swords?" asked Artos.

"There was no word of that. I sought that knowledge, but never was rewarded with an answer." Donel shrugged. He waved his hands, and the images vanished.

"It is told that one group defied their words and attempted

to ambush and murder the four brothers, but as they lay in wait, preparing their ambush, a star fell from the sky and utterly destroyed them. After that, people listened and when Austin told how the lands would be divided, and the power shared, none dared say nay. They renamed the uplands of the Darrellyel family The King's Valley, and the lands there were divided among what then became the Great Houses. They also redistributed the lowlands, with House deDarrellyel given a large demesne to repay them for what they had given up in the valley.

"The brothers traveled to what had been called Crag Castle and found it had become attuned to them with the qulan field set to their blood. The youngest of the brothers, David deDraconis, he of the double-dragons, went across Loch O' Wrens to the Armory and founded the school of magic at Starstone Tower. But he was not to dwell there long, for he was destined to be the first master of this, the crystal tower.

"The next youngest, Charles, he of the star, built the Cathedral of the Four at the mouth of the river Silver and the city of Phoenix grew up around it.

"Austin then began and oversaw the building of what is now the High Kingdom of Veda. He sent his final brother, Braedon, he of the sword, as his emissary, first to the Forge-folk of Deep Earth and then to Fairinlan of the Fairborn and told them the words of the Four. Having witnessed what had come before, they swore their allegiance to the High King as separate lands with their own rule and ways."

Donel stopped and refilled his glass and drank deeply, then looked around at his audience. "But enough of that for now. The history of Veda is fascinating, but that is all we need to speak of those days. I shall now come back to a time closer to our day.

The time of the Great War, House deYung's rebellion."

Donel cleared his throat. "Back when I was young, there was often strife between the Great Houses. Feuds and raids between Houses were not unknown. They settled some disagreements with duels between House champions. They settled others with harsher means; an agreed upon force of each House, or Houses would meet on the field of battle and fight until one side was forced to surrender, or sometimes wiped out to the last man. Duels between individuals were common. For some slight, real or imagined, two men would settle their honor in a duel with pre-agreed upon terms, sometimes to the very death. Only two Houses refrained from such conduct, House deSpryngdal and House deYung. The two lowest in rank.

"Both Houses were known for their secretive natures and kept very much to themselves. Neither House had a large presence in the King's Valley, and House deSpryngdal was secluded in the Spider Peaks in the northwest corner of the lowlands. House deYung complained often that House deDarrellyel and House deHerndar were poaching from their lands, yet never offered evidence in a court of grievance at the King's palace in Phoenix.

"I was not the keeper of this tower before the murder of Denar. I was his apprentice and watched over the Tower when he was away visiting the court at Phoenix or Castle Draconis. Or at Starstone Tower. He was dean of the Mage's school and as such spent much time there, but he was the warder of the Crystal Tower and by the law of Austin Draconis, this tower may not be left unattended. When I was away at Fairinhorst, he stayed here, alone. It was then he was murdered. I was far away, but my teacher felt his death and sent me back here with all haste. Prince Meldien of the Fairborn gave me use of his Eagle,

Cloudracer, and I was back here in a matter of hours, but it was far too late for my master.

"When I returned, I saw a tiny figure in gray scuttle off. I have no doubt judging from its aura that it was an Abomination, one of the Five. I might have given chase, although such would have doubtlessly been folly and perhaps was the hope of the creature. What stopped me was the sight of Denar, face down in the dirt near the doorway. I hoped he was not yet dead. But indeed, he was and had been for hours. I carried his body inside the Crystal Cave and examined him. At first, I saw no wound that would have proven fatal, but there was a small hole and a few drops of blood in the middle of his chest. Something the size of a small nail had pierced his body, into his heart. It had passed right through the bone in the middle of his chest. Only a weapon made of crystal could have made such a clean hole and killed so quickly. There was no sign of a struggle or resistance, so he was likely to have been slain instantly. No normal blade was the murder weapon. The hole was too small.

"It was then the treachery of House deYung was exposed. Within a week of Denar's death, the war began. A small army of Beastmen swept across the heath before Blachaas and began to ravage the King's Valley. This was merely a feint as it turned out and had not luck been on our side, things might well have been a disaster. King Alexavier's war leader Bethel led the combined forces of the Great Houses in the Valley against this force while Alexavier returned to Phoenix and rallied an army to ride to the Valley to destroy the threat. While he was there, he contacted me via the screens and told me to join Bethel in the Valley, for they had learned an Abomination was leading the Beastmen raiders and few were they who could withstand his magic. I was forced to tell him I could not, although I greatly desired to do so. King Austin's Law is very clear. The Crystal Tower cannot be left unattended, and I had no successor.

"Alexavier commanded me to break the Law, claimed he had that right. I had to respectfully refuse. He flew into a rage and called me 'coward' and 'traitor,' just as you have done, Prince Bortis. He would not listen when I tried to explain that Austin's law forbade me to leave here."

Donel tried to keep the bitterness from his voice, but it was plain to Artos that even now, after three centuries, it still burned in his heart to be so branded.

"But didn't you just tell us that the Beastmen died trying to pass the qulan here?" demanded Bortis. "He was your king. He commanded your aid."

"Bortis, why are you here today instead of at Castle Draconis?" asked Donel quietly.

"We were driven … that is, the Beastmen were …" Bortis stopped, confusion clearly visible on his face.

"As I told you, an Abomination was attempting to breach the qulan when I returned here. Should I have left and given it free rein to keep trying? What I didn't tell you was the attacks that took place later. Those twenty odd Beastmen were just a drop in the bucket of what was to come. This tower's defenses were tested many times over during Tomung's Rebellion.

"I did what I could for my nephew. There are ways to see with the eyes of others. No, Angela, I do not mean enslaving them with magical bands, as was done with that harpy eagle." He quickly spoke when Angel stirred uneasily.

"I learned long ago how to see using the eyes of others without harming them and ways to nudge them to look where I needed them to see. Tell me, Bortis, did your Uncle Bretton have any falconers in his troops?"

Bortis looked startled. "No. Why would he? He didn't hunt for pleasure while on patrol."

Donel sighed. "So much is lost. Much more than I had believed and more everyday it seems. I did not mean a falconer who uses a bird to hunt. In Alexavier's army, and Bethel's too, there were soldiers with quanti links to falcons to use for reconnaissance. Knowing your enemy's whereabouts can be the difference between winning and losing a battle.

"I had been using an eagle to watch the battles in the King's Valley. It didn't appear the enemy there wanted to stand and fight. They merely circled around and around the valley, causing mayhem and drawing my nephew Bethel's forces to chase after them. This made me curious why. So I flew higher and wider and when passing high above the beach of the Dragon Sea at the place they call The Giant's Dance, I saw a very disturbing sight. The plains there were filled with Beastmen. And worse, they were divided into three groups, each led by an Abomination. One group was waiting along the shore, and another was already hiding in the vale on both sides of the road that leads to the Valley. The third and largest group was hiding in the forest near the ford that crosses the river Mendos at the mouth of the vale.

"It was easy to discern their plan. They would let Alexavier charge to meet the Beastmen already in the Valley and he would be ambushed, his army split in half with one Abomination attacking their rear, another their middle, and another coming out of the woods to attack the foremost troops. I imagine the Beastmen in the Valley would then stop their flight and turn to battle Bethel's troops.

"I had no way to pass this news to my nephew, but I could commandeer one falcon in his troop. This I did. I was forced to take more control than I wished, for the bird was faithful to its quanti-handler and I had to force my will upon it. I gained control of the bird and flew it above the major group of Beastmen and the Abomination there, then released control back to the handler. When he regained control, the enemy's troops were there for him to see. He made his way to his king and informed him of the ambush. Alexavier grasped what needed to be done and led a charge straight across the ford of the Mendos and took the enemy by surprise. He engaged the Abomination Tomung, still wearing the colors of House deYung. They battled, and with his crysword, he beheaded the foul creature.

"If only he had acted wisely then, things might be very different today."

"What do you mean?" asked Bortis. "He killed the leader and then they routed the rest. He chased them back to the eastern barrens with their tails between their legs like whipped curs."

"I know that is the way you were told it happened, Prince Bortis. But I believe the other two Abominations, seeing their leader bested and their ambush foiled, retreated to regroup, rather than stay and fight. Yes, they lost a battle, but you are dealing with creatures to whom the passing of a century is no more than the passing of a year to you or me.

"King Alexavier should have destroyed Tomung, but instead of burning the creature and spreading the ashes far and wide. He threw the body in the river Mendos and took the head home as a trophy."

"So what? It was dead, wasn't it?" cried Bortis.

"Bort. Duke believed that the head wasn't dead, remember?" interjected Artos.

Bortis snorted. "Duka is just a kid, Art. It gave him

nightmares when he was little. That's all."

"You can't kill an Abomination that easily, Bortis. When my brother Caerwyn saw the head, he advised Alexavier to burn it, but our nephew was too arrogant. He wanted the world to see his prize, a trophy of his victory over an Abomination. He refused to allow the head to be harmed. Caerwyn conferred with me, using the screen in the Hall of Mirrors. I told him to have Alex place the head in a sealed jar of salt water to cure it, while I tried to convince my nephew of the error of keeping such a prize. He grew so angry with me, he painted over the screen that was linked to this tower. As if that solved anything except him seeing me." Donel shook his head.

"A few days later, Caerwyn was visited by a Fairborn who brought him a collar made of silver-crystal. He placed the collar about what was left of the neck of Tomung, and they mounted it in the Great Hall above Alexavier's throne."

"Where it still sits to this day," said Bortis, pride evident in his voice.

"Does it?" said Donel. "Can you be sure it is still on the wall and the collar is still in place? Frankly, I doubt it. I doubt it very much. My guess is the primary aim of the attack on Castle Draconis was to rescue that trophy and the death of your family was secondary. Oh, mistake it not, they want you dead. Of that there is no doubt, but they want Tomung revived most of all."

"What would happen if the crystal collar were removed?" asked Carimus.

"Have you begun your instruction as a healer, Carimus?" asked Donel.

"Not yet," he replied. "I am to begin when I am ordained as a disciple in the Church. I'm only an acolyte now."

Donel nodded. "Have any of you ever witnessed a priest treat a lost limb?"

Angel raised her hand. "I've seen a druid heal one of my father's men after he lost a finger. Would that be the same?"

"Yes, what was the result?"

"The finger grew back. Today you would never know he lost it."

Artos looked at Donel with horror. "You don't mean ...?"

"I am not positive, Artos, but I fear the primary reason for the attack upon Castle Draconis was to retrieve the head of Tomung and then to regrow his body."

"But how could they even get inside?" ranted Bortis. "We have always been told it was impossible for those not loyal to the House to pass through the qulan."

Artos nodded in agreement and Carimus added an emphatic, "Yes. How?"

"I do not know, but I have my suspicions. Castle Draconis has two gates where the qulan could be parted. The Main Gate and the River Gate. Of the two, I would suspect the River Gate. The Main Gate had two places where the Qulan make a seal. The River Gate has only one. If somehow, someone could trick a trusted guard into opening the qulan seal on the river gate and a ship with a load of Beastmen hidden within slipped inside, who knows what the result might be?"

"But the guards wouldn't open the River Gate in the middle of the night," said Bortis. "It would take someone like the Captain of the Guard or Uncle Brett to order the gate opened at such a time."

"I do not know, Bortis. I do not," said Donel. "But it must be some such method that the enemy used. The qulan is still intact. I tested that this morning, when I discovered there were no cryswords within the Castle. No red, green, or white cryswords," he corrected himself.

"I feel there is an Abomination involved somehow. It smells

like their work. I do not doubt that the troubles with House deHerndar in Rainbow Valley will also prove to have an Abomination at its roots.

"The true Abominations are extremely rare. The five have lived since the beginning of the second age and there are stories of others. Lesser in power, perhaps. Or merely less evil and without the ambition to have power over others." Donel shrugged. "I was taught that there may have been others born over the ages, or maybe they just came out of hiding. Perhaps a handful in the entire time since the second age began. They are not the same as shape shifters. Our family has the blood of shape shifters in its history." He looked at Bortis. "Another myth perhaps, but it is said that the blood of dragons is in the blood of House deDraconis. I'm willing to guess you have heard that myth, Bortis?"

"A tale for children," said Bortis, flatly.

"We know of it, Donel," said Artos. "But no one believes it. It tells that if ever a demon of power should threaten Veda, then the King will turn into a Dragon to combat it. The myth states that it happened once and that it may happen again … someday."

"It was Austin's son, whose name was very similar to yours, Artos. Arthur Draconis and it wasn't a demon of power. It was the minion of Tiameng, the monstrous black dragon Sandabur, who had stayed hidden in the great sandy waste of the south when his mistress had fled. After many years of hiding in the desert, the dragon came to decide that time might be ripe for his mistress to return from exile. He came forth from the southern desert, like a colossal storm, laying waste to the southern part of the kingdom."

"Arthur changed his shape into a great golden dragon and

fought it. He slew the dragon, but the cost was high. He paid for it with his own life's blood and his son Andru became king."

"Like I said, a children's tale," said Bortis, but there was less conviction in his voice than before.

"Perhaps, Bortis … perhaps," said Donel.

"That story was told in the Valley," said Rachel. "I mean, my mother told me stories like that when I was a girl growing up."

"Mine too!" added Vix. "The dragon slayer was my favorite bedtime tale when I was little."

"Our mother, too," said Artos quietly.

"I don't remember that," said Carimus. "Oh, I guess she died while I was too young to remember her telling us bedtime stories."

"Father stopped her," said Artos. "He was angry. I don't remember why, but she stopped telling us bedtime stories after that. It wasn't long after that she died."

"You were just a baby then, Carimus. Duka had just been born. Bort was probably three and I, four. Father used to stop in the nursery sometimes and listen to the stories with us. But one night, Mother started telling us the tale of the dragon slayer king and Father got angry and told her to stop such rubbish."

"King Aaron always struck me as being very no nonsense. So I am not surprised," said Donel. "I think he tried to be a good king. He stood up to the council when he thought they were in the wrong. It did not endear him to House deHerndar and House deAnson, two Houses that think what they want is far more important than the lives of mere people. What both those Houses want is power and riches."

"How would you know any of that?" asked Bortis. "You live far away from the problems facing the Great Houses."

Donel tilted his head and gazed at Bortis. "I told you, the

screens connect me with the outside world. Just because my nephew tried to cut me out doesn't mean he succeeded."

"The hour is getting late; the cider is gone. It is time to end this meeting and resume in the morning. There should be enough rabbit to serve as our breakfast. Let us begin again on the morrow."

Donel took the empty glasses and the jug and placed them on the serving tray. "I trust you all can find your beds without guidance, so I shall bid you all a good night."

38

A RESTLESS NIGHT

ARTOS

9/18/1971 ar

8:00 a.m.

ARTOS SLEPT RESTLESSLY THAT NIGHT. The more he considered his path, the less sure he felt he was capable of following it. Just the thought of standing before the Great Council made him feel ill. He could never dominate those men the way his father had. And his betrothal ... Elaine had been a friend since childhood, but he had never considered her as his possible queen.

I guess I was just stupid. Why marriage had never entered his mind baffled him, but until his father had brought up the subject, he had never even considered such a thing. Was it only three mornings ago? It seemed like a lifetime ago. He tried to think about Elaine, but her blue eyes and blond hair always seemed to morph into green eyes and red hair.

Duka is still lost. At least we know he's not dead, that's something.

He finally drifted off, but his last thoughts were not about his bride to be, but rather of Angel, how free her life was as a scout and how he envied that freedom.

When it was time to go down to the commons for breakfast, he trailed his brothers into the library. When they hurried down to the commons, he tarried, gazing at the shelves of books.

"Are you looking for something in particular?" came a voice, making him jump. It was Angel.

"No … Just thinking, I guess. There sure are a lot of books," he said awkwardly.

"It's easier to find something if you know where to look. The Magic Man will show you how to use the index. Then you only have to choose from hundreds of books instead of thousands." She grinned at his look of dismay. "It's really not as hard as it seems."

"What's it like to live so free?" he asked.

Angel tilted her head and looked at him. "Free? What do you mean? Do you think just because I don't live in a Great House, I have no responsibilities? If that's what you are thinking, you are wrong. My father trusts me and my scouts to keep watch for him at our end of the valley. I need to make sure we have enough supplies and a dozen other things."

"No, I didn't mean that. It's just … it seems so different. I look at the life I have grown up in and then I see how you live, in the valley, and it's like another world."

"It's the same world, just another part. That's all. It was different, before the raiders."

"I still don't understand that. We were taught bandits were the greatest threat to the people living here. Now you tell me it was House deHerndar trying to steal the land."

"Sometimes you need to see things with your own eyes. That's what my mother taught me. I need to get back to the kitchen. Joy will think I'm shirking my share of the work. See you at breakfast." She walked down the stairs, leaving him to his thoughts.

39

A STORMY
BREAKFAST

DONEL

9/18/1971 ar

8:30 a.m.

THERE WAS TENSION IN THE AIR at breakfast. The mood was strained, as if a storm was about to break. Donel could tell none of the brothers were happy with the information he had imparted to them the previous evening. He suspected they were unhappy for different reasons, but he could tell they were feeling uneasy from the words they had heard. *Good, they have much to learn. And unlearn as well.*

Rachel and Vix seemed the least affected and discussed plans for after their return to Rainbow Valley. Angel seemed amused by Bortis's discomfort, and Joy seemed lost within her own thoughts.

When breakfast was done, Vix and Rachel cleared the dishes. This time Donel did not ask them to desist, but before they left the room, he spoke up.

"Joy, Vix, Rachel, I would ask of you three a boon. We have devoured the rabbit, and my freezer is devoid of any more meat.

Liv has volunteered to assist. She remembers Joy and is not averse to hunting with her again as they did two years past."

Bortis tried to disguise his disbelief, but his skepticism was plain to see.

"You seem to doubt that Liv and the ladies can hunt us a meal, Bortis. Rest assured, Liv and Joy have proven capable in the past and I have no doubt they will again."

"It's not that. I figure you have her trained, your cat, I mean. It's just the way you act like you can talk with her. Angel did too. She told it to tell you we were here, and the cat ran off. Everyone knows cats can't talk."

"Cats seldom need to," said Joy. "They can make themselves understood to each other or to people very well if they so choose." She stood up and helped Vix and Rachel remove the dishes. "We shall get ready for the hunt." The three girls left the room.

Donel sent a thought to Liv, then smiled. "So, Bortis. If Liv comes in here in a few moments and sits beside me, it will be purely coincidental?"

"Sure. What else could it be? You haven't even called to her."

Liv chose that moment to enter the common room. The mist cat walked up to Donel and sat down beside him at the end of the table. She then stared at Bortis. Amusement shone in her enormous amber eyes.

Bortis looked disgusted. "I suppose you told her to do that somehow?" The skepticism dripped from his voice. "Can you make her speak, sit up, and play dead, too?"

Donel's eyes never left Bortis' face. "I can ask her, but she is not my pet. She is my friend. If she chooses to perform for you, it is entirely her decision."

Artos and Carimus sat silently watching, wondering just

what would happen. Would Donel give Liv hand signals, as some dog trainers do? Or would he just speak to her as Angel had done?

Donel did neither. His hands were folded before him on the table, and he remained looking at Bortis. Liv's ears flattened slightly as she turned to look at Donel, then back to Bortis. Then, to Bortis's alarm, the mist cat stood up and walked around the table and stood a few feet behind him. Bortis turned in his chair and watched, doubt plastered upon his face. "What's she doing!"

"I do not know what she is planning, Bortis, but do not be alarmed, she means you no harm."

Liv stretched her neck toward Bortis and sniffed. Then, as if reaching a decision, she made a loud snarling sound, which caused the three brothers to jump. Angel smiled as if she had expected it. Liv then sat and flopped to the ground, her legs extended and her head on the floor. She lay there for an instant, then leaped to her feet and stood with her head less than a foot from Bortis' face. After a long moment, there was a deep rumbling sound. Bortis thought she was growling, but then realized it wasn't a growl, it was a purr.

"I think she likes you, Bort," said Angel.

"I believe she recognizes a kindred warrior spirit within you, Bortis," added Donel.

Liv stopped purring, turned, and walked toward the southern door of the room.

Bortis let out a long breath. "By the Sky. How did you train her to do that?"

"I did not train her Bortis. I told you, she is a free spirit. She does as she wills. I can ask her to do things for me, like hunt, but she often brings me meals without my asking. We have been friends for a long time."

"How smart is she?" asked Carimus. "I read that mist cats were quite intelligent, but the book said nothing about them doing things like that!"

"I would say Liv is very intelligent, Carimus. Easily as smart as some people. Smart enough to stay away from most of them, I guess."

Donel turned his thoughts to the day's business. "Bortis, what are your minor regalos? I know from your aura and your red sword that your major quans are of the Body, the warrior branch, but from Liv's reaction to you, I would think you have some strength in nature as well." Seeing the blank look upon Bortis' face, Donel frowned and turned to the younger brother.

"Carimus, what are you the most skilled in? I need to think about what training you may need. All of you."

"Uncle Cameron said I was strongest in the quans of nature."

"Yes, of course. You carry a green sword. I knew that already, but where are you strongest? What were your test results? Surely Cameron tested you all thoroughly?"

"Test results?" Carimus looked blankly at his brothers, then back at Donel.

"What tests do you mean?" asked Artos. "We were all trained to use the screens to far-see. We all can control the lights in our rooms or the water temperature for our baths. After we bonded with our swords, they showed us how to call them to our hands. Uncle Brett was working with Bort on the use of his crysword as a weapon. There were some things he meant to teach me as well, but we hadn't progressed to them yet. What more would there be?"

Donel looked at the three brothers with dismay. "Are you

serious? Is such a simple thing as that forgotten now? The small room, just past the schoolroom, with screens on the walls, floor and one overhead. Surely Cameron tested you there?"

"I know the room you speak of," said Artos, as his brothers both nodded. "But it was just a storage chamber, I think. I don't remember ever seeing the inside. Did you Cari?"

Carimus shook his head and Bortis said, "I always thought it was where Camy kept supplies. Books and stuff."

"By the Sky, this is intolerable. How can things have fallen so far?" Anger boiled up inside him. "How can I teach you enough in the short time we have? There is much to do and so little time."

"What do you need to teach us?" asked Bortis. "We need to go kill the Beastmen in Castle Draconis, not sit around having lessons."

"How do you propose to even get inside the castle, Prince Bortis? Call out to the Beastmen to release the gates? Which trusted Beastman can operate the quanti controls? Or will you fly up to the airship dock? Or perhaps the eyrie and enter that way? I didn't realize you could fly. Have you been withholding this information? Maybe you are a skilled climber and can climb the rock wall one hundred feet to the lower battlements and enter there. Surely the Beastmen will unlock a door so you can enter?"

Bortis' face was turning a dangerous shade of red. Artos interjected. "How do you think we should proceed, Donel? What can you teach us that will allow us to regain the castle and defeat the Beastmen there?"

"Before we even talk about a way to regain the castle, I need to teach you enough to live to reach there. You do not understand the terrible power the Abominations may wield against you. Alex was so very lucky. His attack took Tomung by surprise and the Abomination had no time to bring all his power to attack. Another disservice he did to his ancestors by hanging that trophy on the wall. He led all to believe the Abominations were easy to kill. They are not. Not only can they change their appearance, they can cloud your mind. They are master of illusion. They could make the path before you look like solid ground when it is naught but air. You need the skill to true-see. Without a mind-shield, they might even subvert your will and persuade you to take your own life."

Bortis made a loud snort.

"Oh, I do not think you would be easy to control, Prince Bortis. But tell me, can you draw your sword? I never had your word that you would not try to threaten me again, and so I have not released your compulsion. Try it now."

Bortis stood up, almost knocking his chair over backwards. He grabbed the hilt of his crysword and gave a mighty yank. The sword appeared to be locked firmly within the sheath. Bortis strained, but the sword didn't budge.

"Just call it to your hand, Bort," cried Artos. "Like you did when Liv leaped in front of us."

"I can't Art. Last night, I tried. I tried again this morning. He's witched me. I can't! He's a witch."

"Bortis, you are my kin," said Donel softly. "We are blood. I would not hurt you. Any of you. We are family, even if you do not like to admit it. It is the truth. Calm down, relax. I shall release you now. The only reason I didn't last night was I felt you would need to be shown this. The foes you face are far stronger in the ways of the quanti than anyone you have ever known before. They are stronger than I am. You must learn or you will surely die. You must believe me."

Artos spoke before his brother could answer. "Donel, I feel you have spoken true. I don't know why I feel this way. Some things you have said I do not want to believe. But in my heart, I believe you speak the truth."

At that moment, Joy, Vix, and Rachel entered the common room.

"We are ready to go hunting, Teacher," said Joy. "Is there anything in particular you would have us target? As I recall, you were fond of venison. Should we try for a young elk?"

"Indeed, I do enjoy venison, but it really doesn't matter. Haste before taste today. Leave it up to Liv to find what she and her brood might flush. If you can bring us home a few days' worth of meals, it should suffice. But be wary. Stay attuned to Liv. If she senses any dangers, return at once whether or not you have found any game. Be careful."

Angel stood up. "I should go too. I think you have family matters to discuss that are not for those outside to hear."

"No, Angela. I would have you stay. There are reasons. If there are things you should not hear, we shall hunt that dog when it has grown."

Angel nodded, though she had doubt in her eyes. She sat back down.

Joy nodded to Donel, and the three girls left the common room, in the direction Liv had taken earlier.

"Try to call your sword now, Bortis." said Donel. As Bortis reached toward the hilt, he said, "No, do not draw it. Summon it."

Bortis scowled, held out his hand and with a *pop*, his sword appeared in his clenched fist.

"Is it easier when you are angry, Bortis? Easier when you don't think about it? A crysword can be a fearsome weapon and it needs to be kept in firm control, but you have a powerful mind and good control. Why do you worry so greatly about it?"

Bortis looked at the ground, shook his head, and slid his sword back into its sheath.

"Bortis, pretending nothing is wrong will not make the problem go away," said Donel gently. "We will discuss this later, just you and me. Please?" Bortis responded with a slight nod.

"Artos, you say Cameron has trained you to farsee with the screens? And little household uses for the quanti. Did no one ever mention seeing-true? To true-see will be vital when facing these foes."

Bortis answered. "Uncle Brett was going to teach Art and me, but he got mad because I was having … because I had so much trouble calling my sword. There was no use in trying to learn anything more, he said, until I could master the easiest of skills. He could call his sword to either hand and move it as though it were light as a feather, but when I asked him to show me, he refused. He said … he said my skills were too slight. I would never be a sword master like he was. Even though I was the best at swordplay, I could never use a crysword the way he could."

"Bortis, you can learn that trick. Inertness doesn't even need a crysword, it can be done with many things, any weapon, a heavy object, even yourself. A crysword isn't just a magical weapon. Its purpose is to help you focus, but it is not the end result in itself. I admit there are things I wouldn't recommend you try without such a focus. But a crysword isn't necessary for you to turn on a light in your room or warm the water in your bath. Why would it be needed for inertial combat, or to truesee?"

"You just do," Bortis insisted, looked befuddled.

"No. You do not," Donel felt grim. "Alexavier ordered the magic school closed because I refused to break Austin's law, but you are the ones suffering for his wounded vanity."

Carimus spoke up. "The quanti-school in Phoenix isn't closed. The Church teaches the airship pilots and many other things."

"Carimus, your Church now sees no difference in shape shifters and Abominations, and they are not the same thing."

"Yes ... yes, they are! They may not be born dangerous, but they are evil and they—"

"No!" cried Donel. "They are not the same! It was only after the War that people began to think so."

Carimus shook his head, a look of horror on his face. "How can you say this?"

"I do not know how I can prove this to you, Carimus. But the Church has been slowly destroying Veda by sending away innocent children who merely have a defect of appearance. Nothing more. True Beastmen breed more Beastmen. These are what used to be called Beastmen. Humans sometimes breed people with beast traits, but given a loving family life, these children will not suddenly change into ravening beasts. Indeed, it is thought that even the true Beastmen, if not hunted and tormented, would not be the savage enemy they have become."

Donel scowled. "My brother Caer offered to help with the school at Starstone Tower, but Alexavier refused. He told Caerwyn that it would be enough to teach the ways of the quanti at the Church schools. Perhaps for a generation that was enough, but the trained wizards died off with no one to replace them. The priests of the Sky sect now teach enough to serve the needs of the Great Houses, but the wizards are gone. The Sky sect serves the Great Houses and ignores the needs of the common folk except to test for the basics and steal their children if they deem their blood is not pure. I am afraid the rot runs deeper than I thought. If a child shows potential for quanti control Carimus, what are their options?"

Carimus frowned. "They have lots of options. They can learn to pilot an airship if their control is strong and can master the wind to push the ship. Or they can join the church. If they are strong in the martial quans, they become Sky-knights. If they are strong in the nature quans, they may become a weather sensor or a healer."

"When I was a boy, menders could use quanti to fix broken items, lock smiths could attune locks to families so people could protect their homes or valuables. There were the finders who could locate lost items. Are there still shops to offer these things? Do these services still exist?" Donel knew these shops were gone now. *They do not comprehend how much they have lost.*

"I haven't heard of such things, but there might be. I am not sure of all the ways the Church teaches quanti in the school. Uncle Cameron taught me what I needed. He was going to have me spend time with the healers this winter and he spoke of me spending some time with the druids as well, next summer."

"I have never seen such shops. Not in Phoenix anyway. Have you, Bort?" asked Artos.

Bortis shook his head.

A soft bong interrupted the discussion.

"The roost," said Donel. "I turned on a chime this morning to let me know if Oswald had returned. Normally I leave it off, as Oswald comes and goes in the night. Let us check in with him before he retires for his nap." Donel stood up and led the way to the stairs leading to the upper floor of the tower, with Angel close on his heels.

On entering the library, Donel walked to a small alcove in the northern wall and placed his hand on a spot to the side. The wall before him slid upward, revealing another spiral stair leading higher into the tower. He led the way, with the Angel and the three brothers close behind.

CHAPTER TEN:
REGALOMAL AND REVELATIONS

40

REGALOMAL

ARTOS

9:45 a.m.

ARTOS FOLLOWED ANGEL UP THE STAIRS, which ended at a three-way intersection. The lighting was dimmer than on the floors below. The floor was black and absorbed the glow of the everlights, which numbered fewer here. Corridors to the left and right appeared to lead to dead ends. The path ahead curved slightly, the end out of sight.

Donel turned to the left and strode towards the end. He placed his hand upon a protrusion on the side of the wall, and a section slid quietly upward, revealing a large area with the morning light shining in over a balcony at the far end. Two dark alcoves opened on each side, and a gas fireplace stood to the right of the doorway, keeping the mid-September chill from permeating the room.

Donel spoke softly, "He's here, and he's still awake. Follow me." He led the way into the first alcove on the right. Perched upon a wooden pole that seemed to grow directly from the crystalline wall about four feet off the ground was a large gray owl, a sight the brothers remembered well.

"It's your demon, Cari," chortled Bortis, seemingly in the best mood he had been since having first reached the crystal tower.

"All I saw at first were his eyes through the branches. They would have scared you too, Bort," said Carimus defensively.

"Take it easy, squirt. You're probably right, but I bet I wouldn't have screamed like you did."

"Easy for you to say," Carimus muttered.

"Tchokk, Tchokk, Tchokk, Tchokk, tu-whooo." The owl hooted, sounding amused, just as he had when Carimus first sighted him.

"It's good to have you back, old friend," said Donel. "Joycel is out hunting with Liv and when they return, we'll send you up something to eat. Until then, rest. But first, did you see anything unusual on your flight back here from the valley?" There was a long moment of silence, and his eyes narrowed.

"The crow!" said Angel. "It's back and watching the Valley. Oswald? Had Kae returned before you left?" Angel stood silent a moment, breathed a sigh of relief, then turned to Carimus. "I'm sorry Cari, Kae returned safely, but she came home without Duka."

The three brothers all just stared at Angel, dumbfounded looks on their faces.

Artos broke the silence. "How do you know that?"

Angel looked back. "I can mindspeak to Oswald, just like I can with Liv. Words are not really necessary, but it's easier if I do. I am gifted with the mind regalo, Ansuz. The gift of communication."

"Among other things," added Donel. "I suspect you are

gifted with Ansuz as well, Bortis. All of Bethel's Falcon-masters had that regalo. It is very useful for reconnaissance."

"I don't know what you are talking about," said Artos. "Uncle Cameron never taught us anything like that."

"Can you talk with people that way, too?" asked Carimus.

"Do you read minds?" asked Bortis, suspicion filling his voice.

"It is possible for those with that gift to be trained to communicate, even over distance, but unless they are blood relatives or have close bonds of some nature, it is not common, nor is it mind reading, Bortis. Thoughts have to be pushed from one side to be received by the other. Although ..." he trailed off.

"Although what?" asked Bortis sharply.

"Remember, I warned you about the strength of an Abomination's mind. The illusions I warned you of are also a use of Ansuz. Beguiling is another, as is projecting terror or despair. A mind's strength does come into play. Algiz, the regalo of defense is one I hope you all possess in some measure. I think teaching you to form a mindshield is where we must begin. Angel, I know I have already trained you to shield. I think I need to teach all of your band as well. Joycel already possesses it, as does Kaerin. I will test Vix and Rachel before they leave. I think it would be prudent if you bring the other Daughters here before too much time passes. With that crow patrolling the Rainbow Valley, it really isn't safe for anyone there to be unprotected."

Angel nodded. "I can set out tomorrow. We can leave the Valley unwatched for a short time. I sent Cat on an errand to inform my father of what had occurred, but she should be back shortly, if she hasn't already returned."

"No, first I need to test Vix and Rachel. You and Joycel

should not travel alone without us knowing more of this crow. It may easily be the eyes of more raiders, or worse. It will take a few days. We can send Oswald in a day or two. A night flight to avoid the bird. He can inform Kaerin." He smiled. "It will be like teaching my old class at Starstone once again. Come, let us leave Oswald to his nap."

Donel led the way out of the Roost, then turned left when they reached the intersection near the stairs. Artos followed down the hall and passed between another pair of gas heaters. He saw this hall also appeared to be a dead end. Donel stopped partway down the corridor and pressed a spot on the wall with his right hand, causing a section to slide upward. Beyond was a room whose walls were large crystal screens, as were the floor below and the ceiling above.

"I would ask the four of you to all stand between the screens. I know you have done this before Angela, but I would like to measure the result against the tests of three years ago. You four need to do nothing save stand in the room for about five minutes after I start the test. The screens will glow when the test starts. Afterwards, I will come and get you. Questions?"

Angel walked into the center of the room and stood waiting. Carimus looked back and forth between his older brothers as if awaiting a sign.

"I guess not," said Artos, and followed Angel into the room along with Carimus.

"Just what are you going to do?" asked Bortis, looking at Donel, suspicion in his voice.

"After you enter the testing room, Bortis, I will shut this door and go into another room. There I will begin the quan-regalo test. This shouldn't take too long, and the screens will glow during the testing. Different people have different reactions to the quanti during the test. Some hear music, singing, or strange hums. Some see colored lights, or experience scents or tastes. Others feel a tingly sensation, and still others have no reaction at all. I would like you each to tell me what, if anything, you notice." He raised an eyebrow and looked at Bortis, who squared his shoulders and walked into the room to stand beside his brothers and Angel.

The door slid shut and Artos looked at Angel. "What did you feel when you tested before?"

"I smelled the scent of pine trees and it felt like a cool breeze was blowing, except there was no breeze. If that makes any sense?"

At that moment, the screens began to glow with a soft blue light, and Artos heard a note. No, it was a full chord of notes, and it changed as he listened. He looked to see if his brothers were hearing it too, but he was all alone. Somehow, this wasn't alarming. The air in the room grew warmer, but not unpleasantly so, almost like the warmth of a spring day when you enjoyed the sun after a long winter. Then suddenly, it was over. Surely it was too short for the test to have been completed, but the screens stopped glowing.

"Thank the Sky that's over," said Bortis. "He said it would only be a few minutes, and it was at least a quarter hour. What a strange color everything turned. It smelt like hot metal, and such a horrible racket." He looked around and saw the others looking at him with puzzled expressions. "You didn't hear that?"

"I heard music, Bort. But it wasn't an unpleasant sound, and it wasn't long at all," Artos replied.

"I didn't hear anything," said Carimus, "except my heart beating. So I counted the beats. It lasted almost three hundred beats. I was to two hundred and eighty-nine when the funny feeling stopped."

"What funny feeling was that, Cari?" asked Angel.

"Well … at first it felt like we were falling, but I could feel my feet against the floor, so I knew we weren't. Then suddenly, after about one hundred heartbeats, it felt like the floor was rising, pushing us up. Like the whole tower was rising into the sky and taking us along."

"What about you Angel? Was it the same as before?" asked Artos.

"It was the same, except this time I heard some birds singing, but I didn't recognize their song. I know all the birdsong of the Valley, and this was brand new to me."

At that moment, the door slid open and Donel stood outside, looking in at them. "The Regalomal is finished. That wasn't too bad, was it?" he asked. "No ill effects? Anyone feeling a headache, dizzy, or anything of that nature?"

"Reg-al-o-mall?" said Carimus. "What's that?"

"Regalomal just means testing for the quan regalos that each of you possesses, Carimus. What you just experienced."

"I know what quans are. At least I thought I did," he replied. "But I never heard of regalos before you used the word."

Donel took a deep breath and nodded. "I know. I could see that. Cameron did not receive near enough schooling in the ways of the quanti and I fear we are going to suffer for his lack. The quans are the divisions of the quanti. They are Mind, Body, Spirit, and Nature. The regalo are the specific gifts. The Regalomal is the testing for those gifts. But come, let us look at your results."

41

DUKA?

CARIMUS

10:15 a.m.

THE FOUR FOLLOWED DONEL back into the hallway and he shut the door to the testing room. He then walked to the end of the hallway to a doorway that hadn't been opened before. Carimus looked at the way the hall was shaped and thought to himself there was probably another door beside this new one that would open to the left side at the very end, but it was just a blank wall of crystal at the moment. *This place is full of secret passages,* he thought.

The new room's walls were covered with crystal screens. One vast screen nearly filled the entire left-hand wall. The screen appeared to be idle and sat inert. On the right, the wall had two large screens, far larger than any he had ever used at Castle Draconis, though smaller than the one across the room. The one on the right side also seemed to be idle, but the one on the left glowed softly and was lined with four columns, each filled with strange markings in various colors. He recognized several as being the same as the runes on his bracelet. The wall opposite the door had thirteen screens. Three appeared to be in use, and the largest of them, alone on the top, immediately caught his eye, filled with bright red flames. The next two rows were like the screens in the Hall of Mirrors back at castle Draconis, except none of the screens were painted over. Two screens had markings above that he was unfamiliar with. One had what looked like a bat in flight. Another appeared to be some sort of flower. It looked like a chrysanthemum. The one beside it was marked with the double-dragon, matching the birth mark on Donel's arm and that of his missing brother, Duka. A pang in his heart reminded him none of their plans so far seemed to involve finding him. He resolved to speak to Donel about this. Of the remaining two, the other ones not inert, both looked to be views of the tower from somewhere outside. He recognized the entrance to the Crystal cave on the left end screen. The other, on the far right, just showed a view of one of the blue spires. He guessed it was another view of the Crystal Tower from another angle.

"What is this place?" he asked. "It has screens like the Hall of Mirrors."

"Yes," said Donel. "This is my central control. It is very near the heart of the Crystal Tower." He pointed to the large screen on the left. "Here I can view much of the world." He indicated the array of screens on the central wall. "There I can watch the entrance to the tower and to the roost. I could also talk to the Great Houses on their screens." He nodded at the lighted screen on the right-hand wall. "And that screen shows the results of the test." In the middle of the room was a round raised dais with a chair in the center. On each side of the chair was an onyx box, their tops covered with glowing raised buttons of various colors. Donel sat himself in the chair and the dais rotated to face the two large screens. He gazed at the rows and colors.

"Each of you has a column and the markings within show the results of the test. The first column with the white rune on top is you Artos, The next with the red is Bortis—"

"I'm the green one then." interrupted Carimus, who immediately looked abashed at his rudeness and fell quiet.

"Yes Carimus, you are correct," said Donel. "And the last column, also with a green rune, is Angel, I could spend a good amount of time analyzing these, but for now I am inspecting what regalos are major in you all and which are minor. Those are what are important right now. The trace gifts we shall overlook for now. Hmmm … This is fortunate. You all have Algiz as minor quans except for Bortis. Oh, this is interesting …"

"You mean I can't defend myself from illusions?" asked Bortis. "I don't believe in them, anyway."

"No Bortis, you misunderstand. I see here why you are having problems. You have three major regalos, including Algiz, and three minor ones. This is quite rare. Most who are strongly gifted have two major gifts and three minor ones. Without a proper teacher to instruct you, your regalos will interfere with each other's focus. When you call your crysword, your regalos are at odds. Offense tries to dominate, but with two defensive gifts vying for control, your sword is conflicted, and it slows your reaction and manifests itself in your mind as anxiety. Actually, Bortis, this will not be hard for you to overcome." Donel looked at Bortis with a small smile. "You are really quite lucky. What was unlucky is you weren't properly tested and trained."

After looking at the runes on the screen and comparing

them to the ones on his bracelet, Carimus was getting bored. It was nice Donel would be able to help Bort. Maybe Bort would even stop being a bully if he wasn't so worried about proving himself to everyone.

A flicker of light from the screens on the central wall drew his attention.

"Why is my name on that screen?" said Carimus. "Where is Fairinhorst? Why does it say to send me there?"

Everyone turned to join Carimus, looking at the screens opposite the entrance. Sure enough, the screen with the chrysanthemum above it had a sentence written on it. *SEND CARIMUS TO FAIRINHORST* in large red letters. Even as they looked, the letters faded away, leaving the screen blank and inert.

The dais with Donel's chair turned to face that wall. And Donel looked down at the glowing buttons beside him and pushed one. Nothing happened.

"I don't understand. This is unprecedented. That screen connects to the Fairborn. It isn't activated." Donel pushed the button repeatedly. Artos thought he sounded more upset than he had, even with his story of the disagreement with King Alexavier and his disgust with the failings in the teachings of magic. Only the news of the disappearance of Duka had moved him so.

The screen suddenly had the words upon it again, the same words: *SEND CARIMUS TO FAIRINHORST.* There was no soft blue glow as with the screens in use, but the words were there. Slowly, they faded away again.

"Wasn't Fairinhorst where you were when your teacher was murdered?" asked Artos.

"The Fairborn school? Why should I go there? Why would I

want to go there? I won't go," said Carimus loudly.

Once again, the words appeared on the screen, but this time they were larger and appeared to be written in red fire. *SEND CARIMUS TO FAIRINHORST.* This time the words grew larger until they filled the screen. Once again, the words faded away except the word *FAIRINHORST,* which grew larger still, until it filled the screen and then burst into nothingness with a bright flash.

"That screen is the means I have to communicate with Prince Tirinvo when he is home in Fairinlan. According to my controls, it is not in use. I confess, I have no idea what this is about."

On the active screen above the Fairinlan screen, there was movement. "Look. Our hunters are already back. They look burdened. Angel, please take Artos and Carimus down to help the others. You know what needs to be done. I wish to do some work removing the blocks Bortis has acquired. Take charge of the kitchen and we shall join you at lunch. Providing none of you has any objection?" He looked at each of the three princes. "We share the chores here equally. I know you are used to having servants to attend to such things, but there are no servants here."

Artos gave a nod. "Come on Cari. We can do our part, right?"

Carimus tore his eyes away from the screen that had directed him to go to Fairinhorst. "What?"

"Come on, Cari, there are chores to do." Artos pulled his little brother along, and with Angel, left Donel's control chamber.

42

A PROMISE KEPT

BORTIS

10:30 a.m.

"Prince Bortis," said Donel, "it is time I kept my promise to help you overcome your problem of conflicted regalos, but you are going to have to do something you will not like, I'm afraid."

Bortis looked at Donel with suspicion. "And that would be?"

"You are going to have to trust me. You are even wary of your brothers, so I know it will be hard for you. Forget those tales they taught you about me being a traitor and untrue to House deDraconis. I have told you what I did and why."

"I still don't understand that. You did what you thought you had to do, but that doesn't make it right. What was so important that you would defy a command from your king?"

Donel gave a long sigh. "Bortis, when your father was coronated, he took a vow to follow the laws set down by the first king of Veda. All the kings take this vow. It is a part of the ceremony. One of Austin's laws was that this tower was never to be left unoccupied. A trained occupant must always be here to handle … Well, a description of those duties isn't the important issue. King Alexavier wanted me to break that law. Alex was in the wrong, not me. You understand duty, that is very clear. Probably better than any of your brothers. When Artos is crowned, he too will take those vows, and I suspect he will abide by them."

"Of course, he will."

"Then you understand why I could not leave. The details are unimportant. The law is clear."

Bortis gave a small nod.

"You and Carimus must support your bother and be there to guide him when he needs aid. Duka too, if and when we discover his whereabouts and bring him here to be trained as my successor."

"Duka is a good kid. Cari is a scatterbrained, spoiled brat."

"I think you may underestimate Carimus. He is young and his strengths are far different from yours, but I agree, he needs more discipline than your great-uncle was willing to impose. That will require some thought." Donel placed his elbows upon the armrests of his chair, placed the tips of his fingers together in a steeple before him, and began tapping them together.

"That brings us back to where we started, Prince Bortis, a matter of trust. Will you trust me?"

"I … I … I guess I can try," Bortis licked his lips. "What do you want to do?"

"When I taught at Starstone, we had teaching screens that would imprint patterns into students' minds. Then it was all a matter of allowing them to develop the muscle memory and the mental reactions to use them. Do you understand the concept?"

"You mean like reflexes?"

"Yes, reflex can be muscle memory. Your mind sees a

situation and your muscles know how to respond without you having to think, to weigh options. You merely react."

"But we're not at Starstone."

"No, but we don't need to be. All the screens are linked to an extent. The Great Houses have blocks against outsiders controlling their screens. But Starstone Tower and the Crystal Tower have no blocks between them. The records and all the teaching tools are stored here. My mentor was the head of the school there. But he spent most of his time right here. He had to, unless I was present to fill in for him. We swapped occasionally for short periods, but mostly I was there, and he was here."

"What will I have to do?"

Donel rose from his chair and led Bortis back to the room where the testing had taken place. "Stand in the middle of the room and gaze at the far screen. A colored dot will appear. Focus on that dot. I will speak to you through one of the side screens. Do not watch me though. Keep your attention focused on the dot on the screen before you. You may feel as if you are dozing off. Do not fight it. Just keep watching the screen. I know this seems strange, but trust me. This will help you balance the conflicted regalos in your mind. I believe you will see the results immediately and find it much easier to call your sword into your hand."

Donel left the testing chamber, and the door slid shut behind him. Bortis stood uneasily between the screens and waited for something to begin. In a moment, the screen to his right glowed with the faint blue light that meant it was in use, and then the screen before him did the same. "I'm here," said Donel from the screen to his side. "The dot will appear now."

A dim red dot appeared in the middle of the center screen. It brightened and then slowly started to grow and then shrink, grow and shrink, grow and shrink. Bortis heard Donel speaking softly, telling him to just relax and watch the dot. He took a breath and then tried to time his breathing to the pattern of the dot. Suddenly, it was gone.

"How do you feel Bort? Headache? Are you dizzy? Does anything seem unusual?"

Bortis realized his eyes were watering, and he wiped them with his hands. "I guess it didn't work. Nothing happened."

"Try summoning your sword now."

Bortis held up his hand as he had done so often in the past and thought about his sword. With a soft *pop* it was there. Bortis stared at his sword unbelievingly. "It came," he whispered. He sheathed the blade and tried again. Again, the sword came effortlessly into his fist. He tried again and yet again. There was no more mental block.

The door slid open behind him. He turned to see Donel standing there. "I don't think you will have any more problems calling your sword, Bort. Let's go down to lunch. After we eat, we will go to the training chamber. There are a few things I wish to show you that need a larger space."

"You didn't do anything. I don't feel any different, but ..."

"It's an ancient technique, Bort. It's called hypnosis. How long do you think you have been in the test chamber?"

"A few minutes. Why?"

"You were there for most of an hour. Besides removing the blocks your conflicting regalos had caused, I put several patterns into your mind, the beginning training for several other things. But you will need practice to use them. I will show you when we go to the basement. Come along. I am willing to wager you are hungry."

"Now that you mention it ..." Bortis grinned.

Donel turned and led the way, with Bortis following close behind him.

43

A STORMIER LUNCH

ARTOS

11:55 a.m.

When Bortis and Donel arrived in the kitchen, they found it bustling with activity. Vixen and Rachel were making a salad. Angel, aided by Joy, stood beside Carimus as he fried seven venison steaks on the crystal griddle stove top. Artos was washing the breakfast dishes. From the look on Bort's face, he had good news and was eager to share. He made up his mind. He would let Bort have his moment, but when lunch was finished, he would announce his decision. Bort and Cari would just have to understand. Cari at least should understand. He hoped.

"Time to flip them again, Cari," said Angel. "You want to be sure they cook all the way through on both sides and you want to be sure they do not burn."

Joy spoke to Donel, "Angel took a few pounds of meat to Oswald. So he has been attended. Liv found a yearling elk quickly, and several others had left tracks, but we had all we could carry, so we refrained from hunting more."

"You did well, Joy. We will need more soon, so I will ask you to keep at it whenever Liv returns from feeding with her brood." A faraway looked came over Donel's face for a moment. "She informs me she will be back in a few hours. So we have time for a good meal. I think we shall have to ask you and Angel to do most of the hunting until we have everyone trained to form a mindshield. But I shall be able to do so fairly quickly. After lunch, I shall test Vix and Rachel for their regalos. By the time Liv gets back, we shall know where we stand. I think Artos and Carimus should go hunting with you this afternoon, and I will spend some more time with Bortis. This evening after dinner, we shall all go down to the training area, and I will lay the foundations for mindshields. Tomorrow we shall begin the serious training. Anything you bring back just store in the larder. Liv has told me we are welcome to thin the elk population as they are overgrazing the area. She thinks there will soon be a problem for the rabbits. Liv prefers rabbit to elk."

Sure enough, as they were gathering in the commons for the noon meal, Bortis could contain himself no longer and he showed everyone how proficient he had become with summoning his sword.

Bortis's good mood was not destined to last. As lunch finished, Artos pushed back his chair, stood up, and cleared his throat.

"I have been thinking ... a lot. And the solution to our problem finally came to me last night as I lay tossing and turning. Houses deAnson and deHerndar feel they do not have enough control over their own destiny. This is something I understand all too well. I have conceived a plan that will bring them to our side. Make them eager to help us retake Castle Draconis."

Donel frowned, but before he could speak, Artos hurried onward.

"Hear me out. I will not become king. I shall renounce the throne and become the Count of House deDraconis. We shall reform the Great Council so all have an equal vote and have a chair who does not vote, except to break a tie and keep order. Donel will be perfect for this. We shall still be able to keep deAnson and deHerndar in check, because Houses deEagledon, dePenrodyn, and deDarrellyel will side with us against them. We will then unite, march on Castle Draconis and destroy the monsters there! Then we can devote our energy to finding Duka. By the time deAnson and deHerndar realize we have them controlled, it will be too late for them to do anything about it." He sat back down, and for a moment, everyone sat in stunned silence.

"Are. You. Out. Of. Your. Mind?" Bortis pushed back his chair and jumped to his feet, his face growing red. "Art, you can't just abandon your duty! You bear the crown on your shoulder. You were born to be king. What are you thinking?"

"What about me, Art?" Carimus stared at his brother, his eyes wide. "I was born to head the Church. How would that fit into your plan? Yes, we need to find Duke, but this doesn't seem the right way to me."

"The Canon and the Cantor will take you under their tutelage, Cari. Then, when it is time, you shall take up the mitre and lead the Church.

"I have thought this through. Count Eagledon and Count Penrodyn will lead the forces and march to the castle gates. Cari, you will go with them. Bort and I will go with some troops from the gatehouse. Some trusted guards. I think there are some there. Fly an airship to the Eyrie battlements.

House dePenrodyn's ship is small enough, I think. If not, the deDarrellyel ship is even smaller. We shall go in the morning when most of the Beastmen will be asleep. We will sweep down the Winding Way in an all-out charge and open the main gates. Then the troops will march in. We shall destroy the monsters and reclaim the castle!"

Bortis sat back down. "Art, we can do all this without you giving up the throne. That is madness."

Artos opened his mouth to retort to his brother, but before he could reply, Donel spoke up. "Prince Artos, I can see you have thought about this but ..." He paused a moment. "I will not insult you by calling you a child, for you are not. You are a man. But ... you are a very young man. Let me give you my thoughts on this and you may take as much of my advice as you may wish. I will not try to force you to take any path merely because it is what I desire.

"Suppose we follow this plan? You wait until Count Eagledon and Count Penrodyn reach their castles in the lowlands. You contact them, they agree to your plan and return to The Valley with their airships and mustered troops. They organize an assault by the Houses upon your Home. This is what I foresee would follow. Your raiders who enter through the Eyrie would find very little resistance in your charge of opening the main gates. Some 'accident' would happen to Prince Carimus, either on the march to the gates or shortly after. During the fight to clear the castle, both you and Bort would probably also be struck down or 'accidents' would soon befall you both as well. No Abominations will be found in Castle Draconis and the Great Council will appropriate it for the Council to use as there will no longer be a House deDraconis.

"Artos, to some, it will not matter that you abdicate. You

will still have the crown birthmark upon your shoulder. They will worry that you might change your mind, for they could not conceive of giving up such power. Even if you did not, what of your children? What will happen when your son is born with the same birthmark? Would he not want his Crown and Throne returned to your House? Your enemies will think so, no matter what the truth might be."

Donel sighed. "Think more about this. That is my advice for you. We have a little time. Your family's demise will not be known by any who would admit it for a few weeks, but you will need to act soon, whatever fork in the road you choose. You were born to walk the Glory Road, Artos. You cannot change that, whatever you decide. Fate has placed this burden upon your shoulders."

Donel looked at Bortis. "I suggest you let Prince Artos think more about this Prince Bortis. I know you have potent feelings about duty, but this is something he must decide himself."

To Artos's complete surprise, Bortis just looked down and nodded. Carimus looked as if he was surprised, too. He just kept looking back and forth between his two elder brothers with a look that seemed to ask who were these two people and what had they done with the brothers he was used to?

"Angel," said Donel. "I'm going to test Rachel and Vix now. I'm putting you in charge, see to clearing the table and preparing for this afternoon's hunt. You will find a couple of spare bow and arrows in the storeroom. Outfit Artos and Carimus after the kitchen is clean. We should be done testing by then. Joy, if you do not mind, I would ask you to retest so I may compare the results with the ones of a few years back. Bortis, I would like you to come along as well. Liv will return soon. When she arrives, you may set forth. Good hunting."

Angel nodded. "Come on, you two. Let's get these dishes to the kitchen."

Artos suspected Donel was taking Bort merely to separate them. He found he didn't disagree, even if it meant all the washing up was left to him and Cari.

Chapter Eleven:

The Hunt

44

HUNTERS

ARTOS

1:40 p.m.

"WHEN WAS THE LAST TIME you went hunting?" asked Angel.

"Well … I, err …" Artos stammered, suddenly afraid he was about to lessen himself in Angel's eyes.

"Never," said Carimus. "We don't need to hunt."

"Food is brought to Castle Draconis," said Artos. "We have farms that raise cattle, pigs, sheep, and chickens. We have foresters who hunt for venison and pheasant, those kinds of things. I know Bort has hunted on his patrols with Uncle Brett. I have ridden with some patrols too, but I never went with him on any of the extended trips, like Bort has. We always brought enough supplies with us so not have to take the time for hunting."

Angel nodded. "I suspected that was the case. Well, you have bows now, and can try your hand if you wish, but if you prefer, we can do the actual shooting and you two can just watch."

"We can shoot," said Carimus. "We have archery lessons three days a week. Art is an excellent shot. I am too. But not with this kind of bow. I am very good with a crossbow, as good as Bort."

"We should learn," said Artos. "We may need the skill soon and I am sure you are excellent teachers for the things we would need to learn, like skinning the meat. I have to confess I have no idea how that is done."

Angel glanced at Joy, who shrugged as if to say, *Why not?* and Angel nodded. "The first rule is you never leave a wounded animal. If you don't bring something down with your first shot, you follow it and finish the job." The brothers nodded.

"Second rule, follow the huntmaster's directions. That's me for this trip. If I say do not shoot, do not shoot. Understand?" Again, the brothers nodded in agreement.

"Excellent. Let's get going."

Angel looked at Liv, who was patiently sitting a little way off from the group. "Liv tells me there are some yearling elk not too far away to the north and west of here. Joy and I will lead, you follow. Vix and Rach will be rear guard."

"Liv knows directions?" asked Carimus, doubtfully.

Angel looked confused for a moment. "I don't believe she thinks of them in exactly the same way we do. But, she put the direction they are from us in my mind. I'm not really sure how. I'll have to ask Donel about that. I never thought about it before."

"I can answer that," said Joy. "Like many animals, mist cats can detect the magnetic lines. It's as though the land itself tells them."

"Oh," said Carimus. "Like birds."

Joy nodded. "Exactly, Cari. Birds use the magnetic lines to migrate."

"We have homing pigeons at the Castle," said Artos.

"Now that mystery is solved, let's get going," said Angel and she set off, following a path towards the north.

2:45 p.m.

With a finger held to her lips for silence, Angel waved for Artos and Carimus to move up beside her. She then pointed down the slope to a clearing in the aspen and mountain pine. A spring gurgled as it flowed down the rocks into a marshy area. The four young giant elk were grazing on cottongrass and rushes. The elk stood ten feet tall at the shoulder and the buck's antlers were over eight feet across.

"Okay, Cari, Art," she whispered. "You both aim for that one in the front. It's a young doe and will be tender eating. I'll back your shot in case you only wound it. Joy, you take the other doe off to the right. That will give us all the meat we can carry and leave plenty for Liv and her brood." She looked to make sure everyone understood her instructions. Artos and Carimus nodded. Joy gave her a thumbs up to show she understood as well. Vix and Rachel stood a short way behind them, keeping watch.

"Aim just behind her front leg, in the center of the chest. Go ahead," said Angel. Artos made sure his arrow was notched firmly and began drawing the string back, taking a deep breath and then letting it out slowly. He waited for Carimus, ready to release as soon as he heard the twang of his little brother's shot.

Carimus's bow sang and Artos gently released his hold and watched as the arrow struck the doe in the shoulder, at least six inches from where he had aimed.

Carimus's arrow was too high. It narrowly missed the back of the doe and lodged in the hindquarters of the buck, gazing just beyond. An instant later, the other doe, Joy's target, reared up and fell with a splash onto the marshy ground. The uninjured yearling raced off to the east. The doe with Artos's arrow in its shoulder dashed to the north while the buck Carimus had struck charged west.

Indecisive for a moment which wounded animal to target Angel loosed an arrow at Carimus's buck, but failed to fell the frightened beast.

"I didn't mean to shoot that one!" wailed Carimus.

"Blast," muttered Angel. "Joy, take Vix and Rach, track the doe Art wounded. We'll go after the buck. Come on." She hurried down the slope to where the yearling elk lay on the marshy ground. She stopped long enough to make sure the beast was dead. As usual, Joy had been right on target. Joy ran up beside her and then, with Vix and Rachel on her heels, set off to the north, tracking the wounded doe.

"I didn't mean to wound that one," repeated Carimus.

"It's alright Cari. I think I hit it too. We'll track it." She stopped and bent low, looking at the ground. The big red drops of blood proof to her the buck was leaving an easy trail to follow. She set off, with Artos and Carimus following along behind her.

The trail was easy for the experienced tracker to follow, and after a while, she paused. "It won't go much further," whispered Angel. "It's losing too much blood. Try to step quietly, so when it stops, it won't bound off again, and I'll get a clean shot."

Sure enough, after another hundred yards, she held up her arm and stopped the brothers. She pointed at a strand of brush. The outline of the wounded elk was visible within.

Angel crept closer, her moccasins making no sound on the dewy ground. Her bow was drawn, ready to end the hunt with one more shot.

"Wait here, Cari," Artos whispered and moved after Angel, trying to mimic her noiseless path over the rough ground. He had only gone a few yards when he heard the snap of her bow and the crashing in the brush as the elk fell.

"Got him," said Angel triumphantly. "Come help me clear some brush, Art. He weighs too much for us to drag free. We'll have to butcher it where it lies."

Artos's hands were sticky with blood as he helped Angel butcher the young elk. He had never done such work before and found it very distasteful. He followed her directions, doing his best not to appear squeamish in her eyes, tugging the skin back when she directed and doing his best to be useful.

"Art?" Carimus's voice quavered a bit.

"Don't worry, Cari," he answered. "We know you didn't mean to wound this one. It's alright."

"Art, we're in trouble," came the response. "Come here, please."

Something in Carimus's voice made Artos turn his attention away from the task, and he stood up and stepped clear of the brush. He heard Angel standing up behind him.

Twenty feet away, Carimus was in the grip of a large man in black leathers. In his left hand, the man held a large knife inches from Carimus's throat. To the man's left was another man, similarly clad, holding a crossbow aimed between Artos and Angel. To make matters worse, the two men were flanked by a pair of enormous black mastiffs. Not hunting dogs—warhounds—each easily weighing nearly three hundred pounds.

45

WHAT COLORS?

CARIMUS

3:30 p.m.

Carimus stood motionless, quivering in fear. The stink of sweat and an unwashed body nearly made him gag. The man's hand dug painfully into his shoulder and the dirty blade waved back and forth before him.

"Keep your hands up where we can see them or I cut Cari's throat," growled the leather clad man. "Come out nice and slow. Drop the knife, sister. Now!" he roared and moved the blade closer to Carimus's throat as Angel emerged beside Artos, the skinning knife clenched in her hand. She dropped the bloody blade to the ground at her feet. Artos and Angel exchanged a quick glance, then slowly raised their hands.

"We've been scourin' the mountains fer months. Looking fer signs of you valley rats," Carimus smelt his rancid breath. Then heard him spit on the ground. "Now yer goin' to be leading us to yer secret camp an' we can start movin' you out of hiding and put ye to work." He grinned a nasty grin. "Remember, we don't need three guides, so if ye want to keep the blood in little Cari's throat, ye best be nice an' helpful. Got it?"

"You're making a mistake," said Artos desperately. "We're not from Rainbow Valley. I don't know where their hidden village is. We can't guide you there."

"Sure yer not," sneered the big man. "Just who else would ye be, then?"

"I'm Artos deDraconis. You'll be in a world of hurt if you harm my little brother!"

The two men exchanged a hurried glance. "Draconis, eh?" The big man looked back at Artos.

"Kill him," he said to his henchman, who raised his crossbow and took aim at Artos's heart.

The big man moved his knife to the side to slash at Carimus's throat. Time slowed to a crawl as he saw Artos step forward, summoning his crysword to his hand. He knew with despair he was going to die. Artos was too far away to stop the big man from cutting his throat, but he had to do something. Out of the corner of his eye, he saw the second bandit raise his crossbow to kill his brother.

Carimus's sword appeared as if by magic in his hand and swept before him, deflecting the knife and slicing through the wrist holding it. The big man screamed with shock, released Carimus, and grabbed at his bloody wrist. Carimus fell in a heap at his feet. He heard the snap of the crossbow firing and the twang of Angel's bowstring at nearly the same instant. He looked up at his brother, expecting to see him falling with a crossbow bolt in his heart.

The two dogs snarled and leaped forward. One at Angel, the other at Artos. From out of nowhere, a snarling gray streak bowled into the mastiff coming at Artos, knocking it off its feet, directly into the other charging dog. Liv had arrived!

Artos took three quick steps forward and swung his crysword at the big man, who had thrown Carimus down. The man's screaming stopped with a gurgling sound as Artos's sword cleaved through his chest, nearly cutting him in two, and he dropped at Artos's feet.

Liv's snarling stopped abruptly. She stood over the corpse of one dog whose neck was clearly broken by the force of her powerful attack. The other dog had turned to flee, but an arrow from Angel had struck the dog, killing it instantly.

Artos dropped to his knees bedside Carimus, who was sitting on the ground, looking around with a dazed expression, the bloody blade of his sword still clenched in his hand. "Are you okay?" Artos asked gently.

Angel walked over and crouched beside them. "That was good work, Cari. You probably saved Art's life. The one with the crossbow jerked when his friend screamed, and he shot wildly. It gave me a chance to get my bow and finish him. Liv took care of the dogs. We're all safe now."

"He grabbed me from behind. I ... I never saw them coming. He held that knife to my throat and told me to call you. I didn't know what to do."

"You did just fine, Cari," said Artos. "You got our attention and then you cut his knife hand right off. That was well done. Uncle Brett would have been proud."

"Is Liv alright? I saw her attack the dogs."

"She's fine," replied Angel.

Liv was sitting a few yards away, licking her paw and then washing her face, looking as though nothing in particular had occurred.

Artos wiped the blood from his blade on the black leather

armor of the fallen big man and sheathed his sword. Carimus followed suit with a trembling hand.

Angel slipped her bow to its normal spot on her back, walked over to the dead archer and bent down and started searching the body.

"What are you doing?" asked Carimus.

"Checking for any sign of a House. I'm betting these raiders have the blue and yellow of Herndar under their armor."

Carimus looked at the bloody remains of the fallen big man, then turned away suddenly, fell to his knees, and was noisily ill.

Artos patted him on the shoulder and repeated it was okay.

"By the Mother," said Angel.

"Did you find something?" asked Artos.

Carimus retched a few more times and then stopped throwing up; his stomach emptied.

"Not what I expected," she replied. "This guy isn't wearing Herndar's colors."

"So, they weren't from a Great House after all."

"I didn't say that. He's wearing colors, just not blue and yellow. He's wearing yellow and green. Those are Anson's colors. Aren't they?"

Artos gave Carimus a clean rag to wipe his face and walked over to Angel and the fallen man.

Carimus wiped his face, stood up, and walked over near Angel. He looked at the fallen archer. Sure enough, beneath the black leather armor, the man sported a tunic of yellow with thin green stripes.

Artos kneeled down next to the fallen archer, drew his dagger, and cut off a swath of soiled cloth from the dead man's tunic. "This is proof House deAnson is mixed up in this mess. These aren't their lands, but they were backing House deHerndar about the tax increases." He rolled up the piece of cloth and stuck it in his belt pouch.

"Are you okay, Art?" asked Angel. "You're white as a ghost."

Artos swallowed and nodded. "I never killed a man before, but they were going to kill us. What else was there to do?"

"I've shot a few Beastmen," replied Angel. "But that bandit was the first man I've ever killed. I don't regret it, though. He would have shot you if Cari hadn't distracted him." Angel shook her head. "Don't let it get to you. Think of it like a war. Men die in wars. It was self-defense, and you were protecting Cari. You did what you needed to do."

Artos took a deep breath and nodded. "Do we bury them? Or what?"

Angel shook her head. "Leave them lay. The scavengers will take care of them. They don't deserve anything better. Come on, we have an elk to butcher."

They left the bodies where they lay and returned to finish skinning Carimus's elk.

Chapter Twelve:

Mind Shields

46

MINDSHIELDS

ARTOS

7:45 p.m.

ARTOS'S THOUGHTS WERE JUMBLED and turbulent when they sat for dinner. Were those brigands who wore the colors of House deAnson acting under orders of Count Boris? Or were they renegades, mere bandits? Cat had claimed raiders wearing House deHerndar's colors had burnt down her family's home. What was he to believe?

The six hunters were all weary, having carried home as much venison as they could shoulder. Artos let Angel tell Donel the tale of their encounter with the raiders and only added his affirmation, producing the swath of cloth with the deAnson colors when Bort questioned the identity of the bandits.

After dinner, when Donel announced it was time to begin mindshield training. Artos suggested it be postponed, using the extreme tiredness of the hunting party as an excuse. Donel would not hear of it, however, citing that an enemy would never pause an attack merely because someone was too tired to defend themselves. So, after the table was cleared and the dishes washed, he prepared for an evening of training.

Artos did not know what to expect in the after-dinner training session, but from the smug expression on Bortis' face, he expected to be surprised. Whatever training Donel had given Bortis that afternoon obviously met with his approval and, considering the skepticism that his brother had shown to everything here within the Crystal Tower so far, it must have been nothing short of wondrous.

Donel led the way to the lowest level of the tower, past the doors he explained led to his gardens, and stopped before a large door at the end of the hall. Artos noticed that this area didn't seem to have any of the nooks or dead-end hallways that held the sliding crystal doors, just the stairs up and three iron-bound wooden doors. He wondered if this was really the case. As far as he could tell, this tower seemed to have many secret places and although Donel had seemed willing to expose those secret places to them, he wondered if there were rooms Donel didn't wish to reveal. These thoughts vanished when Donel opened the door and proceeded into the room beyond.

"This is the training chamber," said Donel. "The walls are composed of nine different screens, plus the screen which is the back of the door. I can use these in any number of ways to enhance your training in quanti-magic. Although the floor and the ceiling do not look it, they are screens as well. They can project images and they will absorb any stray energy which might rebound from a normal screen and produce unwanted effects, including injury."

Artos looked up at the ceiling twenty feet above him and then crouched down to examine the floor. He rubbed his hand along the surface. "This is crystal? It feels like the stone floor of the Winding Way. But not as soft."

"It is a type of crystal, Art. You will see it in use soon, but not tonight," said Donel. "Tonight is mind-shield training. Down to the end of the room everyone, stand before the screen there. I will go into the control room and begin the lesson."

Everyone followed him to the eastern end of the large chamber while Donel disappeared around the corner and into the control room. Shortly afterwards, a large red rune appeared on the screen before them.

"This is Algiz, the rune of protection, representing the regalo of the mind-shield. It should be easy to remember," said Donel's voice coming from the screen. "It looks somewhat like the letter 'Y' or perhaps a trident as the center line extends up as long as the two forking ones."

Artos looked at the glowing rune. It would be easy to remember, just as Donel said. But how did remembering the shape of a rune help create a mind-shield? When his Uncle Cameron had taught him to farsee with the screens at Castle Draconis, Cameron had used the screen to open up a part of his mind. At least that was how Uncle Cam had explained it. There had been no runes involved, just concentrating on the screens while Cameron lectured.

"The rune will glow, and it will get brighter and then fade, over and over. You need to concentrate on forming your mind-shield while it does this. Everyone has their own way of doing this. Some picture a golden, unbreakable aura surrounding them. Others think of themselves inside an impregnable fortress with walls and a moat. I have always pictured my mind floating atop a soft cloud, high above the world where no one can see or reach me. Find something that feels safe for you. Relax and concentrate on the rune."

A barely perceptible humming filled the room, and the rune began to pulse.

Donel spoke softly, "Find your safety and have it surround you. Know that no matter how confusing or puzzling the world around you becomes, you are safe within your mind. No terror can engulf you, no bedazzling can cloud your thoughts, and you are the master of your own Self. Find your center, your true innermost self. Once you are secure in that place, no tempest can engulf you. Nothing can break through the shield that guards your center, that which makes you truly who you are. Every person is unique. You are the only you that is or will ever be. Inside yourself, you are the master. Fear kills the mind, but you will not be afraid, for you are mind shielded. Confusion is the great divider, but you will remain whole and untouchable within your mind."

At first, Artos was unsure of what to picture as his safe place. A castle was his first thought, but the events at Castle Draconis made the thought of an impregnable fortress seem less than safe. Floating on a cloud? No, that just seemed too silly somehow. What would make him feel safe? The form of Liv, the huge mist cat, sprang into his mind. He pictured his mind as a young mist kitten with its mother standing protectively over it. Then, to be doubly sure, he pictured a lovely green aura surrounding the entire scene. The green hue of Angel's eyes formed a strong, unbreakable shield around an image of Liv, who stood guard over his kitten mind. Donel was still speaking. He could hear his voice intertwined with the soft, low hum that seemed to fill the entire world. The rune Algiz pulsed to the rhythm of his beating heart.

Suddenly, the rune was gone, and everything was quiet. Artos realized his eyes were closed. He must have dozed off. He shook his head and looked around wildly. Everyone else was reacting the same way. What had just happened?

"Is everyone feeling alright?" asked Donel, no longer in the control room but standing before them. "Is anyone feeling dizzy? Anyone have a headache?"

Angel and Joy were standing beside him. How had they gotten there? Artos was sure the four girls were all to his left, but only Rachel and Vix were there now. Carimus was still to his right with Bortis beyond him. They were looking around, appearing confused. Artos' legs felt shaky, as if he had just run a few laps up and down the Winding Way, but that was silly. It was true they had marched home with a full load of venison, but he had rested during dinner and thought he was recovered.

"I'm worn out," said Carimus. "My head doesn't hurt, but my legs are so tired."

"As well, they might. It's been a long session, after a long day," said Donel. "The training screen uses an old teaching method called hypnosis. Angel and Joy have been through it before. After the screens took hold of your minds and began imprinting the rune upon your under-minds, I sent Angel and Joy up to the Roost to send Oswald off with a message to Kaerin. They already have mindshields. I know you feel you were only listening to me for a few moments, but the session was over two hours. It is time for sleeping. You all have Algiz imprinted in your minds, and I also took the liberty of programing your minds so that illusions will not easily fool you."

"Trueseeing?" asked Bortis.

"Yes, however, it's not automatic. A person's mind will normally see what it expects to see. If something seems normal or expected, you can still be fooled. However, you will now be able to discern an illusion if you are searching for it. Whatever is not truly there will become fuzzy, blurry, insubstantial. What is real will appear within it. But you have all had enough training tonight. Tomorrow the actual work will begin. Angel and Joy have prepared a second supper for you all. Nothing heavy, but I think you will find you will sleep better."

"I'm starving," said Bortis, and then looked a bit hurt when everyone laughed.

"You're always hungry, Bort," said Carimus, as Artos nodded in agreement.

As tired as he was, sleep did not come easy for Artos again that night. Memories of the knife to Carimus's throat, thoughts of his betrothal to Elaine deEagledon, the sight of Duka's crysword hanging from the hook on his bed at the castle, all whirled through his thoughts. When he finally fell asleep, it was uneasy, and he tossed and turned restlessly.

ACT THREE

TO BE A KING

Chapter Thirteen:

News

47

A VISITOR

ARTOS

9/19/1971 ar

9:30 a.m.

Artos expected Donel to resume training directly after breakfast, but instead, he took them upstairs and had everyone except Angel and Joy undergo a fresh round of testing.

Afterwards, they all gathered in the control room as he examined the results.

"I am happy to say, it looks as though you all have mindshields, and I can see no signs of any harmful effects from working with the screens."

"What kind of harmful effects?" asked Carimus.

"It is extremely rare, Cari, but sometimes people have suffered bleeding within their brains. Something I have never seen from my time as a teacher at Starstone Tower. It was something we were told to be on the lookout for, with new students. Full testing is not something we will have to oft repeat unless one of you has headaches or other symptoms of damage. A quick scan will show if there are any adverse effects."

At that moment, a soft bong sounded. "The roost," said Donel. "Oswald should not have returned so quickly. There must be news!" He jumped up from his chair and led the way to the roost, but it was not Oswald who awaited them there. It was the bard Varyan and a giant golden eagle.

"Ser Varyan," cried out Donel, "Well met! Is Prince Tirinvo with you?"

"Lord Donel, it is good to meet with you again. Although I wish it was under different circumstances. No, I am alone. The prince is communing with his brother at Alfheim, and I fear I cannot stay here long."

"Have you any word of Duka?" interrupted Carimus. "Have you seen him?"

"So Duka is the missing brother," answered the bard. "Andune told us he had word that three of House deDraconis had come to Rainbow Valley and his daughter was escorting them to you, my friend."

He looked at Carimus and shook his head. "Alas, I have no news of your brother, nor of Cloudbreaker, my old friend, and steed."

"When Prince Tirinvo heard only three of you had arrived here safely, he asked me to come and ascertain which brother was missing, and to deliver his apologies. He is delaying his trip back to Fairinlan so I might accomplish this task, so I must not tarry overlong. But I have sad tidings to convey, although not unexpected ones, I am sure. Donel, may I beg use of your library screen?"

*

When everyone had gathered around the table, the bard reached into his pouch and produced his sapphire-crysharp, which he placed on the screen.

"Over the years, I have developed certain skills with my crysharp, which, as far as I know, I possess uniquely. Being a trained bard requires I be able to memorize an untold number of songs and tales. I am also entrusted to be a bearer of news and happenings around the realm. A crysword grows and adapts to the mind to which it is bound. With some effort I am able to record every event which goes on around me and reproduce them when required. This includes my own past performances, allowing me to correct flaws and to remember songs played long ago and thus refresh my memory.

"I have a recording of that fateful night which I am about to show you. I must warn you there are things some of you may find most disturbing. Would be it was not so. This being the case, before I begin, I wonder if watching this is necessary or desirable for everyone here? Princes Artos and Bortis and Lord Donel need to witness what I am about to reveal. I wonder if anyone else needs to?"

"I'm not leaving!" said Carimus.

The rest of those watching also indicated their desire to stay.

"Very well," said the bard. "I will tell my tale and my harp will provide such detail as needed.

"Prince Tirinvo and I left the Great Hall late after a long, sometimes heated, discussion with King Aaron and Archduke Cameron. As Prince Tirinvo had told Lord Donel via the screens on that fateful afternoon, before we left The Darrell's hall, he urged King Aaron to allow the four of you to come here and study under Donel. I believe the king might have been persuaded if not for the emotional rebuttal of the Archbishop.

Lord Cameron was adamant that Prince Carimus remain under his tutelage, and equally forceful in insisting the training of the rest of the princes was best done under the eye of the Church. The king agreed to speak with Prince Tirinvo once more in the morning before we returned to Fairinlan, but I fear he had already decided. He could not trust his sons to a distant relative, who he had always been taught did not support the best interests of your House.

"As always, Jaek led the way, with Taur following along behind. We had gone no further than a dozen steps up the stairway that led to our quarters when loud voices shattered the quiet behind us. King Aaron was addressing Duke Bretton, heedless of the peace that had fallen in the castle. 'How can I expect Artos to act royally when you set such a poor example, Bret? Where were you all evening?' There followed a crashing sound as if glasses were being dashed to the ground. Prince Tirinvo and I exchanged worried glances, but would have proceeded upwards as it would not have been seemly for us to intrude on a family disagreement. But then, we felt an overpowering aura of unmistakable evil emanating from the room behind us. As one, we turned and hurried back to the Great Hall."

Varyan reached down and plucked a sequence of notes upon his harp and rising from the screen was a scene of the nearly deserted Great Hall of Castle Draconis.

As the Fairborn entered the hall, King Aaron was standing next to the seated Cameron, facing Duke Bretton. The Duke was glaring at them and as they watched, his eyes turned a glowing red. Inhuman eyes! Tirinvo summoned his crysword even as his liegemen attempted to step between him and the imminent danger. Varyan pulled his harp from its pouch and readied for battle.

The creature wearing Duke Bretton's form heard their approach and glared furiously in their direction. Then it quivered, gave a menacing snarl, and its body morphed. In the space of a heartbeat, the creature grew to eight feet tall. Covered with matted dark fur, it had long black talons. As quick as thought, it leaned forward and slashed through the throat of Cameron as he was rising from his seat. The talons of the other arm slashed deeply across the chest of King Aaron. Slicing through his flesh and bone as a sharp knife cuts through soft cheese.

"Father!" shouted Carimus. Artos put his arm around his younger brother and held him close as they watched in horror. Bortis drew a sharp breath and clenched his fists.

A jarring wail emanated from Varyan's crysharp and a brilliant electric blue bolt of energy burst forth and slammed into the creature, sending it flying away from the king, crashing against the wall with a loud thud.

Everyone watched breathlessly as the Fairborn raced to Aaron's side. They could all see Cameron was dead. Not only was his throat slashed, but his head had been severely twisted, his neck broken.

A sob broke from Carimus' throat, and several of the daughters moaned in sympathy.

Tirinvo knelt beside Aaron and looked helplessly at the ruin that had once been his chest. Blood was pouring freely from the grievous wound.

Aaron looked at his old friend and struggled to speak. Tirinvo leaned close and Aaron managed a few words.

"Save my sons … Art … Artos …" he whispered, and the light left his eyes. He slumped and his body gave one last shudder, then went limp.

Tirinvo bowed his head. "I will, Aaron. I promise, my friend, I so swear!"

Artos felt something inside him stir. Whether it was rage or sorrow, he wasn't sure, probably a combination of both.

From across the room came a loud undulating cry as the black furred creature rose to its feet. And the cry was answered. Outside the Great Hall came the howling of many beasts and the surprised cries of men turned to screams of fear and pain.

Varyan raised his crysharp again, but the creature was not to be caught off guard again. As the bard struck his weapon to launch another bolt of sonic energy, the creature leaped up and scuttled up the wall like some monstrous spider. The bolt shattered harmlessly against the wall where it had stood but a moment before. It wailed again as it gained an upper balcony and, in answer to the call, a horde of Beastmen charged into the hall, howling and waving bloody axes and clubs.

Artos closed his eyes and whispered a silent prayer for his father and his uncle. He had known they were dead, but somehow seeing the event brought the weight of his circumstance down more heavily upon him.

"My Lord," shouted Jaek, pulling the prince to his feet, "we must flee!"

Varyan turned to face the horde and struck his harp again. This time there was a loud *CRACK* and the sound of thunder as a bolt of lightning shot forth and crashed into the maddened horde of Beastmen. Bodies flew and fell, but more were howling behind them.

"How many Beastmen were there?" asked Artos.

"How did they get into the Castle?" said Bortis simultaneously.

The twang of a bowstring and the swish of an arrow came from Taur where he stood beside the bard and a bellow of rage sounded from the balcony of the orchestra gallery as the beast ducked out of sight.

"We realized the creature was on an upper floor now," said Varyan, "and that you princes were also somewhere above."

"With me!" Tirinvo shouted, and with the bard and his liegemen behind him, he made haste to the royal entrance and to the stairs that led upward to the rooms of the sleeping princes.

*

Varyan put his hand against the strings of his harp and the vision vanished.

"Of course, you know what happened next," said Varyan. "You ran to the top of the tower and the Eagles took off into the teeth of the storm. Prince Tirinvo and Taur stood with the Tower Captain and awaited Jaek and me to join them. And what everyone knew would follow on our heels …

"I fired several bolts of lightning into the horde of Beastmen that were charging up the Winding Way. It slowed their attack, but never for too long. I could feel the mental urgings of the

Abomination, filling them with anger and a lust for blood."

The bard gazed at his audience. "This was the first part of the events of that night. The next part I am going to show you is what Prince Tirinvo wanted you to see, so you might understand the reason he owes you an apology."

The bard plucked another combination of notes, and a new scene arose from the screen.

Varyan and Jaek were sprinting up the Winding way. They rounded the last curve and, facing them, was a line of bowmen with arrows notched and ready.

"DON'T SHOOT!" bellowed Sergeant McArn and though several of the guardsmen flinched, none loosed an arrow at the running Fairborn. A gust of dark smoke trailed the runners and the howls of the approaching Beastmen could be heard.

"Be ready lads!" repeated McArn as the two Fairborn ran through the qulan field and through the archers who closed ranks behind them.

Around the bend of the Way came the Beastmen, racing up the ramp. In the fore was a burly figure with the head of a wolf, waving a bloody axe over his head. Close behind were three others, two with the snouts and tusks of boars, the third with the horns of a ram, all armed with clubs or axes. Howling with crazed fury.

Carimus gave a gasp at the sight of the onrushing horde as Bortis beat his fist into the palm of his other hand in impotent rage.

"Kill them," whispered Artos as he watched his guard stand their ground bravely against the rush of foes.

"FIRE!" shouted McArn, and the bows of the guards sang. The wolf-headed Beastman dropped short of the end of the ramp, arrows peppered his body. Three arrows lodged in the body of the ram-head, another arrow lodged in the eye of one of the boar-head and they both fell, leaving only one howling Beastman to burst through the qulan field. Before the creature took two steps, Jaek slashed the creature across the neck with his short sword and the beast's club veered wildly over the shoulder of the Fairborn. The Beastman dropped to the Eyrie floor, its life blood pouring from the gaping wound in its throat. A few steps behind were more of the creatures and they, too, were greeted by a barrage of arrows. Only two made the top of the ramp, and that pair each met their end at the hand of a swordsman. More howls echoed from below, but no more of the Beastmen were visible.

"Good shooting, men! Stand ready, there's more coming. Make sure of yer targets. Some of our lads might be a-runnin' up the Way. Let's make those beasties fear the Eyrie." McArn walked behind his men, slapping a shoulder here and there. "Yer doing a grand job, lads. Keep it going. Stand ready."

"Tower Captain McArn is a brave man," said Artos. "A good leader."

"Uncle Brett told me he was one of his best men," said Bortis.

Bestial roars and the sound of slapping feet warned of the Beastmen's approach a moment before the next wave came into view. Tirinvo shouted, "Here they come!" as they charged up the ramp.

This time, there were too many for the bows of the guards to stop them all. Although many of the first wave fell, those following leaped over their bodies and crashed into the row of guards. At that point, it was all hand-to-hand combat. Tirinvo's crysword-rapier thrust into the throat of another wolf-head as Jaek and Taur stood beside him, their short swords weaving a deadly pattern of defense that no Beastmen could penetrate.

Bortis was quivering with rage and frustration as Artos kept his arm around Carimus's shoulder. His younger brother frozen in shock at the onslaught.

Suddenly, the House Anthem of the Draconis rang out loud from behind the guards. Varyan stood playing his harp and the stirring music rang forth. The guards fought on with renewed energy, buoyed by the song-spell of the bard and the wave of Beastmen faltered. A few turned and fled. Soon there were no living Beastmen in the eyrie. But the attack had taken its toll. Three of the guard lay motionless on the floor and two more were bleeding badly. Varyan stopped playing and dashed up to the first of the bleeding guards. He laid his hands upon the wound and chanted a few words. The wound stopped bleeding and fresh pink flesh showed where moments before there had been a grievous wound. He repeated the spell upon the guard and again, the healing chant worked its magic.

"You're a healer," said Carimus.

"Thank you for saving those men," said Artos.

Bortis stood silent, his fists and teeth clenched in anger.

"Yes, Prince Carimus," answered Varyan. "I am forced, at times, to be a warrior. But it is my choice to be a healer. When I can."

Just then, a crashing sound and a shout was heard coming from beyond the eastern guard guardroom door.

McArn looked to Tirinvo, who nodded back to the Tower Captain.

"Everyone stand fast. Watch the Way! Prince Tirinvo's in command! Shawn, ye and Williams with me!"

With that, McArn and two guards ran to reinforce the stairs in the eastern guardroom.

Tirinvo quickly assessed the situation. "Pile up some of those bodies before the Way. Use the stinking beasts for cover. Get your bows ready for another charge." The Fairborn Prince stepped forward and, taking a hold of the shoulders of a dead guard, pulled him back away from the corpses of the Beastmen. His liegemen followed suit and removed the other bodies of the fallen defenders, laying them well behind the line.

The guardsmen hesitated at first, but realizing the wisdom of the Fairborn prince's words, began heaping the dead Beastmen into a pile before the entrance to the Winding Way.

"Captain! Sergeant McArn," came a call from the door to the western guard room. Tirinvo pointed at Taur, and motioned for him to stay with the archers, while he and Jaek hurried to the guardroom, with Varyan right behind them.

Stepping into the room, he stopped in surprise. Standing in the room were four women and a young man wearing the white tunics of kitchen servants. The guards were busy replacing the barricade in the barracks beyond, that they had removed to let the servants in.

"We heard the women calling, and we had to let them in, sir," one guard explained to Tirinvo. "No sign of the beasts. Yet."

"You did right," replied Tirinvo. "Get that barricade back in place and stand ready." He turned to the servants. "Stay here. You are safe now."

The Fairborn hurried back out to the eyrie just in time to meet McArn as he returned from his mission to reinforce the east barracks. The tower captain helping a wounded man stumble along, blood streaming from a slash on his arm.

"There were only four of them," said McArn. "They burst through the barricade and killed poor Dony. Kincaid be slashed badly. Sir Bard, can ye help him?"

Varyan repeated his healing chant, and the blood stopped flowing as the arm knitted back together.

"Four servants made it up the stairs to the other side," said Tirinvo. "I told them to stay in the guardroom. I fear we are now all that remains alive, though there may be a few others hiding away. The beasts will spare none if they sniff them out, I am afraid."

"How many do ye think there be? How did they get in? I always was told none could enter who were not invited or proven trusted men." The grizzled guardsman's eyes were haunted as he gazed at the bodies of the Beastmen. "What of the King, an' the Dukes?"

Tirinvo shook his head. "I do not know how many of the beasts are inside. A great many. I would feign to guess over a hundred from the howls we heard. As to how they breached the castle? I do not know. We saw King Aaron murdered and the Archbishop as well. No Beastman murdered them. There was a creature who looked like Duke Bretton. His aura was pure evil. It changed shape into an enormous beast with red eyes and long black claws. Claws that cut right through King Aaron. It slashed Duke Cameron's throat, and the force of its blow snapped his neck. Varyan blasted it with a bolt and knocked it across the room into the wall. It jumped right back up and when he fired at it again, it scrambled up the wall like an insect ..." he trailed off.

"An Abomination," whispered McArn.

Tirinvo nodded. "It would seem so. Though how such a creature could be inside the qulan is a mystery to me."

"You say some servants are in the guardroom? I better be looking in on them. Keep a watch please. I'll be right back." McArn hurried to the guardroom and went inside.

"Cousin?" Tirinvo looked to the bard. "You saw that thing. Saw it change and scuttle up the wall. Do you agree? Abomination?"

Varyan looked grim and gave a terse nod. "From the evil aura, I would say there is no doubt. One of the Five. Here to recover the head of Tomung, I would wager."

"Shawn!" It was McArn calling from the door to the guardroom. "Come here and replace Sonny for a bit!"

The corporal who had accompanied McArn to the eastern guard and returned with him looked at the sergeant with surprise, but dutifully trotted over to the west guardroom door where McArn waited.

"Donel pled with Alexavier to destroy that head," said Tirinvo. "He would not listen. I fear his grandsons paid for his folly with their lives."

"I know the Angellar sent a warning as well," said the bard. "For I delivered it. All that accomplished was to make King Alex even more determined to keep his trophy and show the world how powerful he was. The fool."

"I hope Windrider can get the Princes to the valley. With this storm, they could blow across the Dragon Sea to Renn or crash into the mountains and perish."

"Cloudbreaker has borne me in foul weather before," answered Veryan. "We always prevailed. Though I must admit never in a storm this fierce. I have faith in our friends."

"I am glad to see I was mostly correct," said Varyan. "I fear for Cloudbreaker and Prince Duka."

"Duka's alive," said Carimus. "His crysword is still hanging in his room. Maybe he and your eagle will show up. Soon."

"That is good news," the bard answered. "Let us hope you are correct."

McArn rejoined the Fairborn. "We can hold this position for a while, but we are too few to hold it long. We were twenty-five, but we have lost four men. It would have been more without yer healing magic, Lord Bard, and I thank ye. But we need to decide what we are gonna be a-doin'. We need a plan. We be trapped here, with nowhere to go, save but to jump to our deaths."

Bortis inhaled sharply. Artos reached out with his free arm and clasped him on the shoulder.

Tirinvo gazed at the grim face of the sergeant. "Your men have done well, McArn. If we can hold this position until our steeds return in the morning, we shall ferry you all to the gatehouse across the loch. We will hold those beasts at bay, never fear."

McArn looked at the Fairborn prince. "Do you think the young lords are safe, sir? Did ye send them to the deEagledon castle?"

"I sent them to their kin. In this weather, we can only hope the Sky Father has spared them. The storm is diminishing. By morning, it should have passed."

"Count Penrodyn is their grand sire," said McArn.

At that moment, the howls sounded loud once again, and the pounding of the Beastmen's feet was heard coming up the Winding Way. McArn turned back and ran to stand with his men.

*

"Prince Tirinvo felt it was better to keep your whereabouts secret," said the bard, halting the narration on the screen. "Some abominations can read thoughts or beguile people into saying things they should hold secret."

Donel nodded. "It was best he let the guard captain think that. I am guessing that would be what the creatures thought as well. Hopefully, we did not set the dePenrodyns in harm's way. I tasked The Darrell to warn them, but he told me no one answered the call."

"What!" said Artos. "You didn't tell us this. The Abomination may have killed them all!"

"The Darrell told me he knew Count Estel's plan was to set out for the dePenrodyn demesne the morning after the party. I hope we can believe that was the case."

"You should have told us," said Artos.

Donel sighed. "Artos, I am sorry, but I believed you had enough worries. I thought adding another thing you were helpless to affect would only add to the difficulties you would have in trying to learn the things you need to know. Would it have made learning to mindshield easier or more difficult with yet another thing to distract you?"

"He's right, Art," said Bortis. "Uncle Brett always said to focus on each task in the order of need. To focus on everything is to accomplish nothing."

"We fought off the next wave and then they stopped attacking," said Veryan. "It stayed quiet, and the storm passed. I believe we had frightened the Beastmen away from attempting to take the Eyrie. At least for a time, but the Abomination who led the Beastmen was not done with us. Perhaps it was making sure the castle held no other resistance. It may have been searching for your whereabouts. That would have been of utmost importance to the fiend. I do not know. There may have been pockets of resistance which kept his attention away from us. There were no more sounds of battle coming up the Way, however. So it may have been merely a matter of the creature making sure the castle was under its control."

"With the dawn, things went from bad to worse. To monstrous, in fact ... Sergeant McArn had his men napping in shifts with six archers keeping watch at the mouth of the Winding Way. We were awaiting the return of our steeds when suddenly there was a commotion outside the eyrie as if the flapping of enormous wings. At first, we thought it heralded the sound of the eagles returning, but it quickly grew too loud. Then there was a loud crashing thump coming from the eastern side of the castle." The bard reached out and plucked the strings of his harp once again.

A new scene appeared showing the battlements outside the Eyrie.

The four Fairborn rushed out onto the battlements along with several of the archers. Hurrying to the eastern battlements, they looked down at the airship dock a few hundred feet below. A horrendous sight awaited them. Perched on the crushed remains of the deDraconis airship sat a monstrous crow.

"The crow!" said Angel.

"I see you have seen this creature," said the bard. "It was flying over Rainbow Valley when I tried to make my way here. It forced me to detour through the mountains and I wandered for a time in the mists. That is why I was not here with this news sooner."

"It was flying above the valley when we left Angel's camp," said Artos. "We didn't know exactly what it was, but we assumed it was looking for us."

"Look closely," said the bard, pointing at the scene above the screen.

Everyone peered closer.

On the creature's back, strapped between the wings, was a howdah. Seated there was an ominous figure, clad in dark gray.

"Varyan, on its back!" called Tirinvo. "Can you blast it with a bolt?"

"It's too far. I could probably hit it with a sound bolt, but at that range, it would only tickle it. Gah!" The bard put his hands to his head and grimaced in pain.

The others felt it too. "What was that?" gasped the Fairborn prince.

"Shield yourself. It has mind weapons," gasped the bard.

Tirinvo's liegemen looked up from the giant bird. "What is it?" asked Jaek, looking at the prince.

At that moment, the three guards started firing arrows at the bird and its rider.

The arrows directed at the monstrous bird made it look up, but otherwise were as pinpricks to the monster. One arrow was fired at the gray-clad figure. Narrowly missing its target, it drew the rider's attention.

The guards suddenly reacted. One screamed, dropped his bow, and threw himself over the battlement, still screaming as he fell. His scream abruptly ended as he collided with the rocky wall of the keep and bounced to the stone floor of the airship dock.

Carimus gasped in horror. Artos swallowed hard. Bortis was swearing softly.

A second guard would have followed, but Taur grappled with him and pulled him away from the battlement, still screaming in abject terror. The third guard dropped his bow, clutched his chest, and crumpled in a heap.

"Get back inside!" Jaek shouted. He grabbed Tirinvo by the arm to pull him away. The Fairborn prince resisted and would have tried to help the fallen guard, but the bard reached him first and threw him over his shoulder, as if he were a child.

"Go! Go!" yelled Varyan and rushed back toward the entrance of the eyrie tower carrying the fallen guard.

Tirinvo pushed Jaek toward Taur. "I'm going. Help your brother." He turned and sprinted back toward the doorway. He could hear the flapping of huge wings.

Varyan stopped at the door and watched as the twins each took an arm and dragged the struggling guard between them. Behind them, the flapping sound increased, and he saw the bird rising as it flew upwards. Fortunately, a crow cannot fly like a hummingbird and the creature had to fly away from the castle to gain altitude.

The scene shifted, and they were back inside the Eyrie. The brothers pulled the still struggling guard into the tower. He stopped screaming and looked around in a confused manner. Tears poured from his eyes, his body quivered, and he let out an abject moan.

Tirinvo slammed shut the door and dropped a bar across to lock it.

Varyan laid the other guard down, shook his head, and looked at Tirinvo. "He's dead, Trin. His heart burst from sheer terror. That rider, it's another Abomination. It can attack with its thoughts." He gazed at the shaking guard, pity in his eyes. He took his harp and played. A sensation of peace and tranquility filled the air.

The guard gave a sob, then shook himself as if awakening from a bad dream, as perhaps he was.

"What is it?" asked McArn as he rushed up. "What happened to Flynn? Where's Scotty?" He locked down at the guard laying on the stone floor. "Is Brock ..."

Tirinvo nodded. "He's dead and the other man, too. He jumped off the battlements. There's another Abomination out there. Riding a gigantic crow. It can attack with its thoughts. It was fear that drove your guard to jump, and this one would have followed if Taur hadn't stopped him. Fear killed Brock. His heart burst."

Varyan kept playing the soothing music. "I can negate his terror aura, but I can't do anything else while I'm doing so. No more lightning blasts."

McArn looked grim. "They haven't come back as yet. But I

be a-thinking it won't be long with that thing out there trying to a-fear us."

The bard's fingers kept playing as he spoke. "The one inside knows the other is here. That pain we felt Trin, that was them communicating. The Angellar once told me they can exchange thoughts rapidly and anyone sensitive nearby would feel it. Painfully. I think we both caught that blast. In the one brief moment, they likely had a long conversation and already have their plan in place."

"With that crow out there, Windrider and the rest cannot return. Prince Tirinvo, I fear they have us trapped," said Jaek, looking grim.

At that moment there was a tremendous beating of wings and then a loud thump from the eastern side of the eyrie. A horrendous "CAAAWWW" rang out, shaking all within the tower. The Fairborn hurried around the central pillar and looked up at the enormous window that served as the aerial entrance on the east side of the tower.

Huge golden eyes peered in at them above a monstrous ebony beak. The crow was there, perched on the eastern guard house and looking in at them. So large was the monstrous bird, its head blocked the entire window. Its beak thrust in, hit the perch beam, then withdrew again. The bird turned its head as if unwilling to stick its head into what to it was a small opening. The enormous eye looked in at them, and then the head drew back and faced the window, looking in at the people within as if looking at mice in a cage.

The beak opened, "FAIRBORN FILTH. I SEE YOU COWERING THERE WITH THE REST OF THE VERMIN," came the croaking voice. "TODAY IS YOUR LUCKY DAY. THERE ARE SOME EAGLES OUT HERE THAT WISH TO JOIN

YOU. IN A MOMENT, I WILL ALLOW THEM TO ENTER AND THE THREE OF YOU MAY RUN AWAY AND TAKE BACK A MESSAGE TO YOUR PUNY PEOPLE! WARN YOUR KING TO STAY OUT OF THE LANDS OF MEN AND WE SHALL LEAVE YOU AND YOUR PITIFUL KINGDOM ALONE! THE HUMANS ARE DOOMED! WE HAVE KILLED THEIR KING AND ALL HIS BROOD! NO BLOOD OF DRAGONS REMAIN ALIVE IN THE CASTLE. THE FEW GUARDS LEFT THERE WITH YOU, IN YOUR HIDEY HOLE HERE ON THE ROOF, WILL SOON JOIN THEM. BE HAPPY WE WISH YOU TO CONVEY OUR MESSAGE AND SO MAY HAVE YOUR ESCAPE!" The bird's head turned and jerked from view for a moment. A tremendous "CAAAWWW," rang out, as if in warning. Then the bird peered back in.

Tirinvo's face seethed with rage. "Stupid fiend! You think the deDraconis are all dead? You are wrong. Last night while your Beastmen were running amok in the castle, we used our Eagles and sent the Princes far away, to safety. They are beyond your grasp now and will return to slay you all."

There was a moment of silence, then the guards all twitched and many gave a gasp of pain. Veryan redoubled his efforts, weaving his musical spell to counter the mental waves the mounted Abomination hurled against them.

The raven's head tipped back and a loud cry of pure rage filled the air and with a tremendous flap of its enormous wings, the gigantic bird took to the air again.

Varyan stopped his playing, watching the guards to see if the mental attack had ceased. When they showed no sign of the creature's malign effects, he brushed his right hand across his temple with a relieved sigh.

But only moments later, the howls of the Beastmen came

roaring up the winding way. Another charge was coming.

The Fairborn rushed back to rejoin the guards and Varyan held up his crysharp and it transformed. The bard now held a sapphire-blue crysbow.

He looked at his cousin. "No spells for a bit. I need to save some strength for healing. I'll join the archers."

Tirinvo nodded and, flanked by his liegemen, he proceeded to the center of the line of waiting guardsmen. He drew his diamond crysword rapier and the blade of the sword flared with white flame. "Let us slay some beasts!" he cried.

"We had only a few moments to wait before a fresh wave of Beastmen came howling toward us. McArn gave the command to fire at will and barely had the words left his mouth, when a crashing sound came from the western guardroom. Tirinvo sent Taur to help guard our vulnerable flank.

"We slew dozens of the Beastmen then, and another dozen turned and fled. By then, two more of the guards lay dead in their wake and four more bore serious wounds, which I turned to mend. Jaek suddenly faltered and called out, 'Taur! No!' then turned and ran toward the guardroom with Tirinvo close on his heels. I followed as soon as I was able." Varyan sighed and shook his head sadly.

"On the guardroom floor lay the bodies of a guard and three large Beastman. The remains of the barricade they had burst through lay scattered around them. By the door to the stairs leading down into the castle lay the body of Taur, face down on the floor. Jaek had rushed to his fallen brother and gently rolled him over. I hurried to join him. No wound was apparent except a small spot of blood in the middle of his leather armored chest.

"The guard corporal, Shawn, was holding a weeping woman in his arms to console her. The other servants stood huddled behind them. Tirinvo asked what had happened, and the young corporal explained." Varyan plucked his harp once again and the inside of the guardroom appeared before their eyes. Artos recognized the young corporal as the one who had shared his cinnamon rolls with him and Duka a few days before.

"It was a child, sir. At least that's what it looked like, at first. When the Beastmen burst through the door, Thomas fell to the bull-headed one with the axe. I was standing between them and me mum, and the others, when your man rushed in and stabbed him in the throat. He and I killed the other two. Your man was looking at the bodies when this wee lass of a girl peeked in the door. She started wailing about her mommy. Well, me mum saw the pitiful girl and rushed over to help her, as anyone would. I was following her myself when your man yelled at us to stop. He jumped between it and me mum and pushed her back into my arms. I didn't see what happened next exactly. There was a flash and sparks flying and your man dropped to the ground. Where the child had been was something else. The thing was still small, but it wasn't a child. It was horrible looking. Bald, with gray skin and blue marks like tattoos on its cheeks. It was shaking its hands and cursing. Then it turned and ran down the stairs. The qulan field is right there at the doorway. I think that caused the flash and the sparks."

*

"Within minutes our eagles entered the Eyrie, but without Cloudbreaker. I used Taur's steed, Skyflyer, and with Starseeker and Windrider, we ferried the remaining men and the servants to the Gatehouse across the causeway at Brierly. Tirinvo left it to Sergeant McArn to explain what had happened to Captain Jarid derDraconis." The bard shrugged. "I know not what he shall do, but Prince Tirinvo told McArn we would relate to you what happened. That at least he, his remaining guards, and a few servants had escaped. I fear the good sergeant still carries the thought that you are at House dePenrodyn. Until you discover how the Abomination and its minions gained entrance to Castle Draconis, it is better that no one knows where you are. Tirinvo told me to express his sincere regret that in his anger, he let it be known you had escaped."

Artos shook his head, not knowing what to answer.

"I think Prince Tirinvo's instincts were correct," said Donel. "We shall make our plans now that we better understand the situation."

"Prince Tirinvo spoke briefly with Captain Jarid after sergeant McArn had explained the situation. He confirmed we had seen the death of King Aaron. I believe your cousin is a wise man. He did not ask where you were, he only asked if you four were safe. We told him we believed you were. He said that he and his men would hold the gatehouse and await your return, Artos. As we were leaving, I heard his announcement to his men. He said, 'King Aaron is dead. Long live King Artos!' There was shock and grief in the reactions of the men, of course. But the last thing we heard as we flew off were your men cheering for you, Artos."

Artos felt his eyes brimming with tears and he could only nod to the Fairborn bard.

Veryan picked up his harp. "I must go. Prince Tirinvo awaits me. We have a cremation ceremony to attend to. Prince Artos, Prince Bortis, Prince Carimus, I offer my deepest condolences for your loss. I counted King Aaron as my friend. Farewell Lord Donel, Lady Angela."

Donel escorted the bard back to the roost as the rest sat in silence, considering all they had witnessed.

When Donel returned to the library, Carimus was sitting huddled in a chair while Artos stood and stared down at the screen. Bortis paced back and forth like a caged beast. The daughters sat silently apart, leaving the brothers to their thoughts.

"How many people were at the Castle, Prince Artos? Do you know?" asked Donel softly.

"Nearly three hundred," said Artos. "That's counting all the staff, guards, the groundskeepers, and the wives and children."

"Do you think he's right? ... They are all dead?" asked Carimus, looking up from where he sat.

"Yes, I fear it is so. I think the five would spare no one serving our House. It is possible some may have been taken to be their slaves and sent back to the Beastlands. But I doubt it. The beasts were in a killing frenzy. The Abomination's mind projections had them in a blood-lust rage. It wanted to retrieve their Lord, Tomung, and take revenge upon our House. No, I doubt they spared a single man, woman, or child. Curse them."

"We ... we have to do something," Bortis was pale with rage. He stopped pacing and stood clenching and unclenching his fists. "The elves didn't see Uncle Brett, only an Abomination that looked like him before it murdered father. Maybe he's still alive."

Donel sighed and shook his head. "The only sword in Castle Draconis is that of Duka. The others are gone. The creature using Brett's form, the one who murdered you father and uncle, would have killed him first. It probably beguiled him into inviting it through the qulan. If something which looked like the Duke ordered a trusted guard to open the river gate, perhaps saying a grain ship was sinking and needed succor and couldn't wait until morning. The guard, befuddled by the late hour and being ordered by the Duke, could have opened the river gate and let in a ship with a cargo of Beastmen. Then when the ship docked, the beasts flooded out, overwhelmed the guards, and sacked the lower village."

Donel shook his head. "I was hoping the Abominations would think you were all dead, killed in the carnage of the attack at the castle. It becomes imperative you retake the castle quickly, Artos. Whoever the allies of the Abominations are, they will soon know you live. If they do not already. They will move to find and destroy you as well. You must appear too strong for them to risk exposing themselves. We have to advance with your training. You and Bortis must learn to shield your bodies now that you learned to shield your minds."

48

FAIRINHORST?

CARIMUS

1:30 p.m.

AFTER LUNCH, DONEL ONCE MORE brought everyone back to his testing chamber and reassured there was nothing amiss in any of his trainees.

"This afternoon I am going to begin teaching Artos, Bortis, and Carimus how to create and hold a body shield. I am afraid such training would not be of any use to you, ladies. At least not in the time constraints we find ourselves in. Liv has returned and is waiting below to make another hunting expedition. She tells me her brood is getting quite spoiled with all the remains from our trips. But we need to prepare enough supplies to last me for a time and for the expedition that will undertake to reclaim Castle Draconis. Therefore, may I ask for you Daughters to go hunting for us again?"

"Of course, teacher," began Angela.

"There it is again." Carimus interrupted, his voice cracking. Sure enough, the screen beneath the sign of the chrysanthemum had the message, *SEND CARIMUS TO FAIRINHORST.*

"Why should I go there?" he asked defiantly.

Before Donel could reply, the words faded away, and then another single word appeared. *DUKA.* It then slowly faded, and the inert screen showed nothing more.

"What about Duka? Where is he?" shouted Carimus. The screen remained blank.

Donel turned to Carimus. "I think that is all the screens will tell us, Carimus."

"Tirinvo mentioned the Angellar," said Artos. "He said she sent a message to Alexavier about destroying the trophy. Who is she? How could she be sending for Carimus today if she was advising the king over three hundred years ago? I know the Fairborn live long lives, but that long?"

"She's a witch," said Carimus softly.

"Prince Tirinvo was born during the reign of Alexavier's son, Artos. The Bard Varyan is nearing his four hundredth year. Yes, the Fairborn live long lives. Often four times that of a normal man. But the Angellar? I do not know how old she is. Although she was my teacher for a time. I never met her. At least not exactly." Donel looked down and rubbed the back of his neck. "Most of my instruction was from other teachers there. She sent me visions. Only once did we mindspeak. When she informed me of the murder of Denar. I believe she meets with no one except the seers of Fairinhorst, but I was not there very long and most of that time was spent in my chamber and in the gardens."

"She's a witch!" cried Carimus again. "Uncle Cameron told me to beware the witch Angellar. He said she is evil."

"No! Carimus. She is the High Priestess of Mother Veda to the Fairborn Race. Cameron would not like her because she was not under his ecclesiastical jurisdiction. The Forge-folk and the Fairborn both have their own hierarchy outside of the human Church of the Four. They agreed on this in the days of King Austin. Cameron should have taught you this, not told you tales of witches and of evil." Donel shook his head in disgust.

Carimus felt aghast. "But the Church of the Four is the high church of Veda. How can they be apart? That makes little sense."

"What of Renn? What of the lands to the east and west that are not a part of Veda? Do you think you should be the Archbishop to the entire world, Carimus? But this is not the time to discuss theology. We have more pressing things to decide."

"Yes," Bortis agreed. "We need to make plans to avenge father and to reclaim Art's throne, Cari. Not to argue over who is the religious leader of the elves."

"Bort, you need to learn not to call people childish names," said Donel. "Artos is going to need the aid of the Fairborn. You have picked up some vulgar habits from your uncle Brett. If you truly are to serve as your brother's right arm, realize that when you speak, you speak, not only for yourself, but for him.

"I will help train you in the quanti, but you must train yourself to speak respectfully regarding all. If they prove themselves unworthy of respect, then by all means, treat them as they deserve. Until then, you need to give respect, or no one will ever respect you." Donel looked into Bortis' eyes, and he stared back defiantly for a long moment and then looked away.

"People respected Uncle Brett. He was a noted warrior, a skilled swordsman. No one challenged him," Bortis' voice quavered. "He thought I could never fill his shoes. He never said as much, but I could tell. When I failed to master the lessons he was trying to teach me, I could see the disgust in his eyes."

"That's not true, Bort," said Artos. "You were always his favorite. Everyone knew that."

Carimus nodded in support. "He was hardest on you, Bort, because he knew you were his successor, and he was afraid that people would judge him through you. Just like Uncle Cam was with me."

"You two weren't there in the private lessons. When he tried to teach me the light blade, or to truesee. He would end the lesson and give me some stupid busy work to do and stalk away in disgust."

"Duke Bretton was an impatient man, Bortis. I see he was also not a very good teacher," Donel spoke gently. "A teacher needs to inspire his student to achieve, not be angry with slow progress. I have told you why you were conflicted in your regalos. Bretton and Cameron should have been working together with you all to strengthen your use of your gifts. It was a case of the blind trying to teach the blind to see. Neither Bretton nor Cameron were trained enough in the ways of the quans to teach others. Now we must try to overcome this deficiency in a short time. We have less that six weeks to work with. Artos must secure the Dragon Crown and Throne before the solstice."

The enormity of the situation filled Carimus with fear. "We must have someone we can turn to for help," said Carimus. "The Canton of the Sky Church is at Eagleroost with Count Eagledon and the Cantor was with our grandfather at the dePenrodyn keep."

"I would not count on the support of the Sky Church too strongly, Prince Carimus. You face a similar situation as Artos. Bishop Neubre stands to become the leader of the church in Veda as far as the human community in the Lowlands is concerned," said Donel.

"Bishop Neubre has always been friendly to me," protested Carimus.

"Hmmm, yes, it's usually a good idea not to disparage your future superior. However, I suspect he would gall at the prospect of you now being his senior. Years from now would be different in his mind than tomorrow. You are naught but a disciple in the church and he is the Canon with eight bishops answering to him. The same arguments concerning your age and inexperience will be used against you, as with Artos."

"Acolyte," said Carimus in a small voice. "I haven't been giving my disciple's vows yet. Uncle Cameron started calling me disciple this autumn when I showed I was ready in his eyes to advance. I am due to take my vows at the Convocation on the Solstice."

"Teacher? What is your plan?" asked Angel. "How can the Daughters help?"

"Why would you want to help us?" said Bortis, glaring at Angel. "You hate the Houses. You said so yourself."

"I think I can see for myself why Artos needs to be king. Why would I want a council controlled by Herndar and Anson to take over Veda? Even if he has a rude rockhead for a brother!"

"Please! Let us stay on the issue at hand," said Donel. "We all agree that Artos needs to regain his crown. To do so, he must remove the Abomination and the Beastmen from Castle Draconis. For this to be done, all three of you need to be trained in the proper use of the quanti. What I fear we lack is time. I can train you to perfect your shields in a few days, but the proper ways to use your cryswords will take longer, and then there are the remaining major regalos. Partial training of the quanti can be dangerous not only to those who have the gifts, but to all around them as well."

"Can you train us enough?" asked Artos. "And if so, then what can we do? How can the three of us do anything against the enemies Tirinvo told us about?" He glanced at Angel. "Even with your help, Angel. Creatures like the monstrous crow? And the Abominations? It seems so ... so hopeless." He held up his hands and shook his head.

"I will begin training you today, Artos. It is Sevenday now, by Secondday you will be able to mindshield and to truesee. These are relatively basic things..." Donel broke off, lost in his thoughts, then sighed.

"Artos, I can teach you enough to make a difference. I can tell you where to go to find a way into Castle Draconis. I will reveal to you some secrets that I alone know. Things that may be enough to tip the scale in our favor. But ..."

"But what?" broke in Bortis.

Donel looked at Bortis. "As the eagle flies, we are about forty miles from Castle Draconis. On foot it is nearly double that, through very rough terrain. You have no experience with the mountain trails between here and Starstone Tower. You do not have anyone to show you the way there."

"Starstone Tower? Why would we want to go there? We can follow the same trail I took with Uncle Brett two years ago, the Heartbreak Road, he called it. I never understood why it was called that. It was an easy enough road to follow."

"Walk right up into the deAnson demesne? There are four villages along that road. Would you stop at one for supplies? The road goes almost directly beneath the walls of Ansonburg and is close to the deHerndar village of Stopgap." Donel sighed. "Bortis, haven't you been paying attention? Neither of those

Houses are your friend. Both would benefit if the three of you were never seen again. Why Starstone Tower? I think I am the only man alive who knows of the back door to Castle Draconis."

"Back door?" asked Artos. "How can there be a back door? Except for the main gate and the River gate, there is no way to gain entrance to the castle without an airship. Or an eagle, or some form of flight. Water surrounds the Castle. Loch O'Wrens to the north and Dragon Loch to the south, with the Dragon Falls on either side connecting the two."

Donel smiled, "Quanti-magic, Artos. Quanti-magic." The smile left his face. "I wish the quanti-masters of old had the foresight to use it here as well. It would solve so many of our problems."

"Actually, there are two back doors into Castle Draconis. Both from Starstone Tower. Besides the quanti-gate, there is an underground tunnel that runs beneath Loch O'Wrens. It joins somewhere with the Dark River and runs along its bank. I have not seen this tunnel myself, but my mentor told me of it before his untimely passing. He was preparing me for the time I would take the mantle of Head at the Quanti-school at Starstone Tower. I would have served there for perhaps a decade and then he and I would switch roles off and on. Unfortunately, he was murdered before he had the chance to retire from his duties here at the Crystal Tower. This is something I plan for myself, but first I must have my successor here." Sorrow was apparent on Donel's face. "Once we locate your missing brother."

"We have made no plans about that yet," said Carimus with some agitation. "Who knows what he must be going through, lost and all alone? The only one who has even mentioned him is the witch."

"The Angellar is not a witch, Carimus," said Angel heatedly.

"Father spoke of sending me to Fairinhorst last summer, but the needs of Rainbow Valley arose. I stayed here with the Daughters to help guard the Valley against the raiders. My father spends time here, but he has other places he watches and defends."

"I'm sorry, Angel. I do not mean to be disrespectful, but I am worried we will never find Duke."

"We all are Cari," said Artos. "I promise you we will find him somehow."

All their plans are fine for Art, but they are not going to do anything about Duke. Carimus took a deep breath. *Finding Duke is going to be up to me.*

"How far is this …?" Carimus's voice cracked a little. "This Far-in-horst place? You said it's over a hundred miles away? How would I get there? Walk all the way?"

Artos looked at Carimus in surprise. "Cari, what are you talking about? You can't go off on your own."

"You are staying with us, squirt!" said Bortis. "We're not going there. We have to stick together. Duke is already lost. You can't go off on your own."

"Rachel went with Kae and Joy to Aranothrond last spring," said Angel thoughtfully. "Kae told me she will need to go again soon to replenish some of her healing supplies. We could send Rach and Vix with Kae and Joy to escort Cari to Fairinhorst. A road leads there from Tarcitime, the city down river from Aranothrond. It's only about thirty or forty miles from there."

"We could take him," said Vix, as Rachel nodded in agreement.

"It's out of the question," said Bortis. "Cari can't go off on some wild goose chase. We need to stay together."

"I'm of age, Bort!" said Carimus with some heat. "This is the only clue we have to finding Duke now."

"He's right, Cari. We need you with us," said Artos.

"Prince Bortis, how old were you when you led your first patrol?" asked Donel.

"I was sixteen. It was two summers ago, but that was completely different. We never went out of sight of the Castle. We never left the deDraconis lands."

Donel just nodded and looked at Artos. "And you, Prince Artos, how old were you when you first sat at the Great House's Council?"

"I turned fifteen during the meetings," said Artos.

"So you were fourteen when you first attended and turned fifteen during the three days?"

Artos nodded. "But that's not the same at all. I was sitting right beside father and all I did was watch and listen. Father chaired the meeting, of course, and he would have flayed me had I dared to interrupt the proceedings."

Donel looked back at Bortis. "How old were you when you rode out with your Uncle Bretton on your first patrol?"

"Fourteen," muttered Bortis. "But what does that have to do with anything? I have been trained to be a warrior since I was a child. Carimus was training to be a priest, not a soldier. He spent his time with books, not with swords."

"You know that's not true, Bort," said Carimus with some heat. "I had sword practice with Uncle Brett every day. Just like you did. Well, maybe not just like. You had two sessions a day for my one, but I know how to use my sword."

"I know you want to stay together. The three of you. That may not be possible, I am afraid. I will train you all to use a bodyshield and to truesee in the next few days. I will also help you, Prince Bortis, with a few new things to do with your crysword. That will not take overly long, a few more days, perhaps as long as a week, because I must spend most of my time teaching Prince Artos. He has the heaviest load to bear. I must teach him how to enter Castle Draconis undetected. To open the magical gate, and other things he will need when he arrives at the Castle to combat the Abominations that wait there."

"Yes, Bortis," he added quickly. "You will have your part to play when the combat begins. But you have the warrior regalos. You will master those much faster and easier than your brother. He must learn much in order to survive and it must be clear to all that he is worthy to be the King. I know you do not doubt it, but it is not you that Artos must impress."

Donel stood up and pointed toward the screens with the House symbols above them. "He must show his grandfather, Count Penrodyn, and his future father-in-law, Count Stephan, that he, not they, will lead Veda. He must show them, although he will need their help and their wisdom, he will not be their puppet. He must put fear into any who may think to supplant his rule. Count Boris and Count Charlton must see that Artos is strong enough to defeat them if they try to stand against him."

Donel looked at Carimus as he sat back down. "I am sorry, Prince Carimus. If there were more time, I would teach you in the ways of your regalos. But time is one thing we are not blessed with in abundance. You are strongest in the quans of Nature, where I am weakest. My strengths are Mind and Spirit. I have been trained to teach those of the Body. The Angellar is who you need to give you the proper teaching. Also, she is the greatest Seer that I know of. If anyone can find Duka, it is she. Indeed, from what clues we have, she may already have that knowledge."

"A fortune-teller?" said Bortis with some scorn. "Does she

have a pretty crystal ball and predict where you can find the love of your life as well?"

A half smile appeared on Donel's face. "Tell me Prince Bortis, how did your father, or your uncles, explain your cryswords to you?"

"Huh? What in the Sky does that have to do with anything?" asked Bortis, as puzzled as Carimus felt.

"What do you mean?" asked Artos. "Explain what?"

"Where did your cryswords come from? Did none of you ever ask?"

"Of course I did," said Artos. "I asked father the day I bonded with mine. He and Uncle Cam both. They were both there for my bonding."

"Uncle Brett was there for my bonding, as well as Art and Camy. But that's not when I asked him about it. I asked him once when we were training. I was there when Cari bonded. Both Art and I were. But you didn't ask about it, Squirt."

"No, I asked him a day or two later. I was too excited to think about it on my bonding day, my birthday."

"Well …?" asked Donel.

The brothers all answered at once.

"Prince Tirinvo," said Artos.

"The Elves … err Fairborn," said Bortis.

"The Fairborn," said Carimus.

"So our cryswords came from the Fairborn. So what?" said Bortis.

"You're missing the point, Bort," said Artos softly. "I never thought about it before."

"What point?"

"Father told me that on the night of his pre-marriage celebration, Prince Tirinvo came to Phoenix and gave him that sword box. You know the box, I mean. That polished wooden box that held our four swords."

"So?"

"We weren't born yet. Father wasn't even married then. But Tirinvo gave him a box with our four swords. White, red, green, blue. How did they know?"

"As I said, the Angellar is the greatest Seer in the land. They give every person whose offspring is due to receive a crysword the proper crysword or swords before the children are born. Do you think that is the act of a charlatan, Bortis?"

For once, Bortis had nothing to say.

"If anyone knows where Prince Duka is, it will be the Angellar," Donel paused and Carimus's heart lifted. "I have never heard of her being involved with something like this, and unsolicited at that. There must be a reason for that message, in answer to your question, Carimus. Though I admit I am puzzled as to what that could be. She rarely gets involved in the affairs of humans, except for the gifts of the cryswords. I can only think of one other time besides the collar she sent to my brother to fit upon the neck of Tomung. That would be when she sent word to my master, Denar, for me to be schooled there."

"Well, I think I should go. We can't just abandon Duke," said Carimus. He gazed defiantly at his brothers.

49

DECISIONS

BORTIS

4:00 p.m.

Bortis could see the indecision on Artos' face. *This is ridiculous. The Squirt can't go running off on his own, not with a few of these outlaw girls, even if they aren't really outlaws.* He had always felt Carimus was the most immature of his brothers. The one who most needed others for support.

Carimus and Duka had almost always been together. Duka may have been the youngest, but Carimus had always been the more childish of the two. It wasn't as though the brothers had never been separated before. Just last summer, Artos and Duka had spent two weeks with the Darrell at Daryelhaas, leaving Bortis and Carimus behind at Castle Draconis.

Bortis had gone out with Uncle Brett on patrols every summer for a week or more for many years now. He knew, next year, Uncle Cameron had planned for Carimus to spend time with the Druids at one of the Circles in the lowlands. But with Uncle Brett gone, this was different. The burden of deciding these things might be on Artos's shoulders, but the duty of protecting the family fell squarely on his.

"As I was saying, Artos," Donel continued. "You will need to travel to Starstone Tower, and you will need to do so secretly. The road through the King's Valley will be watched and not only by the Houses that oppose you, but also by the eyes of the Abominations. A far greater danger. The Mountains of Myst offer concealment. The enemy has used the harpy eagle, and we know now, the monstrous crow is actively seeking you. You will need to find someone to guide you through the mountains, and I can only think of one person who can do so safely."

"Who would that be?" asked Artos.

"Andune, the West Wind."

"The Bandit?" gasped Bortis. "Why would he? How could we trust him to …" Bortis broke off and looked at Angel. "My uncle … I mean. He always said …"

Angel's face grew stony and her eyes narrowed as she took a breath.

Donel held up his hand to forestall the outburst he knew was forthcoming. "Andune has no cause to help you or your House, Bortis, or House deEagledon. But his feud with your uncle was not yours. He has no love for the Houses deAnson or deHerndar, and that may sway him to help Artos. Without the help of someone familiar with travel in the mountains, there may be no way to gain entrance to Castle Draconis. And the one who will need to persuade him is you."

Bortis shook his head. "Me? … No … If anyone should do that, it's Art. I'm no good at persuading people."

"I told you, Artos needs to learn things that will take time. I can teach you what you need to know to defend your mind and your body in a few days. Also, the way to become a weapon in ways few will be able to stand against. It will take at least two weeks, perhaps more, to train Artos. Time during which you can stand around idle and do nothing. Or you can be your brother's right arm as Braedon was to Austin. As Bretton was to Aaron. Or should have been, had they not their quarrel."

"What would I do?" asked Bortis. "Just ask him to take us to Starstone Tower? Do I tell him what happened at Castle Draconis?"

Donel looked at Artos and arched an eyebrow. "What is your suggestion, Prince Artos? Prince Bortis is your liegeman."

"Tell him the truth, Bort. Ask him for his help. Explain to him we need a guide through the mountains to take us to Starstone Tower."

"I would stress you tell him you are not looking to him for warriors in this endeavor, Bortis," added Donel. "Just a guide through the Mountains. This is not a war party to storm Starstone. You merely wish for you and Artos to gain access to the tower. I'll give you instructions on how to proceed from that point. Once there, his guide can stay with you or return as Andune wishes."

"Starstone Tower isn't my chief concern," said Bortis. "It's deserted, right? The battle will be once we return to Castle Draconis."

"Starstone Tower has been empty for over two hundred years. I don't scry there often. It saddens me to see it so empty. I have fond memories of my time at the school, first as a student and then later, my years as a teacher." Donel sighed and slowly shook his head. "I will farsee there soon. Have no worries in that regard."

"I think we will need to discuss these things among ourselves, Lord Donel," said Artos. "But I fear you most likely have the truth of it."

"Bortis, Carimus, have either of you ever learned to cook? Simple meals? Trail food?" Donel turned his eyes on the two brothers.

Carimus shook his head. "The first time I ever cooked anything was here, yesterday."

Of course I can cook. Does Donel think I'm a helpless baby like Cari? "Uncle Brett made sure I took my turn when on patrol," said Bortis. "He said every man must know how to feed himself. He said the men would follow me better if I took my turn at the chores with them and didn't expect to be waited upon. I can cook."

"That is something I can agree with. Duke Bretton may not have had the knowledge or ability to train you well in the ways of the quanti. But he was a natural leader of men," said Donel. "We shall resume training after lunch. Angel, would you lead Bortis and Carimus to the kitchen? The venison you brought home yesterday will get us started. Bortis, if you would, prepare some of the meat for smoking. Angel, please show Bortis the ways of my kitchen and give Carimus another lesson in cooking basics. I know my kitchen is far different from a campfire, but he can start there. I need to spend a few moments with Artos, alone."

Bortis felt as though he should object, but at a nod from Artos, he complied, and he and Carimus followed the girls to the kitchen.

Chapter Fourteen:

What Comes Next?

50

MEN PLAN

ARTOS

11:55 a.m.

THE DAIS TURNED, and Donel gazed upon the screen, which held the results of the tests. Artos looked too, although he did not know what the various runes and other markings meant.

Donel touched a glowing gem on the obsidian block beside his chair and Art watched the runes fade, except the column that Donel had said were his gifts.

"I have put off discussing this with you Art. I needed time to consider your gifts. You have a significant group of regalos. Far more potent than I had expected to find, and I expected a powerful collection. I wish we had more time than we do, but fate has set our path before us."

Donel drummed his fingers on the arms of his chair. "Your two major regalos are Mannaz and Skjebne. Mannaz is the gift of Self. Knowing yourself is a rare thing, Artos. Most men blunder through their whole lives, seeking to find who they are. Some find this and some never do. It is also the regalo that relates to shape shifting," Donel glanced at Artos with an appraising look. "Don't look so shocked. We don't have to tell Carimus. You are not an Abomination. The other major regalo, Skjebne, is the unknowable, fate, destiny. When speaking of the Church of the Four, the Sky Father and the Earth Mother get most of the attention. But it is the Church of the Four and the other two facets are Time and Fate. Skjebne is the symbol of Fate. Linked as it is in your testing with the minor regalo Sig, it means that you are gifted indeed. Sig is the regalo of wholeness, completeness. With proper training you are capable of using every regalo. Every one. This essentially makes your trace gifts minors, and your minors as strong as most people's majors. Your other minors are Algiz and Tiu. Which are two of Bortis's majors, by the way, the third being Eihwaz, which is protection. If need be, you will match Bortis as a warrior. However, I hope you will never find the need to stand against each other."

Donel sighed. "What we do not have is the time to train you to the utmost of your capability. I will strive to give you everything you need to retake your crown and throne. If we accomplish this, we will try to find the time to train you fully. Indeed, you have the potential to become one of the most powerful quantimasters of all time."

6:35 p.m.

It was decided that after lunch Angel and the daughters would continue to hunt with Liv and procure more elk to be smoked and turned into trail rations. The brothers would return to the training chamber and concentrate on training.

Dinner was a time for discussing plans. Donel proposed Angel, Joy, Kaerin, Vix, and Rachel escort Bortis and Carimus to Alfhiem, where Joy, Kaerin, Vix, and Rachel would continue south through the Mountains of Myst to the Fairborn lands, taking Carimus to Fairinhorst. Angel would present Bortis to her father, where he would ask for a guide through the mountains to Starstone Tower. After which they would return to the Crystal Tower. Artos and Bortis would prepare to set forth with their guide, journey to Starstone Tower, and begin the assault on the Abomination and the Beastmen at Castle Draconis.

"I still say the Squirt should stay with us," said Bortis.

Carimus's face clouded, but before he could speak, Artos cut in. "We haven't decided anything about Fairinhorst yet. The three of us will discuss this among ourselves later."

"Is it possible to keep a mindshield continually, Donel?" asked Carimus as they walked down the hall towards the training chamber. "How do you know if you are doing it?"

"That is an excellent question," said Donel. "There are situations in which you may wish to stay continually shielded. However, there are drawbacks that must be considered as well. If I am shielded, I cannot mindspeak with Liv or cast spells, even summon my crysword. If you are using a mindshield, you will find you cannot use the quanti to do all those minor tasks to which you are accustomed. You know how to turn off and on the lights in your room or to adjust the temperature of your water for bathing. These are all impossible when you are cloaked within a mindshield. Also, the use of a shield consumes energy, though not a great deal. These are things you must consider. The best use, that is to say, the most efficient use, is to cloak yourself within your shield instantly, whenever needed, and to only use it in such situations." Donel sighed and shook his head with a sad expression on his face.

"This is the type of skill that was taught at Starstone. I was teaching classes of this nature at the time the Angellar invited me to learn at Fairinhorst. Unfortunately, the mastery of this skill isn't something taught in a few hours, days, or even weeks. The class I taught usually lasted a month, and some of the young lords took twice that long."

They reached the door to the training chamber. Bortis proudly placed his hand on the screen, opened the door, and waved everyone through.

"Just exactly who were you teaching, Donel?" asked Artos.

"The Starstone Tower had two types of students, Artos. We taught the sons and daughters of the Great Houses the basics of the quanti. The same type of things that your Uncle Cameron taught you, as well as many skills that seem to be neglected of late, such as shielding. The others we taught were those who were to teach at the lesser schools. At one time, every demesne had its own quanti school. Places where those who were gifted with the regalos could learn to utilize their gifts. There was such a school in Brierly at one time, but Alexavier's son, Arlond, closed it, when teachers became scarce, saying that it was unnecessary. The Sky Church school in the deEagledon demesne was sufficient for the needs within the King's Valley. The House deDarrellyel didn't agree with Arlond on that issue. There was another school in the deDarrellyel demesne, which lasted until the death of the last teacher there. That was about one hundred years ago. There were no teachers to replace him and so the school was shuttered. There is still a druid Circle there, where any who feel a calling to serve the Earth Mother may go."

Artos nodded. He remembered his visit to the Circle of The West Wind two summers ago. "They teach quanti-magic too, don't they?"

Donel sighed. "Yes, but they are primarily teachers of the Nature quans. Growth and healing mostly. Farmers rely on the druids when they have crop issues, blights, and things of that nature, mostly. The Sky Church has tried for years now to make itself the ascendant Church."

"Well, they are," said Carimus. "The Canon is second in the church and the Cantor, third."

Donel grimaced. "Did Cameron tell you that, Carimus?"

Carimus looked confused as he thought. "Well, no. I don't think so, but …"

"They are equal in rank, Carimus. Remember that when it comes time to take your place as the Archbishop. Cantor Aubrie has an equal voice with Canon Neubre.

"We are getting off topic. We really need to stop wasting time."

9/20/1971 ar
4:30 p.m.

By late afternoon, Artos and Bortis could shield themselves against whatever Donel projected. But Carimus was nearly in tears at his failure. He could shield his mind, but not his body, and when he tried, he lost his mindshield as well. Donel had taken pity on him for the last few tests and had him come into the control room to wait. Artos knew it was weighing heavily on his little brother, and when Donel dismissed Artos and Bortis to rest before dinner, he waited behind.

When Donel and Carimus came out from the control room, he was waiting by the door. Carimus walked with his head down and just stared at the ground before him.

"Cari, I've decided about you going to Fairinhorst." Carimus looked up with a bleak expression, expecting the worst.

Donel looked at him with a doubtful expression, but before he could speak, Artos added, "Bort will undoubtedly object, but as the head of the household, I'm going to let you go with Vix and the rest. But you have to learn how to shield yourself and truesee first. Do think you can do that?"

Carimus looked up and then threw his arms around his big brother. "I'll try Artie. I'll try really hard."

Donel nodded to Artos. "We were just going up to the top floor, if you'd like to join us. I'm going to give Cari another session with Algiz. This isn't unusual, you know. Not everyone can assimilate these things at the same speed. It's nothing to be ashamed of, Carimus. Both Artos and Bortis have Algiz as strong gifts. For you, it is a minor regalo. I think you will find it easier after a reinforcement session of hypnosis." Donel looked at Artos appraisingly. "Yes, much easier, I think."

The three ascended to the top floor, where Donel left Carimus in the testing chamber and walked with Artos to the control room. Donel sat in his chair and the dais spun to face the west wall with its two screens. Art watched as Donel touched a few glowing gems. Both screens began to glow. The right-hand screen showed Carimus standing in the testing chamber. On the left-hand screen, the column of Carimus' regalos appeared, then shifted from the middle to the left side. In the center, a large red Algiz rune appeared.

"Watch the rune, Carimus," said Donel. "Concentrate upon it and think of your safe space. Think of nothing, except those two things. Build your safe space around you, let it envelop you. Watch the rune and build your safe space."

Donel pushed a glowing button on the onyx table beside him and the speech he had given in the training room below repeated, just as it had when Artos had stood there. Donel pushed another button, and the voice faded away. "Hopefully, this reinforcement added to your words of encouragement will pull him through. That was good thinking. He respects you very much."

"How is the screen repeating your words?" asked Artos.

"The training speech I used was a recording. I only spoke for the very beginning, then I replayed the same speech I used when I was a teacher at Starstone Tower. I recorded most of my lectures at Starstone. As I told you before, I have access to many recordings made by my predecessors as well. But I find it is better to use a voice the students expect to hear, instead of a stranger's. The mind reacts much better to familiar things. We are creatures of habit and instinct. We acclimate best to things we expect. It will take nearly an hour for the recording to repeat the lesson. I think he will respond better to the hypnotic suggestion this time. Your words will help a great deal. He is deeply worried about Duka."

"I am too. Do you really think this Angellar knows where he is? If so, why didn't she just tell us? Tell you?"

"I don't know Artos. As I told you before, she is the greatest seer I know. I can use the quanti to try to foresee the future, but the future is not set in stone. It is best to think that foreseeing shows what might be rather than what will be. I can farsee and use that knowledge as well, but my mastery of the quanti to foresee is far from perfect. If my time at Fairinhorst had not been cut short, I might be better able to answer you about what she can do. Sometimes knowing a potential future and trying to bring it about can change it completely. The glimpses of the future in which I foresaw your coming here differed from what happened. In one vision, all four of you arrived here with Angel along with Prince Tirinvo, his two liegemen, and the Bard Varyan. We both know that wasn't how it came to pass. The Angellar may see a future where Carimus is needed at Fairinhorst to find Duka. Or it may be something very different. I just do not know. But Artos, my mentor told me what I will now relate to you. The Angellar will do what she perceives to be the best for Veda and the Fairborn first and foremost. He also told me to trust she will not violate what she believes is right."

Artos thought for a moment and nodded. "Do you believe I made the right decision to allow Carimus to go there?"

"Yes, but it also removes Carimus from your task. He will not travel to Fairinhorst and learn what he must learn, then travel back here in time to aid you in recovering Castle Draconis. I expected to stay at Fairinhorst a long time, many months at least."

Artos gazed around Donel's control room. It had become a familiar place. Although it seemed much smaller than the Hall of Mirrors at Castle Draconis. It also seemed much less forbidding somehow, less formal. "Well, in a way, I am glad. I know taking back the castle from the grasp of the Abomination and the Beastman will be extremely dangerous. At least Cari will be safe."

"The trip through the mountains has its dangers, but I

agree, you and Bortis will face the brunt of the danger, going toward the castle rather than away from it. I plan on helping you the best I know how, so you can combat the evil there. The shielding I have taught you and Bortis will help mitigate some of the danger."

"I used hypnosis to tell Bort's mind that his three major gifts could work in harmony and not battle against each other for domination. Also, I took each of his gifts, both the minor and the major, and placed the runes within his subconscious where he will draw upon them once I begin his training. I plan on doing this with you as well. The lesson Cari is being given will reinforce the uses of Algiz in his mind. I do not think I need to do anything more with Carimus in the matter. As I said, your words will help a great deal. You have given him an incentive to succeed."

Artos stood a long minute, considering Donel's words, and then nodded. "I believe you."

The dais with Donel's chair turned, so he was facing the center wall of screens. "I told you of the time before the Reckoning when the quanti-masters of old tricked Demigoran and imprisoned him within the Hellesgate. What I didn't tell you was the true purpose of this tower, or the task that is laid upon its master. There are several, actually. But the one that concerns us now is my duty here. I am warden of the prison of Hellesgate, a prison which holds only one inmate, the Demon Demigoran."

"What do you mean? What prison?"

"The top screen. What do you see?"

"Fire ... flames, just reddish fire. What am I supposed to see?"

"What you are looking at is the outer seal. The Red Flame

Seal. Less than a mile from here stands a circle of six red spires. They enclose a magical gate which is filled with a deadly red fire, as you see on the screen." Donel put fingers on buttons on each of the onyx blocks that flanked his chair and the scene on the screen changed. The flames grew closer, closer and then parted, revealing a dark circle. As Artos watched, they seemed to enter the circle and pass through the fire, only to see more flames, but this time, they burned a pure white. "This is the White Flame Seal." The white fire grew closer and then parted, and there was another wall of brilliant blue flame. "The Blue Flame Seal." As the flames grew closer, Artos could see something in the middle of the blue fire. It looked as though someone or something was standing motionless in the middle of a blue inferno, totally wrapped in chains of bright, emerald-green fire. It was impossible to make out any details, but he felt a revulsion, nevertheless. Whatever was within the blue flame, it was foul, an enemy. A horrible, powerful enemy. Then the picture reversed. The blue fire was replaced by white and then, finally, once more, with red.

"Besides myself, you are the only person to gaze upon the imprisoned Demon Lord, since my mentor showed me what you have just witnessed. I have told no one what I have just told you, although I plan to tell my successor someday. Duka, I hope. I feel if Alexavier had seen what you have just witnessed, he might have done things differently, but my mentor never saw the need. Alex thought the Abominations were long past, dust in the centuries gone. By the time the situation arose, it was too late, and Alex would not listen. There was no way to expose him to what you have just seen.

"As powerful as the Abomination which murdered your father is, this being is a hundred times more so. It must never be loosed. Never. I am the watchman. The warden of his prison. There are weapons within the red ring which are controlled here. If any enter that ring and attempt to free the demon within, I must be here to stop them. Now you understand why I cannot forsake my post. I am as much a prisoner as the demon lord."

At that moment, a soft chime sounded and the screen to the right of the test results suddenly burst into activity and the screen filled with blue fire. The screen slowly faded to black, leaving words of blue flame remaining on the dark background.

"The Prophecy," whispered Donel upon reading the first few words.

King's Blood flows like Dragon's fire...

Yet from the Darkness... Light!

Young Falcons' flight begins in peril…

As Black doth conquer White,

But Mystic Flames shall banish night,

And wake Stone Giants at time's hour.

From Crystal Eyrie comes the Spell…

To bring a new light unto flower.

"What is that?" asked Artos. "Is it a song?"

"Those are the words of the prophet Davidka. He was the keeper of this tower over a thousand years ago. What it relates to, I am not sure, however appearing at this time, it probably relates to you and your situation. There is more. This is only the first part. I must think about this."

"What is the rest? Is it long?"

"No, not very long. Let me see…" Donel thought a moment, then recited:

"Things to see with eyes of stone,
Blood and fire, earth and bone.
Everywhere to go, but home…
Wander lonely, all alone…

Learn to see through eyes of stone...
Eyes of fire, wood, and bone...
Cast your fate upon the foam,
To sail through Time, to sail alone...

Dawn brings the day, new comes the light...
The Oracle ends now... with the night."

As Donel finished reciting, the words faded and the image of Carimus was back.

"What does it mean?" asked Artos. "Why did it appear?"

"It must relate to you, at least what is written here, that would be my guess, but as to the meaning? I must think."

51

AND FATE
LAUGHS

ARTOS

9/21/1971 ar

5:40 p.m.

Bortis disagreed with Artos's decision to allow Carimus to travel to Fairinhorst when it was revealed at dinner. But later that night, when Carimus proved he could finally shield, he grudgingly gave his assent. He wasn't happy, but when Artos explained he saw the trip south as a lesser danger than traveling with them to Starstone Tower, he was forced to agree.

Donel spent all the next day training. In the morning, they practiced their shielding and after lunch he introduced them to the art of seeing-true. First sending minor phantasms to confront them, then making the floor of the chamber seem to be covered with imaginary obstacles or pits and potholes.

At dinner that night, he announced they were all able to shield themselves and truesee as well as expected in the short time they had.

"Angel, as soon as Kaerin arrives with the rest of the Daughters, the seven of you should set forth for Alfhiem.

Once there, you shall present Bortis to Andune. Joycel, you and Kaerin, along with Vix and Rachel, will escort Carimus south to Fairinhorst. I shall test the rest of your band of scouts, Angel, and the Mother willing, train them in mindshielding. Hopefully, all will have at least traces of Algiz and be able to learn to mindshield. The majority of my time will be spent training Artos, of course."

Angel nodded. "I am surprised they aren't here already. Perhaps they will be here this evening, although Liv tells me she has not yet caught their scent."

"How are our supplies coming, Angel? Joy?" asked Donel, looking at his chief foragers.

"I think we have enough jerky smoking for both trips," said Angel. She looked at Carimus. "You will need to carry a lot of food for the trip. There are villages after you get below the falls at Lake Deth. If you have money, you can buy supplies at Elpeler. But in case of the unforeseen, you should carry several pounds at least, along with your other gear. Your pack will be at least fifteen pounds. I know that doesn't sound like a lot, but you will be on mountain trails, like the trip from the nest to here only much further. Think you can manage that?"

"Lake Death?" said Carimus, sounding a bit put off.

"D-e-t-h, nothing dead. It's just the name," said Angel. "No one can carry your supplies for you, Cari."

"I'll have to … but … I will need to carry more than that. We don't have any money. We didn't have time to grab anything away from the castle that night. At least I didn't." Carimus looked at Artos.

"Sorry Cari," Artos shook his head. "I wasn't thinking about much of anything that night."

"We have money," said Bortis.

Both brothers' jaws dropped in surprise, and they looked at him incredulously.

"How were you able to bring money along with you, Bort?" asked Artos.

Bortis looked down at his plate. "I have three gold pieces in my jacket. In the inner pocket. The hidden one."

Artos smiled as he realized why Bortis had some hidden gold. "The story uncle Bretton used to tell us about the soldier and the ambush. You sewed three gold pieces over your heart."

"What of it? It means we have some money, doesn't it?"

"Keep your gold, Bort," said Donel. "I have silver, and that will be easier for Carimus to spend in the Fairborn village. Tomorrow, we shall take the morning off from training and prepare your packs for the trek."

"I expect Kae, Cat, and the rest to show up any time," said Angel. "Since they didn't come today, I expect they will be here tomorrow. Cat wouldn't have stayed long in Alfhiem after she gave father the news. So he will know some of your story already, Bortis. I had to report your arrival and why I didn't escort you to him straight away. I think he will forgive me for bringing you here instead of taking you to see him first. It's not like you were raiders from Herndar, burning villages."

Artos was glad to see that, for once, Bortis didn't bristle at Angel. Things were finally looking better, he thought.

9/22/1971 ar

By lunchtime the following day, they had loaded six packs with needed supplies. Donel gave Carimus a small leather pouch containing twenty five silver pieces. Rachel had even offered to take the hems out of the trouser legs of the pants Susi had given Carimus. They now fitted much better for his upcoming trek through the mountains.

Donel spent the afternoon with Bortis, training him in using Tiu, the regalo of the warrior. The rest went hunting once again, for although they had enough smoked jerky for travel supplies, they still needed food for the table. Besides, as Angel remarked, Liv seemed to feel a need to continue to thin the elk population and Donel had a large freeze room.

It was quiet at the dinner table that evening. Donel seemed lost in his thoughts, and everyone else was tired. The hunting party had brought down another fair-sized elk yearling and since the kill had taken place several miles away, all the members of the hunt had staggered back to the crystal tower with all they could carry.

Bortis had turned out to be a quick learner, now his regalos were not at odds with each other. He could utilize what Donel called the principle of inertial control and had worked up a good sweat whacking at the images Donel produced with a padded wand from one of his storerooms.

"Do you remember how Uncle Brett could flick his sword around as if it were light as a feather, Cari?" asked Bortis. "Well, I'm getting a feel for it. I'm on my way to becoming a master with the sword. Just like Uncle Brett was."

"You have made a good start, Bort," said Donel. "However, you will need to practice holding your shield as well, while you wield your inertialess sword. Not to mention holding a mindshield and using truesee as well. It wasn't bad for a first day, but it was far from being remarkable. A true quanti-master must be able to hold many runes in his thoughts at once. But you are showing excellent progress."

"I'm worried," announced Angel. "I thought Kae and the rest would be here waiting for us this evening when we returned. We sent Oswald out on Sevenday. Kae would have gotten my note that evening or on Firstday at the latest, and it's Thirdday eve now."

"Perhaps Cat was delayed coming back to the Nest from Alfhiem," said Joy. "Kae would wait for her return."

"I probably shouldn't have sent her off by herself. But there was no one to go with her. Ava and Sherri had been patrolling until late, Kae was out looking for Duka, and Susi was loading packs and making breakfast," said Angel.

"No need to borrow trouble," said Donel. "I will try to contact Oswald tonight after moonrise. I doubt he will know Kae's plans, but he may have picked up some idea of when she is going to set out."

"Why don't you just mindspeak with Kae?" asked Carimus. "Or isn't that one of her regalos?"

"No Cari, I'm hoping Kae may have said something about her plans near Oswald, but she cannot mind-speak with him as Angel, and I do. Or I with her. Oswald is a clever fellow, and Liv is very intelligent. They both understand a good deal of our speech, but their minds are not the same as ours. Liv might tell me she has brought me a rabbit for dinner, but she doesn't tell me that in words in my head. She thinks of the rabbit and a meal for me, and I understand the concept. Between people it's different, or rather I should say it can be different. People who are related closely and share the regalo of Ansuz can learn to share thoughts, but it isn't an easy skill to master. It will probably be easier for you to learn to mindspeak with Liv than to Bortis, or to me."

"Why is that? It seems it would be the opposite. I mean, I can tell what Bort is thinking half the time, anyway."

Bortis snorted. "Hah! Sure you can, squirt."

"It's not the same thing, Cari. You know your brother well, you can read his body language and his expressions. But those are not the same as his thoughts," said Donel. "People have complex minds. Animals, even extremely clever ones like Liv and Oswald, have simpler minds. It may even be the fact that we have speech, which makes it harder for us to communicate directly with our minds. You will, perhaps, be able to instruct me on this at a later time."

"Huh? How could I teach you?" asked Carimus in bewilderment.

"There is only one person I have ever known who used direct mindspeech with me. And that only once. It was something I believe she may have planned to teach me, but circumstances …" Donel shrugged, a sad expression on his face.

"The Angellar? Oh." Carimus looked thoughtful.

At that moment, a soft bong rang out.

"The roost! Oswald has returned!" said Donel and led the way as everyone rushed to the stairway.

Donel untied the scroll case tied to Oswald's leg, then frowned, and turned to Angel. Her expression mirrored his.

"Strangers at the nest," said Angel. "Fairborn, Oswald says. I could see father sending people to escort her back to the Nest, but why would they stay there? Oswald says everyone seems very upset. Are there more raiders in the Valley?"

"Kae addressed this to you, Angel. I believe that is her hand," said Donel, handing her the vellum from within the case. "Let us leave Oswald to rest."

Angel nodded and led the way back downstairs to the library.

Once in the library, Angel broke the waxen seal and unrolled the piece of vellum. Artos noticed it had only three lines.

"This isn't good," said Angel. She handed the note to Joy, who quickly scanned it and looked thoughtful.

"Well … what's it say?" asked Bortis.

"Maybe it's none of our business, Bort," said Artos.

"I'm to go to Alfhiem, at once," said Angel.

"Well, good. Isn't that what we want?" asked Bortis, looking confused. "Just what we planned."

"Father also states that I am to stay out of the affairs of the … err Valley dwellers. I'm to give you no aid. That's all it says."

"Valley dwellers? You mean us?" asked Artos.

"He used a rude word, but yes."

"He called you 'the Orqui of the Valley'," said Joy. "That's like a human calling a Fairborn an 'Elf'. It's rude. He has had troubles with the raiders from Herndar, and he's just lumping all of you from the King's Valley together."

"He called us Beastmen, didn't he?" Bortis bristled.

"No, the Fairborn word for Beastmen is 'Orch'," said Donel. "I don't see how this changes our plans. Except, now, Prince Bortis, you are going to have to try extremely hard to win his help."

"You can do this, brother," said Artos, clasping Bortis's shoulder. "We need his help. You just need to put on your best court manners." *And not act like Uncle Brett.*

"What about me?" asked Carimus. "Does this mean I can't go to the Angellar?"

"Andune won't want Kae and I escorting you, Carimus," said Joy. "At least I think he would not. Perhaps it would be better not to inform him of that trip?"

"I should have waited and sent Susi with Cat," said Angel. "It's his rule that we always travel in groups. But I wanted him to get the news about the Beastmen in the King's Valley as quickly as possible. He is probably upset with me over that. Kae will have to come with me instead of going along with the others to take Cari to Fairinhorst."

"Rachel and I can take him," said Vix. "Rach has been south before."

"It's better that I go as well," said Joy. "There are those in Fairinlan who would think it improper for three humans to be traveling unaccompanied. Especially south of Tarcitime. Once you entered the Hidden Vale, you would be stopped and sent away for certain. No, I best go with you."

"I'll manage a private word with Cat," said Angel. "I'll have her bring Susi and rest here. Kae and I will make our way to see father, with Bortis. Then, after he is through lecturing me and speaks with Bortis, we'll come back here."

"I only met Andune once, and that was years ago," said Donel. "Tirinvo would visit here once or twice a season when Angel was my student. Varyan has visited me often as well. He and I share a love of music and song. Andune came only after Stephanie insisted I teach their daughter in the way of the quanti. Andune preferred she go to the Angellar for her schooling. Once Andune was convinced I was proficient with the knowledge Angel needed, he agreed she could be taught here. He sent Joy to learn as well and Kae to oversee, as she had been schooled in Fairinhorst. I thought him to be a fair man, Bortis, though there was some bitterness about him. I attributed much of that to his relationship with his father, the king."

"I suppose we should set out first thing in the morning," said Angel. "The sooner Father rakes me over the coals for breaking his rules, the sooner he will get over his anger, and better the likelihood of him listening to Bortis."

Artos detected the doubt in her voice. "Do you think I should I send him a letter? Is there anything I could offer him to influence his judgment for our cause?"

"It wouldn't harm your cause, Artos," said Donel. "I think a letter from the future High King of Veda offering his friendship would be a proper thing for you to do, especially when you are asking for his aid." Donel thought for a moment. "I think it's a good thought. I shall get you some paper and a pen."

Chapter Fifteen:

To Be A King?

52

WHAT MAKES A MAN A KING?

DONEL

9/23/1971 ar

2:00 p.m.

WHEN ARTOS FAILED TO ATTEND his afternoon training session, Donel felt a moment of concern. It wasn't like Artos to be remiss in such things. He had said he was going to take in a breath of fresh air after lunch. This might have given him some apprehension, but Liv had padded right after the young man and there was very little in the Blue Spires that would endanger Artos if Liv was keeping him company.

Closing his eyes, he concentrated for a moment, trying to attune himself to Artos's presence. If he was still outside, he might need to use the screens, but no, he could feel Art's distinctive aura. He was in the Crystal Tower.

"Now that's interesting," he mused to himself. "I wonder how he got out on the Porch? I guess it's obvious that passage must lead somewhere, just like the other direction leads to the Roost, but how did he open the door?"

Donel left the training chamber, walked up the three flights of stairs and down the hall to the front overlook, the place he called his Porch, a balconied area high above the front entrance to the Crystal Cave. He placed his hand in the proper place and a panel in the crystal wall slid open noiselessly. Artos stood at the far edge, his back to the doorway, gazing eastward into the mist that shrouded the spires and gave the mountains their name.

Without looking back, Artos said, "I don't have a choice, do I? If one of the Houses helped in the attack, we can't allow them to gain more control, more power. I see my idea of a stronger council would be a disaster."

"It is only speculation at this time. But my thoughts are that one or both Houses were involved somehow."

Artos nodded. "I used my trueseeing when I was outside and saw this place from below. Is it a property of the qulan field that masks it?"

"Yes, once the entire tower was concealed, but I removed the glamor from the front door. It bothered Liv. It didn't really seem to matter. The Abominations know where I am, the qulan keeps the uninvited out. I offered to remove it from the roost, but Oswald didn't mind. I feel he rather enjoys flying through what looks like a solid wall. He has an interesting sense of humor."

Artos nodded. "Cari said he thought Oswald was laughing at him, back when he first called him a demon."

"He probably was. He was looking for you and, although he probably doesn't know the word 'demon,' he would have recognized that Cari was afraid of him and that would amuse him."

"I'm sorry. I guess I'm late for training. I saw this place from outside and wanted to see it, so I came up here. Then got lost in my thoughts."

"Time is precious, but so is reflection. May I ask what thoughts you were lost within?"

"What makes a good king?"

"I can only give you my opinion on that, and I might be biased. Every man sees the world colored by his experiences in it."

"I think your opinion would carry much weight. You have seen more kings than most men."

Donel shrugged. "My grandfather, Arheur, was king when I was born, but he passed while I was still a boy. I really remember nothing that stands out about him for good or ill. My father, Aregis, died in an accident after a brief reign, as did his son, my brother Allison. You know my views on Alex and his son Arlond. I think your grandsire, Attios, was a good man and a good king. I know he had plans to undo some things his father and grandfather had set in motion, but he died young as well. As did your father. Do you see a pattern here? Four of the last six High Kings died untimely deaths. Three in accidents, although I truly wonder now if accidents they were, or murder. There is no doubt about King Aaron. His death was murder, most foul. He stood up for the people when House deHerndar would have exploited them. He tried to be a just and fair king. Like you, he had his kingship thrust upon him early, but I think he had the makings of a good ruler."

Artos turned and asked what Donel suspected was his genuine cause of concern. "Do you regret living the life of a wizard and not marrying? Did you ever love someone and were forbidden her?"

"Why do you think I never married?"

Artos looked at Donel, his eyes wide with surprise. "I just assumed … You live here alone."

"My bride was chosen for me soon after I finished my time as a student at Starstone Tower, before I was an instructor there. I was very lucky. Although we had never met before our betrothal, we discovered we were kindred spirits. Love followed quickly, and we were happy in our time together. We both knew it could not last forever. We both had our own destinies to follow." Donel shrugged. "I was born with the double dragons and bore the blue sword." Donel turned and looked away into the mist. "Is that what's really bothering you, Art? Your betrothal to the deEagledon girl?"

"No! Yes. I don't know, I, I just am not sure ..."

"My father once told me that the surest path to disaster was worrying about tomorrow's problems before you had solved today's. If you do not learn to use your regalos to master your gifts, what are the chances you will ever exchange the vows of matrimony? Family is very important, Art. You are lucky. Your brothers care for you and you for them. I know it has been hard, losing your father and your uncles, but you have Bort and Cari, and hopefully Duka will be found and return home as well."

"I still have one uncle." Artos reached out and touched Donel in his chest. Donel suddenly found a tear forming, and he had to blink rapidly a few times.

"Yes, you do. And I have a family again." Both stood silently for a few moments.

"I believe you will be a good king, Art." *If you live*, he added to himself. "Let us proceed with your lessons."

Donel followed Artos back into the Crystal Tower.

APPENDIXES

The Calendar of Veda

The calendar of Renn and Veda consists of three hundred and sixty-four days in twelve months. Eight months of thirty days and four of thirty-one. The months with the equinox and solstice are the longer months. There are six holidays: New Year Day, Spring Equinox, Summer Solstice, Autumnal Equinox, Winter Solstice, and Year End Day (also called Old Year Day). The equinoxes are especially Holy for the Earth Mother Veda. The Solstices are dedicated to the Sky Father Quai. New Year Day is dedicated to The Unknown, and Old Year Day to Time.

Janus	30 days	New Year Day on the 1st
Febrous	30 days	
Marcous	31 days	Spring Equinox on the 15th
Aprilous	30 days	
Maymont	30 days	
Junmont	31 days	Summer Solstice on the 15th
Julous	30 days	
Augous	30 days	
Ninmont	31 days	Autumnal Equinox on the 15th
Tenous	30 days	
Minquos	30 days	
Rastous	31 days	Winter Solstice on the 15th
		and Old Year Day on the 31st

The days of the week are known by number names:

Firstday - Monday

Seconday - Tuesday

Thirday - Wednesday

Fourthday - Thursday

Fifthday - Friday

Sixthday – Saturday

Sevenday - Sunday

The First Age of Man ended with the First Quantum War. There followed a period of time when the world was in chaos, which ended with the Second Quantum War and the Reckoning. This was followed by the rise of the Great Houses in Veda. The calendar starts after the Reckoning. The years are labeled as xxxx ar, which stands for After the Reckoning. The Glory Road begins in 1971 ar. This is roughly two thousand years after the end of the First Age.

Dramatis Personae
The Great Houses

<u>deDraconis</u>

Aaron Draconis
High King of Veda

Evelyn Draconis ne`dePenrodyn (*deceased*)
Queen of Veda

Cameron deDraconis (uncle of Aaron)
Archduke Archbishop of Veda

Bretton deDraconis (brother of Aaron)
Duke Grand Marshal of the Armies of Veda

Artos deDraconis (son of Aaron)
Crown Prince of Veda

Bortis deDraconis(son of Aaron)
Prince of Veda

Carimus deDraconis (son of Aaron)
Prince of Veda

Duka deDraconis (son of Aaron)
Prince of Veda

DEEAGLEDON

Stephan Eagledon
Count Eagledon

Stephanie Naurfindl ne'deEagledon (*deceased*)
Viscountess deEagledon
(elder twin sister to Stephan by 13 minutes)

Renee Eagledon ne'deHerndar (wife of Stephan)
Countess Eagledon

Jon deEagledon (brother of Stephan)
Baron deEagledon

Ellis deEagledon (son of Stephan)
Viscount deEagledon

Elaine deEagledon (twin sister to Ellis)
Viscountess deEagledon

Samuel deEagledon (son of Stephan)
Viscount deEagledon

Juneau deEagledon (daughter of Stephan)
Viscountess deEagledon

DEPENRODYN

Estel Penrodyn
Count Penrodyn

Ravena Penrodyn ne'deHerndar (*deceased*)
Countess Penrodyn

Walter dePenrodyn (son of Estel)
Viscount dePenrodyn

Ruth Diana dePenrodyn ne'deDarrellyel
Viscountess dePenrodyn (wife of Walter)

Johan dePenrodyn (son of Estel)
Viscount dePenrodyn

Katlyn dePenrodyn (daughter of Walter)
Viscountess dePenrodyn

Marx dePenrodyn (son of Walter)
Viscount dePenrodyn

Violeot dePenrodyn (daughter of Walter)
Viscountess dePenrodyn

Roberta dePenrodyn (daughter of Walter)
Viscountess dePenrodyn

DEANSON

Winston deAnson (brother of Boris) (*deceased*)
Viscount deAnson

Boris Anson
Count Anson

Yanet Anson ne'deHerndar
Countess Anson

Kramer deAnson (son of Boris)
Viscount deAnson

Floyd deAnson (son of Winston)
Viscount deAnson

Viki deAnson (daughter of Winston)
Viscountess deAnson

DEHERNDAR

Charlton Herndar
Count Herndar

Annis Herndar ne'deAnson (wife of Charlton) (*deceased*)
Countess Herndar

Fredrick deHerndar (son of Charlton)
Viscount deHerndar

Jaccque deHerndar (son of Charlton)
Viscount deHerndar

Pitor deHerndar (son of Charlton)
Viscount deHerndar

Liza deHerndar (daughter of Charlton)
Viscountess deHerndar

DEDARRELLYEL

Glendon Darrellyel
Count Darrellyel

Yasbeth Darrellyel ne'deSpryngdal (wife of Glendon)
Countess Darrellyel

Tenna Fey deDarrellyel (sister of Glendon) (Druid)
Priestess of the Green Bough

Yoshua deDarrellyel (son of Glendon)
Viscount deDarrellyel

Seth deDarrellyel (son of Glendon)(Druid)
Priest of the Green Bough

Brandigim deDarrellyel (daughter of Darrell) (Druid)
Priestess of the Green Bough

DESPRYNGDAL

Maria Spryngdal
Countess Spryngdal

Rubyia deSpryngdal (daughter of Maria)
Viscountess deSpryngdal

Cassia deSpryngdal (daughter of Rubyia)
Viscountess deSpryngdal

Persons of Interest

Castle Draconis Guards, Staffs, etc.

Guards

Captain General Daneel derDraconis
Marshal of Castle Draconis

Captain Jarid derDraconis
Captain of the Gatehouse Guards

Sargent Ian McArn
Captain of the Eyrie Guards

Corporal Shawn Dorime
Corporal of the Eyrie Guards

Staff

Elaer Prindar (half Fairborn)
Tutor to the Princes

Agnes Dorime (Widowed mother of Shawn)
Cook (pastry chief)

The Church of the Four

Pietro Neubre (Grand Bishop of Quai)
Canon of the Sect of the Sky

Stanley Aubrie (Great Druid of Veda)
Cantor of the Sect of the Earth

The Magic Man

Donel the Magic Man
Wizard

The Fairborn

Farnir Naurfindl
King of the Fairborn

Claudian Naurfindl
Queen of the Fairborn

Meldien Naurfindl (younger brother cf Farnir)
Prince

Andune Naurfindl (eldest son of Farnir)
Fairborn Prince (removed from the royal line)

Tirinvo Naurfindl (second son of Farnir)
Fairborn Crown Prince

Taur Ka'Naurf (liegeman of Tirinvo)
cousin to the royal house

Jaek Ka'Naurf (liegeman of Tirinvo)rh
cousin to the royal house

Varyan Beiniot` (Bard to the royal house)
cousin to the royal house

Angela Andunsuruessa (daughter of Andune)
not recognized by the royal house

Kaerin Arastina
senior Daughter of the Wind

Joycel Arastina (Kearin's younger sister)
a Daughter of the Wind

THE DAUGHTERS OF THE WIND

Angela Andunsuruessa
Leader of the Daughters of the Wind

Kaerin Arastina

Joycel Arastina (Kearin's younger sister)

Catlyn Petrie

Susi Petrie (Catlyn's younger sister)

Vixen Fauntaneer (Sarah)

Ava Fauntaneer (Vixen's younger sister)

Rachel Symtth

Sherri Lucarn

THE BALLAD OF HOUSE DRACONIS
(THE KING MUST DIE)

The silver moon salutes the sun as tears fall with the night,

The White King's forces are depleted. He cannot win this fight.

The Leaves of Fall give ancient call, add anguish to the plight,

As day's light fades, the sentry sighs and whispers soft

"The King Must Die!"

As vultures gather at a kill, the Dark Ones soon arrive,

Only the strong will survive!

Awaiting weakness to appear to move in for the kill,

Only the strong will survive!

So we'll ride away, fly away to freedom. (freedom)

We'll fly away unto a distant shore...

We'll ride away, fly away to freedom. (freedom)

And tomorrow we'll begin to strive once more.

We must away lest light of day should come to find us dead.

This treachery we cannot best, now Royal Blood's been shed.

The Dark One comes with evil's power, demon eyes glow red,

To empty eyries be them led, young falcons with all haste have

fled.

With hissing cries of maddened fear, the Dark Ones scream
with rage.
Only the strong will survive!
Somehow the quarry's disappeared, vanished into air.
Only the strong will survive!

We'll ride away, fly away to freedom. (freedom)
To learn and grow, to return when we're strong.
We'll ride away, fly away to freedom. (freedom)
Someday the bards will tell of us in song,
Of loyal sons return to right old wrongs

So we'll ride away, fly away to freedom. (freedom)
We'll fly away unto a distant shore...
We'll ride away, fly away to freedom. (freedom)
And tomorrow we'll begin to strive once more.
And tomorrow ... and tomorrow ... oooh ... ohh ... oh.

N
Lake of The Setting Sun
Where the Eagles Left them
X
Camp of the Daughters of the Wind
X
Rainbow Valley
Tower of the Magic Man
X
To The Kings Valley
Alfhiem Village of the Westwind
FIVE MILES
Map By Inkarnate

ACKNOWLEDGMENTS

The team at diyMFA:

Gabriela Pereira - My first mentor, who has guided me from the beginning.
Jeanette Smith - Who first lessons added so much to the starting of my book.
Jenn Walton - early readings and advice.
Laura Highcove - early readings and advice.
AK Nevermore - pure spunk

The team at The Book Incubator:

Mary Adkins
Liz Pickart
Harrison Gale
Gayle Brown
Ashley Strosnider
Lucas Schaefer

The Team at Paper Raven Books:

Morgan Gist Macdonald
Megan Buttaro
Brianna Shaffery
Rachel Yoldi

Christine Roberts

Charlotte Zang

M.A. Hinkle (my *Fantastic* developmental editor)

Brian Dooley

Colleen Tomlinson

My Beta readers:

Theresa Cross - my alpha beta

Mitch Howard - also my first line editor.

Pam Warren

Ed Daniel

C. William (Bill) Heinowski

Darrell Hopper

THE GLORY ROAD
BOOK TWO:

THE LAY OF STARSTONE TOWER

CHAPTER ONE:

ARTOS ALONE

1

ARTOS

9/22/1971 ar

5:00 p.m.

ARTOS LOOKED AROUND THE CLEARING, an uneasy feeling in his gut. Just moments ago, the air had been alive with the normal bird calls and the rustling of the wind blowing through the autumn foliage. Now a brooding silence had descended upon the forest. The wind still stirred the reddish-brown leaves of the oak trees that surrounded the clearing, but the birds had fallen silent.

He took a deep breath and forced himself to relax. He closed his eyes and turned to his inner sight, probing the forest in front of him for anything out of place, anything out of the ordinary.

There! Ahead, still a short distance away, was the distinct feeling of anger. Something was hunting, and the malice he detected brought a shiver to his spine.

Summoning his crysword into his right hand, he felt the familiar weight and grip, offering him a sense of comfort. Standing in the center of the clearing, he felt vulnerable and quickly scanned his surroundings for a strategic spot to defend himself.

The old forest trees were all huge, some of the trunks being over eight feet in diameter. The scrub in-between the trees was taller than Artos, making visibility more than a few yards outside the clearing all but impossible.

Artos backed up into a space between two of the smaller giants and continued to scan the surrounding woods, keeping his inner focus on the things hunting him. They weren't men. He was sure of that. *Not dogs either.* The emotions felt alien, unfamiliar, unlike anything he had ever encountered before.

Using the mental probing techniques Donel had taught him, he tried to determine how many enemies he faced. He didn't have much range. He knew they had to be within a couple dozen yards for him to detect them. There were three, not too distant, probably almost to the far edge of the clearing. And there was another group, also of three, further away. That was all he could locate, but that was enough, too much really. How could he defeat three foes at once, much less double that amount?

He needed a plan! Suddenly, he could hear a humming noise from across the clearing. No, not a humming, a buzzing like the sound of a disturbed bee's nest.

Bursting from the brush on the opposite side of the clearing came three black and gold hornets, each at least six inches long. Buzzing belligerently, the formation came to a halt, hovering in midair and slowly turned, the three creatures moving in perfect unison, surveying the empty clearing.

Artos froze, hoping the creatures would fail to notice his motionless form, but to no avail. The creatures stopped turning, their formation aimed at where he stood between the two oak trunks. Then, with the angry buzzing increasing, they shot forward directly at him.

Artos instantly realized his mistake. By positioning himself between the two trees, he had protected his left side, but had very little room to maneuver his crysword. He swung the sword up before him defensively as the hunter hornets streaked to attack.

The three hornets crossed the small clearing in a matter of seconds. The lead hunter twisted its body as it approached so its stinger aimed directly at his face.

Artos swung his crysword in a short stroke and felt the razor-sharp blade cleave the nasty thing in twain. He felt a burst of triumph, but his joy was short-lived as the remaining hornets, following close behind the leader, each scored a direct hit to his exposed sword arm.

The pain was excruciating, and the sword flew from his hand as he lost all feeling in his fingers. The two remaining hornets pulled away from his arm and hovered before him. Without thinking, he summoned the sword back into the grasp of his left hand and made a desperate swing at the creatures.

His uncle Bretton had made all the brothers spend countless hours using their swords with either of their hands and the practice served Artos in this moment of need. The crysword sliced through each of the two monsters in one smooth stroke.

Where are the others? He looked wildly around the small clearing. *I need to move away from this clearing, so they can't come at me so quickly.* He moved to his left, walking around the clearing in the general direction he knew the other hunters had been moments before.

Artos held his crysword at the ready as he slipped from behind one tree trunk to another. The pain in his right arm made him break out in a cold sweat. Leaning against the rough oak bark, he listened for the faint buzzing of the flying hunters he knew were seeking him. He should use his mind to pinpoint them, he knew, but he needed a few moments rest before he could concentrate.

He took a moment to thank his deceased uncle. If not for Duke Bretton's relentless training, he wouldn't have been able to summon his sword instantly to his other hand. He would never have struck down the remaining hunters. They would have each scored another sting.

Then he heard the buzzing sound again. It came from somewhere before him. His right hand was numb, but shooting pains flooded his right arm from his wrist to shoulder as he pushed himself upright again. He bore two large, red welts from their stings now and knew he couldn't take another.

The buzzing sounds grew louder. They must be almost upon him! There were only three of them left. The buzzing sound stopped, and a faint scraping sound alerted him. The hunters had landed on the tree, crawling around the trunk to attack! He opened his thoughts to pinpoint their locations. One was coming from the right and another from the left. Where was the third?

He stepped to the left, choosing to attack the one on his sword side while frantically probing to locate the last hunter. The six inch long black and gold striped body of the hunter hornet appeared. Artos sliced it cleanly in two, then quickly took a step back and waited for the second to appear. Before it came into view, something landed on his shoulder, and Donel's voice sounded in his ear.

"That's three, Art. You lose."

There was the third hornet, perched on his left shoulder.

"It's dinnertime, so I took pity on you. But I could have stung. Denar would have never spared me the third sting."

The trees faded away, replaced by the training chamber

wall-screens glowing with their faint blue light. The bodies of the dead hunters melted away just as they had after the first exercises.

"But then, my master would never have gone from beginning exercises directly to an advanced one, either. You did very well, considering." The hunter on his shoulder vanished.

Artos chuckled ruefully. "I think you cheated, Donel. The last hunter wasn't buzzing."

As the screens went inert, Donel emerged from the control room. He walked up to Artos and began applying almas to the welts on his right arm. The pain and swelling quickly dissipated.

"I set only four of the six to buzz on that exercise, Art. The second one you hit, the first to sting you, hadn't buzzed. You must be more aware of your surroundings. I felt you probe, but you only probed before you, where you heard the buzzing. The direction you expected them to attack from. An enemy will seldom be so polite as to inform you of their location. How does that feel now?"

Artos flexed his arm. "Better. Thanks. I'll be ready for another round after dinner."

"That's the spirit. I'll take it a little easier on you after dinner. I'll try a more intermediate setting. I really should have used it for the last match, but you did so well with the first two. I wanted to make it a challenge."

"I think you succeeded."

With only the two of them at the large table, Artos thought he had never felt so alone as he did now. "How long do you think it will take Bort and Angel to persuade the West Wind to give us a guide, Donel?"

"I really don't know ... not long, I would think. Bort, and whoever Andune should choose to send, should be back here within a few days. It may be longer. Four or five, perhaps. However, from the tone of Andune's letter, he may not allow Angel to return. I expect he may send Bort back with the guide and no one else. Andune knows where the Crystal Tower stands. He sent people here once or twice when Angel was being taught."

"But he has to let Angel go. She leads the daughters."

Donel just shook his head, took a bite of his venison steak, chewed and swallowed before answering. "The giant raven watching the Rainbow Valley will give Andune pause. He is not without skill with the quanti. He may have sensed the Abomination. When we met, when he was deciding if I would be the proper teacher for Angel, he told me he believed one of them may have murdered Stephanie, her mother. He may decide that he wants his daughter where he can see she is in no danger."

"But what about the Daughters? Angel told me he was using them to watch that part of the valley."

"I do not know Andune's mind, Art. He may tell them to all to go home now and post his own men to watch the western part of Rainbow Valley. The raven has changed the situation."

"That would be terrible. Do they even have homes anymore?"

At that moment, Liv entered the commons and sat down a few feet from the table. Artos was amused to see that she turned her head and watched whoever was speaking, just as if she was following the conversation. Which, as he considered, she probably was. For although she was a Mist Cat, she was a very intelligent being.

"The human families that farmed the Valley now reside in a remote dale to the north, in a tiny village called Cedars. I think it's pretty crowded. Only seven or eight families dwelt there originally. Now there are more than double. It may even have been a reason Andune assigned the daughters to keep watch from the Nest. Fewer mouths to strain the resources at Cedars. Angel told me the valley folk all hoped to return and start their farms again next spring. With that raven patrolling, I don't see that happening. I think it depends on you now."

Donel smiled at Liv and tossed her a bite of his steak, which she caught neatly and swallowed.

"On me? What do you mean?"

"The Abominations want to find you and your brothers. You, above all else, you are the symbol of everything they wish to destroy. That harpy that wounded you was likely being mind controlled by Anndr, the Raven's master. The legends say he is the most adept at regalos of the mind. He is most certainly seeking you. The raptor saw likely subjects, and Tirinvo told him he sent you away to safety. They know I am here, and Andune is in Alfhiem. Two havens where you might hide. Both places with shields to cloak you and your brothers. They will divide their attention between us until they find you. It is fortunate he does not have any of your minds patterned."

"What do you mean?"

"To someone who is skilled, every mind has a distinct pattern. All three of you have powerful auras. The auras of House deDraconis. I knew you were Dragonbloods as soon as you entered."

"That means Bort and Cari are in danger! How could you send them out with that thing flying around above the Valley?"

"To detect your auras, he would need to be much closer. A few yards away, at least. If he had your patterns, he might find you from further away. Not miles and miles, but within a few hundred yards, perhaps. He is looking for you, there is no doubt, and if he thinks he sees you, then he will come closer to detect your aura. Both Bort and Cari will stay on the forest trails. I discussed this with Angel and Joy. They won't allow your brothers to be exposed to his sight. The sooner Cari is removed from the Valley, the safer he should be. Bort will be safe in Alfhiem. Liv knows the scent of them, and she has not detected it near the Crystal Tower for several years. She and her brood are watching over us. I think the Raven and its rider will keep watching the Valley until you give it a reason to go elsewhere."

Artos looked at the Mist Cat again and she gazed back at him solemnly and he felt she was agreeing with Donel's words.

"But we are going through the mountains to keep the Abominations from detecting us. From following us."

"When you return to Castle Draconis, they will converge on you. I think Tomung will try to unite them all again. We know that two of them, at least, were involved in freeing him from your trophy wall. I think when you strike at the Abomination, who we know was at Castle Draconis, the one who will have freed Tomung, then the rest will converge there as well. Tomung will summon them, I think."

"How long will it take Tomung to be whole once more?"

"I do not know, but it will take some time. This is another reason you must act with haste."

"What more do you know of these creatures and their regalos, Donel?"

"Very little, I'm afraid. Just the myths and legends. As I have said, Tomung is the leader. Legend states his lieutenant is named Mohattri. That one is cloaked in mystery. The legends say nothing more. Anndr has mind regalos, and the reputation of being a master craftsman. He is most likely the source of the black crystal. Constructing crystal is a feat that no one besides the crystal-masters of Fairinhorst, the disciples of Angellar, are known to possess. He is the most adept at mind control. Which makes him undoubtedly the most dangerous. Of the other two, Babich and Kargyn," Donel shrugged, "the tales say they are little more than ravening beasts, totally enslaved to the will of Tomung. For three hundred years, they have been free of his direct control. Who knows how things will stand once he is whole again? But they are all masters of deceit and users of illusion, creatures dark of heart, totally evil and, of course, shapeshifters."

"You could see Duke's crysword at the Castle. Can you see Bort's and Cari's too?"

Donel gazed at Artos for a moment and then nodded. "Of course. You are missing them, aren't you?"

"I've always had them around. At home, we'd always be together for meals and most of our classes. Occasionally, one or another would be away. Bort was gone with Uncle Brett a lot, sometimes for weeks. Duka and I spent some time at House deDarrellyel last year, but now there's only me and you, and I just feel empty, like something is missing." Artos realized how that sounded and glanced up at Donel. "I don't mean that you aren't good company..."

"I understand, Art," said Donel. "The Glory Road can be

very lonely. I had three brothers, too. They are all long gone now, of course. Allison was the king. He was your great-great-great-grandfather. My other brothers were Baeddan and Caerwyn. I missed them all when they finished their classes at Starstone Tower. We all went there together at first, but only Caerwyn and I stayed there after the first term. Later, when Caer went home, I was lonely, but Denar was there, and other students were coming and going. Daimion deDraconis was still alive then and the keeper of this tower. His brother Charales was alive then, too. He was the Loremaster of deDraconis and Caer's teacher after he left Starstone. They were both quite old. But you don't wish to hear ancient history. You want me to go find Bort and Cari on the screens so you can see them and reassure yourself they're safe. We'll do that after dinner."

"I don't mean to seem childish, Donel. It would be nice to see them, though. I am the eldest, and for all Bort saying we are his duty to protect..."

"I understand. It is the king's duty to watch over all his own. And Bort and Cari are your brothers." Donel sighed. "I wish I could show you, Duka. I hope the Angellar has good news for Cari."